PERFECT BONES

Samantha Willerby Mystery Series – Book 3

A.J. WAINES

First published in 2018 by Bloodhound Books

www.bloodhoundbooks.com

Print ISBN 978-1-912604-88-3

Also by AJ Waines

Standalones:
The Evil Beneath
Girl on a Train
Dark Place to Hide
No Longer Safe
Don't you Dare

Samantha Willerby Mystery Series:
Inside the Whispers
Lost in the Lake

Writing as Alison Waines:
The Self-Esteem Journal
Making Relationships Work

Prologue

Friday, June 15 – Three weeks earlier

It's not often a journalist is offered first bite of the cherry – not on a plate like this.

Pippa French glanced over her shoulder, wondering if anyone else could feel the dynamic shift in the air. The water-cooler gurgled. Someone behind the photocopier sneezed, but no one seemed to notice the electric charge fizzing around her. No one spotted the way she tightly squeezed the receiver, nor heard the galloping thud of her heartbeat.

Her secret was safe.

He was speaking again. 'It's a genuine Cézanne and it's been hanging in a lawyer's front room for a decade. She'd mistaken it for a copy all this time. Make a great headline don't you think? Interested?'

Interested? Of course she was interested! This was the real McCoy. The exclusive that could take her career to the next level.

When Mr Morino told her not to say where she was going, to keep the whole thing hush-hush, it didn't ring any alarm bells. Pippa wasn't listening out for them. All she heard was the velvety voice in her ear telling her what she wanted to hear.

'You can bring your colleagues up to speed once you've seen the painting and have something to squeal about,' he said. 'We don't want anyone else jumping the queue.'

His caution was understandable, to be expected. It was common practice for journalists to follow a lead without even telling their boss – to make sure no one else snatched the glory. Journalism is a cut-throat business. Everyone knew that.

So, she didn't say a word to anyone.

Pippa's follow-up checks were just as convincing as the phone call from Philippe Morino. She'd heard of the Sotherby's expert before. One of her rivals from *Art Monthly* had done a piece on him. Still, she'd decided it would be better to call him back on the main Sotherby's number just in case – she'd been scammed before by fake leads.

But by the time she'd finished her meeting with the editor, Mr Morino had left for the day. Just missed him, apparently. She checked her watch. That would add up. In his earlier call, he'd arranged to meet her at Languini's wine bar, only a short walk away, in ten minutes time. He'd be on his way by now. There was no question in her mind. She had to follow this through, before anyone else got their hands on this exclusive.

It wasn't difficult to slip away. Most of her colleagues had already gone home. Before she left, she wrote the time and location on a Post-it note and stuck it to the computer monitor. It was just a precaution. The office operated a hot-desking system, so whoever got to the spot first in the morning would see it. Then she realised it was Friday and no one would see it until Monday. It would be a bit late by then if she'd run into trouble. She screwed it into a ball and threw it into the bin.

As she rounded the corner of the street and the green-striped awning of the bar came into view, Pippa got another call.

'Ever so sorry… change of plan,' he said, his voice plummy and polite. 'Much better if you come straight here. I'm sending a taxi for you. It'll pick you up outside the wine bar any minute now.'

She slowed her step, a flicker of doubt crossing her path. It was all getting a bit cloak 'n' dagger. Some tiny part of her knew it was too good to be true. She should turn around. Let it go. Something wasn't right.

But she ignored the niggling voice and didn't turn back. She was blinded by the prospect of her own personal scoop and wasn't thinking straight. Part of her – the ambitious, tenacious, go-getting side of her – hung on to the belief that she'd struck it lucky.

But her instincts were wrong.

This was a well-coated honey trap.

Chapter 1

I should have known it was never going to happen. As I rolled up two more T-shirts and tucked them under my gold sandals, I ignored the niggling voice that said this suitcase wouldn't be leaving the flat tomorrow morning.

Getting away on holiday is straightforward for most people, but that's rarely the case in my experience. Something always gets in the way; a terrorist attack, hospital colleagues calling in sick or Miranda – my effervescent but unpredictable sister – having a mini meltdown. This time, I'd been forced to cancel twice due to work and Miranda had begun making snide quips about me finding excuses to not go. But this time I was adamant. We were absolutely, definitely, one hundred percent going to make that flight.

I dragged my case to the front door, ready for the crack-of-dawn taxi I'd ordered and returned to my checklist. Sun-cream, passport, European plug adaptor; all ticked.

I'd originally hoped for a week in Prague, sightseeing, but my sister wanted 'more fun', so scuba diving, beach-volleyball and jet-skiing on the Greek island of Lefkas won through.

I emptied the bins, made sure there was nothing in the fridge that would turn green in my absence, pegged up the last of my washing on the indoor airer and flicked on the TV in the sitting room to catch the late-night news. A map of north London filled the screen, then cut away to the newsreader in the studio, but my mind was elsewhere; *did I need to leave a note for Mrs Willow upstairs to remind her to water my plants or would she remember? Were there any online deliveries I should have re-arranged?*

That's when it happened.

A camera zoomed in to reveal a scene I knew only too well, cordoned off with blue police tape. I snapped to attention. The outside broadcaster sounded grave:

'…where an artist from the Camden Community Art Project was found critically injured on the towpath last night. Police are appealing for witnesses…'

A stab of panic pitched me to the edge of the sofa. *CCAP.* I resisted the impulse to grab my phone. She'd be fine. She wouldn't have gone out last night, she would have been packing. My sister was hopeless at deciding what to take away with her and always started several days early, making various aborted attempts at filling her suitcase and tipping everything out again. She was probably knee-deep in her wardrobe this very minute putting back dungarees and trying to track down her sarong.

I made the call anyway. No reply.

I went to the bathroom to splash water on my face; my early night was out of the question now. There's no way I'd be able to sleep until I knew for certain that she was okay. Over the buzzing of my electric toothbrush, I heard my phone ring.

It was Terry's number on the screen. Again.

'Terry. Hi.' My voice was flat. I needed to keep this short.

'I'm glad I caught you,' he said, the words wilting apologetically at the end. 'Listen, Sam, I know I saw you earlier, but I've got someone who'd like to speak to you.'

'Now? It's late, Terry. I'm going on holiday tomorrow. You know that.'

'Sorry, but it's important. It's a colleague in the Metropolitan Police. Someone pretty high up, actually…'

'Police?'

There was a scuffle at the other end and before I could get an explanation from him, a fresh voice came on the line. A woman; stern and loud.

'This is Detective Chief Superintendent, Elsa Claussen. I'm calling from the Central North Command Unit in Camden...' I let my weight fall into the wall beside me. *Oh, God – Miranda.*

I couldn't swallow. I didn't hear any more.

I felt my body slide down the wall, my stomach about to cave in, when I realised my mind was going in the wrong direction. A chief superintendent wouldn't break this kind of news over the phone. Surely, there'd be uniformed officers looking pained and awkward outside my flat door. Then I registered her next words.

'...your help.'

'Sorry?'

'We need *your help*,' she said once more.

'Help?' It came out like a whimper.

'We need an expert in Post Traumatic Stress Disorder. Your name came up.'

I forced myself to stay focused. 'This isn't about my sister, Miranda Willerby?'

'I think we're talking at cross purposes.'

I was confused. 'Can you put Terry back on, please?'

There was a clunk. 'What's going on?' he hissed. 'This is really important, Sam.'

'Is this about Miranda?'

'No, it's–'

'Is this about the woman found last night on the towpath near Camden Lock?' I said, bulldozing over him.

He stalled. 'Yes, it is. We–'

'Who is it? Who was critically injured?'

'She was from the Camden Community Art Project–'

'I know, but *who* is it? You know my sister... she's an artist at CCAP. She uses the towpath. I can't reach her.'

'It's not her,' he said firmly.

I got him to repeat it. 'It's *not* Miranda. This woman had long dark hair, she was–'

'You're sure?'

'Absolutely.'

I blew out a bucketful of air. If the victim had long dark hair that was all I needed to know. My sister had a blonde buzz cut; her hair couldn't have been more different.

The phone went back to Claussen. I had three seconds to shift from panicky relative to self-assured professional.

'Are we on the same page now?' she said stiffly. She didn't wait for a response. 'We need a PTSD specialist as a matter of urgency.'

'Right, well, I'm sorry, but I'm about to go away on my first annual leave in three years and—'

Her voice ploughed over mine, informing me that two other prominent PTSD specialists were unavailable. 'One is in the Caribbean and the other was rushed to hospital this evening with a burst appendix. In terms of professionals we can call on... well, it looks like you're all we've got.'

Mmm – probably not the best way to win me over.

'Like I said to Terry – he *knows* this – I've got a flight booked tomorrow at eight thirty in the morning. There's another person involved. I can't let her down. It's only for a week.'

'I know. We called St Luke's earlier today to see if you were available.'

'You've already checked up on me?' I was having trouble keeping up.

She sniffed. 'We've cleared this with your department.'

'You've what?'

'We did our utmost to find someone else, believe me. That's why I'm calling so late. As I say, the guy we had lined up has been carted off to intensive care. It's a crisis situation.'

'But, there *must* be someone else. There's a register of PTSD experts in London the length of my arm – they can't all be having surgery. Let me switch on my laptop and—'

She sounded agitated. 'That's not going to help. It's a tricky scenario.'

I let her hear my heavy sigh. 'What *is* the scenario, exactly?'

'A nineteen-year-old appears to be the only witness to a savage murder attempt. This witness was moored on a boat on the

Regent's Canal – right where it happened. Found at the scene in a catatonic state.'

'She's your sole witness?'

'It's a *he* actually. We're convinced he saw the whole thing, but was traumatised by the situation.' I heard a sharp intake of breath. 'When I say savage attack, I mean *savage*.' Her voice wavered. 'The victim was almost decapitated – her head practically taken right off. She's in intensive care – no one can believe she survived.'

I flinched at the thought of it. Claussen carried on. 'The witness was seen by our psychiatrist, but he hasn't been able to tell us what happened. His brain has kind of shut down. Heavy trauma, we gather. It happened at an isolated spot, at dusk, beside the water. No one else has come forward and we don't expect them to. It's a miracle there were any witnesses at all.'

My voice came out as a whisper. 'Why do you need *me*? This witness could talk to any number of PTSD specialists, surely?'

'None of the other experts can give us a devoted period of time away from their commitments. We need someone to work with him immediately and intensively.' Claussen didn't sound like the kind of person who failed to get her own way too often. 'As you already had annual leave booked, all your patients and staff are expecting you to disappear for a while.'

Her next words come out cool and slightly smug. 'Besides, the witness is an art student and we understand you have specialist art therapy skills.'

Ah, there we have it. *Thanks, Terry.* I reran the conversation I'd had with him only nine hours ago. It was meant to be a friendly catch up, but I should have cottoned on as soon as he started asking an inordinate amount of questions about my work. *Just interested, eh?* I'd been set up.

'You can't push someone with PTSD,' I pointed out. 'He will only be able to reveal what he saw in his own time.'

'I'm afraid that time is exactly what we don't have. As I said, he's our only witness. Witnesses are unreliable at best, but leave it too long and they start thinking red was green, up was down – and every bit of the incident goes pear-shaped.'

She was absolutely right, of course.

'We need to get a statement from him as soon as possible,' she persisted. 'We need to catch whoever did this and we think this witness saw the whole thing. We've already lost a day and if we don't get information soon, whatever he can offer us is likely to be worthless. We reckon you've got a week with him. That's our cut-off point. Seven days.'

She wasn't making sense. 'If this witness is suffering from PTSD, it's going to take a lot longer than a week for him to face a police line-up or describe exactly what happened. I've known colleagues who've worked for *months* with patients following a trauma. You can't give him a deadline.'

Besides, this might only be a week, but it was *my* week; my week to be with my sister.

'There's a further complication,' she added, gravely. I suppressed a strong desire to groan down the line. 'We don't think it's simply a case of PTSD.'

My eyes clamped shut. 'Why? Why not?'

'He won't talk to anybody.'

Oh, great.

'And what makes you think he'll talk to me?' I laughed. 'A complete stranger?'

'No, what I mean is – he can't speak. At all. The psychiatrist says he's been rendered mute by the situation; he was diagnosed this afternoon. He hasn't uttered a word to anyone in twenty-four hours. Not one word.'

Chapter 2

I switched off the television that had been rolling on in the background and stared at the black screen. DCS Claussen had broken off to deal with another call and said she'd get back to me, but I could already feel the smouldering sun slipping down behind the ocean waves, the sand between my toes rapidly dissolving.

It was all Terry's doing. I backtracked to the conversation I'd had with him over lunch that day. Something told me at the time that he wasn't being upfront with me. I should have followed my gut instinct and questioned his motives there and then.

Terry Austin was an old friend from my PhD days at university, long before he'd joined the police force. We hadn't been in touch for years until I met him at the hospital where I was working as a clinical psychologist about two years ago. He was having a check-up following surgery and we'd ended up chatting in the waiting room. He'd been shot in the leg during an armed robbery and had been signed off for months. After that chance meeting, we'd followed each other on social media, but had no proper face-to-face contact. Then out of the blue he rang me this morning, asked if we could meet for lunch.

'Just thought it would be nice to catch up,' he'd said.

I was taken aback, but there was a tight edge to his voice that gave me the feeling it could be something serious. I'd told him if he'd left it another day I'd have been lounging on a beach by the Ionian Sea munching feta cheese.

'Romantic getaway?' he threw out with a smile in his voice.

'Hardly. I'll explain when I see you.'

I'd spotted him as soon as I stepped inside The Archduke, awkwardly perched on a stool at the bar. A carved walking stick hung over the back. His leg must not have properly healed.

The bar was open-plan and airy, nestled within the railway arches outside Waterloo Station. It still retained the bare brickwork of its original construction with additional broad windows, mezzanines and cosy alcoves. I'd not been here before and was startled when the first train rumbled overhead, making the glasses tremble, harking back to the structure's original raison d'être. Somehow, the atmosphere of grimy nostalgia wasn't at odds with the upmarket clientele.

I dropped my bag on the stool beside him and leant over with a casual hug so he didn't have to get up.

'Looks like I just caught you before you disappeared,' he said.

I nodded. 'Early plane in the morning. I'm getting away for a while with my sister.'

I glanced down at the tall glass with a straw and lemon in front of him. Not drinking. I should have taken that as confirmation he was still 'on duty'.

'What can I get you?' he asked.

'Chablis, please.'

'Drinking at lunchtime?' His smile belied any judgement. 'What's got into the cool and consummate professional I used to know?'

I threw up my eyes with a huff. 'Dr Samantha Willerby finished work this morning.' I flung my jacket over my bag with a flourish as the barman plonked the glass in front of me. 'This is my first holiday in years and it starts now.' I chinked my glass against his. 'I've got the afternoon to pack and I'm *more* than ready to slip into vacation mode, I can tell you.'

Terry knew me well. Most people regarded me as detached and never ruffled, like any good psychologist should be. But it wasn't just about my job. Long before I worked at St Luke's I'd had a reputation for being an ice-maiden. Miranda once said that if she was a tagine of spicy, multi-coloured kedgeree, then I was a plate of cucumber sandwiches with the crusts cut off. She's wrong, of course. As are all the others who think I breeze through life with a natural resilience against everything fate throws at me. In truth, I'm often curled up into a little ball inside, fighting silent battles over making the right decision, struggling to hold my own against self-doubt. Terry understood that. He was one of the few individuals who'd seen me at my worst. He knew I was more like a Creme Egg; solid on the outside, soft and melty in the middle.

'I'd join you, but I've got meetings this afternoon,' he said, wrinkling his nose.

'Shame.'

I shuffled onto the stool, but it was too high for me, forcing my skirt to reveal more of my thigh than I intended. I nonchalantly hoisted it down.

'Where are you off to?' he said, glancing at my leg, then back to his drink with a tiny flicker of his eyebrows.

'Somewhere warm in the Mediterranean. It's Miranda's choice. To be honest, it's only partly pleasure.'

A fold appeared in his forehead. 'How come?'

'In a nutshell, I'm going away with her partly as her sister, but mainly as a psychologist.'

He winced. 'Whoa – sounds a bit technical. Not a break at all then?'

I laughed. 'It will be – I hope. Miranda was involved in a minor hit and run about a month ago and since then, she's definitely lost weight.'

'She was a slip of a thing to start with if I remember correctly. Was she badly hurt?'

'No, just bumps and bruises; the car tipped her into the kerb and didn't stop.'

He glanced down at his own knee.

'She was lucky…' I said, my gaze following his. 'But, I need to find out how she's coping. *Really* coping. It's not that long ago that she was in intensive care after a fire. I won't go into details, but she suffered nasty burns on her arms, legs and back.'

'I'm so sorry.' He reached out for my hand, then once he'd taken it, awkwardly let it go.

'She dealt with the aftermath of the fire incredibly well at the time, but I'm not sure if this recent incident could have triggered something. I don't want to suddenly discover she's struggling with hidden anxiety that's escalated into anorexia or self-harm or–'

'Can't you talk to her here, in London? Invite her round for coffee or go shopping together?'

'It's not quite as easy as that. Miranda is terribly slippery and the world's best at avoiding her feelings. She hates me interfering, as she calls it, and regularly goes through periods when she blanks me or stops answering my calls. On holiday – just the two of us – I can wait for the right time and do it all very slowly, inconspicuously.'

'So, you're going to spend your well-earned break sussing her out?'

I took a long sip of wine. 'I won't even dare to broach the subject until we've settled into our rooms and knocked back our first cocktail. In fact, I'm going to wait until she's had her first dip, shaken the sand out of her towel and peeled the bikini straps from her shoulders, then I'll ease my way in, ever so gently.'

'So she'll hardly notice...' he gave me a wry smile as he sipped on his straw.

I laughed. 'Yeah, I know. It's rather optimistic, isn't it? It's so annoying when you want to be there for someone, but they refuse to let you in.'

Terry's expression slid into a knowing grimace. He knew about Miranda's delicate mental health, about her past. He'd been there many times at University, when I'd come back from a fraught family weekend pulling my hair out. He'd helped restore my sanity, sitting up with me well into the night as we shared bottles of wine.

While many sufferers of schizophrenia show signs of depression and withdrawal, Miranda tended to have 'outbursts'. These symptoms had started during her childhood, when we didn't know about her diagnosis and thought she was going through random episodes of attention-seeking behaviour. On one occasion, she tossed over twenty packets of frozen peas onto the floor of a supermarket before my mother was able to catch up with her. One winter, she set fire to her bed, because the voices in her head were telling her that the room was gradually being frozen by the snowman on the neighbours' front lawn.

Miranda told me, much later, that she'd spent most of her upbringing believing she was in a different reality to everyone else; one where other people lived behind sheets of glass, but she was out in the open, vulnerable and unprotected. That was before she was getting the right medication, but even now she only had one foot in the same world as the rest of us. I'd never stopped being on my guard; any new upset could set her off.

I pulled a shameful face. 'Miranda would kill me if she thought I had any plans to throw therapy into the mix.'

Terry put his hand over mine and held it there, this time. Even though I hadn't seen him for two years I felt as if we'd last met only a few days ago. Some friends are like that. Terry had always been a rock; reliable, straight down the line and gentle. I'd always thought he'd fit snugly into the role of brother, if we'd kept in touch better. I'm not sure why, but I'd never considered him as potential boyfriend material, which was a shame, because he probably ticked all the right boxes. He was loyal, uncomplicated and made an amazing mushroom risotto. But there was no spark. You can't make someone fit the part if a crucial bit is missing, no matter how perfect they might seem on paper.

'Are you still working at the same mental health unit?' he asked innocently.

'Yep. Same old.' I was about to ask how his own work was going, but he had another question.

'What sort of issues do you deal with?'

I halted, suddenly cautious. Was Terry looking for a counsellor? Was this the reason he wanted to see me? Getting shot, then coping with a long-term disability must have been a tough ordeal for him. Not only his leg, but his career in the Met had been shattered. I'd learned via social media that he'd been forced to give up his role as a detective for a position in data training instead. He must have had support through work at the time, but it would have only been for a few months.

I stayed on course with his question, remaining neutral. 'Any sort of trauma. I'm brought in when the nightmares and flashbacks won't go away. When patients jump at the slightest noise, lose their appetite, withdraw into themselves… can't cope any more.'

'So, your work involves all kinds of accidents, terrorist incidents, domestic and street crimes?'

I couldn't play the game any longer. 'What's this about, Terry? Are you in trouble?'

'Me?' he snorted. 'No. I'm just interested, that's all.' He snatched a sip of water too quickly and I knew he was covering something up.

I carried on, hoping all would be revealed eventually. 'I've been doing research into art and play therapy; not with kids, but with adults instead. To recover repressed or distressing memories.'

He fingered his chin looking thoughtful. 'You get them to draw or paint?'

'Not just drawing; some patients would run a mile if I gave them a blank sheet of paper and a crayon. We use lots of different methods.' I laughed. 'My office looks like a toy shop. I've got Lego bricks, pebbles and shells, a sandpit, Tarot cards, dolls, model cars – you name it. You should come and see sometime. It's all about symbols. I often work using fairy tales or ask patients to describe themselves using characters from a soap opera or film. Sometimes it's easier for them to describe what happened through another persona.'

He tapped his lip. 'Wow…'

Was this really an idle interest? It was rare for anyone to be this enthusiastic about what I did, but Terry seemed genuinely entranced. It spurred me on to tell him more.

'I had one guy last week who could only tell me about himself if I referred to him as Captain Picard. I had to be Counsellor Troy.' Terry gave me a dubious look. 'I know – it can sound a bit kinky at times, but this guy was above board. He talked me through various scenes from *Star Trek*, through the eyes of the ship's captain. Using that means of separation he was able to explain how he felt in a way that was safe for him.' I leant forward. 'That's confidential by the way. I use all kinds of approaches to help patients express themselves, often without using any words at all.'

'You have patients who don't speak?'

'They can but they don't *have* to. Words can get in the way sometimes. Speaking can seem too direct and confrontational at times. Sometimes it's easier, safer, to *show*...'

He stared into his glass. 'Sounds fascinating.'

'Okay, Terry. Spill. Why are you so interested all of a sudden?'

I saw his chest rise and fall. 'No reason.'

'Oh, come on, all you've done is fire one question after another at me. It's very flattering, but I'm rather mystified. What's going on?'

For one strange moment, it crossed my mind that Terry might have fancied me since our paths crossed at Manchester University, and had only now chosen this obscure moment to pluck up the courage to tell me. My life was certainly low on love-interest at the moment, but with all the will in the world, Terry wasn't 'the one'. I was starting to panic about how I was going to let him down without offending him.

He got to his feet. 'Let me get you another drink,' he said.

I was still standing in the sitting room, holding the phone in my hand when it rang again. In the light of that odd lunch date, Claussen's request now made perfect sense. At least I didn't need to worry about any possible romantic interest from Terry; instead I'd walked straight into his trap. Once he'd realised I was just the person they needed, he'd confirmed with Claussen and I'd been 'requisitioned'.

'Sorry about that,' Claussen said, her tone clipped. 'Drugs bust just gone tits up.' She cleared her throat. 'Right – we'll send a car over at seven-thirty tomorrow morning for the briefing, okay?'

I paused, trying to gather my thoughts. We hadn't actually had the part of the conversation where I'd agreed to anything, but I knew there was little use in pointing that out.

'Let me make a call,' I told her. 'Let me do that first – *one* call – before I agree to this.'

'Sure,' she conceded. 'I'll wait for you to ring me back.'

It was after 10pm. I hit redial, with an entirely different quality of trepidation to twenty minutes ago. This time she answered.

I jumped straight in. 'Miranda, I'm really sorry to call so late, only I've got bad news…'

'So have I, as a matter of fact.' There was tremor in her voice; she'd been crying. 'I was going to call you.'

'Why? Are you okay?' I said, 'what's wrong?'

'I can't go… on the trip…' she spluttered, 'something terrible's happened.' She'd borrowed the words I was about to use, almost word for word.

'I can't believe it…' She broke down into heaving sobs. 'It's Kora … someone's tried to kill her.'

Chapter 3

The patrol car pulled up at Stanhope Street Police Station in Camden promptly at 8am. As a 'civilian', I wasn't allowed into the major incident room, so I was taken by the desk sergeant into a space reserved for general meetings; comfy chairs, a white board, coffee in silver pots in the corner. There was an oily smell of new carpet. As I scanned the area I was immediately able to put a face to the robust female voice I'd heard late last night. DCS Elsa Claussen was reprimanding two uniformed officers, one of whom was visibly cowering. Her voice blasted across the room like a polar vortex, filling the space with icy fumes, sucking out all the air.

I braced myself as she headed towards me and gripped my hand without a smile. She'd sounded on the phone like she was Danish; but from what I could see she was about as far removed from the delicate pastry variety as you could ever imagine. Everything about her was bulky with straight lines; the back-and-sides haircut, balcony bosom, clompy lace-ups. Not a curve in sight. She looked how I'd imagine a female Sumo wrestler would look.

I reined in my cruel assessment of her, but I knew where the negativity was coming from. I was angry with her. Angry that she'd stolen the precious time I'd set aside – at last – for my getaway. In thirty minutes time, I should have been soaring above the city, switching off from patients and crises, and looking forward to my first tequila. Finding a way to check on Miranda after the hit and run had been my main motivation when I'd booked the break, but its status had shifted since then. Once I'd packed my bags yesterday,

I saw how desperate I was for time out and the trip had recast itself as a blissful retreat that I not only needed, but deserved.

When I accepted this case last night, my first thought was that I'd let myself down. But that self-reproach had been short-lived once Miranda revealed that her best friend had been involved in a brutal attack. Getting pitched off the road at Baker Street was nothing compared to this. Now Kora was at death's door. Even for a 'normal' person the impact could be devastating, but for Miranda, diagnosed with schizophrenia, the after-effects could be far more damaging.

The Chief Super introduced me to DCI Keith Wilde. He was tall and frowned slightly as he offered his hand. His handshake was flimsy, but his pupils were hard, like rivets. A difficult man to please, I surmised. Next in line was DI Jeremy Fenway with whom I'd be working most closely. He had a tiny scrap of tissue stuck to his neck where he'd cut himself shaving, which warmed me to him straight away. He was the only one so far who looked vaguely human.

Several other plain-clothes and uniformed officers joined us and I took a seat on the second of three rows. DCI Wilde outlined the gist of the situation: a nineteen-year-old art student, Aiden Blake, had rung police from his mobile just after 9.30pm on July fourth, having witnessed a gruesome incident.

'Carry on, constable,' Wilde instructed, stepping to one side.

A young male officer loped forward, holding a spiral notepad in front of him with both hands, as if it was a hymnbook. He cleared his throat. 'Right… Mr Blake managed to mutter something about a woman with her throat cut,' he explained. 'He sounded pretty confused, but he did tell us a figure came out of nowhere, right up to the boat.' The officer's eyes darted about the room as if expecting a big bang to occur at any moment. 'Then Mr Blake went silent and couldn't say a thing after that. When we got to the scene, we found him squatting beside the victim, but he wouldn't say another word.'

DI Fenway stepped forward, holding a photograph. The TV monitor was on the blink, apparently, so he was using more antiquated methods to give us the details. 'It looks like a very cruel booby-trap,' he explained.

He stuck a picture of the crime scene on the top of the whiteboard, pressing it flat. I made out the towpath, the fence behind it, a twisted bicycle lying at the water's edge and a trail of blood, before I took my eyes away.

'The victim we now know to be Kora Washington, twenty-seven, was riding her pushbike from the Camden Lock direction, going pretty fast by the look of it. Looks like someone had set up some kind of tripwire at head height.' He glanced down at his shoes. 'It nearly took her head clean off.'

A whoosh travelled the room as everyone sucked in a sharp breath.

'It was a vicious and calculated attack. We assume the perpetrator tied an invisible wire from the fence at one side to a lamp at the front of Mr Blake's boat. They must have removed it after the victim had fallen, because there was no sign of it. There's barely anything for forensics at the scene apart from a lot of blood and skid marks, very little to pin on the offender.'

DI Fenway pressed another photograph onto the board of Aiden Blake's boat, and beside it, further shots of the crime scene. He added times in black marker pen as he spoke. 'We're checking CCTV in the nearby car park and going over the area for footprints, but it's a busy public footpath before dark...'

Someone along my row called out, 'Is Mr Blake a suspect?'

'Unlikely, unless he's the world's greatest actor. There was a pile of fresh vomit near the door of his boat and he's been in a terrible state since it happened.'

Another officer piped up. 'If you were going to do something like this, you wouldn't do it on your own doorstep would you, sir?'

'Unless he's a complete nutter...' said a voice from the back row. It raised a tense snigger.

'Which we're pretty sure Mr Blake isn't,' said the DI. 'Everyone says he's a smart lad with a bright future. No police record.' He strolled up and down, his hands behind his back looking like a bobby on the beat. 'The canal boat is his home. It looks like he was getting ready for bed. Neighbours said he often brought his washing in late… left it drying on a wooden rack outside his front door. There was a laundry basket, tipped over, by the boat when we found him. He might have seen the tripwire at that stage, we're not sure. He might have heard the bike coming, turned round and…' DI Fenway tossed what looked like a bad taste around in his mouth. 'There were no marks or scratches on his hands… only fluff, and an officer said he could smell fabric softener on Mr Blake's fingers. Looks like he'd been handling laundry. We've searched his boat; nothing untoward, so far.'

'And the guy's not speaking? Is that right?' asked the officer in uniform, beside me.

'That's correct. Medical condition induced by the trauma. Can't utter a word.'

'What exactly did he manage to say before he stopped speaking altogether?' asked the same officer.

DI Fenway glanced over at the young male officer who referred again to his notebook.

'His exact words were… "She's off her bike… you've got to help… throat cut… oh, God, there's blood everywhere…" then he started kind of howling. The operator asked where he was and Mr Blake said "Camden… towpath… someone in black… out of nowhere… right here…" The operator asked his name, but he was just crying. They couldn't get any more out of him after that.'

'Why bother to take the wire away?' came a voice. 'Why did the maniac put himself at risk of being seen?'

'We're not sure yet,' replied the DI, thoughtfully.

'It was definitely a tripwire, not a knife or long blade of some kind?' someone asked.

'Our police surgeon confirmed that the neck wound and the victim's injuries were consistent with a thin wire being used. We've also had forensic guys in to check the position of the victim when she fell… the bike and the blood spatter… it all confirms that MO. There was no evidence of a struggle. We found fresh scratches in the paint on the lamp and marks on the fence directly across from it, so we think that's where the wire was attached. Just hooked around and pulled tight.'

I asked the next question. 'Mr Blake was taken to hospital straight away?'

DI Fenway nodded. 'By the way, this is Dr Samantha Willerby, everyone – she's our consultant psychologist on this case.' He gave me a little bow as faces in the front row spun round. 'Mr Blake was in shock, in quite a bad way, actually. Seems a pretty sensitive chap. He'd soiled himself at the scene and was catatonic. He spent the night in The Royal Free where they gave him a brain scan, to check he hadn't banged his head before we got to him. All clear. He was seen by the police psychiatrist and by the afternoon, physically, he seemed fine. Apart from not uttering a word, there was no reason to keep him there. We took him back to his boat and he immediately tried to move it.'

'You stopped him?' I asked.

'Only until we'd thoroughly checked out the boat. It's now back at his usual mooring spot at Limehouse, about six miles away along the Regent's Canal. As I said, he's not a suspect, at present, but we need to know where he is. We took his laptop and tablet – we're checking them out – and his mobile.'

'Did he know her, the victim, do you think?' came a fresh voice from the front row.

'He's at art college and the woman was from the Camden Community Art Project, but no one, so far, seems to think they knew each other. The victim's partner said he'd never heard of Mr Blake and she wasn't due to meet anyone that night, but we're looking into her online footprint to see if there's any connection on social media or email. Kora has an eighteen-month-old child. She should have been cycling in the opposite direction… on her way home.'

'And the attacker saw Mr Blake, presumably?' I queried.

DI Fenway shrugged. 'Very likely, I'd say. Probably standing there in shock, unable to move when the attacker came forward to take the wire. And that reminds me. Everyone, listen up. The press must *not* get wind of Mr Blake's identity or his whereabouts. If they track down his boat, it will not only make his life hell, but we'll end up with a ridiculous game of cat and mouse up and down the canals of England.'

There was a rumble of consent.

'When the assailant came back for the wire, why didn't he attack Mr Blake, if he was just standing there?' I added.

The room sank into an extreme hush. Only the fan continued, beating frantically beneath the ceiling. DI Fenway looked at his shoes and then up at me. 'Good question… as yet to be adequately answered.'

A uniformed officer tapped on the door and scuttled across the room. He held up a phone in front of DCI Wilde, who quickly scanned the message.

The DCI clapped his hands together. 'Right… everything else you need is in the online report… that's it, for now.'

After the meeting broke up, I hung around at the back of the room waiting to speak to DI Fenway so I could arrange my first meeting with Aiden. He was discussing something with the DCI, nodding as he fiddled with the strap on his watch. He came over when he'd finished and stood in front of me looking somewhat shell-shocked.

'Right,' he said, his left eyelid twitching as if he had something in his eye. 'Coffee?'

I declined. I didn't want to spend any more time here than I needed to; my next priority was to get over to see Miranda. Find out what kind of state she was in.

'Have you seen Aiden's medical history?' I asked. 'Has he ever been mute before? Any other mental health issues?'

'It doesn't seem so. Clean as a whistle. Looks like he hasn't even been registered with a GP during the last three years. I'll get his records over to you.'

I nodded. 'I think it's best if I see him at St Luke's, where I work,' I proposed, 'rather than at a police station. It'll be less intimidating for him.'

'Ah…' He looked sheepish. 'No one's told you?'

'Told me what?' My hands were on my hips before I could stop them. I forced myself to peel them away. None of this was DI Fenway's fault.

'There's a snag.' He sunk his hands in his trouser pockets and jangled his keys. 'Mr Blake clung to the door frame of his narrow boat when we tried to get him to come to the station this morning. He got terribly distressed. We have an officer there with him now. He's refusing to leave the boat.'

Chapter 4

I had to weave my way through a high-tide of summer tourists to get from the Tube station to Miranda's flat. It was a glorious day – heat rising in shimmering zigzags above the pavement, inviting surrender and abandon. But I barely noticed; instead my head was buried inside entangled thoughts about how I was going to handle this. Miranda didn't know I'd been called in to help with the very same incident that had knocked her for six. A cruel coincidence to say the least.

My phone buzzed against my hip. I stepped into the doorway of a vacant shop to hear properly. It was Terry making a brave attempt at an apology. I left long silences and made him grovel, refusing to end his agony with mollifying statements to let him off the hook.

'Why didn't you just tell me?' I asked eventually.

'Honestly, Sam, I feel terrible.' His voice was breaking up, brittle with repentance.

'Good – and so you should.'

'I couldn't explain properly at lunch yesterday, it had to be under wraps. They were still trying to reach one of the other trauma specialists to save having to get you on board. I kept telling them they must find someone else… that it wasn't fair on you, with you going away and all that, but…'

He admitted that what he'd done was unforgiveable. I agreed with him.

There was a prickly pause. 'Would an expensive dinner for two cut it, do you think?' he suggested.

I let him wait.

'At The Dorchester?' he added.

'I doubt it,' I said, neutrally.

'Really?' I had him worried.

Another pause. 'Throw in champagne and you might be in with a chance,' I said.

'You're on,' he said, relief saturating his voice.

He knew he owed me – big-time.

Miranda looked like she'd been up all night when she answered the door. She was still in her dressing gown and had trouble parting her eyelids. Her white-blonde hair was stiffened by a build-up of styling gel and resembled a scouring pad. She mumbled something that I took to mean *come in* and backed inside.

Miranda's flat was effectively an extended art studio. What had once been an open-plan sitting room barely lived up to its name any more, with a single lumpy sofa pushed to one side in front of an old television set. The rest of the space looked like a warehouse. There were two easels, each holding a canvas in progress; finished canvases leaning in stacks against the walls and battered trunks acting as tables for paints, jars of brushes and palettes. Wherever there was room for something to hang; the end of the iron staircase, the edge of a door, there was an oily cloth or a paint spattered T-shirt. It was the kind of place where you'd leave after a visit with a wet splodge on your backside if you weren't careful.

The bare floorboards creaked with every step and I found myself crossing the room swiftly to get to the kitchen in order to stop the noise.

I made us both coffee. Miranda took the sofa and, after careful scrutiny, I sat beside her on the arm. I always found it hard to relax at Miranda's, but it wasn't all about the inhabitable conditions. At least I wasn't constantly on the lookout for another person's belongings, like I used to be whenever I came here. A crumpled black shirt, a discarded wrapper of his favourite snack, a notepad open at one of his poems – items I'd recognise that would turn my stomach and bruise my heart in equal measure, every time my eyes rested on them. Thank goodness those days were over. He was long gone.

'I'm so sorry about Kora,' I said, wrapping my arm around her shoulders.

She was huddled over, her hands jammed between her knees. I noticed how prominent the bones in her wrists were, the sunken skin around her mouth.

'Why Kora?' she whispered. 'What has she ever done to anybody?'

I'd met Kora several times at openings and special events at CCAP, where she'd exhibited her sculptures. She was girlishly pretty with thick hair halfway down her back. I'd seen her recent work; faces emerging from veils all made of wax. They looked like the ghosts you might see in a 1930s horror movie. Unnerving, yet beautiful.

'Come here,' I said, pulling my sister into both my arms. She leant into me, allowing me to stroke her hair. Simple actions such as this weren't always so straightforward.

'Have you been to see her? Will they let you?'

'No. Family only at the moment. She's not… in a good way.'

She buried her head against my stomach.

'I don't know what to do,' she spluttered. 'That poor little boy. Raven isn't even two years old, how is he going to cope if his mother… if she…? And Sponge. He's in a dreadful state.'

Sponge was Kora's partner. I first met the two of them in a café on Camden High Street. He was a happy-go-lucky Geordie who also worked at the art project. No one seemed to know his real name.

'She's such a sweetheart. Wholesome and totally trusting of people, possibly a bit too naïve at times.' She sniffed. 'Everyone thinks the world of her; so radiant and carefree.'

A handkerchief was permanently squashed into Miranda's hand and she pressed it against her eyes and nostrils from time to time. It wasn't her fault, but I'd missed out on a lot of my childhood because of her manic behaviour. She was two years older than me, but had always felt like the younger sister, forcing me to grow up fast. I love her to bits, but with professional parents focused on their careers, I was the one who had to keep an eye on her. Whenever she left the room, I'd be on red-alert; listening, waiting, poised to rush out and stop her from breaking something or hurting herself. That sense of foreboding had never fully left me.

She gripped my wrist. 'You do understand, don't you, that I couldn't go away on holiday... after this?' she added.

'Of course. I know.' I wiped a stray tear from her cheek with my thumb. Even if I hadn't been railroaded into helping the police, I could never have taken off and left her like this.

'You could still go,' she added, pulling away. 'You don't have to worry about me. You could catch a flight today.'

'No, no. It's fine. I've got work, now, as it happens.'

That was the moment I should have told Miranda that I'd agreed to help with the case, but it felt beside the point, somehow. What mattered most was how Miranda was going to get through this.

'Have you eaten?' I asked.

She wasn't really hearing me. 'I might go over to see Sponge, later.' She exhaled heavily. 'I might need to go to the project...'

Almost everyone at CCAP, like Miranda, had a troubled background; a history of drugs, gambling, self-harm or some psychological affliction that had blighted their lives. The ethos of the place was built around acceptance and a non-judgemental approach, and it had become the backbone of my sister's existence, fulfilling her need for identity, purpose and structure. I hoped that after what had happened, it wouldn't alter the safe status that place held for her, in her mind.

'Have you taken your—'

'Don't fuss!' she hissed, flapping me away. I took a quick glance around the room and spotted a bottle of tablets, open, standing on a tin palette.

It had taken Miranda until last Christmas to tell me that she'd heard 'voices' in her head from as early as five years of age. I've always tried to be supportive and sympathetic towards her, especially in the last few years, so I don't know why it had taken her so long to tell me. Maybe it was my job that put her off. I'd never told her that my choice of career stemmed not from a fervent desire to understand and help other people, but to help *her*. Perhaps she'd guessed at some point and found it all too humiliating. So, yes, I'd kept secrets from her, too. We were both as bad as each other.

With the right medication, Miranda had managed to tame the errant voices. She described them as a bland commentary, like a radio playing in the background that she could now turn down at will. On good days, the voices were absent altogether. Under times of stress, however, they had a tendency to get louder and more demanding. They came in many forms. During a particularly bad episode, Miranda found triggers in traffic signs and number plates. One time, she believed she was receiving instructions to march onto Waterloo Bridge and drop her purse into the water and another time she found herself in a church, stripping off, having been 'instructed' to leave all her clothes on the altar. With this level of potential instability, I needed to know how resilient she was after Kora's appalling assault.

'I'm sorry,' she said, nuzzling into my neck. 'Thanks for coming.'

'What about extra support, to see you through?' I suggested. Following previous lapses, Miranda had ended up being sectioned and sent back to a secure unit at Linden Manor. I couldn't bear to see her being taken there again.

'Is this a consultation?' she said, drawing back.

'Of course not. I care about you.'

'I'm not going to do anything stupid, if that's what you're worried about.'

'It would be good to have people around you.'

'I've got friends,' she said defiantly. 'I know what I'm supposed to do.'

I reached out to pat her knee and thought better of it. I rubbed my sweaty palm on the sofa instead. 'You know you can call me any time, okay? And I'll regularly check in with you.'

'Fine.' She sounded like a grounded school kid. Miranda's moods were like that; she could swing from loving to hostile in a matter of seconds. Especially, it would seem, with me.

I got up, ready to go. 'What are you going to do now?' I asked breezily. With someone in distress, it was always good to help them put a few plans in place, very basic ones, to get some order into their day.

'Drop in to see Sponge, then go to the project. See if anyone knows any more about what happened. Hang around. Drink decaf coffee.'

'Sounds good,' I said. 'And you'll cook a proper meal tonight?'

'Yes, *Mum*. I've got some salmon.'

Her mention of food made me realise I was hungry. I checked my watch to find I only had a few minutes to grab something to eat before I needed to head off to the east end of London. I decided now wasn't the time to tell Miranda I was due to meet the sole witness to Kora's attack. I gave her a kiss on the forehead and left.

Chapter 5

Friday, June 15 – Three weeks earlier

'Are you getting in, or what?' the cab driver calls out. Pippa French had been standing outside Languini's Bar on her phone and bobbed down to the window.

He said her full name. 'That's you, right?'

'Yes, but I'm not sure where I'm supposed to be going.'

'It's fine, love,' he said. 'I'm to drop you off at the corner of Ferndale Road, EC2. It's only a few minutes and it's all been paid for.'

It wasn't exactly the usual way she met a source for a story, but she *had* checked this guy out thoroughly, hadn't she? Philippe Morino was a bona fide dealer at Sotherby's; it was all on the level. In any case, it was still light, there would be plenty of people about.

As the taxi darted through the back streets, he phoned her again. She heard a slight clunk as the call was connected and he admitted he was using a public phone box.

'I know, it's not very professional, is it?' he said, sounding embarrassed. 'I've made so many calls about this painting today, my phone's dead, can you believe it?'

He had further instructions for her. Once she left the taxi, she was to cross at the traffic lights by the hotel and take the street down the side of the bespoke tailor. After that she should keep going until she reached the square with a church in the centre. She hurriedly scribbled down his directions. He asked her to come to the third house on the right with the dark red door.

'What's the number?'

'That's all you need,' he said.

Pippa almost got cold feet at that point, perched on the edge of her seat in the taxi. Why the need for this silly treasure hunt?

He had to placate her. 'I know, I'm sorry it's so covert. But I can't risk bringing the painting out into the open. It would draw too much attention and I know you'll need to see it before you run a story. You can't just take my word for it. Speak to Carlo Hennings at Sotherby's if you like, he's the only other person who knows about the scoop.'

Pippa recognised the name – she'd done a recent feature on art restoration and had got a quote from him.

'Look, I don't mean to be rude, but I think I will check,' she said. 'Just… you know…' She laughed nervously and he chuckled along with her.

'No problem. I can give you his direct line.'

'It's okay thanks, I'll go through the switchboard.' She wasn't going to fall for him giving her some dodgy number.

'Sure. I'll call you again in a few minutes.'

She tried Sotherby's main number again and was put through to Hennings' office, but of course, it was outside working hours and she reached only his answerphone.

Now what?

She was torn, but the ambitious competitive streak in her was winning over. Sometimes you had to take a leap of faith as a journalist, run the gauntlet and hope for the best. Okay, she hadn't got to speak to Carlo Hennings, but everything Mr Morino had said so far added up. If she got this story her kudos would go through the roof. If it turned out to be a wild goose chase, she'd just go home.

Mr Morino rang back minutes later. 'Oh, yes, I'm sorry, I forgot Carlo would have left by now. He had a charity thing to go to in Bond Street.'

Pippa happened to know that was true; the receptionist had mentioned it just now when she'd checked to see if there was another number she could try. Bolstered by this comforting reassurance she waited for the taxi to pull up on Ferndale Road and went on her way.

Chapter 6

Friday, July 6 – Day One

I left the train at Limehouse and dropped the wrapper from the sandwich I'd wolfed down en route in a recycling bin at the station.

The Docklands Light Railway came into operation over thirty years ago, but the station here still looked fresh and clean. I was struck by the imposing broad Victorian archways, although the angular metal and glass the architects had added seemed oddly disrespectful in contrast. When I looked up, the design jutted out of the old brickwork like a see-through umbrella.

I turned left at the bottom of the steps and headed straight towards the boats. My first impression of the marina was that there should have been more people about. It was lunchtime, on a giddy summer's day and I'd expected a hubbub of activity. Instead, apart from a perpetual string of joggers and a cluster of fishermen, their legs dangling over the water, the area was deserted. It became clear why. There were no benches inviting visitors to sit and enjoy the view, no bars or cafés, no amenities apart from an estate agent, a dentist and an art gallery. Perhaps it was a deliberate ploy to keep non-residents at bay.

Each of the new apartments had its own balcony, but some of the high-rise blocks were already in need of repair, strapped up with scaffolding and flapping blue tarpaulin. It was quiet in an eerie rather than tranquil kind of way, as if something bad had happened here recently. Only streets away, the customary buzz of traffic, horns, sirens and people going about their business felt more real and inviting.

Ahead, beyond the basin of water was a white church and to the right in the distance, the tall sparkling tower-blocks of Canary Wharf. I spotted a uniformed officer across the water and followed the path around the edge, crossing several bridges and a large lock leading out onto the Thames, to meet him.

The boat in question, *Louisa II*, was moored on the third of three pontoons, berth number thirty-four. Aiden Blake must have been no ordinary student. Not many nineteen-years-olds owned a narrowboat at all, never mind one this impressive. Access to the pontoon was through an imposing iron gate, locked with a key pad and surrounded by coils of galvanised razor wire. PC Spenser Ndibi, one of the officers I'd met at the briefing that morning, came along the gangway to let me in.

'He's expecting you,' was all he said.

I followed him along the wooden platform and stepped onto the front of the boat. Once I'd ducked inside, it wasn't just the size of the boat that took my breath away. Aiden, slight – but around six feet tall – stood holding the back of a chair, his hands tight around its wooden frame. He had hair the colour of golden syrup down to his shoulders, held away from his face with a footballer's headband. I couldn't see the colour of his eyes but they were wary, warning me to keep my distance. I'd rarely been so struck by anyone on first meeting.

He looked away when I said hello, so I stayed where I was, not wanting to crowd him. This was a tricky situation that needed to be handled with the utmost sensitivity.

Constable Ndibi came alongside me. 'Aiden? This is Dr Sam Willerby. She's a clinical psychologist,' he said. 'She's going to help you get back to normal.'

Aiden's chilled stare punctured the air. A barbed wire fence, like the one at the entrance, was between us right from the start. I smiled, but Aiden wasn't looking my way. He continued his opaque, unfathomable gaze into no man's land.

I quickly scanned his clothes to get a sense of how well he was looking after himself. He wore scruffy black jeans, a polo shirt and had bare feet. A typical student. I noticed the label of a well-known shoemaker printed inside a shoe on the floor to my left. Handmade, no less. Perhaps not a typical student, after all.

Aiden looked clean and groomed, but his whole being seemed to convey mixed messages; proud and helpless, all in one. His polo shirt hadn't seen an iron and was incorrectly buttoned. There was patchy stubble dotted around his chin and his jaw bone twitched as if he was grinding his teeth. I had the feeling he was using every ounce of energy to prevent himself from falling apart. My guts squirmed at the daunting task that lay ahead of me.

'When I got here, he was hiding inside the wardrobe,' whispered PC Ndibi, pointing to the far end of the boat. 'He's looking more perky.' I made a mental note that Aiden's current blanked-out appearance was, in fact, an improvement. 'When we brought him back from the hospital, he curled into a ball. Like he thought he was in an earthquake and everything was collapsing around him.'

The constable beckoned me past Aiden through the saloon into the kitchen area. Aiden stayed where he was, still gripping the chair. A grim determination was holding him inches from an unseen cliff edge.

'I don't think you're going to get much out of him, not right now, anyway,' he said. 'I might as well give you the grand tour of the boat.' He pointed to the glossy wooden sink unit. 'This is the galley.'

I drew back. 'We can't snoop about like we're thinking of buying it. Not while Aiden is here.'

The constable looked affronted. 'He's not going to mind, is he?'

'How do you know?'

'Well, we can ask him, but he's hardly going to refuse, is he?' The flippancy in his tone appalled me. He seemed to be finding this whole situation quite amusing – and I wasn't having it.

'We are intruders,' I said firmly. 'We have to respect Aiden's privacy.' I turned away refusing to insult Aiden any further by whispering behind his back. PC Ndibi shrugged and stayed in the galley. I returned to the saloon and sat on a banquette a little distance from Aiden.

Now we were alone, I wasn't quite sure how to begin. Having never treated a patient in their own home before, I was aware of how entirely different the dynamic felt. I didn't deliver my usual introductions, nor did Aiden break the ice by offering me coffee or asking whether I'd found the location without any trouble – the usual social niceties offered by a host when receiving a visitor. Aiden did, however, let go of the chair. Then he sat down on the opposite banquette, pulling his knees into his chest, staring through the tunnel between his thighs in a frozen state. He didn't seem to be affected either way by my presence.

My instinct told me to allow the silence between us to linger for a while, to show him that I was neither uncomfortable nor annoyed by it, rather than bombard him with questions he couldn't answer. In that silence, I gazed past his shoulder but found myself being drawn back to refocus on his face.

I couldn't say that he was handsome, exactly. There was nothing macho or rugged about him. It seemed ridiculous to define him in this way, but I could only describe Aiden's appearance as beautiful. It was the only word that seemed to fit. 'Beautiful' carried a soft magic within it, transcending sexual attractiveness. Perhaps it was his silence that was alluring – the old cliché of the taciturn artist, with ideas simmering inside his head, perpetually unreachable.

Not only was Aiden not speaking, but the police psychiatrist had explained in his report that he wasn't communicating at all to anyone – no smiles, nods or shakes of the head. He was fixed in one expression, locked in some dark trance he couldn't shake himself out of.

It was my job to try to reach him.

I'd heard of children rendered mute from cases at St Luke's. One girl of six couldn't speak after being involved in a car crash that killed her mother. And a colleague worked with a boy aged nine who had seen his father fall from their garage roof. I knew post-traumatic mutism existed in adults, but I'd never actually come across it before. In the child cases I knew of, it took several weeks before the patients were able to speak again. With Aiden, I'd got exactly one week to work miracles.

The seconds ticked by and I continued to sit opposite him, neither of us making a sound. His elegant bare feet resting on the banquette implied some kind of intimacy between us and I found myself simply wanting to watch him; the delicate angles of his cheeks, the long line of his neck. His back was straight and in the midst of his detachment there was a defiance; like that of an exotic bird, caged for reasons it could not understand, but determined to maintain its dignity.

I'd had plenty of long pauses in sessions with patients who refused to, or were emotionally unable to speak for certain periods. It's hard when working with such people not to feel frustrated and impatient. At times their unresponsiveness might seem belligerent to an outsider – no doubt what PC Ndibi experienced – although this was rarely how the patients themselves felt. Nevertheless, I was immediately fascinated by Aiden. Even though he didn't utter a word nor acknowledge my existence, there was a charisma, a bohemian quality that vibrated from him like electricity.

Eventually, I let my eyes drift away from him and noticed a small battered musical box with a ballerina on the top, on a shelf beside us. It looked like it had been around for several generations.

'I used to have one just like this,' I said, getting close to it, but not touching. 'My grandmother gave it to me. Does it still play a tune, I wonder?'

I glanced round, but he wasn't looking at me – cut off like he hadn't heard. His skin was of the same rich colour as those who live in the Mediterranean; it made him look like he regularly slept under the stars, rarely spending time indoors. 'Mine used to play "Blow the Wind Southerly",' I said lightly. 'It used to send me off to sleep when I was little.'

I stood to look at the frames on the wall. There was a series of pencil portraits; one of a young woman looking coy and another I instantly recognised as a self-portrait. Aiden had completely captured the soft, vulnerable quality of his own face.

'These are beautiful,' I said.

He acted as if he hadn't heard me, remaining subdued and listless, then abruptly got to his feet and padded to one of the doors at the far end of the boat. He went inside and closed it behind him. I stayed where I was for a moment then re-joined PC Ndibi in the galley.

'Told you,' he said, folding his newspaper. 'I've been here once or twice since it happened.' He yawned. 'He's done nothing but stare into space or sleep.'

'It's early days,' I said, sounding more hopeful than I felt.

'You finished now?'

'I'm not sure. I'm just going to sit in the saloon for a while… see if he comes out again.' I tried to smile, not wanting to alienate him.

'Okay, I'll wait,' he said.

'Aren't you staying with him the whole time?' I asked. 'To make sure he's okay?'

'No way,' he replied. 'I was only here to meet you and make sure you got to see him, that's all.' He flicked back his shirt cuff to check his watch. 'I'm going to stretch my legs for a minute.' He winked as he came past me, then left the boat.

I'd spent a holiday on a canal boat once on the Norfolk Broads, but it was nothing like this. My lasting memories were of constantly bumping into people, cramped oily and dark spaces where I kept banging my head and a bad cabbage smell lingering by the toilet. The vessel was constantly chilly, even in July. Aiden's boat was palatial by comparison.

I'd learnt from the police report that it was the maximum size allowed for a canal boat to navigate the waterways, with two berths, each within their own enclosed cabins. The rest was open-plan. The interior of the saloon was immaculate with granite worktops and wood panelling in a shade of gold. Special touches of gold light switches and decorative door handles made it appear luxurious – almost romantic.

On bookshelves beside me were novels by Will Self and Salman Rushdie, biographies of Che Guevara, Banksy and Martin Luther King. He was obviously a wide reader and the subjects told me a little about his interests. The way a person sets out their home, whether it's a tent or a palace, reveals a great deal about who they are. In Aiden's case, all I had were his belongings, his artwork and people who knew him to tell me who he was. They were the only signposts I'd have to assist me in helping him.

Loose press clippings were scattered on the Welsh dresser opposite, next to a printer. I picked one up; a review of a recent fashion show for which Aiden had designed a collection, all in white. Beside the dresser was a framed poster advertising one of his exhibitions at the Chelsea College of Art & Design, labelling him a 'cutting-edge textile designer'. The police report stated that this was the end of Aiden's second year, but as he was only nineteen, he must have started a year earlier than usual. I couldn't deny that his work looked impressive to an untrained eye such as mine.

I wandered back into the galley. Above the sink were a series of books about martial arts alongside vegan cookbooks. I remembered from the report that Aiden was vegetarian.

I wrote my phone number in large digits on the back of one of my business cards, together with the words, 'Any Time', and slipped it under a mug on the draining board.

'No point in doing that,' said Ndibi, folding his arms as he came up behind me. 'How's he going to talk to you?'

'I know,' I said, 'but it's an offering.'

'He hasn't been given his phone back yet,' he smirked, leaning against the washing machine like he owned the place. I ignored him and took a closer look at the walls, which were covered, end-to-end, in works of art. As well as the sketches, there were framed photographs, based around shades of white.

'I don't get these, myself,' said Ndibi, turning up his nose. We stared in turn at images of a white telephone on a blank wall, spilt white paint on a bare white floor, a chipped chalk landscape against white clouds. All white on white.

'I rather like them,' I said. 'I've never thought about different shades of white before. So subtle. He's really got something.'

I'd always been intrigued by artistic people, although Hannah, my best friend, would put it a little stronger than that. In fact, on her advice, I'd had intensive therapy in the past year to deal with my annoying pattern of falling for impressive, high-achieving men who were invariably unavailable. I'd been single since then, so I hadn't exactly put it to the test yet.

Hannah had a new private therapy practice in Devon, having committed the worst sin imaginable by moving over a year ago. I was gutted when she left London and missed our impromptu get-togethers. Video chats didn't cut it for either of us, but she and her husband had their hearts set on starting a family alongside rolling hills rather than bumper-to-bumper traffic on Wandsworth High Street.

I stopped at a pastel portrait of a child. 'Can't draw, personally,' said Ndibi, looking bored. 'What about you?'

'Hopeless,' I confessed.

I hated to admit it, but Aiden's work certainly seemed more accomplished than the pictures my sister Miranda was producing. She'd made only a few attempts at portraits, claiming they 'upset people'. It was easy to see why. Her paintings were invariably aggressive and garish. These days, she'd moved on from ugly images resembling mutilated body parts and was churning out 'landscapes' with gaudy splodges of orange, pink and red. I could barely bring myself to look at them, but I made a point of never making it obvious. I knew they were important to her, so that was the main thing. In fact, the reason I'd done additional training in art therapy was because I'd seen how much of Miranda's disturbed internal world was hidden inside her paintings. For her, splashing her feelings onto a canvas was the only way to fully express herself.

'Has Aiden drawn anything while you've been here?' I asked.

'No. Not a thing. Apparently he's never without a piece of charcoal or paintbrush in his hand, but he's done nothing since the incident.'

It was clear that art consumed Aiden's life, but since witnessing the assault he was in a bad way; deeply traumatised and shut down. I left with a heavy heart. It wasn't just that time was against us and Aiden couldn't utter a word. What worried me most, was that any creativity – the one avenue we had left open to us – may have completely dried up.

Chapter 7

As soon as my first 'meeting' with Aiden was over, I darted back across London. DCS Claussen had moved on to other pressing CID matters, but DCI Wilde had demanded I meet the core team at Stanhope Street station. I only just made it.

I rubbed the spot on my wrist where my watch was cutting into my skin, kept thinking that if things had gone to plan, I'd have been on a flight that morning to Greece. So much had happened, it was hard to believe it was only last night I'd got the phone call that threw everything up in the air.

Wilde was standing, glaring at the door when I came in, as if on the verge of giving up on me. By contrast, DI Fenway offered a bright smile and introduced me to two new faces; Crime Scene Manager, DS Edwin Hall and Major Incident Room Manager, DS Joanne Hoyland. This time, we were in a small room with a TV screen on the wall, seats dotted around a large white table. I threw my jacket over the back of the chair and sat down in the empty seat next to Fenway.

'And this is our police psychiatrist, Dr Melvin Herts,' said DCI Wilde. I gave Dr Herts a formal nod, taking in his shiny bald head, offset by inordinately bushy eyebrows. It struck me as a rather cruel stroke of fate that the only hair he possessed was nowhere near his head. Instead, it had been lavishly distributed above his eyes.

'Have you met the witness yet?' Wilde asked.

I nodded. 'I've just come from his boat. I think we have a remedial case on our hands. Coaxing Aiden into revealing anything could take a *long* time.'

'That's one thing we don't have,' the DCI pointed out, unnecessarily.

'I have to get him to trust me first,' I stated, calmly. 'Nothing will happen without that.'

Wilde cut straight to the point. 'How long is he going to be in this state?'

'I can't answer that. If he witnessed the whole thing it must have had a profound effect on him. The victim must have been hurtling along the towpath on her bike, and then all of a sudden, she's almost decapitated. She fell right outside his boat. It must have been ghastly – a shock to his entire system.'

The psychiatrist chipped in. 'Is he still refusing to take antidepressants or sleeping pills?'

'As far as I know.' PC Ndibi had told me as I left the boat that Aiden wasn't accepting any medication. 'But, I'm worried about his state of mind,' I stressed. 'Has he made any attempts to harm himself?'

'It's hard to give an accurate assessment when the patient isn't speaking,' said Dr Herts, his pudgy hands folded together on the table. 'But, I'd say he has too much to live for to go and do anything stupid.'

'Except he may feel this incident has shattered his life forever,' I said, unable to hide a frown. 'Has his family been contacted? Can't anyone come and stay with him on the boat for a while?'

'We can't track down any family members,' chipped in DI Fenway. 'He might have changed his name. We've been in touch with various friends, but he's refusing to let anyone he knows on the boat, apart from his neighbours next to him in the marina.'

'Is it possible to have a police officer on-board round the clock to keep an eye on him?'

DCI Wilde made a noise that sounded like a cross between a choke and a howl. 'You seriously think we have money or resources for round-the-clock supervision?'

I should have realised. Only that morning, I'd seen a report on the news about the Met with the terms 'spending cuts', 'limited resources' and 'unsustainable pressures' being bandied about.

DI Fenway stepped in again. 'If we thought Aiden was in danger, from the attacker or himself, we'd have to consider some form of protection. As it is, there's nothing to suggest he's a target and nothing in the psychiatric assessment, in so far as Dr Herts has ascertained, to indicate that he intends to harm himself.'

Dr Herts nodded and his fulsome eyebrows twitched. They reminded me of hairy caterpillars; it was hard to take my eyes off them.

'We've got officers dropping in to check on him,' the DI added, 'and the harbour master and neighbours are keeping an eye on the boat.'

'Thank you,' I said. More for taking the sting out of the situation than for what he could offer. 'Have any other witnesses come forward?' I added, hopefully.

'No. Mr Blake is our only one,' grunted Wilde.

'Can we go back to what Aiden saw?' suggested DI Fenway. 'Dr Willerby; could Aiden have *known* the victim? Is that why his reaction is so extreme?'

I sat back so I could turn to him. There was no longer any sign of that morning's shaving injury on his neck, but I noticed a faint line of blue biro near his ear.

'It's possible,' I said. 'The report said you'd spoken to a few of his friends and so far, it looks like he didn't know Kora, but they were both artists.'

Melvin Herts jumped in again. 'It could be that Aiden is just a particularly sensitive guy.'

'But will anything useful come back to him?' pressed the DCI.

I looked over at Dr Herts, but he was waiting for me to speak. 'There are no guarantees,' I said. 'All I know is we need to tread carefully, it's a delicate situation.'

Herts pushed back his chair abruptly. 'Got to go,' he said, rubbing his hands together. 'Busy, busy…' The meeting had only been underway for five minutes.

A weighty silence followed once he'd closed the door, bristling with frustration from both sides of the table. 'I'll tell it to you straight,' said DCI Wilde. 'I've got a bad feeling about this. I think this maniac is going to strike again. We've had reports of someone loitering at various points along the same stretch of towpath. Of course, that could be the public getting jittery, but we need to get Mr Blake talking, or drawing, or whatever he's going to do – and we need him to start doing it *now*. Like DCS Claussen explained to you, we've got a maximum of seven days. Probably less, if we're being realistic. After that time, I don't think whatever he has to offer will be of any use to us.'

I was almost on my feet, poised to wave a belligerent finger at him, but managed to stop myself. I needed to remember that he wasn't interested in Aiden's mental state. He wanted him solely as a credible witness.

DI Fenway broke the impasse. 'Moving on, what do we know about Kora Washington?'

DS Hoyland piped up, without looking at her notes. 'Victim is white, twenty-seven, five-five, weighs a hundred and thirteen pounds, pretty,' she said. 'A sculptor at Camden Community Art Project. Former drug-user, but no relapses in the last two years according to her partner and therapist. She does waitressing at the café at CCAP, as well as exhibiting her work there. She's been with Sponge, her partner, for four years. They have an eighteen-month-old boy, Raven. Devoted mother, apparently, lots of friends. She's being described as lively and spontaneous, wholesome, loyal…' She glanced down at her report. 'Outgoing and selfless.'

I remembered Miranda's other term. *Naïve.*

'Oh,' she said, her finger running down the page, 'they ran tests at the hospital when Kora was admitted and her stomach was virtually empty, which rings alarm bells, because users at the project said they remembered her having lunch that day. There was residue of diarrhoea and traces of a laxative – a pretty strong one – in her system. Her partner Sponge said they didn't keep any such product in the flat and he didn't believe Kora would use something over the counter like that.'

'We'll need to check that with her, if she… survives,' said Fenway.

'What was she doing the night she was attacked?' I asked.

'Caretaker saw her just as he started to close up at about twenty-five past nine,' said Joanne. 'She was getting her bike from the shed round the back. He said she was in a bit of a fluster, because she couldn't find her helmet, but she rode off without it anyway. He checked the building and did the final lock up.'

'No helmet – a coincidence that she was totally unprotected, or not?' I asked of no one in particular. 'Which way did she cycle?'

'He said she cycled off to the right.'

'Which isn't the obvious route home for her,' added DI Fenway. 'To the right took her towards the towpath.'

'And he said she looked like she was in a hurry,' added Joanne.

'Okay… so where was she going at that time of night?' Fenway pondered.

There was a lingering silence.

'Did the caretaker see any other vehicles in the car park or outside the gates?' I asked.

'He said the place was empty,' said Joanne. 'The cleaner had left a few minutes before.'

'What about the missing helmet?' I asked. 'Did she usually keep it with her bike?'

'Caretaker said she did, in the bike shed.'

'Locked to her bike?'

'No, but the shed itself is locked. Anyone from CCAP could have had access.'

'Any CCTV?' I asked.

DCI Wilde gave me the kind of stare that implied I'd just dropped in from another planet. 'Community resources don't usually stretch that far,' he said, brushing a piece of fluff from his sleeve.

'Was it usual for Kora to use a bike?'

'Everyone at CCAP says she used it all the time,' said Joanne. 'Definite "green" type; vegetarian, into recycling, sustainability, all that.' She gave a cautious glance in my direction, as if concerned she may have sounded dismissive.

'You said Kora was clean, but could this be drugs related?' I asked.

The DI wiggled his pencil between his fingers. 'It's an ongoing line of enquiry.'

'Have you established whether Kora was happy?' I interjected. 'Whether she liked being at CCAP?' I'd been to CCAP many times and had been impressed not only by the quality of the work on display, but by the serene ambiance of the place. I'd seen Miranda blossom into a confident and charismatic woman ever since she'd been involved. I even envied her, she seemed to have more of a social life than I did; more friends, people admiring her work, blokes queuing up to take her on dates. But, not everyone might feel that way about the place.

'General consensus is that she was doing very well; selling her work, cheerful, friendly, her usual self,' said Fenway.

'What about the scene of crime report?' I asked. 'What was visibility like at half past nine that night? How much could Aiden have actually seen?'

Edwin Hall cleared his throat. 'Sunset was around nine fifteen, but there were lights in the car park and street lights along the Ridgeway Bridge.'

'Okay, so how much light are we actually talking about here?' I asked. 'Are we asking the impossible from this witness?'

'No,' said Edwin. 'When we found Aiden, the lamp outside the boat was on. There was also a lamp clipped onto the front of Kora's bicycle pointing directly along the towpath. Visibility is largely a subjective measurement, but at a range of up to five metres, I'd say we're talking about seventy to eighty percent visibility, considering the conditions. Good enough for recognisable detail and Mr Blake is clearly tuned in to seeing things better than most people.'

A low hum of approval went round the table. Edwin sat back and briefly let his tongue hang out with the look of someone who had just got his first hole in one. Fenway had told me earlier that this was his first case.

'What evidence was there at the scene?' I asked.

'Virtually nothing,' said the DI. 'The path was dry, so we have no decent footprints. There's a wire fence between the towpath and the car park the other side, so if the attacker climbed over there won't be fingerprints, but there could be DNA from sweat or skin flakes. We've picked up partials from the stairwell nearby and on Aiden's boat near the lamp where the assailant pulled the wire away. None of the prints so far are Aiden's. There are no matches on the database and if the attacker had any sense, he'd have been wearing gloves, so they might not be his.' His chest swelled up and sank. 'The problem is whoever did this didn't get anywhere near Kora.'

'The attacker must know the area well,' said Joanne. 'He knows there's a car park beside the towpath for access; he knows where the boats are and where to tie the wire. He also knew that the towpath gates wouldn't be shut until later.'

'Gates?' I queried.

'There are security gates that close off sections of the towpath to protect the residents after dark. That section beyond Ridgeway Bridge is for visitors' moorings – owners are issued with a key. We spoke to them to check who actually closes the security gates, and when. British Waterways have an official who comes down daily at about ten, during the summer.'

'He showed up while we were cordoning off the scene,' said Edwin. 'He confirmed that he'd been closing up at ten o'clock for about four weeks. It depends on when it gets dark.'

'So the attacker knew the area, knew how things worked,' I mused aloud.

We sat still for a while, each of us waiting for someone else to add anything, but nothing happened. Then, that was that. DCI Wilde must have given a surreptitious sign and the team started gathering their papers together and closing their tablets.

Before he left, Wilde turned to me and delivered one final command. 'See to it that you give this your full attention Dr

Willerby, because we don't have much to go on.' There was an uncomfortable silence. 'And *that* mustn't go beyond this room, nor should any details of this case. None whatsoever. Understood?'

The entire room quivered as he slammed the door, followed by an aftershock of shuffling and straightening of ties. Once everyone had dispersed, I found myself in the corridor standing by the coffee machine.

'Don't *ever*, whatever you do, get a drink from this machine,' came a voice in my ear. 'It will either drop a clump of powdered milk in at the last minute or shoot boiling water over your hand when you reach in for the cup.'

I laughed and Fenway straightened up beside me. 'I'm afraid you're going to be stuck with me a fair bit over the next few days,' he said.

'I think I might just be able to cope with that,' I replied, puffing out my cheeks, relieved DCI Wilde wouldn't be the one breathing down my neck. 'In any case, it's only supposed to be for a week.'

'It's not going to be, though, is it?' he said, with a frown. The chill in his tone unnerved me. 'You've got a tough job on your hands.'

'I'm not the only one,' I pointed out, raising my eyebrows.

'Listen, here's my personal number.' My phone beeped with his text. 'We'll be in daily contact, but if you need to ask me anything, anything at all, or it all gets too much, just ring. Day or night.'

Before I could answer, an officer hurtled towards us along the narrow corridor, shunting me face-forward into Fenway as he darted past. The DI was forced to take a sudden interest in my lapel until I was able to get my balance and step away.

'Sorry…' we both muttered awkwardly, in unison.

As I turned to go, he held up his arm. 'Hang on a moment,' he said, before disappearing into a nearby office.

He returned holding a sheet of paper. 'Here's a list of Aiden's main friends. We've made contact with most of them so far. We'll also be talking to his college tutors and other students and raking through Facebook contacts and so on. We're struggling to find any family at the moment.'

'Thank you,' I said, taking the list from him. I fanned my face with it. 'Anyone know how Kora is doing?'

'Still fighting for her life in ICU. No change a couple of hours ago. There's something incredibly ruthless, almost inhuman, isn't there, about deliberately hanging an invisible wire across a cycle path, then waiting to see what would happen?'

'Then creeping out to unfasten the wire, afterwards... unbelievable...' I gasped, shaking my head. 'It can only have been carried out by an utterly heartless individual.'

He had a way of standing with his hands in his pockets that made him look both shifty and playful all at once. 'Call me Jeremy, by the way – it will put you one step up from all the others around here who have to call me *sir*.' He looked about him to see if anyone had heard.

I laughed, feeling self-conscious. 'Okay.' I swung my bag over my shoulder ready to leave. 'Likewise, I'm Sam.'

He rocked on the soles of his feet. 'I think we'll all be needing therapy after this,' he said, giving me a sad shrug. His manner made me feel as if I was in safe hands; not only did he seem on the ball about this case, but realistic too. As I wandered out into the roar of the busy street, I wondered who was taking care of him once he got home.

Chapter 8

Natalie Beauvoir was wringing out a shirt in the sink and Didier, her husband, was peeling garlic when I climbed aboard that evening. Jeremy had told them I'd be in touch. Didier was offering me a glass of red wine before my foot even touched the floor.

'We're French,' he said, rolling the 'r' unashamedly. 'After six o'clock, the French drink only wine.'

I accepted gratefully. It had already been a long day and it was far from over. They invited me to join them at the saloon table.

'How long has Aiden been based here at the Limehouse moorings?' I asked.

Natalie responded. She was strikingly pretty, around twenty-five, I guessed, with straight black hair and tiny features. She wore a white embroidered blouse that was virtually see-through, complimented by snug capri pants. I wondered if Aiden found her attractive.

'Aiden was already here, for a year, maybe?' she glanced across at Didier for confirmation. He nodded. 'We came here in March.'

'Do you get on well as neighbours?'

'Yes,' they both said at once. 'Some of the boat owners keep to themselves, but the rest of us… we knit together into a little community,' added Natalie, nudging her phone away on the table with her glass. 'We look out for each other. It can be… how you say?... vulnerable being on a boat, you're that much closer to the elements and there are always fears for security. But Aiden is wonderful. He feeds our cat, brings in our washing when it rains, takes in grocery deliveries.'

'We do the same for him,' said Didier. He was wearing shorts that revealed chunky legs the colour of mahogany, cross-hatched with thick black hair. He dangled his wine glass between his knees, staring into it.

'He's like a different person now,' said Natalie, dropping her voice as if he might hear from the adjacent boat. 'All silent and cut off from everything. You're going to help him, the police said.'

'I'm going to try. I work with people affected by trauma.'

'We'll look after him any way we can. The detective said Aiden won't leave his boat, but he lets us in, so we can check on him.'

'Do many people come to his boat?'

They looked at each other. 'Now and again,' said Didier. I listened for any undercurrent in his voice, but there was nothing.

'He's not one for throwing parties,' said Natalie. 'He's totally focused on his art. Always with a crayon in his hand.' She got up and came back with a framed portrait. She handed it to me with pride. 'It's good, no?' Aiden had caught something startlingly sexy about Natalie as she sat, beaming at him over her shoulder.

'He doesn't seem interested in drawing me,' said Didier, curling his tongue.

I smiled. They seemed a friendly, welcoming couple who obviously took an interest in Aiden.

'When he isn't sketching, he's taking photographs or working with cloth. He invited us to one of his exhibitions. It was very good. He designs clothes, too. Where is that magazine, Didi?' She looked about her, but I told her not to bother. I knew I'd be able to gather any factual information I needed about Aiden from the police or his own boat.

'Any partner you know of? Any romance?'

'We know he's into girls.' Didier stopped himself. 'What I mean to say is, he isn't gay, as far as we know. We've seen different girls staying over, but no one regular, I don't think?' He gave Natalie an enquiring look.

'That's right. No one regular and none recently. I think he's too involved with his work to get serious.'

I finished my wine and took the last few minutes to ask how they occupied themselves. Natalie was a dancer, working temporarily in a troupe based in Islington. She invited me to a performance they were giving that week at the National Theatre. Didier said he was researching medieval documents for a PhD and spent a lot of time in the British Library. I got the impression neither of them were strapped for cash, although their boat was smaller than Aiden's and was nowhere near as plush. I thanked them and said I'd no doubt see them soon.

Once on the pontoon, I took a couple of steps towards Aiden's *Louisa II* and listened. The boats were all moored head-on to the wooden platform, so by checking from side to side, I could see that all the curtains were closed. I wondered if he'd eaten supper yet, or maybe even gone to bed. The door at the front end was closed and, for a second, I felt a shiver of concern that he might have taken off somewhere, until a puff of smoke wafted out of the chimney on the roof. I smiled to myself and headed back home to Clapham.

My suitcase was still sitting packed, looking hopeful, at my front door. I hadn't had chance to empty it and didn't feel like doing it now. It was late and I was running on empty. Then I realised my toothbrush was embedded inside, as was the bedside novel I was reading… and my hairbrush. I dragged the case onto a chair in my bedroom and pulled out what I needed. The rest of my belongings would have to wait until tomorrow.

I pondered for a while on what someone would make of *me,* if they only had the contents of my flat to go on. From the outside, the property was wedged between a former bakery on the corner and a row of tall Victorian houses with sash windows, all broken into flats. I rented a one-bedroom place on the first floor, living alongside people I had nothing in common with other than a shared front door. Mrs Willow lived upstairs, a sparky widow in her eighties. We took in each other's parcels and I always had an ear open for the floorboards above, satisfied when I heard the familiar rhythm of creaks. I knew the others to speak to, but that was all. It wasn't the kind of place I would ever buy; too scruffy with visible flaws, such as damp and cracks that were gradually eating into every wall and ceiling. When I moved in, it was only meant to tide me over until I 'sorted myself out', whatever that meant.

That was over four years ago.

I cringed when I thought of how I must look to a psychologist. A professional, attractive woman in her mid-thirties still living in 'student-style' accommodation with no close family, aside from a sister who needs special care and a best friend who's moved away. The nearest I got to homely chats were with Mrs Willow. Under such scrutiny, my situation felt bleak and, frankly, embarrassing. To an outsider I probably looked like I was waiting for something, some event to break the stalemate. But what exactly?

As I put my passport back in a drawer, I mourned the loss of my holiday. Another area of my life that never seemed to get off the ground – literally. I felt a twist of fear tug at my stomach, warning me that if I didn't watch out another summer was going to pass me by and I'd plunge headlong into a grim winter never having felt alive. I needed to take a long hard look at myself and work out what I really wanted, before my life turned into one extended Groundhog Day.

I didn't have enough energy for supper other than to tip a few flakes of cereal into a bowl and flood them with cold water. I'd forgotten to pick up milk. I gave myself a moment as I crunched through them to pretend I was watching the sun go down on the beach, with the twang of Greek musicians in the distance and the waft of oysters in the air. But I wasn't even to be allowed that luxury, because my phone rang.

There was silence at the other end, but the kind of silence when you know someone else is there. I said hello a few times and when there was no response I swiped the screen to disconnect. Then it rang again.

'Who is this?' I barked.

There was a tiny click followed by the chimes of a bell. No, not a bell, the tinkling notes of a musical box. It was playing 'Love Me

Tender'. I could hear the tick of the mechanism in the background and I knew exactly what it was.

'Aiden, is that you? It's Sam,' I said. 'Are you okay?'

There was a short silence.

'Has something happened?'

The tune played again.

'Do you want me to come over?'

Silence again. 'I'll come over,' I said, knowing I was never going to get any reply.

After I hung up I rang Jeremy. 'I'm sorry it's late.'

'It's okay – there's no such thing as a sleeping policeman,' he chuckled, but he sounded like he was fighting a yawn.

I explained what had happened.

'Are you sure it's Aiden?' he said. 'We've got his mobile phone.'

'He must have borrowed one from Natalie or Didier,' I said.

He asked me for the number.

'Yeah, that's Natalie's. But it's late and it's a long way over to Limehouse,' he said wearily. 'Ring back and tell him you'll go over first thing in the morning.'

'No, I don't want to wait. I might miss something. This is a good sign. He's making contact, he's trying to make a connection. And don't forget what everyone's been saying about time being of the essence.'

'Yeah, yeah, I know.' I could almost hear his bones creak as he rallied. 'Okay, I'll send someone to let you in. I don't want you being there on your own. Keep a note of all your expenses, won't you? Can't have you out of pocket.'

I thanked him for his concern and was about to leave when I decided I wouldn't go empty-handed. It was a heavy job lugging the boxes all the way down the stairs, but there was the slimmest chance it might be worth it. I left the pile inside the communal front door, then set out into the night in search of a taxi.

Chapter 9

It was almost 11pm by the time I returned to the marina, but I'd already resigned myself to getting minimal sleep over these seven days. The message could only have come from Aiden; the nature of that little musical box, plucking its little tune in my ear, seemed both intimate and desperate. What did it mean?

PC Ndibi stepped out of the shadows by the marina gates and helped me with my boxes.

'Been shopping?' he said.

'Just tools of the trade,' I said, enigmatically.

The bow door was already open and I stepped inside. Ndibi followed me and made us all a coffee.

'I'll wait in the galley,' he said, pulling across the wooden partition, 'and give you two some privacy.'

Aiden was sitting on a banquette, his elbows on the pull-down table, head in his hands. The phone I'd seen earlier near Natalie's glass of wine, was beside him. No one knew how Aiden wanted to be treated, but my aim was to be as normal with him as possible.

'Are you okay? You wanted to see me?'

He was constantly trembling as if we were in a different season altogether. There were red patches on his cheeks, blotches around his eyes from crying. I wanted to hug him; he looked like he'd been washed up after a disaster at sea – the sole survivor.

There was an open sketch pad behind him on the dresser. I moved over to get it. He flinched as I got near him. It was common for people with PTSD to jump at the slightest of movements.

'I'm sorry,' I said. 'I didn't mean to startle you.'

The pad was open at a blank page and it made me think Aiden might have been trying to draw something. 'Can I see?' I flicked back a page to the last one he'd done. It was an unfinished drawing of Natalie stroking a cat, with a date four days ago scribbled in the bottom corner.

I found a pencil in a tray on a small table and left it on the notepad beside him, then sat opposite, waiting. He sat back, his head hanging, avoiding all contact with me. His eyes were empty; there was nothing behind them. Perhaps he'd changed his mind and didn't want me there after all.

I waited in silence; no sighing, no fidgeting, no huffing. When nothing happened, I leant over and examined the drawing again and told him what I saw. 'It's lovely… the whiskers of the tabby, the light in Natalie's hair… fluid shapes, shading, careful detail.'

He looked over at my sandals for a second, then dropped his head again, shutting himself off. I couldn't see his face to read what inner turmoil he was going through, but everything about his body was uptight and jittery.

I waited a while, then folded the pad over to the blank page again and slid it towards him, holding my breath. He didn't lift his head, but his hand reached out for the pencil. It was the first positive action I'd seen since we'd met. I sat back, forced myself to stay completely deadpan.

As he rested the point of the pencil on the sheet I could see his hand shaking. He gripped the pencil awkwardly, like he'd never held one before and didn't know what to do with it. Then he dragged the point in a wobbly, uncontrolled line from one corner to the other. A pained expression claimed his face and he swapped the pencil to his other hand and tried again. With the tip on the paper, he attempted to get it to do what he wanted, but the pencil merely scraped across the page again.

It was like watching someone who had lost all feeling in their hands trying to draw something recognisable. It was hopeless. He looked fraught and humiliated; he couldn't even doodle. He screwed up his eyes, slammed down the pad and hurled the pencil across the room. It was all too much for him. When I stopped to consider what he must have witnessed, I wasn't surprised. Imagine bringing in your washing and seeing someone getting thrown off their bicycle, getting their neck sliced open right in front of you. I shuddered at the thought.

'It's okay,' I said, 'you gave it a go. That took a lot of courage. Don't push yourself if you're not ready.'

Aiden propped his chin into his hands. He didn't look at me, but he didn't get up and walk away either.

I blew out a silent slow breath. We were a million miles away from a pristine representation of the assailant's face. That's all the police wanted, but asking Aiden to draw was like asking him to put his hands into a scorching flame. He just couldn't do it.

Time for Plan B. 'Is it okay if we try something else?' I asked.

He stayed completely still, then put his hands together into a prayer position, his fingers resting against his mouth. Was that a *yes* or a *no*? This was a whole new language I didn't understand. He didn't look horrified, so I took it in the affirmative.

I dragged the cardboard boxes into the saloon. Ndibi heard the commotion and thought I was leaving. His face fell when I told him I was far from finished, but he'd been well behaved, this time. He hadn't interfered or talked behind Aiden's back. Occasionally his radio would crackle and startle me, but most of the time he'd sat silently out of sight with his newspaper.

'You'll need the code to the keypad when you do leave eventually,' he said, handing me a small scrap of paper. 'You'll be on your own with Mr Blake from tomorrow.'

Someone overseeing the purse strings at the Met had obviously realised they didn't have the resources to provide me with a regular gatekeeper.

Aiden watched me as I pulled out a series of plastic topped containers; the type that keep biscuits or cheese fresh. When I peeled off the lids, instead of food, they revealed a selection of miniature models; realistic figures of animals, people, ships, cars, a helicopter, an aeroplane. Another tub held shells and bones, another stones and eggs, one with miniature fruit and veg, one with items from a doll's house including a grandfather clock, armchair and cot. There were tiny bridges, gates, a castle, figures of Batman, Peter Pan, Darth Vader, Cinderella, a witch, dinosaur, octopus. A cornucopia of fantasy people and objects, all from my office that I'd taken home to clean and mend once I'd returned from Greece. Last of all I placed a flat wooden box, the size of a large tea tray, on the table beside them.

Aiden stared, open-mouthed, at my every move. It was the first time I'd seen an expression bearing any resemblance to interest on his face. I took the lid off the box to reveal a layer of sand, four centimetres deep.

'I'll need a wet cloth,' I said, addressing the PC. He disappeared for a moment and came back with a damp tea towel. He looked as intrigued as Aiden, but I had to usher him back to the galley to give us privacy.

We started first with the sand itself. I invited Aiden to put his hands in the tray to get a feel for the grains of sand. He did as instructed, pushing his fingers deep into the box. I then asked him to see if he could find any items in the containers that would represent what he could smell at this precise moment. It was a 'here and now' question designed to be as un-emotive as possible, simply to get Aiden into the routine of using the tools.

I inhaled and was aware of the sweet smell of an overripe banana on the window ledge, the constant diesel overtone on the boat, coffee from the dregs in our mugs. He looked into the boxes, but didn't reach out and touch anything. He kept his hands firmly in the sand and hid them there. I asked him a few other simple questions and each time he looked into the boxes, but didn't move. I stopped after a while. We weren't getting anywhere. He bit his lip and looked perplexed. It was beyond him.

I thanked Aiden for giving it a try and handed him the wet cloth so he could clean the grains from his hands. With my disappointment came an overwhelming desire for sleep. I was starting to feel nauseous from riding high on adrenalin for so long. I explained this to Aiden. He dropped his head.

'It's not your fault. I'm not blaming you. I'm just exhausted.'
I tried to stifle a yawn. 'I think we'll call it a day. Thank you. I'll
come back tomorrow.'

I called Ndibi and when there was no movement from the
galley, I walked through and found him slumped over the table.

'Spenser?' I whispered close to his ear. 'Time to go.'

He snorted, adjusted his uniform and tried to make it look
like he'd been on his guard all along. Keen to get going, he left the
boat first. As I moved to follow suit, in one deft movement Aiden
slipped in front of me and gently pressed the front door shut. As
I took another step forward he blocked my path. I froze, not sure
what to do. Aiden held his ground, standing right in my way.

'What's going on?' I said calmly. Had I left something behind?

Spenser was knocking on the door. 'What's the hold up? Why
have you shut the door?'

'It's okay,' I called back. 'Wait a minute.'

Aiden was looking at the sand tray. I didn't know what he
meant at first, then when I got closer I saw that he'd put something
inside. He'd rummaged around in the selection of dolls, knick-
knacks and stones when I was talking to Spenser and had placed
two china hedgehogs side by side in the sand with a little padlock
underneath.

I looked at it for a moment. 'I don't know what this means,'
I said gently.

He didn't move.

'Two hedgehogs together with a padlock...' I mused. 'Safety?
Together?' Then I got it. 'You want me to stay?'

His lip twisted to one side; it was almost a smile, but fear kept
his eyes wide, making him look like a helpless child.

'Have I got it right? You want me to stay here with you on
the boat?'

He nipped his lips together and dropped his head.

I was aware of how young he was beneath his bold, sophisticated
veneer, but my immediate impulse was to decline. It would be
awkward. Too close.

'Aiden, I can't. Thank you for your trust in me, but you're my patient – it's a bit too... intimate.' There, I'd said it, but honesty seemed the best way.

There were no histrionics, no tears – he politely showed me the two figures in the sandbox again. He drew a box around the objects with his finger and waited. He didn't want me to leave. He didn't want to be alone.

The notion of sleeping a few feet from each other, therapist and patient in this small space was entirely inappropriate. It was unheard of in my profession. Regardless of breaching professional boundaries, Aiden was a man I knew very little about. He didn't have a police record, but it didn't mean he might not be dangerous, especially if he wasn't in his right mind.

On second thoughts, if my approach was going to work, I needed to reduce the amount of stress Aiden was under to the absolute minimum. Only once he felt safe and in control, would he be able to reveal to me what he'd seen. What better way to have him open up to me than to be beside him as much as possible, where I could work intensively with him on both his recovery and secure evidence for the police?

But, I'd had an issue before with patient boundaries and it hadn't ended well. That said, it wasn't always easy to see what was best and this case was so entirely different from any other I'd come across. Before I made my decision I told Aiden I had to make a call. He let me open the door where I found a bemused PC Ndibi on the other side.

'What's going on? Everything alright?'

'Yep.' I patted his arm and asked him to call the police psychiatrist on duty at the station. He handed me his phone once he was put through.

'This is Dr Molliford,' a female voice told me. 'Dr Herts went off duty early today.'

I gave her the gist of the situation.

'You want to move in with him?' she scoffed. 'It's highly irregular.'

'It would be entirely above board and professional. Purely a working relationship.'

'How can you possibly justify it?'

'Aiden's barely an adult. He doesn't appear to be communicating with anyone else. He has no available family and he's blocking all his friends, but he's made a connection with me...'

An uncomfortable silence hung between us.

'This isn't just about Aiden's recovery,' I ploughed on, 'it's about finding a maniac and Aiden is our only witness. This is a sign we're making progress. He's trying to engage with me. If I'm here all the time, it could make all the difference to his recovery *and* the case.' Instead of asking for her opinion, I realised I was willing her to approve.

'Well, it's highly unorthodox. Is there no other way?'

'He won't leave the boat. He's traumatised in a way I've never seen before. He needs to feel safe and he's started to trust me.'

'Okay. I'll authorise it,' Dr Molliford relented. 'As long as you don't undermine any police procedures or ethical considerations. You're his therapist, not his mother...'

With that she cut me off.

I handed back the phone. I was staying. I popped my head round the door and told Aiden. He stood gazing at his bare feet as though he hadn't heard.

'I need to go back home for some things,' I said, holding the door open, 'but I'm coming straight back.' I saw him glance over at the two hedgehogs in the sand, but his expression didn't shift. 'I promise.'

Chapter 10

Friday, June 15 – Three weeks earlier

Pippa followed Mr Morino's directions past the tailor and into the square with a church in the centre. She stood on the corner and peered along the row of houses to the right, searching for the dark red entrance. True enough, it was the third house down.

The heavy front door had been left slightly ajar, and when Pippa rang the bell she could hear a voice, but couldn't see anyone. She stepped tentatively inside and was disconcerted at first. The hallway was long and dark, with no lights on.

She called out, 'Mr Morino? Are you there?'

'Is that Pippa? I'm just down here,' he shouted. 'Come inside and follow the light – I've just had a power-cut and I'm trying to find the trip switch.'

Her heels tapped hesitantly along the bare hallway before she reached the doorframe to the cellar.

'I'm really sorry about this,' came his voice from the shadows. Pippa could see a torch flicking around below. 'The electrics have blown. I'm not sure if it's just here or the whole street. Isn't Mildred there to meet you?'

Pippa turned and stared into the gloom, listening for footsteps. There didn't seem to be anyone else around. 'Mildred?' she called out. Then louder, 'Is anyone there?'

Her voice bounced off the walls and bare floorboards, ringing in the air.

She could make out two closed doors in the hall, but one didn't have a door handle, so she tapped on the other one. No response. She retraced her steps towards the entrance and glanced up the stairs. She didn't fancy straying up there. The place was chilled and smelt musty, as though no one had lived here for years. The only signs of life were coming from the cellar.

'Mildred has probably popped out for torch batteries,' came the voice. 'Are you any good with fuse boxes?'

She returned to the cellar doorway. 'Not really.'

'Why don't you come down anyway? Four eyes are better than two.'

She faltered. 'Can't you come up?'

'Not much point if we can't see what we're doing. I've closed all the curtains to make sure the painting doesn't get seen by anyone snooping around… you know… looking in the windows. You can't be too careful. I've got a special lamp we can use, so I can show you how we know it's an original. But only if I can get this damn power back on. We can hardly take the masterpiece out into the street!' His laugh sounded easy and wholesome.

She peered down the wooden steps but held her ground. It really didn't look inviting down there.

'I'm terribly sorry,' he went on, 'I'm useless at anything electrical. But, we might as well try as you've come all this way. I'd hate to send you away and then give the story to someone else…'

He waited in the silence, holding his breath.

That was the point at which everything could swing either one way or the other. He had it all meticulously planned. He just had to be patient.

He heard a shuffle and thought he'd lost her, then one step at a time, her shoes clunked down the steep steps. Before he saw her, he could smell her perfume pervading the space. He briefly closed his eyes letting the waft wrap around him. She needed a few moments to adjust to the light and it was then, as soon as she reached the bottom step, that he nipped into the space behind her and charged up the steps. Then – *bang*. The cellar door was shut and bolted.

Like a rat in a cage, he'd got her.

She didn't know it then, but in a few weeks' time Pippa French would become the star of the show.

Chapter 11

My buzzing phone brought me sharply to an upright position. I answered it and stared around me, trying to work out where I was.

'I tried your flat first and got the answerphone.' It was Miranda.

'I'm not there at the moment,' I muttered, holding the phone towards me so I could check the time. Nine am.

'Not at home?'

'No.' I spotted my slippers beside the bunk, my opened suitcase on the unfamiliar rug, spilling out the clothes and toiletries I'd grabbed from my flat late last night.

'Shit, Sam – have you gone to Greece without me, after all?'

I laughed. 'No. I'm at Limehouse.' I was still sleepy and it came out before I realised a barrage of further questions were bound to follow.

'Why?'

'I'm working with the police...'

'What?'

'I'm sorry, I can't tell you anything else.'

'That's where that witness lives, isn't it? Oh God, this is connected to Kora's attack!'

Miranda wasn't stupid. She'd spoken to the police. My silence confirmed her assumption.

'You're involved aren't you? Why are you involved?'

'I can't tell you anything more, I'm sorry.' I winced, recoiling from the frustration wheezing through Miranda's gasps, aching to slide back under the covers.

'Sponge said an artist guy saw the whole thing. Is that what this is about?'

I didn't answer.

'Oh, I get it,' she said, a smug edge to her voice. 'Sponge said the witness has got PTSD and won't say anything. You're treating him, aren't you?' Miranda often put two and two together and got five, only this time she was spot on. 'Did he do it?'

'What? No, he's a key witness. It isn't him. We just want him to tell us… what he saw.'

I could hear her brain tracking from one question to the next. 'Are you at a police station?'

My mind wasn't sufficiently in gear to make up lies. 'No. At the marina. On a boat.'

'Why are you on a boat?'

Another silence.

'Sam – are you mad?! You're with *him*? What's going on?'

'Miranda, listen to me. You know this is confidential, okay? *Completely* confidential. I can't say anything else and nor must you. Not to Sponge, not to anyone, you hear me? I've said too much already.'

'But, he might be this crazy maniac who beheads people.'

'Don't be silly,' I said. 'He's in a really bad way, poor guy.' I was touched by her rare display of concern for me.

'You had the chance for a week off and you're still working. I don't understand it.'

'I was asked to help.'

'You can't say no, can you? Not when it's work. You say no to everything else, though. When did you last go on a date? When did you last sleep with a bloke? Or even have a spontaneous snog in a back alley somewhere?'

I laughed. 'I'm not sure the last one is on my "must do before I'm forty" list.'

'You know what I mean. You've got to loosen up, Sammie. You should be letting go. Putting yourself out there.'

She hadn't called me Sammie for months. 'Thanks for… caring. I've got to go,' I said wearily. 'I'll ring you later.'

'Do your best, Sam. Sorry, I know you will. Kora deserves…' Her voice crumbled away into nothing.

'I will. I promise.'

I slipped the phone under my pillow and thought about what she'd said – especially the part about me saying no to everything except work. Her words had stung, but she was absolutely right. It was career all the way for me, it always had been; the value of 'achievement' had been ingrained in me since before I could walk. It wasn't difficult to see why. I was pushed by both parents, both established pillars of the community; my father a respectable barrister, my mother a senior lecturer in architecture. For them, academic success and status meant everything. My mother, for certain, always saw the job before the person, 'David Smith is a window cleaner,' she'd say distastefully. 'He can't possibly know what I'm talking about.' Or conversely, 'David Smith is a professor of cultural anthropology; he'll be the perfect person to invite to our garden party.'

You pick up bad habits from your parents and, before you know it, those habits become trusted codes to live by, unexamined and deep-seated until it's too late and they're embedded into your psyche for life. For me, this has played out in my constant struggle to feel good enough; the dread of failure looming at my shoulder with more terror than the Grim Reaper. As a result, the idea of 'letting go' as Miranda suggested, was about as unnatural for me as it was for the Queen to be seen eating chewing gum.

I curled onto my side and stayed in that seductive wilderness halfway between sleep and waking. But not for long. My phone buzzed again, like a bluebottle trapped under my pillow.

'Who is it?' I said through a yawn.

'DI Fenway… Jeremy… are you okay?'

'Sorry, long day, long night.' I hitched myself to the edge of the bed. There was nothing for it, I was going to have to face the day.

'Spenser told me you stayed with Aiden. That he wouldn't let you leave.'

'Something like that. It's probably not a bad idea. The second cabin is comfortable, and—'

'Yeah, I know,' he interrupted, 'you'll have more opportunity to get to know him and find out what he saw.'

'That's the idea.'

He cleared his throat. 'We've got a meeting this morning to discuss the case in more detail. Can you be here? Eleven?'

'Absolutely.'

I slid into my dressing gown and wandered out of the cabin with the sole aim of finding the kettle. Aiden's cabin door was closed and when I couldn't find him elsewhere, I assumed he must be still in bed. Mornings were often tough for people with depression, clearly another of his trauma-related symptoms. I made a strong coffee and had a quick look in his fridge. There was cheese, leeks, mushrooms, an opened jar of pesto and soya milk. In the cupboards there was plenty to eat; peanut butter, baked beans, cereals and several packages, many unopened, which was understandable given Aiden's poor appetite.

I cut two chunky slices of bread from the crusty cob, dropped them in the toaster and once they'd popped out, spread thick layers of vegan margarine and blackcurrant jam over them. The bright sunlight was bursting to get inside, so I slid aside the curtains to invite it in. Eager rays splashed instantly over the interior, scattering gold geometric shapes across the rugs. I unlocked the door at the bow of the boat and sat on the step with my dripping toast, listening to the ripple of water, the chirrup of birds. It was a rare moment of bliss.

Aiden still hadn't stirred by the time I left, so I stood outside his door to listen, not wanting to leave without knowing he was safe. I waited and waited, until finally there was a creak and a huffing sound, the noise when you exhale after a yawn. I wrote a note telling him I had a meeting at the police station and would be back as soon as I could – and pushed it under his door.

DCI Keith Wilde stood at the entrance to the same meeting room as last time, waving people in as though he was directing traffic. Jeremy was already seated, with DI Karen Foxton, who I'd met in passing when I first visited the station. With silky blonde hair plaited into intricate thin braids, she looked a fraction too dainty to be a police officer.

'I gather you haven't got anywhere,' said Wilde bluntly, before he'd even offered me a seat.

'I wouldn't say that.'

Jeremy pulled out a chair and poured me coffee from a stainless steel jug, as everyone settled.

'Where's Dr Herts?' I asked, noticing his absence.

'Too busy,' came Jeremy's hushed reply, with a curl of the lip.

DCI Wilde closed the door, but stayed standing. I sat back, assuming he was going to say something until I realised all eyes were on me, waiting for me to declare there'd been some sort of breakthrough.

I stared at my twitchy fingers, then took a shallow breath. 'Aiden has indicated he wants me to stay with him. It's a good start.'

'Has he *said* anything? Has he communicated?' pressed Wilde. He was pacing around with his shirtsleeves rolled up, dark rings already mushrooming under his armpits. I couldn't help wondering what kind of state his shirt would be in if he was really under pressure.

'Yes,' I said definitively. 'He's started to communicate through a sand tray, but… er, not about the attack, as yet. We're just establishing a connection, although I'm expecting him to communicate visually before he actually speaks. I think that will be the way forward. Images are second nature to him. I hope he might be able to draw–'

'A *sand tray?*' He spat the words out. 'What use is that?' He wandered behind my chair out of sight then took hold of the back of it. I could feel him pulling against it and fought the urge to snap round to tell him how irritating it was.

'Okay, let's look at what else has come to light,' suggested Jeremy. His soft, calm voice came as a welcome respite; a lullaby in a storm. He pressed the remote in his hand and the TV screen on the wall came to life, showing shots of the crime scene; the towpath, the wire fence, the bicycle cast to one side, the puddle of blood beside it. I averted my eyes and focused on what I recognised of Aiden's boat.

'If we had a motive, we might be closer to finding who did it or at least know where to start looking,' said Wilde.

Edwin Hall, the crime scene manager, spoke. 'From what we've got so far, the assailant set everything up, like he knew Kora was on her way and about to come whizzing along the towpath. Everyone at CCAP knew she rode a bicycle.'

'Maybe it wasn't about Kora,' said Wilde, still behind me. 'Maybe he was just hoping some random person would head that way.'

'But, in that case, there was no guarantee it would be a cyclist,' said Jeremy. 'It could have been a group of pedestrians, or one of the boat owners. They would have walked into the tripwire, for sure, but most likely not been injured by it at all.'

'Presumably timing was key?' I suggested.

'I'd say so,' agreed Jeremy. 'Someone knew exactly when and where to rig the wire, exactly when she'd be coming under the bridge. That person knew she would be there. They were expecting her.'

I nodded. It made sense.

'What about the method, what does that tell us?' Wilde asked. I could feel him right behind me, heat from his breath in my hair. I turned round sharply with a frown, so he'd get the message. He let go of my chair and straightened up.

'There was no rape, no sexual interference, no disturbance to her clothes, no theft,' said Jeremy. 'No contact at all between the attacker and the victim at the scene itself.'

'Almost like it was meant to be an execution,' I muttered, hardly aware that it had slipped out of my mouth.

Jeremy nodded, looking over at me with a collaborative glance. 'He... let's call the attacker he, for now... most likely got there by car.' He flicked forward to scenes inside the car park. 'Except the CCTV wasn't working…' He tailed off mumbling something I couldn't catch.

Wilde finally stopped pacing around and took a seat near the door, his forehead sticky.

'It was extremely well planned,' said DI Karen Foxton, addressing us for the first time. I'd noticed she'd been looking over at Jeremy several times, even when he wasn't speaking, fixing her gaze on him a fraction too long each time. It was in my nature to notice these things. Are they having an affair? There was certainly something, although it was hard to tell at this stage if it was a one-way street or not. 'The wire was set up for a specific time,' she said, 'perhaps for less than five minutes, at the perfect height for garrotting a cyclist. Clean across her throat, like he'd measured it. Without her helmet the attacker knew she'd suffer maximum injury.'

'Kora was pedalling fast, right?' I said. 'The damage caused depended on that. But how could he know she was going hell for leather? I mean, if that was me on a pushbike, I'd be going at a steady pace. It was a narrow path, getting dark. The wire might have knocked me off for sure, but I doubt it would have… done the damage it did to Kora.'

'It's a good point,' said Jeremy.

'Maybe she thought she was being chased.' Karen Foxton's cheeks had gone a blotchy pink since she'd started sharing her opinions.

'Mmm,' I said. 'Or else she was in her own rush to get somewhere.' I rubbed my lip. 'The method itself is extremely impersonal, don't you think. Almost as if it was about getting a job done and getting away as quickly as possible. No hanging around, no interference, not even touching the body.'

'No pleasure in it. Just expedience,' said Jeremy.

'It could indicate he had no emotional attachment to Kora. It wasn't an emotional outburst, it was pure logistics,' I concluded.

'And why was Kora there in the first place?' said DS Joanne Hoyland, speaking for the first time. 'At nine thirty at night, along a lonely towpath? She had a little kid and a partner waiting for her at home.'

'Was she dressed differently to usual?' I asked.

'Her colleagues said not.'

'And any calls to or from her phone?' I asked.

'We couldn't find her phone. She didn't have it with her,' said Edwin.

'That's odd,' I said. 'So the attacker could have picked it up. Can you trace the last calls made or received on it?'

'Kora's phone has been switched off,' said Jeremy, 'so we can't locate it, but we've been able to trace the calls made to it through the service provider. We're looking into the last number, to a mobile, made at nine twenty-two. The calls before that were to her partner's mobile and her home landline.'

'That call at nine twenty-two could give us the answer, then,' I said. 'It must have been just before she set off.'

'It's our best hope, so far,' agreed Jeremy.

Why Kora was there was a big question, but there was an even bigger one staring us all in the face, as far as I was concerned. I spread my fingers out flat on the desk. 'Is Aiden in danger because of what he saw?'

No one answered at first, then Jeremy spoke. 'Limehouse Basin is twelve locks away from Camden, but if the attacker saw the name of the boat and went looking for it, it could be a problem.'

'The attacker must have known he'd been seen. Aiden wasn't hidden when whoever it was made a grab for the wire. He was standing out in the open.'

Jeremy digested my concerns. 'I think something would have happened by now. The assailant wouldn't want to risk Aiden blabbing to the police. I think he would have done something.'

'Unless there have been so many police officers around, that he's waiting for it all to calm down,' I said uneasily, knowing that there was no police presence at the boat any more.

He didn't reply. I knew Jeremy couldn't give me an answer – certainly not one that would set my mind at rest. The update appeared to have ground to a halt. Jeremy fiddled with the remote, DI Foxton examined her nails and Edwin took his glasses off to give them a clean. Just as I was getting twitchy, there was a knock on the door and a female officer came in. She headed straight for the DCI and whispered something in his ear. He shot to his feet as though a wild dog had been let in.

'Right... Kora Washington died in hospital a few minutes ago.' Everyone in the room froze.

He prodded his finger into the air. 'Fenway, my office, two minutes.'

DCI Wilde's shoulders stiffened and his fists clenched into tight balls. I waited for his final words, briefly closing my eyes, because I knew what was coming.

'This is now a murder investigation.'

Chapter 12

I scurried out of the police station with only one destination in mind. I wanted to get to Miranda's flat to break the news before she heard it from someone else. I had to be there to deal with the backlash; I had no idea how she was going to handle it.

I broke into a run on the high street; it wasn't far.

My phone buzzed on the way and I slowed to a brisk walk to see who it was. Miranda. I swiped the screen to answer.

'Why didn't you tell me?' she shrieked.

'I've just heard. I'm on my way to you right now.' I was already at the bottom of her road. 'Are you at home?'

She was sobbing and incoherent. I heard a moan that sounded closer to a *yes* than *no*, so I bolted to her front door. It was already ajar.

She fell into my arms as I pushed it open. 'I'm so sorry,' I said, practically holding her up. 'The news came through. I was at the police station.'

'Sponge just rang. I can't believe it,' she blubbered into my jacket.

I guided her inside, let her sink onto the sofa.

For the next hour I made her hot drinks and let her rant and wail about the shock, the loss, the unfairness of it all. The doorbell rang and one of her friends from the project, a tall and spindly-thin woman I'd never met, arrived ready to take her over to Sponge's place.

'He doesn't want to be on his own,' she explained. 'We're all going to do shifts to look after him... and babysit Raven.'

Miranda clung to me in a prolonged hug as though she was about to fly off to Australia for six months. 'Thank you for being there,' she said. 'I'm sorry I was–'

'Shhh,' I said, wiping a stray tear from under her eye.

My phone pinged with a calendar reminder. I'd completely forgotten. Since joining Aiden on the boat, I'd arranged an emergency session with my supervisor. I was supposed to be at Tower Bridge.

'You'll help them get the bastard, won't you?' she said, as I left her. 'Promise me…'

'I'll do everything I can,' I said and meant it.

Dr Petra Hall had insisted we meet at a hotel near St Katherine's Dock. She was never one to use an office if she could get away with a more comfortable setting, especially if it happened to be at lunch time.

Supervision is non-negotiable for all NHS psychologists, no matter how experienced. Working with the fragile minds of patients requires regular meetings to discuss cases, debrief – and ask for help. For months I'd been stuck with a crusty old-school analyst, Dr Rosen, and we were like chalk and cheese. Not long after he was assigned to me, I discovered his core philosophy was: 'Follow the rules no matter what and don't *ever* rely on your own instinct'. The total opposite to me. Putting us together was a disastrous match and led to all kinds of problems, although I'd had to wait nearly two years before I could finally make the swap. Thankfully, Petra was entirely different. She believed in paying attention to gut feelings, going with the flow and trusting professional instinct.

As my supervisor, she'd never meet Aiden, but she'd be an additional experienced mind in the wings, making sure he was getting the most appropriate treatment.

I was five minutes late, but she was talking to the barman and didn't seem to notice. As usual, she was dressed as though she was on her way to an awards ceremony at which she was about to receive the most prestigious honour. Her hair was always immaculate; tied up into a soft grey roll at the back, all the pins invisible. We found two comfy chairs on a balcony overlooking the dock and ordered open sandwiches and cappuccinos. They arrived with extra pistachio nuts and olives. I gave her the full picture, covering everything I knew of Aiden and his symptoms.

'Sounds like typical Post Traumatic Stress Disorder,' she confirmed. 'Lack of sleep, nightmares, flashbacks with agoraphobia and depression.'

'That's pretty much it.' I explained how he was unable to speak or draw, but had used the sand tray.

'As you know,' said Petra, 'with this kind of trauma, victims usually go over and over the *telling* of an event, trying to understand it, make sense of it, integrate it. If Aiden can't do that, he must be exploding inside. He's probably mentally and emotionally exhausted.'

'Absolutely,' I said, pausing to chew a mouthful of cheese and tomato. 'He's lethargic, listless, like there isn't enough energy in his body to hold him up. He's unmotivated, socially withdrawn and doesn't want to see people. He's jumpy, too, he can't watch the news or read a newspaper. He can watch certain films, mainly cartoons, maybe because he knows they're not real.'

'Okay, so what's the way forward with this guy?'

'The police want a sketch of the killer by Friday.'

She gave a prim snort. 'Forget it. Out of the question. In any case, your first and only allegiance is to your patient. Let the police do their own work.' She stabbed an olive vehemently with a toothpick.

I looked down and took my time over what I had to say next. 'There's one thing I need to mention.' She turned to look at me. 'I'm staying on his boat with him.'

'You're what?' Her reaction sent a teaspoon spinning to the carpet.

'I had to make a decision and it seemed the right one, based on my therapeutic assessment at the time.'

'O-kay…' she dragged the word out waiting for more explanation. A waiter came over to pick up the spoon. 'We need two brandies,' Petra told him.

'Just the one,' I called after him. Much as I would have loved to join her, I needed a clear head for the rest of the day.

'You've had problems in the past.' She folded her arms, giving me a knowing look.

I swallowed. 'Only once.'

But once was enough. I'd allowed a patient to get too close to me and it had led to all manner of complications. 'It's different this time. Let me explain,' I said tentatively. 'The world used to be a rational and safe place to Aiden. We know that, right? Bad stuff only happened on television. And now that's all changed for him. The attack – it's murder now – will have shaken his entire belief system about security and normality. Life is suddenly *intensely hazardous* for him and in his mind, it's best not to go out or get involved with humankind at all.'

Petra nodded, but slowly, waiting to be convinced.

'He's only nineteen, with no immediate family in the area,' I went on. 'In his closing down, he's likely to act as if he's younger, to need consolation, comfort, reassurance. You agree?'

She pulled a *maybe* face, not entirely persuaded.

'By staying with him, I can give him continuity and support. I'll be undemanding company for him; he knows he doesn't have to entertain me. I won't get upset when he doesn't speak. I can help him express his fear, shock and outrage about the tragedy when he's ready. I'll be there to catch the moment he starts to let it out. If that happens to involve drawing a picture in the next few days – then everybody's happy.'

Her brandy arrived and she inhaled its fumes then set it down in front of her like a trophy. 'Fair enough,' she said unexpectedly. I felt a sense of relief wash over me. I thought I was going to have to work a lot harder to win her over. 'But you must keep your distance from him.'

I nodded vigorously. 'Of course.'

'I can see you know what you're doing,' she said, rolling the stem of her glass between her fingers. 'You said he's not communicating with anyone else–'

'He's not really communicating properly with *me*, as yet,' I corrected her.

'Do some desensitisation work with him on leaving the boat, so he can reintegrate. Just stand on the threshold with him at first, then let him watch you go to the end of the landing strip, or whatever it's called. Take it in simple stages.' She took a small sip of brandy and savoured it. 'And make high energy foods and fresh juices for both of you, bump up his vitamin intake, especially if he won't take medication.'

'That's one big advantage of being with him on the boat,' I said. 'I can make sure he eats well. I found stacks of halloumi cheese in his fridge. Can't bear it myself, but never mind. He's vegetarian, apparently,' I said, nibbling on a pistachio.

'Even better,' she said. 'Fresh vegetables. Cook him spinach pasta, rice dishes – be creative. Get him planting seeds, using soil...'

'Coax him back into the basics of nature, you mean?'

'Exactly. Work with things he can control. Let him see that the world is still working as it should. Sounds like a bright boy. He'll come round. You'll see.'

On my way back to the boat I jotted down a few notes so I wouldn't forget the points Petra had made. Normally, I'd leave them in my 'supervision' file at work, but I'd have to keep them folded in the bottom of my bag for now.

Then I rang the first number on my list of Aiden's friends and got through to Jessica, a young woman his age who'd known him before he went to art college. I'd caught her at work, but she gave me a few minutes over the phone.

'Have you been in touch with him recently?' I asked, explaining I'd got her details from the police, but there was nothing to worry about.

'I left a comment on his Instagram and he said he'd be in touch, but that was a few days ago.' Her tone changed. 'What's this about exactly?'

I gave her a sketchy overview of the situation and once she was assured Aiden was unharmed, she told me more.

'We both went to the same sixth-form college in Ealing,' she said, 'Aiden was really good at his art, he won loads of competitions and awards. We met at the pub, went for walks, that kind of thing. I never went to his house. I got the impression he was living with a relative. He didn't say who, but I don't think it was either of his parents. He didn't talk about his family.'

'What was he like at sixteen, seventeen?'

'Humble... very unassuming... in fact he was always surprised when people were interested in his work. People either admired him or were jealous of him. He was on a bit of a pedestal, although he didn't do anything to rub it in anyone's faces. Everyone else put him there; the tutors, the press. We knew he was destined for great things; you know how some people just seem to shine above the rest? They look good, they're articulate about what they do, they're talented, modest, really secure about themselves. That's Aiden.'

'Can I ask if you were his girlfriend?'

'No,' she chuckled. 'I must admit I quite fancied him, but he wasn't into me in that way, more's the pity. He's gorgeous, isn't he?' She moved on swiftly when she could tell I wasn't going to respond. 'There's a side to him that's completely unavailable. I mean, he's a real sweetheart; open-hearted and funny, but it feels like the real Aiden is hidden all the time. Sorry... am I making any sense?'

'Absolutely. He sounds like a very private person.'

'That's it.'

'Did he seem emotionally stable to you?'

'Oh, yeah. He's the most together person I know. Totally committed and so clear about his ambition. The rest of us faffed about, not knowing which subjects to study, which career path to follow, but Aiden had it all sorted out. He's super sure of himself – quietly confident, I'd say.'

I could hear a phone ringing at her end. 'Listen, I've got to go,' she whispered. 'Ring me back another time, if you need to know any more. I'll try to call him, but send him my love anyway, will you? Just in case he doesn't pick up.'

I ended the call, a leaden feeling in my bones. I couldn't quite explain it. Something like the kind of dull heartache that hits you when you've just heard that an old friend you lost touch with has passed away. With everything I knew about Aiden, Jessica's description made complete sense, but that simply wasn't the man I'd met. That man; passionate and driven, was gone and in his place was a feeble imposter.

I wanted to meet the man she'd known. I wanted nothing more than to find him and bring him back.

Chapter 13

Aiden was up when I got back, standing by the washing machine in his bare feet staring at nothing in particular, his eyelashes flickering constantly. He'd boiled a kettle and was now filling two mugs, though his hand was shaking so much that the boiling water splashed onto the surface and dribbled down the door of the cupboard.

Had someone told him that Kora had died? Was this a further reaction to hearing he was now the sole witness to a murder enquiry? Aiden had been avoiding the news and the police still had his phone, so perhaps that was yet to come. Anyway, now wasn't the time to bring it up. He'd need to be more robust than this to handle the shock.

I didn't make a sound, I simply reached for a cloth and mopped up the mess.

His hair was awry and his shirt was half-tucked into his jeans. Jessica's description of him came into my mind. A young man with panache and verve. Here and now, he looked positively wretched, more like someone living on the streets.

'Bad start this morning?' I asked, giving him the hint of a sad smile.

Aiden looked perplexed, biting his lip and breathing hard, like he was desperately grappling with a complex mathematical calculation. He was expecting, like we all do, to have a thought and translate it instantly into words, but no sounds were coming out. The skin crumpled between his eyebrows.

Until then, I'd assumed the police psychiatrist – Dr Herts – had explained all about post-traumatic mutism to him. Now, faced with Aiden's bewilderment, I began to think otherwise. Perhaps Herts had been 'too busy'.

'I might be repeating what you've already heard,' I said, 'but I want to make sure you know as much as possible about what it is you're going through.'

Aiden set down the mug of mint tea intended for me beside his own on the galley table. It was an invitation to join him, a step in the right direction. Progress between Aiden and I might have appeared non-existent to an observer, but there were tiny shifts and I was aware of each and every one of them.

He sat opposite me, stiff and uncertain, pressed against the back of the seat as though forced back by a ferocious wind. 'It's an anxiety disorder – a reaction to the traumatic event you've witnessed; called Reactive Mutism.' I didn't say that it was extremely rare in adults, but then Aiden was only nineteen. 'The inability to speak is a temporary reaction. I think the psychiatrist will already have mentioned that to you.'

Aiden continued to sit bolt upright. I searched his expression for any sign of recognition, but nothing changed. There was nothing to suggest he was even hearing what I said. I pressed on regardless.

'What people often fail to grasp is that it's not a wilful refusal to speak. You might find yourself *wanting* to communicate, but nothing is coming out. It can leave you feeling distressed and disempowered.' I sat forward, keeping solid eye contact. 'I need to stress that it is temporary. Your voice *will* come back; we just don't know when that will be.'

I became aware again, in that moment, of the potential hornet's nest I'd been brought into. The conflict of interests. The police wanted Aiden to divulge everything he knew about the attack as a matter of urgency. My concern, however, was first and foremost with Aiden's recovery. What made things even more complicated was that I couldn't treat Aiden's situation as straightforward mutism. I also had to consider his other symptoms; agitation, anxiety, hypersensitive to noise, as well as withdrawal and depression – a huge bundle of malfunctions all at once. Normally therapy would take place over at least twenty weeks. I had seven days. Down to six, by now. Get his treatment wrong and it could push Aiden further away from us into his silent isolated world.

'I'm not going to trick you or push you into reliving what happened. We won't be going there until you're ready, I promise,' I said. 'We'll go at your pace – forget about the police. They can wait.'

I got up and placed the sand tray on the table between us. He'd already used this medium to 'send' me a message; it was worth trying again. At the side I set up a small cardboard doll's house from one of my boxes, showing a traditional family with mother, father and two children standing in a line outside the front door. Aiden didn't react, nor did he shift his gaze from the spot he was staring at in some distant place. But, the fact that he hadn't got up to leave was a good sign. He was totally still apart from a faint tremble, as though he was sitting inside a van with the engine running.

I placed the opened tubs and containers to one side of the tray. At some point Aiden had already cleared away the figures he'd used last night, so I smoothed out the sand, ready for us to start afresh.

I decided to jump a few stages. I had the feeling that with his artistic prowess, Aiden would be able to make sophisticated use of this method without much practice.

'Can you find any object or objects that could represent any members of your family?' Jeremy had said they were having trouble tracing any relatives. It was as good a place as any to begin. 'Use anything here that you think symbolically fits a brother, sister, your mother or father. Try to find items to embody them as closely as you can.'

There were plenty of figures to choose from; small plastic superheroes, soldiers, a doctor, miner, farm worker. There were figures dressed in ordinary clothes of all ages, from a baby in a cot to an elderly man in a wheelchair. Aiden suddenly moved. He abruptly reached forward and held up the female figure from the doll's house, then put it back.

'Okay, so was that your mother? You've put her back.'

He reached into another tub and pulled out three small flat pebbles, balancing them in the sand in the middle, one on top of the other.

I took a chance. 'So *this* is your mother?'

Aiden adjusted the stones, placed them unevenly on top of each other. They looked like they were about to fall over. Was that the point?

'She's right in the centre of your life…'

In this kind of play therapy, the idea is to simply explain what I see. Interpretations needed to be tentative and I'd normally avoid them, but I was aware of how little time we had to get the ball rolling.

He scooped the stones into his hand and reset them again as they were.

'Ah – so your mother is wobbly, unstable, about to fall over any moment…'

Gradually, carefully, my job is to creep under the surface of the obvious towards the hidden.

Aiden reacted to my words with an inconclusive sniff.

'How about your father?'

Aiden dipped his hand randomly into the same tub and took out a pebble without looking. He hid it in his hand before burying it in the sand, so neither of us could see which one he'd chosen. He straightened up.

'So… we don't know which pebble is for your father…' I said hesitantly, '*any* pebble will do for him? And he's hidden? You don't know who he is?' I was taking a huge leap of faith with that notion, but I hoped I'd be able to read his body language if I'd got it badly wrong.

He took a sip of tea and stayed still. Perhaps I wasn't too far off.

I pointed to the pile of pebbles. Time to risk another interpretation. 'Your mum was a single parent?'

He nipped his lips together and rocked back and forth a little. If I'd got it wrong would he correct me? I could only assume he'd stop playing 'the game'. Surely he'd even walk off if I was wide of the mark.

Aiden proceeded to put a figurine of Snow White in front of the small tower of pebbles. I smiled at the choice, given Aiden's predilection for shades of white in his work.

'Snow White is kind, gentle, yeah? So, that's how you see your mum?'

Another sip of tea.

'Any brothers or sisters?'

He looked down, folded his arms, his face hidden behind his hair. Maybe he was an only child.

'What about you? What will you choose to represent *you*, Aiden?'

In front of Snow White, he placed an empty cot from the selection of doll's house furniture. He pulled a scrap of tissue from his pocket and thumbed it into a tiny bundle which he carefully placed inside it. He patted it gently and pushed it close to Snow White.

'Your mother looked after you – she cares for you very much,' I said in a whisper, a sudden wave of tearfulness bubbling up inside me.

Aiden removed the cot and put a figure of a nurse next to Snow White and, using plastic segments, built a castle wall around the two of them. I was astonished at his psychological awareness. He'd got the knack of this, straight away.

'Okay,' I speculated. 'Your Mum is ill, in a confined space, needing special care…'

It would explain why the police hadn't been able to reach her.

He took the Snow White figure out of the sand, gently blew off the sand and put it in his pocket. I waited a moment. 'You want her close. I think you love and miss your mother a great deal.'

Aiden sat back. I thought I caught a bead of moisture inside the rim of his eye. I also thought I saw a passing glimmer of relief on his face – but, equally, I might have got it badly wrong. There was so little to go on. He and I were working within a considerably reduced framework of communication, even his body language was down to about twenty percent of what it should normally be.

He leaned forward and cleared the sand, flattening it out, like I'd done at the start. He was ready for more. This was so positive. Then he pushed the box towards me. I pushed it back. In a firm move, he sent it my way again and folded his arms, indicating it was my turn.

'Well, I suppose that's only fair,' I conceded. 'I find out about you, you find out about me.'

It was a long time since I'd done this exercise myself. I felt a shiver of nerves, knowing how complex my family was and not knowing how much I wanted to convey to a fragile patient.

Finding a figure for my mother was easy. Without hesitation, I chose a witch on a broomstick and for my father, a toy rabbit. Miranda was an iridescent peacock feather and for me, I plucked out a rubber Womble that looked like it had fallen off the top of a pencil. I put the witch and the rabbit at opposite corners of the tray and the last two in the centre. Aiden leant forward and removed the rubber Womble. He dropped it back in its tub and plucked out a figure of a garden fairy instead. A pretty and delicate porcelain figurine with gossamer wings which he pressed firmly in its place.

I felt like I couldn't breathe. So touched by what he'd done, I couldn't trust myself not to well up. An embarrassed silence filled the space between us.

'Okay…' I said, desperate to keep my voice from cracking, 'the Womble isn't me… I'm the fairy, instead.' I sat back, then pushed the feather and the fairy closer together. 'That's it. That's my family.'

I stood up. We'd done enough for now.

'You can carry on, on your own, if you like. I'll get lunch ready.'

He smoothed out the sand, then got up and walked away. He, too, had done enough. After lunch Aiden was about to go to his cabin when I asked him to sit with me for just a few minutes in the saloon area. He had candles and lamps dotted around the place and I lit a plain one and set it between us on the coffee table.

'I've got something difficult to tell you,' I said, as I invited him to sit.

He looked nervous, his knees tightly pressed together, jiggling up and down.

I spoke in an even tone. 'The incident you witnessed… the woman you saw… well, she died in hospital this morning.'

He began shivering feverishly, as though he'd just been dragged from the Arctic Ocean. I wanted nothing more than to reach out to him, to wrap my arms around him and hold him close, but as my patient, I knew it would be wrong. I had to remain detached, consistently professional.

His jaw trembled and he began to sob.

'I'll stay on the boat as long as you like. I won't leave you on your own, if you don't want me to.' I got up to pour us both a glass of water.

For the next half hour Aiden stayed where he was, his head down, inwardly managing the turbulence within him. I didn't want to embarrass him with my sympathetic stares, so I got up and turned to his books. I traced my finger along the top shelf and came across a large volume, *A Hundred Years of Modern Art in Britain*. If I was going to be here twenty-four seven, I might as well learn something about Aiden's favourite subject.

When he wandered over to the sand tray, I tried not to look. I heard him rummaging in the tubs and deliberately didn't react as he sauntered over to the candle. Out of the corner of my eye I saw him straighten up and only then did I shift my gaze.

'That's beautiful,' I said.

Using white shells, he'd created a simple heart shape with the candle at the centre.

I didn't know if it was simply a pretty design or meant something deeper, but it was a start. At least one good thing had come out of today's tragedy; Aiden might not be using words, but he was certainly communicating.

Chapter 14

Monday, June 4 – Five weeks earlier

Honoré Craig-Doyle made little squeaking yelps eager for Trisha to pick up.

'Darling… you'll never guess who I've just spoken to,' she burst in, snatching a breath.

'Who? What's happened?' said Trisha.

'Henby's just been on the phone! Well, not in person, obviously – his agent.'

Honoré waited for her words to sink in.

'What? *The* Henby? You serious?'

'The genius himself! I know! It's *got* to be about using the gallery.'

'Shit. That would be amazing.'

'His agent probably wants to sell some of his smaller pieces through us once his Tate Modern exhibition is over.'

'Perhaps they've heard about your success last month with Maurice Bray?'

Honoré dropped to the edge of her desk, then sprang up again. 'His agent didn't say, but that might have swung it. We've been getting some pretty awesome media coverage lately.'

'So, where are you meeting her… him? Who is it?'

'Romana Warner. She's sending a cab for me at the gallery in about half an hour.'

'Sending you a cab?'

'I know. She must be really keen. She just rang out of the blue and said "Let's meet". We'll probably go to some wine bar or other and talk it over. She said to keep it all under wraps for now; you're the only person I've told. Keep schtum, darling.'

'Of course. How exciting. Have you dealt with her before?'

'No. I've heard of her, of course. Spoken to her PA, tried to get to speak to her personally a thousand times, but you know how it is… she's at a press conference, at lunch with some A-lister, or in L.A.' Her voice rose an octave. 'And now, suddenly she wants to speak to *me* and Craig-Doyle Gallery is flavour of the month!' She squealed like a teenager.

'Go for it girl. I'm so pleased for you.'

'Pleased for us, darling. Pleased for us. You're a part of this, too.'

'Give me a call later to let me know how it goes, won't you? I'll get the champagne on ice ready for when you get home.'

Honoré blew her a resounding luvvie kiss through the receiver and was already inhaling that sweet smell of success.

Chapter 15

Mid-afternoon, I caught the Tube over to Pimlico to meet Howard – another name on my list of Aiden's friends – at the Chelsea College of Art & Design. Once belonging to the Royal Army Medical College, it sits next to the Tate Britain overlooking the Thames. I took a few moments, standing on the large cobbled forecourt, to take in the grand scale of the architecture, before I strolled inside.

Howard said he'd be in the refectory wearing a T-shirt with *Artist at Work* written on the back. When I joined him he introduced me to another art student, Valerie, who also knew Aiden. Valerie was sitting cross-legged with her stocking feet beneath her on the wooden chair. She had pigtails and looked far younger than nineteen.

'Aiden came to college a year early,' said Howard, half-heartedly offering me a crisp then absent-mindedly moving the bag out of my reach before I could take one. He had long hair like Aiden, but it was flat and straggly, aching for a comb to be run through it.

Valerie chipped in. 'He'd already had commissions, articles on his work in magazines and done a fashion show with Donna Karan in New York,' she said. Her voice betrayed awe rather than jealousy. She was holding a can, sucking the last of her fizzy drink with a straw.

'Why do you want to know about him?' said Howard. 'He's not a suspect is he?'

'No. I'm a psychologist. The more I know about him, the more I can help him to assist the police.'

'Cos he saw it, right?' said Valerie, rubbing her sleeve across her mouth.

I nodded. 'How would you describe him?'

'He's very sensitive… and private,' said Valerie, shaking the empty can. 'Not in a freaky way or anything, he's just so focused on whatever art piece he's working on – he kind of goes in on himself.'

'Has he ever been depressed that you know of, or struggled to cope?'

Howard laughed. Splinters of crisps flew out of his mouth and landed on his jeans. 'Man, Aiden is the coolest person I know. He's *so* got it together. He's good-looking, has an amazing talent and money to get things off the ground, he knows all the right people, he's smart… he's got it all… I should hate the guy.'

'But you don't?'

Howard brushed away the crumbs. 'No way. There's such a good vibe about him. A real positive energy.'

'He helped you with your installations, didn't he?' cut in Valerie. 'Up all night with the two of us, wasn't he, the other week? And he bought me a beautiful paint pallet for my birthday. He's a sweetheart.'

'And before this unfortunate incident, he's never had panic attacks or been agoraphobic, that you know of?'

They gave each other a look that suggested I'd asked if Aiden had ever been on the moon. 'No way,' said Valerie. 'He's *so* in control.'

I didn't mention that it was the ones who needed to be in control who suffered the most when things went off the rails. 'I assume the police told you that Aiden isn't able to speak to anyone at the moment.'

'Yeah,' said Valerie, dropping her eyes. 'We've left him loads of messages. When we heard how it had happened, well, it…'

Howard took over. 'I mean, to have been there when it… *shit,* man.' He rubbed his forehead.

'Is he particularly close to anyone? A girlfriend?'

'No girlfriend that I know of,' said Valerie. She opened another bag of crisps and offered me one, within reach this time. I helped myself to be polite. In turn, she fished out a small crisp and posted it into Howard's mouth, with an alluring grin. It looked like she and Howard were an item, so I decided not to ask if she'd ever had a thing for Aiden. 'He was everyone's friend, really,' she said, 'but I only saw him in groups outside of college; at the pub or maybe at a party on his boat.' She pulled her legs out from under her in an abrupt movement. 'Have you seen his boat?' she exclaimed, wide-eyed.

'Yes,' I replied. 'Quite something.'

'Everyone knows he's got money, but he doesn't bandy it about,' said Howard. 'He's always modest. Generous, but not flashy.'

'Do you know where his money came from?'

He hesitated, then shrugged. 'He's sold work and won prizes, of course, but I don't think it can account for that much.'

'Do you know anything about his family? His parents? Where he grew up? That sort of thing.'

Howard sent out his bottom lip and shook his head. 'Not really, to be honest. Come to think of it, he doesn't talk about his parents, or the past. He's very much in the here and now, you know?'

'Only child,' added Valerie. 'I'm sure of it.'

I thanked them and made my way back to the Tube station. On the journey, I went back over Jeremy's list. There were no childhood friends listed. Everyone was from the last three or four years in Aiden's life. Where were the people from his early school days? Who had been looking after him? The police said they'd traced his birth town to Northern Ireland. If my hunches were right from Aiden's sand tray scene, his mother was unwell, possibly mentally unstable and perhaps in a hospital somewhere. I made a note to see if the police had tracked her down by now. Having his mother in the picture could spark a turning point for Aiden.

I mulled over what his friends had told me so far. It was all an 'image'; he was generous, humble, talented and stable. What about the man beneath the groomed public persona Aiden presented to the world? Who was he? He was a student, so where had all his money come from? I came to the conclusion that none of the people I'd spoken to so far knew much about him at all. Just peripheral stuff. He was proving to be a dark horse.

My phone rang during my changeover onto the DLR line, jolting me out of my ponderings. It was Terry inviting me out for dinner.

'Is this the penance we agreed on for doing the dirty on me?' I asked.

'It's long overdue regardless, even if I hadn't got you involved in the case, but… yeah, a bit of penance thrown in as well.'

'You promised me The Dorchester.'

'Did I? Shall we try Soho first and aim higher if we're still friends?'

'I hope you're not wriggling out.'

'Absolutely not – maybe we can do The Dorchester when you're done and dusted with the investigation.'

'Okay – I accept.'

'Tonight?'

'Why not?' I needed time away from the case. Aiden and I had shared some poignant moments recently, but he was still a patient. It would be good to talk to someone freely without having to be on my guard. To talk to someone who wasn't fragile, who would roll with the punches and share a laugh. I felt like I hadn't laughed in ages. Terry said he'd see me at Bar Chico in Soho at 8pm.

As soon as I saw him – idly swinging from one foot to the other, his hands in his pockets – I knew the evening was going to be a breath of fresh air. The best thing was that he was *easy*; easy to be with, to talk to, easy-going. Just what I needed.

The first bar we went to was too noisy, so we moved on to the sushi bar he had in mind for the meal. It was bright and buzzing, with a fast turnover and moments of hilarity as novice diners tried to judge the speed of the passing conveyor belt. One girl tipped a pile of edamame beans into a fruit jelly by mistake. Another sent a chopstick flying. It landed out of sight, but caused havoc with the belt mechanism. It sped up, slowed down, came to a halt and suddenly sprang to life again sending noodles and tofu everywhere. It was all handled with good spirits and I was glad Terry had found somewhere that wasn't awkwardly romantic.

He starting telling me how all his friends seemed to be getting married.

'I used to see Jerry, my best mate,' he said, 'nearly every weekend, and now he's "going to the garden centre", "clearing out the garage" or "choosing wallpaper for the lounge".'

'I know,' I mumbled, as a rice roll fell apart in my mouth. 'Couples get so bloody boring. Two of my friends got married recently and disappeared down large holes in Edinburgh and Northumberland respectively. We used to go out every week – now I'm lucky if I get a Christmas card.'

I thought about my best mate, Hannah, with her new life in Devon. I hadn't yet told her about my latest 'case'; she still thought I was sunning myself on a Greek island.

As if reading my mind, Terry moved on to the subject of holidays and asked where I'd been lately.

'A big fat nowhere…' I told him, flopping back. I didn't dare say out loud how many times I'd passed up on vacations for work commitments in the last few years. 'I'm missing out and I'm determined to do something about it,' I said, pulling a piece of green plastic, shaped like a banana leaf, out of my mouth. 'Why do they always put these things in?' I left it on the edge of my plate. 'I watch documentaries about places like Thailand and India and I haven't even made it as far as Dover. Well, things are damn well going to change.'

We found our discussion sinking into a barrage of moans, fuelled by alcohol, but it felt good.

'Women take one look at my walking stick,' he grunted, 'and assume I've got a degenerative disease. I can see it in their eyes; flashes of Zimmer frames, stair-lifts and incontinence pads.'

I couldn't help but laugh. I knew he wasn't angling for sympathy. I asked, tentatively, about the armed robbery that had left him with a bullet in his knee.

'Did you suffer PTSD, do you think, after it happened?'

He looked down. 'I think everyone does in their own way.'

I nodded. 'Sorry – stupid question.'

'Like most traumatic events, it happened so fast. At the time, you just cope with what's thrown at you, follow orders, respond instinctively. It's afterwards – that's when the rot sets in.' He hunched forward. 'I had nightmares, flashbacks, was afraid to go out, couldn't eat; classic reaction. But it worked itself out, with therapy, debriefings, medication.'

'Was it hard going back to work?'

'I effectively lost my job as a detective and was put behind a desk,' he said. 'But, actually, it's turned out in my favour.'

I admired his positive approach. I'm not sure I'd have been so accepting. 'What is it you're doing now, exactly?'

'I'm part of the HOLMES2 team.'

'I've heard of that.'

'It's the second incarnation of the Home Office Large Major Enquiry System, used by all the forces in the UK. Every piece of information that's gathered in the course of an investigation gets logged as either evidence or intelligence.' He nibbled a piece of avocado. 'I started out transcribing CCTV footage as the system holds unstructured data, as well as vehicle colours, registrations and so on. Now, I mostly train SIOs in how to make full use of it; interpreting data, researching the databases and so on. It's really good, actually. I've discovered I'm a bit of an info-nerd.'

'I'm glad. You deserve something rewarding after losing your position.'

I waited until his smile had faded. 'Are you involved in Kora Washington's case?'

He hesitated. 'Not directly. Other officers do all the inputting these days. I'm aware of where they are in the investigation.'

We had slipped into talking about work; my fault, and I wanted to change the subject back again. 'So, now you've got weekends to do your own thing, what do you do with yourself?'

'Don't laugh, but I've discovered a penchant for extreme sports,' he said, 'despite the gammy leg.' He shifted his left knee a couple of inches with his hands as if it wasn't part of him. 'I did a tandem skydive last month and have started kayaking. I've completed the flat river courses so I'm moving up to white water runs.' He piled slices of ginger onto his raw salmon roll and smothered it with wasabi sauce. 'Then there's scuba diving. Always wanted to try that.'

I glanced down at my two fully-functioning legs and felt a pang of guilt for not making the most of them.

'You're braver than me,' I said. 'I've done some extreme ironing and vacuuming in the past week – that's about it.'

He wiped his hands on his napkin inhaling deeply. 'I fancied you way back when, you know?' he said, not looking at me. 'From the first time I saw you peering at a noticeboard outside the lecture theatre. You looked so earnest and forthright.' The alcohol had made him brave. He looked up briefly. 'And too good for me.'

I swallowed hard. 'You never said...' It was a stupid thing to say. Of course, he'd never said – I'd been far too aloof and unapproachable.

'I never saw the right signs from you,' he said. 'You always smiled *after* I'd said hello, never before.'

'Did I?' I didn't know what else to say.

He looked hurt for an instant, then clapped his hands together.

'So, what are your hopes for the future?'

My eyes sprang wide open. 'Hell, that's a big question.' I took a glug of wine. 'I hardly ever plan beyond next week, to be honest. That's probably why I never get any holidays booked. I have a friend who actually sits down with her partner on the first of January every year and plots out all their breaks for the next twelve months. Easter, summer, bank holidays; the lot.'

'That's a bit OTT,' he said.

'It does the trick, though. My highlight of last year was winning the British Psychological Society Practitioner of the Year Award.'

'Wow...'

'Only in the London area,' I conceded. 'I see myself at the annual dinner, wading through hordes of people clapping, then shaking hands with the chairman – and it makes me glow all over.' I felt ashamed all of a sudden, admitting to such brazen egotism.

'That's brilliant – why so glum?'

'I should have other memories, better memories; of *people*, you know – getting married, buying a house, having a baby – personal things. My achievements are all about work – they feel so narrow, so detached.' I felt a prickle behind my eyes.

'Your time will come. If you want it, that is?'

I didn't know how to answer him and put my energy into chasing my last prawn around the dish with a chopstick. I told him how I loved food, but hated cooking and he said that one of the upsides of working normal office hours was having time at weekends to bake his own bread.

'Not cheating with a machine – all kneaded by hand,' he boasted.

'I'm impressed.'

'You must come over sometime and I'll put on a decent spread for you.'

'Now there's an offer.'

'Sorry – that sounded a bit crude.' He sniggered. 'I don't want to hear any dreadful puns about bloomers or warm buns.'

I nudged his arm, 'Oh, not even one or two...'

The Chablis was slipping down a treat and flirting was effortless. We shared a string of rude and terrible puns, howling at how lame they were. Eventually we paid the bill and by the time I got out onto the street, I was most definitely on the wrong side of tipsy.

'I've got to go back to the boat,' I said suddenly serious, stifling a hiccup.

'You coping?'

'It's hard to make Aiden out.'

As we began walking towards the Tube, I linked my arm through his instinctively. 'It's amazing how much we, as humans, rely on language. We're so used to paying attention to the words people use, how they say things. The way silences become meaningful, because of what comes either side of them.'

He turned to me and pressed my hands together between his. 'I'm sorry I got you into this.'

'No, I'm glad. I love a challenge and I'm living on a luxury boat instead of working at the hospital – it's almost like being in Greece.' I rolled my eyes. 'Seriously though, it's put us two back in touch with each other.'

He smiled. 'Why don't you book a holiday, so that once this is all over with, you can get away?'

'It's a good idea, but getting this bizarre situation resolved feels a long way off. When Kora's killer is arrested and in jail. When Aiden is speaking again and back at college as the shining star.' I squeezed his hands and let them go. 'It doesn't feel like any day soon,' I said wistfully.

We parted at the underground; he was going south; me, east.

I woke shortly after I settled down to sleep that night, still unaccustomed to the movements of the boat. The waterfall at the nearby tower block had gushed on for a while, then stopped. In its place the wash slapped the sides, so we were constantly dipping and bobbing with the gentle motion of the water. I closed my eyes and was startled by the sudden rumble of a nearby train that, coming out of the stillness, sounded like it was heading straight for us. The trains too stopped eventually.

I realised then how exposed I felt in this floating home. How safe were we with a maniac on the loose? He must have seen the name of Aiden's boat. The vessel itself no matter how luxurious, still felt flimsy and insubstantial. I'd always hated camping for the same reason. I preferred the solidity of four brick walls with foundations reaching down into the earth; rooting me, protecting me. I didn't like the idea of potentially floating away like Ophelia in that famous painting by Millais.

Chapter 16

At first light the boat was juddering. I wasn't sure if I was in the middle of a dream, then I felt the pull of the hull and heard the diesel engine chugging like a little tractor. We were on the move.

I quickly got dressed and stepped out to find Aiden at the stern leaning on the tiller. His face told me this wasn't simply a tour for my benefit; he was purposeful and grim. We were leaving the basin and heading along Regent's Canal towards central London. I didn't know where our destination was, but I knew it would be important.

The sun broke through the tall buildings that lined the canal at regular intervals, throwing long shadows across the ripples and I watched the spume of wash froth up behind us as our boat cut through the water. It was early and there was no one else around. Up close, the colours were sharp, but ahead of us they were draped in mist. Even at walking pace, our passage created a refreshing breeze, strong enough to take the hair out of my eyes.

Aiden stared into the distance and I wondered what he was thinking, what he was looking at, what his mind was tugging against. During the night, I'd heard him call out in his sleep, but I hadn't been able to make out what he'd said.

He was an expert at operating the locks on his own, using the windlass to wind up the paddles to open and close the gates. I thought again about the gushing way his friends had spoken about him. It was strange to learn about someone through the eyes of other people. Patching together his personality from the information his mates, surroundings and limited body language gave away about him. He was like a shadow on the wall.

Once I'd been below for breakfast I gave him a hand at the next lock. As I counted the gates, I realised where we were heading. Towards the spot where the attack took place.

Two hours later, as we drew closer to Camden Lock, I took more notice of the geography of the area. This was where Kora had come, pedalling like fury on her bike. When we got through the lock, with help from some Sunday morning revellers already worse for wear, there was a stretch of towpath with lights attached to the buildings. Had no one here seen anything that could be useful to the police? On the far side of the water were balcony apartments, but there was no path that side; if you dropped something from your window, it would be gone forever.

The first bridge we went under was Oval Road. It opened out into a little basin with canoes stacked against the far wall and a pontoon. Then came three bridges in a row ending with Gloucester Avenue. There were locked gates beside the path before the bridges, unused and overgrown with sprawling weeds. Then came Ridgeway Bridge. After this were the first boats: the visitors' moorings. The houses opposite looked upmarket, possibly Georgian. This was the last bridge Kora rode under before the wire cruelly sent her to the ground.

Another boat came past us and I called out to a tanned man wearing a string vest and shorts.

'Is the canal open for boats at night, do you know?'

'Open twenty-four hours a day at the moment,' he replied with a wave.

Aiden skilfully brought us into the bank and I knew from the photos that this was where it had happened. I stayed still for a while waiting to see what Aiden did next, our boat groaning and creaking against the ropes as other boats came past, disturbing the water. He didn't move.

'Are you okay?' I asked.

He clenched his fists, staring at the grass verge.

'Are you looking for something?'

No response. Aiden sat down on an upturned bucket on the bow, his chin in his cupped hands. Was he trying to remember? Was he getting a feel for the area again?

I mulled over the logistics of the killer coming from a boat. Either from the open water or already tied up here, in the visitors' moorings. I'd need to ask the police how far they'd looked into that.

Eventually I stepped onto the towpath, trying not to look at the trailing brown stain on the tarmac to my right. I walked over to the fresh carnations in crisp plastic wrappers, strapped with sticky tape to the arm of the iron staircase. Dandelions and daisies were embedded in the overgrown grass at the base. On the other side of the wire fence was the car park.

Aiden stayed on the boat and began making a little square window with his fingers and looking through it. Every so often, he stopped and pressed his palm to his forehead. His chest was heaving and from the colour of his face, I thought he might be about to vomit. Nevertheless, I was amazed he'd been able to get this far; he'd returned, voluntarily, to the scene of the most harrowing event of his life.

He parted his lips and half-opened his mouth and I braced myself for a distressed cry, but he'd lost the rest of the process and no sound came out at all. His eyes darted about as if desperate to find something that was missing. I didn't know what to do. I was waiting for any signs I could take as instructions, but none came.

Eventually he flung up his arms in despair. He'd had enough. He went back inside the boat and I followed him. I found him hunched by the window, covering his face with his hands. I expected him to get up and take the boat straight back to Limehouse, but we stayed where we were.

Half an hour later, Aiden began his first drawing.

Chapter 17

I found myself moving in slow motion, quietly washing the breakfast dishes, checking what food we had left in the fridge, keeping my distance and trying to act normal so as not to distract him. All the while Aiden had his head down, his hair falling over the sketch pad. My chest was exploding with anticipation. When he'd finished, he left the open page on the table and slipped past me, to his cabin.

I drifted over to where he'd left it and spun it round with my finger.

Within two minutes I was on my way to the police station. Dr Herts said he could offer me twenty minutes out of his demanding schedule.

I asked Aiden's permission to take the drawing before I left and told him I wouldn't be long. It was hard leaving him. I knew he wanted nothing more than to be on his way back to Limehouse.

'It looks like a piece of rock,' said Dr Herts. He seemed to have a permanent bubble of spittle attached to his bottom lip. 'No, wait, it's a volcano. No, hold on, a shoe?' He flipped the page upside down, side to side. 'What do you make of it?' he asked, pushing the drawing towards me.

'I'm not sure...'

'It looks like a Rorschach inkblot. Make of it what you will, but it doesn't look like definitive evidence to me.' I'd been hoping the psychiatrist might have seen something I couldn't. 'I think you'd better come back when you've got something more recognisable.'

With that, I was dismissed.

I was about to leave when I had a text from DI Karen Foxton. She'd heard I was at the station and asked if I had time to watch some video clips of Aiden they'd managed to get hold of.

Karen showed me into a tiny room with only a desk and a television. Before she left me to it, she warned there wasn't much to see. Part of me was relieved; I didn't like the idea of leaving Aiden too long.

'Some of the footage is from camcorder videos we've had copied onto a DVD.' She gave me the remote. 'The rest is from mobile phones, handed over by Aiden's friends.' She sighed. 'Don't get your hopes up; his appearances are short and sweet. And for some reason, there's no soundtrack on the first bit and the rest is too muffled to hear properly.'

She slid the disc into the machine.

I folded my arms, already disappointed. It looked like I was still going to be deprived of Aiden's voice.

Karen unnerved me for some reason. 'Anything is better than nothing,' I found myself saying, superficially. I felt clumsy and inept in her company.

I thanked her and she left me alone. Any footage that showed Aiden in action before his trauma could be useful for my therapy with him. I wanted to see the Aiden everyone else knew; the person he really was.

The first clip showed a sedate gathering of people inside a poorly lit hall, but as DI Foxton warned, there was no sound. Students were getting up one after the other to walk to the front. An awards ceremony. Faces were hard to distinguish in the gloomy shadows, but they were each handed a certificate and shook a dignitary's hand before returning to their seats. I found myself yawning as the trail of students continued as if on a loop. Then there was a hiatus and a large trophy was lifted onto the table on the stage. The camera made a wobbly attempt to zoom in.

Then everything changed. Aiden sprang up the steps at the side. Light from the windows suddenly splashed over him as if it had been planned that way. The audience stood up, hands clapping wildly, mouths open in cheers. Even without sound, the energy in the hall grew to a frenzy; the pictures seemed sharper, the colours brighter. Aiden gave a flourishing bow as he accepted the prize. He placed it at his feet and said a few words, animated and smiley. Flash bulbs went off as photographers huddled beneath him. He looked genuinely overwhelmed. Several times he stopped talking and held up his hand, waiting for laughter or cheers to die down. Then he scooped up the trophy and disappeared behind a curtain. A crowd of photographers and members of the audience flocked after him before the film abruptly cut off.

I waited for the next clip. It appeared to be at a party, but it wasn't on Aiden's boat; the pictures showed a hallway, living room and kitchen inside a small house, people milling around. Everyone looked close to Aiden's age. The camera panned round and settled on him as he stood leaning against a fireplace with four girls and three blokes each clamouring to reach him. A girl on a sofa leapt up and thrust another girl aside so she could be by his side. A young guy offered him a can of beer, but he declined. The girls were preoccupied with flirting, finding excuses to touch his back, his hair – in fact, the guys looked like they were doing the same.

More people piled into the room and Aiden turned a fraction to face them. Someone must have invited him to say a few words, because all eyes shot in his direction, but all I could hear was a cacophony of chit-chat. He dropped his head, reluctant to speak at first, then three of the group stood up and began a slow hand-clap. The whole room was on its feet, applauding. He shook his head then began to speak, grinning, looking playful and unpretentious, but the sound stuttered and broke up all together. I couldn't hear a word. Aiden bit his lip, seemingly embarrassed by all the attention. Someone slapped him on the shoulders, one of the girls slipped her arm around his neck.

It was hard to see him like this, when in real life I'd only known him lacklustre and defeated. I felt uneasy. It seemed sneaky watching him, spying on him, without his knowledge. Like I was a peeping Tom while he was undressing.

Another girl came up to him and gave him a lingering kiss on the cheek. He backed up, overawed by the attention. And that was it – the screen went blank.

As I ejected the disc, a raw sadness got the better of me, as though I'd just watched a heart-breaking movie. Aiden had been a different person then. The one I knew was like an anonymous imposter filling out his clothes. Not only had his voice been stolen, but his entire personality too.

On the way through the reception area, I bumped into Jeremy Fenway. He'd just ended a conversation with the DCI.

'I heard Aiden's made a sketch,' he said excitedly. 'Where is it? Have we got something?'

'Not yet,' I said. I showed him.

'Dear me...' The same flummoxed look I'd seen on Dr Herts' face anaesthetised Jeremy's. 'Well, at least he's drawing.'

'Exactly,' I said, knowing there were only four days left to hand over something useful, before whatever evidence Aiden produced was no longer considered reliable. 'By the way,' I added, 'something Aiden showed me implied his mother could be mentally ill, possibly in long-term care somewhere.' He looked bemused, not sure what I was getting at. 'Only, I gather they're close and having her with him might help. We need all the optimum conditions for Aiden that we can get.'

'Okay, I'll see what I can do,' said Jeremy.

I was about to walk away, when he spoke again. 'There's something that bugs me,' he said, rubbing his chin. 'We've spoken to a number of Aiden's college contemporaries and no one has a bad word to say about him. Not one. It's a bit unrealistic, don't you think? He's coming across as a saint even on a *bad* day.'

I let out a tense laugh. 'Hmm… I've noticed the same thing.'

'Where are the students who've been elbowed into the shadows, the tutors who have been humiliated by his precociousness, struggling artists who can't compete? There must be plenty of people out there who find Aiden's "five easy steps to fame" somewhat galling.'

'Do you mean the murder was aimed at *him*, rather than the victim?'

'I don't know. I just know something doesn't ring true…'

A frown stayed firmly etched into my forehead all the way back to the boat.

Chapter 18

Aiden was sitting on the upturned bucket on the bow of the boat. He must have been waiting for me. As soon as I approached, he wasted no time getting the engine running again. As he took us into open water, I told him that neither the psychiatrist nor I could make out what his sketch was about, but I made sure it sounded like that was our fault, not Aiden's.

'I thought it might be what you were seeing inside your head, something abstract...'

The oncoming breeze swept back long swathes of his golden hair. 'But, I think it's incredible that you've managed to do anything at all, Aiden. You've already come such a long way and I need you to know I'm very impressed with your progress. I don't want you to rush anything. The police are in a hurry, of course they are, but we can't let ourselves get involved in that.' I was probably telling myself this advice as much as giving it to Aiden.

Between locks he let me take the tiller for a while, but I couldn't enjoy it. I was aware of time ticking away and it was nearly dark by the time we got back to Limehouse. Several boats had left our area of the marina, so he moored the boat parallel to the pontoon, this time, at the usual spot.

Aiden didn't return to his sketch book, but I noticed he'd left a thick scrapbook with the title 'Concepts' open on a table. He disappeared and when I heard the shower running, I took a look at it. It was too bulky to shut, bulging with swatches of silk and linen, photos, doodles and postcards. I carefully turned over one page after another, taken aback by the plethora of creative ideas.

He'd also left sketch pads in different sizes around the place, with various grades of pencils and boxes of charcoal and pastel stubs. For the first time in my adult life I was tempted to have a go.

With Aiden still occupied, I sat under a lamp opposite the wood burner and pressed open a small pad to a fresh page, trailing my fingers across the bevelled surface of the paper. Taking a 2B pencil, I began making tentative marks, curving this way and that, looking back and forth between the page and the stove. The lines went awry several times, but I kept going. After twenty minutes or so I held the page away from me and decided it wasn't a bad effort. The angles weren't right and the chimney was too thin, but you could tell what it was meant to be.

I felt a tickle brush the hairs on the back of my neck and realised I was no longer alone. Aiden had been standing right behind me. I slammed the pad shut but I knew he'd seen my drawing. For once I was the one avoiding eye contact. Instead, I got up and went outside, finding the box seat on the stern in the sultry evening air.

Aiden stayed inside and I let time pass, inhaling the charcoal drift of wood smoke as the nearby waterfall splashed its soothing, meditative rhythm. A dog barked, then a door shut and the barking stopped. Gradually everything stopped. The evening fell still. It was oddly mystical and bewitching, slowly rocking as the darkness seeped into the spaces around me. I couldn't remember the last time I'd done something as simple as this; sitting doing nothing, except take in the dying end of the day.

When I returned to the galley I found a glass of sherry on the table where I'd been sitting. Aiden was in the saloon staring at a book, but I wasn't convinced he was reading. He'd done this before. He never seemed to turn the pages and his gaze was at the wrong angle, like he was looking through the book to whatever was beyond it, rather than at the words themselves. It was the same with the television. He sat through films staring at the screen, but I'm not sure what he was seeing. He didn't react to anything; humour, drama, kids' programmes. It was as if he was waiting for the programme he really wanted to watch. Only it never came.

I raised the glass to him in thanks, joining him in his silent landscape.

I sipped slowly, watching him out of the corner of my eye, contemplating this odd situation; the two of us thrown together. To an outsider, it might look as though we were a devoted couple, living our dream on a luxury narrowboat, so able to read each other that words were unnecessary. I sighed; it was so far from the truth.

I couldn't work out how Aiden perceived me. As a therapist? A doctor? A detective? A friend? It was tempting to hope he saw me as a companion, walking beside him as he tried to step into his unbearable nightmare for the sake of justice. But, of course, being his 'friend' wasn't possible. I remembered what Petra had said; I had to be careful.

Since I'd moved in, I'd noticed the different paths we made through the confined space. Aiden had a way of coming out of his bedroom and curling into the bathroom in a single swoop, keeping close to the wall. He also had a little ritual of approaching the table at the centre of the boat and gently resting his index finger on the edge, halting for a moment, then moving on into the galley. When both of us were on our feet at the same time I tended to wait to see where he would go first, before making my move. It was all part of a strange background dance going on between us.

When I next looked at Aiden, he had a sketch book in his hand.

Chapter 19

Monday, June 4 - Five weeks earlier

Honoré was standing on the pavement outside the gallery, hopping from one foot to the other barely able to contain her excitement. Moments later a taxi drew up alongside her.

'For a Mr Craig Doyle?' queried the driver, craning his neck.

She laughed. 'No that's me... *Honoré* Craig-Doyle...'

He glanced over at his hands-free phone. 'Oh, okay... that must be it.'

'Where are we going?' she asked, as she opened the rear door and slid inside.

'Knightsbridge,' he said.

The flutters in her stomach escalated into uncontainable shivers as she tried to figure out whether this was a business lunch with just an agent, or whether Henby himself might actually be there. Thank goodness she'd worn her sexy grey suit to work, that morning. The rose-gold earrings Trisha had bought her worked a treat as an accompaniment. Made her look not only elegant, but bang on-trend. At least she'd be able to stride in with her head held high.

Now she was on her way, the temptation to ring and break the news of her invitation to all and sundry was almost too much for her. She punched in the number for *Monty's*, her rival gallery in Soho, then as her thumb lingered over the final digit, she changed her mind. Better to announce it once the deal was done; she didn't really know at this stage what kind of offer was going to turn up on the table. It could be excruciating if she'd misunderstood or if Romana was only interested in letting her have one or two of Henby's early, unremarkable canvases.

As they pulled up at traffic lights her phone rang.

It was Romana's PA, this time – a guy named Bruce.

'Okay… Henby's running a bit late and Romana thinks it would be better if you meet at his studio. Where are you?'

Honoré leant over to the window and took in the surroundings. 'Just by Cartier's on Sloane Street… in the taxi,' she said.

'Okay, can you get out and catch the Tube to Bank.'

She wasn't expecting this. 'Can't I just stay in the taxi?' she grunted. 'If you give me the address, I can tell the driver where to go.'

'Not sure where it's going to be yet. Might be Henby's studio, might be a hotel. Romana thinks it's better to get to Bank Station, then she can send someone to meet you there.'

'Oh…' she tutted, 'alright.'

'The taxi fare's been covered, so if you could just go back to Sloane Square Tube…'

'Yes, I know how to get there,' she snapped.

She tapped on the glass partition and explained the situation.

Twenty minutes later she reached the pavement at the busy junction at Bank. She hung around for a further five minutes looking out for someone who could be in search of her, before Bruce rang again.

'If you could walk down Threadneedle Street, then take a right and take the street down the side of the bespoke tailor towards the church.'

'What?' She pressed her finger into her right ear, to block out the din from the traffic. 'I thought Romana was sending someone to fetch me.'

'Change of plan… Henby's definitely heading over. Once you get to–'

'Hold on, hold on, let me get my bearings… right, Threadneedle Street, I'm on it.'

She was starting to get decidedly cheesed off with this expedition across town. The soles of her feet had started to burn inside her new platform sandals.

'When you reach the square with the church in the centre, it's the third house on the right with the dark red door. It's not far.'

'What number is it?' she grunted, then groaned as the strap of her sandal caught the ballooning blister on the back of her heel.

'Henby doesn't have a number on the front...'

'Oh... so that's his studio?' This was more like it.

'Yeah... hold on... I've just been told he's arrived.'

If ever anything could put a spring in her step, in spite of the blisters, hearing those precious words was it.

'Okay, I'll be there as soon as I can.'

Only once she ended the call did she experience a flutter of confusion. Weren't Henby's studios in Rotherhithe? Had he moved? If she hadn't had to focus so hard on trying to remember where on earth she was supposed to go, she'd have looked it up on her phone.

He was waiting for her when she rapped on the front door. He knew from the meeting they'd had, months ago, that she was a glamour puss and he'd banked on the fact that she'd be wearing the most unsuitable footwear imaginable. He was bang on the money. Shoes designed for standing still, not for making a quick getaway. She was doomed before she even set foot inside.

He spotted the glimmer of recognition in her eyes when he let her in. Then, as he led her into the back room, he saw the frown of concentration consume her face as she tried to place him.

'Who did you say you were, again?' Then when she got no response, 'Where's Henby?'

The room was sparsely furnished with tatty armchairs and a lopsided sofa. Under their feet lay bare floorboards, the ragged curtains at the windows, closed, the only light provided by several flickering candelabra on a long table down the centre. He led her to a wooden chair.

'What's going on? Why is it so dark?'

'You know Henby,' he said, with an easy chuckle, 'he likes a bit of mystery. The champagne should be here any minute, then he'll come through to give you a very special welcome.'

She sat down gingerly, her handbag propped on her knees, gawping at the open door, listening for the sound of footsteps. She didn't notice him walk behind her. And that's when her life took a dramatic turn for the worse.

She didn't know it then, but *she'd* be welcoming people in, in her own unique way, in no time at all.

Chapter 20

It was late and I was about to turn in when my phone rang. I slipped quietly outside the bow door to answer it.

'Why are you whispering?' It was Miranda. 'Oh,' she exclaimed. 'You're still with that bloke on his boat, aren't you? Isn't that a bit dodgy, you know, sleeping with the enemy?'

'Miranda, he's not the enemy – and in any case, I'm not...' I started again. 'It's completely above board. I'm his therapist.'

She tutted. 'Made any progress? Do you know who killed Kora, yet?'

'No. And I can't share any of this case with you, anyway, I'm really sorry.'

'Yeah... yeah,' she said in a sing-song voice.

'How are you holding up?' I asked.

'Crap, but I'm alright. Been seeing Sponge and trying to keep busy.' There was a short gap. 'Before you ask, I've been taking my tablets and I've got loads of support here.'

In other words, she was doing perfectly fine without me.

'Look, got to go,' she said. 'Speak soon.'

'What did you want to–?'

In a flash, the line fell dead. That was Miranda all over. I never knew what to expect. Why had she rung, exactly?

I stayed outside and looked around at the collection of masts and ropes in the moonlight. Each shape was mirrored in the still water, two of everything – and my thoughts turned back to my sister.

On the surface Miranda's life looked like it was going swimmingly, but as ever with her, it was hard to separate illusion from truth. She had a history of hiding things and putting on a brave face. Before all this happened I'd hoped seven days away in each other's company would have given me enough time to cut through to the bedrock of her reality. I wanted to get her to sit still long enough for me to ask some simple questions. *'How are you really getting on these days?' 'Are you worried about anything?' 'Are you happy?'* Questions I'd been unable to squeeze into our truncated conversations since her own accident. It would have required my most artful skills to do so, without Miranda smelling a rat and accusing me of interfering. She had an uncanny antennae for anything remotely patronising, for any suggestion from me that she wasn't holding it together.

The bottom line was I wanted to convince myself I'd done my level best to be a good sister to her, but I was starting to think I was approaching it all back to front. In some ways, I was anything but her sister; her carer, her therapist or surrogate mother, perhaps – but never her sister. She was probably right to be fed up with me.

When I returned to the saloon, Aiden had put the sketch pad on the galley table, open at a fresh drawing he'd just finished. I took a look at it and recognised it straight away as the place we'd visited earlier. The crime scene; the iron staircase, the patch of grass, the fence. It was shadowy, with grainy hatching in pencil depicting dusk, but a tremendous improvement on what he'd tried to sketch so far. He had even got as far as outlining the bicycle lying on the ground, but there was no figure beside it. Aiden had stopped there, with no detail in that section of the picture.

I shook my head. 'I don't know how you managed this, Aiden. It must be so harrowing for you to try to picture it again.'

He winced and closed his eyes, then walked away.

I went out onto the pontoon and phoned Jeremy. I hadn't realised how late it was.

'Aiden has drawn the crime scene,' I said. 'But don't get too excited. There's no victim and no assailant.'

'I see. Well, that's not much use to us, is it?' he said with a sigh. 'If he can't speak to us, we need at least a portrait of the *killer.*'

'I know. It's frustrating, but we're making progress. At least he's started to draw recognisable images. It's the first step, it means he's allowing himself to face the situation.'

Monday, July 9 – Day Four
Aiden was sketching again the next morning. I made him a camomile tea and sat at a distance, noticing that a fresh batch of *Thinking of You* cards had been propped up on shelves and cupboards. Well-wishers weren't giving up on him.

I watched his hand move across the page, his wrist flick instinctive as he drew a line here, filled in a patch there. He worked away for about ten minutes, then suddenly stopped, looked at what he'd done in horror and immediately started ripping it to shreds.

'No, no, stop!' I called out, rushing towards him.

Tiny fragments scattered around his chair. I wasn't sure if he was upset because the likeness of his attempt wasn't good enough, or because he was re-traumatised.

I hung back as he diligently picked up the pieces and put them in the galley swingbin. The strain in his face, the cowering in his shoulders and leaden shadows under his eyes as he straightened up, showed me how all-encompassing his plight continued to be. All I wanted to do was rush over and wrap my arms around him.

I stayed still and let my arms fall to my side.

He shuffled to his cabin and closed the door.

All went quiet, so I crept into the galley, removed the bin liner and took it to my room. There, I tipped the contents onto a pull-down surface, isolating all the torn pieces of paper. With a roll of sticky tape and a great deal of perseverance, I tried to fit them back together. It was a daunting task, the scraps were the size of postage stamps and the pencil strokes were faint.

Two hours later I had the complete picture and there was more to follow. When I emerged to make coffee, Aiden was nowhere in sight, but he'd torn out three more pages of completed sketches and left them on the galley table.

By 3pm I was striding into Camden police station with a carry-case under my arm. Jeremy came to meet me at the reception desk.

'Well done!' he said.

I sighed. 'It's not down to me. Aiden has put himself through considerable distress to do this. He's been amazing.'

Wilde, Ndibi, Dr Herts and DI Foxton joined us in the meeting room. Edwin Hall and Joanne Hoyland, the two detective sergeants, had also been called in. I placed Aiden's latest drawings, including the one I'd patched up, on the table. Everyone crowded over them as if they were newly discovered works by Monet.

Silence.

'Is he drawing the victim or the killer?' asked Wilde. 'Have you made it clear that he has to draw the killer?'

'It looks like a woman,' said Karen Foxton. 'The shoulder-length hair, the shape of the coat.'

'In that case, it looks nothing like the victim,' snapped Wilde. 'Why is she on her feet? She was knocked off her bicycle.'

Aiden had drawn the crime scene several times from different angles, but the woman he'd sketched was alive, standing on her own by the fence, her face in the shadows, but otherwise shown in considerable detail. She had a short fringe and delicate features. Kora had longer hair and a broad nose and chin. It definitely wasn't her.

'I don't think it's meant to be the victim,' I said.

'Is he saying this woman is the killer?' Edwin Hall offered tentatively.

I held out my palms. 'I don't know. He can't tell us that. He's doing his best.'

Edwin and Karen flopped into their seats.

'What *exactly* is the point of this exercise?' growled Wilde. He was on his feet, dallying behind my chair again. 'Does he have a photographic memory?' I wondered if the DCI ever spoke without a snarling undertone in his voice.

'His drawings are extremely accurate,' I said.

'It's true. Just look at the crime scene,' added Joanne Hoyland. 'It could be an exact copy of one of the SOCO photographs.'

I slid a self-portrait Aiden had let me bring onto the table. Alongside it I placed a recent photograph of him. 'You see? The likeness is incredible. If anyone can provide a realistic representation of the killer, it's going to be him.'

'So the killer is a woman,' said the DCI, scathingly, hands on hips.

Dr Herts spoke up. 'We must bear in mind that eyewitness testimony can be highly unreliable. Creating a self-portrait is one thing, but when a bystander is in danger they're more interested in fight or flight, than if the killer has curly or straight hair.'

'So, this guy is not only mentally disturbed, but was too freaked out to notice anything, anyway,' snapped Wilde. 'This has been a complete waste of time.'

I fought to keep the exasperation from my voice. 'You have to remember that we all memorise events in a way that makes the most sense to *us*. These may not be literal.'

'Are you saying that what Aiden has drawn is *symbolic* in some way?' asked Jeremy. 'Are we meant to read something into it and figure out what he's trying to say?'

He looked at Dr Herts who shrugged and held out his hand inviting me to answer.

'That's a difficult one,' I admitted.

Joanne stood leaning on the table, her palms either side of one of the sketches. 'Aren't his portraits accurate representations? His other work might be symbolic, but not these, surely. The self-portrait is remarkable.'

I didn't know how to respond. I had no inkling as to what Aiden meant by the repeated sketches of the unknown woman.

Jeremy tried to drag a positive out of the proceedings. 'I think we've got to stick with this. Mr Blake is our only witness and so far we haven't got much evidence from anywhere else. What we really need is for him to regain his speech and Dr Willerby is helping him take crucial steps in that direction. He might have more useful information about the crime, such as which direction the attacker came from, how tall he… she was, mannerisms, whether anything was said and so on. Let's carry on.' He glanced over in my direction and I nodded a silent *thank you.*

'Right, well, I'll leave you to it,' said Wilde and brusquely left the room. Edwin's shoulders dropped by at least an inch.

'We're still waiting for details on the last call from Kora's phone, but it shouldn't be long,' said Jeremy, standing his notes on end by way of rounding things up.

The room cleared and I picked up Aiden's drawings. As I did so, I spotted something I hadn't seen before. None of us had. It threw an entirely different light on the situation. I caught up with Jeremy before he disappeared through the doorway.

'Look…' I said, 'I've only just noticed. Aiden has put a series of dates on the back of the last sketch he did.'

I showed him.

'July tenth, eleventh, twelfth… What does that mean?' he muttered.

I thought about it. 'The sketch isn't of Kora – he's drawn a different woman, we can all see that.' I rapped my finger against the sheet. 'In the same spot as the tripwire attack, with dates from tomorrow onwards.'

'I don't get it,' Jeremy went on. 'Why doesn't Mr Blake just write down what happened? I know he can't speak, but if he can make a note of these dates, why can't he jot down information about the crime?'

'Because writing down a date is purely factual. It poses no emotional threat to him. But speaking, drawing, explaining – that means allowing himself to re-experience the trauma in a way that he can't right now.'

He looked nonplussed. 'Okay, so he's written down a few dates…'

I narrowed my eyes. 'We're asking him about the past – but he's referring to the *future.*' I bit my lip, thinking. 'He's used three dots to indicate his list of dates is unfinished. It *has* to be significant, like he doesn't know exactly when…'

I pictured the moment before I left the boat, when Aiden put these pictures in his carry-case for me. There was concern on his face when he did so. Grave concern. I'd put it down to reliving the attack, but now I had second thoughts.

'He was worried when he gave me them,' I muttered, holding the sheets against my chest.

Jeremy stared at me, as puzzled as ever.

'What if these aren't memories?' I said, holding them out again. 'What if this is Aiden showing he's concerned about something else... something to come?'

Jeremy took a step back. 'Something *to come*? And what might that be? How are we supposed to know?'

I stared at him. 'I'm starting to learn how he thinks, how he does things. I've been observing him very closely. These are the only recognisable sketches he's done and they're *not* about Kora. They're not about the attack at all.'

He waits for me to get to the point.

'This is about the future,' I said, my tone emphatic with a spur of the moment flash of certainty. 'Someone else is in danger.'

Chapter 21

'So what are we looking at? Who is Aiden referring to?' Jeremy asked, dismayed. He ushered me back inside the meeting room and closed the door.

'Have any women gone missing in the area recently?'

He sighed heavily, throwing me a ferocious glare. 'You're kidding me...'

'Okay, stupid question. But this is a *different* woman,' I insisted, flapping the sheets at him, trying to get him to understand. 'It's someone Aiden's worried about. He knew I was bringing the sketches to you. This has to be significant.'

He shook his head. 'Over ten thousand people go missing in London every year. Who are we looking for?'

I traced my finger around the outline of the drawing. 'She looks smart, maybe mid-twenties, classy.'

He stared up at the ceiling, sucking his teeth. 'It's too broad.'

'You've got a missing persons' database, right?'

'Of course.'

'And you can apply different filters, I assume?'

He nodded, his eyebrows wavering in disbelief.

'Well, can we check women who've gone missing in respectable jobs – not runaways from hostels? Can we narrow it down to women matching that profile in London?'

He sighed. 'Hold on a minute and I'll get the files up. See how many we're looking at first.'

He came back. 'A hundred and twenty-seven women between the ages of twenty and thirty have been reported missing so far this year,' he said. 'And that's just in Camden.'

I clenched my teeth. 'Right…' I leant against the desk. 'How about in the last thirty days?'

'Let's go and see…' He beckoned me through to his office, an all-glass affair that looked out over a buzzing open-plan space. He drew me alongside him at the computer and brought up a series of missing persons' files. 'Twenty-one women in the Borough of Camden,' he said, his palms flat either side of the keyboard. 'Now let's add the other thirty-one boroughs to get the whole of London…' He made a clucking sound and straightened up. 'Over five hundred.'

'Okay, I get the picture.' I fiddled with my lip, refusing to be defeated. 'What about ethnic background? Would you say the woman Aiden's drawn is white?'

'Could be mixed-race,' he said, scrutinising the sketch as I held it out for him.

'True. How about cutting out certain definite categories? Not black, not Asian?'

He huffed, but punched the keys.

'And women holding down respectable jobs?' I added. 'She certainly doesn't look like she's on the streets. Look at the coat Aiden's drawn, her boots…'

'Okay. That narrows it down to…' he pressed enter, 'eighty-one.' He turned to me and folded his arms. 'We don't even know if this is what Aiden means. You're basing this on a few dates, a pretty portrait and a huge assumption.'

'I know,' I admitted, fully aware I was testing his patience. 'Do you have the photos of these eighty-one missing women?'

'To look for a match, you mean?'

'Yes.'

He cleared his throat. 'You won't be able to take them away – you'll have to go through them here.'

'No problem. Thank you.'

That seemed to remind him of something else. He rummaged through his intray and handed me a brown envelope.

'This is a set of Kora's scene of crime photographs,' he said. 'I think you should have them. It might move things along if you showed them to Aiden... when you think he's ready. Might jog his memory.'

I drew my chin back with a jerk. 'And re-traumatise him in an instant?'

What was he thinking of? In that instant, the DI plummeted in my estimation. I couldn't expect every police officer to be psychologically aware, but I thought I'd seen signs of more solicitude than this from Jeremy Fenway.

'It's not his memory that's holding him back, it's abject terror. Of facing the reality of the situation, of reliving the gruesome nature of it.'

'Well, just in case,' he said, his tone insistent.

I took them reluctantly. They might be useful in some other way, but certainly not for jogging Aiden's memory. In my view, Aiden could remember everything perfectly well already. I quickly flicked through the shots; most were of the crime scene from different angles; Kora's twisted bicycle, her bag cast aside, her sandal near the water's edge. The scarf from around her neck lying in a clump, soaked in blood. It must have been yanked off her neck by the tripwire. The caretaker had remembered her wearing it before she left CCAP, that evening.

But that wasn't all. There were further photos of her injuries, taken when she was admitted to the hospital, showing the gaping wound slicing her throat. There were more after her death. I tried to pretend they were stills from a film, but found my stomach flipping over in a fierce lurch nevertheless. The DI must have seen my face change colour and rushed for a glass of water.

'Sorry...' he muttered as he put it in my hand and eased me into a chair.

'You forget I'm not used to this,' I said, patting my chest.

I carefully placed the envelope in my bag, out of sight.

After a few deep breaths I was ready to take a look at the missing person's photos. Jeremy showed me to a small empty office, barely bigger than a cupboard and flicked on the light. He opened the laptop, the only item on the table, and set up the database for me.

'Twenty minutes max,' he instructed waving his finger at me. 'Someone else needs this room at half past.'

'While I do this, can you see if you can refine the search?'

He slumped his body weight to one hip. 'How exactly?'

I chewed the inside of my cheek, thinking. 'Art is Aiden's entire world by the looks of things, so that's the obvious connection to check out first.'

'You think his drawing could be of another artist?'

I shrugged. 'It could be someone who met Aiden through his art, don't you think? It's worth trying. A fellow student, maybe. Or someone at Chelsea College. Or from one of the other art colleges in London.'

He huffed and backed out of the door.

By the time he came back twenty minutes later, I'd found something.

'Look,' I exclaimed. I held the sketch Aiden had drawn next to the photograph on the screen. 'It's her, isn't it?'

He puffed out his cheeks. 'Jeez... you could be right.'

'Can you find out any more details about her?' I asked, scribbling the police file number from her photo on a scrap of paper and handing it to him.

He straddled the chair beside me and angled the laptop so I couldn't see. 'Sorry, this is strictly confidential.'

I nodded and waited as he punched in an authorisation code for further access. Seconds later he began reading from a missing person's report.

'Okay, she's a journalist,' he said. 'Pippa French... aged twenty-eight, disappeared in Blackfriars. Journalist at *The Bulletin*. Went missing after work on Friday, June fifteenth.'

'*The Bulletin*, what's that?'

'Looks like they cover London culture: trends and fashion, contemporary art, cinema and theatre.'

'Art…' I mused. 'Sorry, go on.'

He reached into his back pocket. 'While you were looking at the photos I ran various art establishments through the database as you suggested, but no missing women came up, so I widened the age range to forty and came up with this.' He pulled out a small notebook and flipped it open. 'A gallery owner. She was last seen getting into a cab in Chelsea at lunchtime on Monday, June fourth.'

'Eleven days before Pippa?'

He nodded. 'Name of Honoré Craig-Doyle, thirty-seven, owner of the Craig-Doyle Gallery in SW3.' He tapped his chin with his finger. 'But neither of these missing women are under our jurisdiction – different London boroughs.'

I took a deep breath.

'But you're right,' he concluded, straightening up. 'We should look into these. It's possible there's a link. We need to talk to Aiden.'

'Let me do it,' I said. 'He'll be less intimidated by me. I'll ask him about it and keep you posted. I promise.'

I left him striding purposefully towards his team and hurried back to the boat.

I found Aiden dozing on the sofa and waited for him to stir. As he sat up and stretched, I knelt on the carpet beside him.

'I've come from the police station. We've been looking at women who have gone missing recently. Are you okay for me to ask you something?'

He blinked hard, but didn't flinch or make any move to escape.

I handed him a sheet Jeremy had authorised showing Pippa's photo and details of her disappearance. He sat forward with a jolt and clasped it to his chest, swallowing hard.

Next, I held out the sketch he'd made of the woman at the fence at the crime scene. 'Is this her?' I said, keeping my voice steady. 'Is this Pippa French? Is that who you've drawn?'

He nodded. A single movement. Firm. Unmistakable. The first clear reaction I'd seen from him, a genuine breakthrough. I forced my voice to stay steady, bubbling inside with elation.

'The police say she's missing. Do you know what's happened to her? Do you know where she is?'

He was breathing hard. A frown and a shake of the head.

'Are you worried about her?'

Another nod. Inwardly my heart was cheering with joy. We really did have a quantum leap forward. Aiden was communicating!

Jeremy had let me have a copy of Honoré's photograph and I studied Aiden's face closely as I showed him. She was older than the other two women; glamorous Latin-looks with frothy bed-head hair and dangly earrings. There was no flicker of recognition, before he turned away.

I called Jeremy, but was put through to voicemail.

'I don't think Aiden knows the other woman, Honoré Craig-Doyle,' I said, 'but he gave a positive response about Pippa. Aiden's definitely worried about her...' I didn't know what else to say, so I ended the message.

I realised it didn't change anything, except that Aiden appeared to *know* a woman who had gone missing. But, surely lots of people knew her. He wasn't indicating he knew where she was or what had happened to her. He was worried about her, that's all – like all her friends and family would be.

'The City of London Police already have her details,' I told Aiden, 'but the Camden team will be involved now. To see if it links up in any way with what happened.'

I watched his face, but there wasn't a flicker.

There were no more sketches of Pippa after that. I took that as a sign that there was nothing more to explore right now – that I'd got the correct message and passed it on to the right people. Nevertheless, Aiden kept drawing from memory: the staircase on the towpath, the side of the boat, the bridge under which Kora rode, the fence beside the car park. Images were coming thick and fast now. But none of the maniac behind her death.

It was frustrating. I wanted him to shift the lens of his internal camera a few degrees to the left, to focus on the wire attached to his outside lamp. I wanted him to freeze frame right there and show us what he'd seen. The figure who must have reached out directly in front of him.

As he drew, I mulled over this new information. I jotted down the names of the three women on a sheet of paper:

Kora Washington (sculptor at CCAP, Camden, dead)
Pippa French (drawn by Aiden, journalist, Blackfriars, missing)
Honoré Craig-Doyle (art gallery owner, Chelsea, also missing)

I added a few details; all were slight, pretty, with dark hair. I looked up *The Bulletin* magazine and took down the address. That was about all I could piece together.

After a while, Aiden dropped his sketch pad and went to sit on his own in the bow. When he came back, I asked for any photographs or press-cuttings I could look at from his past, his school days or recent college days. The police had taken all his online devices so they would check his social media sites, but I was hoping for a more personal angle. I wanted to look for a mention of Kora, but also for the names of the other missing women, Pippa and Honoré. Maybe Aiden himself had some connection to the Craig-Doyle Gallery.

He returned from his cabin with a shoebox brimming with newspaper clippings and snapshots. I saw familiar faces straight away; Howard and Valerie, paintbrushes in hand; Natalie and Didier holding long forks over a barbeque. There were none of Aiden's family that I could make out, none that could be his mother. Nothing earlier than around three years ago, in fact, when he was sixteen. I moved on to the clippings. Awards and accolades followed one after another, praising Aiden's 'outstanding talent', his 'youthful vision' and 'fresh dynamism'. It wasn't telling me anything new.

I was about to put them back into the box, when a photo from *Vogue* caught my eye. It was from a fashion show in Kensington and showed a woman advancing down the catwalk. There was something familiar that I couldn't place. It wasn't her face; she had the androgynous look of many size-zero models, it was something else. Something I'd seen, earlier that day.

I retraced my steps in my mind's eye. Aiden had torn up a drawing and I'd tried to patch it together, then I'd been at the police station. Jeremy and I had talked about the two missing women. Aiden had done more sketches when I got back and I'd looked through his box of memorabilia. What was it? What had I seen?

Instead of forcing my brain to make a connection, I decided to focus on something else. Give myself time. I picked up the TV remote and noticed a prospectus underneath it. It was for Chelsea College and as I gave it a quick flick through, I spotted some of Aiden's work, used as inspirational examples.

That's when I spotted it.

A distinctive silver feather design on white silk; one of Aiden's scarves. I went back to the photo of the model on the catwalk for comparison and it was definitely the same design. Where else had I seen it that day?

Then it hit me.

So Aiden wouldn't see, I took my bag into my cabin and eased out the prints from the crime scene photographs Jeremy had given me. There it was, tossed on the towpath after being torn from Kora's slashed neck. No longer white, but unmistakeable, nevertheless. Aiden's scarf.

Chapter 22

My loyalty to Aiden could only go so far. I had to tell the police about the scarf and rise above the loud voice in my head that screamed: *It didn't mean Kora and Aiden knew each other.*

Jeremy said he'd ring me back. I stepped off the boat and paced up and down the pontoon, waiting. When nothing happened I began chopping leeks for a pasta dish and his call came in as I moved on to grating cheese.

'We've checked the records at his college – pretty inconclusive,' Jeremy said. I went back onto the bow to make sure I was out of Aiden's hearing. 'He sold a selection of items through the end-of-year shows and exhibitions.'

'Is that where students sell their work?' I asked him.

'Some students have market stalls at Camden or Portobello Road, but not Aiden, he's aiming at a much higher market and is getting retailers on board. Tutors told us he's talking to stores like Selfridges and Liberty about producing his range, because he can't keep up with demand.'

I laughed. 'That figures. So, someone could have bought the scarf for Kora, as a gift.'

'Or Aiden could have given it to her.'

'Or she could have been at one of the college shows and bought it herself.'

He made a non-committal noise. 'We're looking into it, but sales at the college events made in cash have no details of the buyers, so it's going to be tricky. Kora's partner certainly didn't know where she'd got it from.'

'I could ask Miranda, my sister; she was Kora's best friend.'

'No, don't you dare! *We're* asking the questions, okay? I don't want you talking to anybody. We've got it covered – leave it to us.'

His breaths were clipped and throaty. 'By the way, we've traced the last call from Kora's mobile phone, made around ten minutes before she was knocked off her bike,' he said. 'It was to a guy called Murray Kent.'

'Who's he?'

'We're trying to work out what connection he had with Kora, but there were a number of calls made to and from the same phone in the last month or so.' I waited. 'Her partner had never heard of the guy. He lives locally. Owns a place called *The Flower Basket*. It's a florist Kora had liked on Facebook.'

'So this guy might have been the last person to have had contact with her?'

'Or been the one to lure her along the towpath. We're talking to him.' There was a beat's silence. 'Don't mention Kent's name to Blake, but bear it in mind… and while you're on the boat, keep a look out for anything else that could be connected. Strict confidentiality goes for any other information that we pass on to you, of course. It's to give you a context for getting information out of the witness, that's all. And don't even think about doing any amateur sleuthing yourself, okay? As soon as he's speaking, it's over to us. Got it?'

'Loud and clear,' I said. 'Therapy is my job, interviewing is yours, right?'

'Exactly. You just get him talking.'

'By the way,' I said, 'is it possible that the killer was either moored in the area or passing by, along the canal?'

'In a boat, you mean?'

'Yeah.'

'We've already checked that out. There were five boats moored alongside Aiden's that evening. Two have left the area now; a couple in their sixties and a young pair with a baby. The others are still there; a retired Dutch guy, a young couple with a yapping dog and a woman on her own, around fifty. We spoke to them all. We've looked into river traffic, too. No one saw anything unusual.'

'What if a boat had been passing and the killer jumped off and then got back on again?'

'Three of the boat folk heard the commotion and climbed onto the towpath straight after it happened. Nobody recalls hearing a boat engine, any water movement or lights from a passing vessel.'

'What about a rowing boat – something small and quiet?'

'Like I say, post-crime witnesses were on the scene very quickly, but no one saw anything on the water. There's a canoe club near the lock, but none of their boats were missing. We've had officers over at Little Venice to the West and no boats came through there at that time – nor were there any stray boats heading east towards Camden. There's the lock there, of course, which would hold them up. And before you ask,' I could hear the smile in his voice, 'we've considered someone swimming too. There were no splashes of water at the crime scene, which you'd expect if someone had come out of the canal.'

Tuesday, July 10 – Day Five

I was in the middle of ordering online groceries when I got a call from the police. They'd traced Aiden's mother. She was called Coleen O'Leary, aged forty, and my hunch from Aiden's sand tray scene had been right; she'd been in a psychiatric hospital for the past ten years. Aiden had changed his name, which explained why it had taken some time to track her down.

'What kind of state is she in?' I asked. It was DI Karen Foxton who'd rung me.

'Not good,' she said. 'Coleen had a breakdown in 2008. She was admitted to St Patrick's Psychiatric Hospital in Belfast, suffering from psychosis. According to the psychiatrist, she'd lost touch with reality and was unable to take care of herself.' I heard her sniff. 'She's been having intermittent electric shock treatment, with medication and psychotherapy, but basically she's spent her time there believing she's Mother Mary.'

I suppressed a sigh, noting the complete absence of sympathy in her voice. 'Imagine having to cope with your mother in that state, when you're only ten,' I said, swallowing hard. 'Sounds like she's not going to be any support for Aiden, for certain.'

'I'll email over the report,' she said. 'One interesting thing, though. Coleen has got a criminal record. She attacked a woman with a knife, in 2008…'

I wasn't sure what she was getting at. 'At the time of Kora's death, wasn't she miles away surrounded by alibis in white coats?'

'Yeah, but it might run in the family,' she said, provocatively.

Aiden seemed slightly brighter when he emerged this morning. He'd washed his hair and walked a little taller than he had during the past few days. We shared a pot of fresh coffee, sitting on tiny canvas stools at the front of the boat, in the sweet calm air. I decided to try a fresh tack.

'Can you imagine something for me?' The muscles in his jaw froze. 'It's nothing awful, I promise.'

He swept a strand of hair out of his eyes and stared back at me.

'Can you *imagine* yourself standing… just a few feet away… on the pontoon?' I pointed to the planks on dry land. 'Right beside the boat, holding on to it, perhaps?'

A look of abject terror came over his face and he glanced sideways towards the door.

'How about one foot on the boat and one on the pontoon?'

He shuddered, then got up abruptly. Keeping his eyes on me the whole time, he backed away, as though he thought I might make a grab for him.

'I'm sorry…' I said hopelessly.

He disappeared into his cabin. He wasn't ready to go anywhere.

I wouldn't be giving that another go in a hurry. It was obviously far too soon for him. I blamed the pressure of time slipping away for my faux pas, together with Claussen and Wilde's bullheaded tones in my head, demanding results. I needed to put them right out of my mind and stick to my own judgement from now on.

I stayed where I was, tipping my face upwards towards the tingling rays of the sun, wondering what to do next. Overlooking this particular setback, Aiden's ability to take up his pencil and draw sketches of the crime scene was impressive for someone so deeply traumatised. Having said that, there must have been around fifteen by now and none of them showed any trace of an assailant. I began to wonder if he'd seen him at all.

My ruminations were interrupted by my phone.

'What's Blake up to?' It was Jeremy.

'Nothing. Gone to his cabin. I suggested leaving the boat and he's not ready to even contemplate the idea.'

'Any chance you can get away and join me for a short lunch break? My treat. I haven't taken a proper lunch hour in weeks and I need a break from home-made sarnies with sausage and ketchup.'

'Yuck, I don't blame you!'

The idea of being back on dry land for a while was certainly appealing. 'I'll need to see if someone here can keep an eye on Aiden, first,' I told him.

Natalie was ironing when I tapped on her front door. She was dressed in a see-through wraparound skirt and bikini top – she'd had the afternoon off from rehearsals.

'I'll just get my knitting.' she said. 'The rest of Didi's shirts can wait.'

Moments later she joined me in Aiden's saloon, with a pile of magazines and a bag trailing pink wool.

'What if he comes out of his cabin?' she asked, nervously fluttering her lashes. 'I don't know what to say to him.'

'Just talk to him normally, but try to avoid asking questions. Tell him what you've been doing – easy, ordinary things – like a verbal postcard. He needs as much normality around him as possible.'

I left her unravelling a tangle of fluffy angora.

Chapter 23

I was getting used to the journey from Limehouse to Camden. Whilst it looked a long way on the Tube map, it was only eight stops via Bank, and it took less than thirty minutes door to door on a good day.

I spotted Jeremy waiting outside *Bartoli's*, a swish place in a secluded passageway, hidden from the bustling high street.

'Woo, this is lovely,' I said. 'I wasn't expecting a proper restaurant.'

'I'm glad you could come,' he said. 'I'm all too aware that you've given up your holiday for this case. Shouting you lunch is the least I can do.'

The waiter took us through to a small courtyard at the back and brought a collection of warm bread rolls. Hanging baskets spilling over with electric-blue lobelia lined the terrace and wafts of boxus and rosemary enveloped us from wooden planters by our feet. Each table had a crisp linen tablecloth and a glass with white roses set amongst sapphire-coloured delphiniums in the centre. It looked divine. Just the chance to sit here for a breather would have been a treat, regardless of the food.

'Wine?' Jeremy offered, opening the drinks menu.

'Oh, no – not for me.' I said. 'I'm officially working.' He nodded and reluctantly closed the menu.

I broke apart a freshly baked roll as we waited for our order to arrive and thought of Terry and his new passion for bread-making. He'd have to pull out all the stops to match the texture and flavour of this. I toyed with suggesting we come here, instead of The Dorchester – our running joke.

Jeremy caught me smiling, but I was saved from having to explain myself by lunch arriving.

'I've decided I'm in love with truffle oil,' I said, as I tucked into my plate of coated gorgonzola and walnuts. I'd chosen to stick with vegetarian, having got a taste for the clean freshness of non-meat dishes on the boat.

We fell into an easy silence.

'By the way, we've interviewed Murray Kent,' he said eventually, manoeuvring a wayward piece of rocket between his lips. It was inevitable that after a while, we'd talk about the case. 'No harm in telling you that he lives in Kentish Town.' He wiped his mouth with the napkin, which was so thick it was almost a flannel. 'He's admitted to knowing Kora. He claims they'd been discussing the possibility of selling her sculptures in his flower shop. They were due to meet that evening.'

I finished my mouthful. 'Why so late?'

'Mmm… exactly… he claimed she suggested it was the best time for her.'

'Do you believe his story?' I asked him.

'Not sure,' he admitted. 'Murray said Kora didn't want to tell anyone about the shop deal until it was definite.'

'Were they having an affair?'

'Murray denies it and Kora's friends and family say absolutely not. They say Kora was totally devoted to Sponge and the boy, but…'

'People do act out of character,' I said, tipping my head from side to side.

'Of course, Murray *might* have been stringing her along, perhaps hoping to introduce some fringe benefits into the deal, if he hadn't done so already.'

'What's Murray's side of the story for what happened that night?'

'He said that as he drove into the CCAP car park to collect Kora he had a call from the caretaker, Lou Tennison, ringing on Kora's behalf, saying she'd been unwell and had just left in a taxi. Murray tried her mobile after that and couldn't get through, so he turned round and went home. He said he got home at around 10.15pm, but there's no alibi for that.'

'So, he thought she'd already left… not on her bike, but in a taxi?'

He shrugged, then pulled a face as he dragged a fish bone from his mouth, leaving it on the edge of his plate.

'We know that's not what happened, but does his version of it fit?' I asked, relieved I didn't have to negotiate my way through fish remains in each mouthful.

'Basically, no,' he said, sitting back. 'Lou said he didn't make a call using Kora's phone. He said he never touched it.'

'So Murray Kent is lying.'

'Not necessarily. Someone else could have made the call and said it was the caretaker. Kent doesn't know Lou. He doesn't know what he should sound like. It could have been someone else who was with Kora and took her phone.'

'Did anyone see Kent leave when he said he did?'

Jeremy scraped his nails over a patch of eczema on the underside of his wrist that I hadn't noticed until then. 'We're checking that out. It took Kent a long time to get from CCAP to his place in Kentish Town, over forty-five minutes. Should have taken around ten minutes at that time of night. Kent said he stopped off on the way home and bought groceries in an all-night place on the corner of Padua Street. Paid cash. It could account for the delay in getting home, but we need to see if there's any CCTV or if they remember him. That could be his alibi.' We both held still for a second as a siren wailed in the distance. 'A call was certainly made to Kent from Kora's phone at nine twenty-two and the caretaker told us Kora left on her bike at nine twenty-five. We know that's true, but she wasn't in a taxi. Obviously we're talking to Lou again, because we've got a story that doesn't add up.'

'Is Sponge a suspect?' I asked, the idea suddenly occurring to me. 'Maybe somehow he'd got the idea Kora was cheating on him.'

'He seemed pretty shell-shocked when we told him about the late meeting planned with Kent, but his only alibi is that he was at home babysitting their son Raven.' He opened his eyes wide.

'There's one more thing,' he said, looking grave. 'Murray Kent has a criminal record for GBH.'

I put down my fork and stopped to take in what he'd said. Something was definitely off-kilter. Someone was messing about with the truth over Kora's last movements.

Jeremy gave a sign to the waiter to bring the bill. 'Maybe next time we can meet *after* work and have a decent glass of wine, eh?' He shook his water glass which rattled with the remains of ice cubes.

I smiled and felt it fade, uncertain over what this lunch was really about.

The bill came and I put my credit card alongside his on the saucer. 'Fifty-fifty,' I said emphatically.

He looked awkward. 'It's okay…'

'No, I insist. We're in this together.'

His eyes flicked briefly to mine. 'Actually, this isn't on me.' He handed back my card.

'Oh…' I tried to catch his eye, but he wouldn't look at me. 'What's going on?' I asked.

He cleared his throat, sounding serious all of a sudden. 'Now that you're on the boat with Blake, we'll be able to cover one hour of therapy a day and your travel expenses to the police station, but that's all. We can't cover for anything beyond that or for loss of earnings…'

'Oh, just as well it hadn't occurred to me to charge by the hour, then!' I laughed, but soon realised that Jeremy was looking straight through me.

I felt my stomach sink. 'Did someone – Wilde or Claussen, perhaps – put you up to this?' He avoided my eyes. I was bang on.

'I see.' I got to my feet.

His mouth twisted awkwardly to one side.

'How very disappointing,' I said, taking a step back. 'So, this was designed to buy me off.' I pushed my chair under the table. 'It had genuinely never occurred to me to ask for a bigger fee. I made a commitment to Aiden, no matter what. That was my choice. I wasn't doing it for the money.'

I grabbed my bag and left.

Chapter 24

When I got back, Natalie had left a note to say she'd slipped out to put on a load of washing. Aiden was gluing together a wooden stand for a ship he'd built inside a bottle. He let me hold it up to the light. The detail on the miniature galleon inside was outstanding; the billowing sails, the cotton-thin rigging, even tiny canons poking out of wooden slats in the side. As I stared at it in awe, he fumbled with the final pieces of the plinth; his fingers twitchy and clumsy like those of an old man.

'It's incredible,' I said.

'He did most of it a few weeks ago,' said Natalie pointedly, appearing at the doorway. She pulled me to one side. 'Making the stand is all he can manage now,' she said in a whisper.

'At least he's involved with something,' I whispered back.

Before she discreetly disappeared she insisted I call on her to look after Aiden any time. 'He's no trouble,' she said. 'It's just so sad seeing him like this.'

I told Aiden I'd already eaten, so he put together a fried halloumi sandwich for himself while I rattled on about my father's fascination with building tiny model aircraft.

'He always wished he'd had a child who could have joined in,' I told him, 'but I've invariably been someone who uses my mind to work at things, not my fingers.'

I had no idea whether he was actually listening or not.

As the day wore on it got hotter and hotter. Aiden seemed restless and itching to do something. He dragged the seed compost I'd had delivered to the bow and began tipping layers into a series of small trays. I watched him painstakingly plant chicory and sunflower seeds; the idea Petra suggested to help him feel grounded. I stretched back in a deckchair on the pontoon and thought about the case, read intermittently, then fell asleep for a while.

I'd probably stayed out a little too long, because by supper time I had a headache and my skin was blotchy. Aiden dragged four fans from the cavernous space under the deck and set them whirring throughout the boat. It helped, but after the meal I needed to get fresh air again. The problem was, there wasn't much room to sit outside on the boat and I didn't want to park myself on the pontoon all the time knowing Aiden wouldn't be comfortable joining me.

I was standing by the door, dithering, when he came past me carrying two rolled up towels. I wondered where on earth he was going with them. As I stepped back, he reached up and draped them on the flat surface of the roof, side by side. He then went back inside and poured two small glasses of brandy.

I laughed, pointed to the roof and shook my head in an exaggerated fashion.

'You think I'm going up there?!'

There was a narrow ledge running around the hull only four inches wide, reserved for those with deft feet. In three steps, Aiden sprang onto it and nimbly hoisted himself up to the roof, two feet above me. There was nothing for it. Using the same footholds he had and gripping his guiding hand, I followed him up. It felt higher above the water than it looked and the boat seemed to lurch about with a mind of its own. Struggling to keep my balance, I sank down onto my backside and gratefully accepted the glass as he passed it over. I needed that first gulp of brandy. When I looked over again, Aiden was stretched out with his eyes closed. I followed suit. As the evening wore on, it brought a wafting breeze, skimming the surface of everything, soothing the bite out of my burnt skin.

When I opened my eyes I found him sitting up with his arms wrapped around his knees, looking intently into the distance. I followed his gaze and spotted a fox on the far side of the marina creeping around the recycling block. As the light faded, we watched bats dive across the water like they were on strings of elastic. They darted past us, caught on the edges of my vision, making me doubt whether they were really there or not.

Only five days ago I'd felt like an intruder on Aiden's boat, disturbing him, invading his privacy, goading him to emerge from the internal strife he was going through. But the dynamic between us had shifted in tiny increments since then. Sitting there, I felt included. He'd invited me into his world and although he was still silent, we were part of something together. Besides, there was so much going on around us, words felt superfluous.

Once the sky had melted from a rich Persian blue to inky black, we lay on our backs again, gazing at the stars that stood out like diamonds on pins.

Although Aiden was still without words, he appeared to have warmed to me. There were times when he held my gaze without looking away, appeared to listen, the inkling of a smile on his lips. It wasn't much to an observer, but to me it felt like a major step forward – like I'd got one foot on the moon.

At times, instead of words, we'd started using facial expressions and simple signs to 'speak' each other. Aiden seemed more comfortable doing this than hearing my words and being unable to take his turn. The hand signals, half-shrugs, narrowing of the eyes, the lift of an eyebrow felt like a secret language between us. We learnt to read small movements from each other, tiny messages passed between us that others could easily overlook or misinterpret.

Aiden moved and inadvertently brushed the hairs on my arm – or so I thought. Instead of taking his hand away he left it where it was, his warmth merging into mine bridging the gap between us. I realised that he probably hadn't been touched – with any form of care – by anyone since the trauma. Shoved around by the police, perhaps, but nothing comforting.

It dignifies someone when you touch them. Not only that, it is the most basic of human connections; it conveys reassurance, shows concern, soothes and consoles. It would have been insensitive to pull away, so I patted his arm and he shuffled closer, resting his head in my lap, just like a child.

Instantly, I held myself in check, acutely aware of my position as a professional. I heard Petra's warning words about maintaining strict boundaries hissing in my ear and wondered what to do. I had to keep my relationship with Aiden entirely above board. If I failed to do so, I could find myself getting struck off. More to the point, I didn't want Aiden to get mixed messages when he was in such a vulnerable position.

But to pull away after such an innocent gesture felt cruel and rude. He wasn't making me feel uncomfortable and it certainly wasn't sexual. I made a decision. I'd let him stay like this for a few minutes, then I'd go and make us both a bedtime cocoa.

All of a sudden I felt him shiver. The shivers turned into trembling and I realised he was sobbing. Within seconds, great convulsive waves were buckling his body. I sat up and held him, rocked him, like a mother enveloping her wounded son. As his sobs escalated into loud howls, Natalie and Didier came charging out of their boat, wondering what was going on. I put my finger to my lips and sent them away with wafts of my arm. I continued to gently hold him as he let out everything he'd been bottling up for days.

Eventually he got up and pulled me to my feet. He gave me a broad, all-encompassing hug. My face was pressed into his shoulder; his arms locked around my back. For a second, I felt precarious, standing on the roof of the narrowboat, then I didn't care. If we fell in the water, we'd fall together.

He didn't know it but as he held me, a few of my own tears landed on his shoulder. Partly, it was relief that Aiden was finally breaking out of his dark cave. It was also a sense of privilege that he'd trusted me with his emotional outburst. Mostly, however, it was an acute recognition of my own loneliness. I hadn't been held by a man like that for what seemed like an age.

Chapter 25

I was so hot I took a wet flannel to bed with me and laid it across my forehead. As I wrestled with the duvet, forcing it to surrender and crumple to the floor, my phone buzzed with a text from Terry.

Sorry it's late. Hope all is going well on the boat. I've booked myself in for scuba diving in Malta and I'm checking up on you to see if you've made any progress with your holiday plans? I won't be letting it lie…

He ended the message with a big 'X'. He really was taking an interest, after all this time.

As I finished reading it, a call came through from Karen Foxton. She was working late.

'We've found out a bit more about Aiden's background,' she said. 'The hospital records are sketchy, but it looks like Coleen, his mother, was born in County Tyrone, Northern Ireland. She had Aiden when she was twenty-one, there's no record of his father. Coleen's parents – her father was Irish, her mother from London – were both killed in 1998 by a bomb, the year he was born. Might have been the Omagh bombing, it doesn't say. Coleen was left alone with Aiden. He was five days old.'

I let out a sad sigh.

'She and Aiden came to London later the same year to start a new life,' Karen continued. 'There was plenty of money from her parents and she bought a house in Notting Hill. But, in 2007, she sold it and went back to Northern Ireland with Aiden, who was nine by this stage. She put money in trust for him for when he reached sixteen, and more for when he turned eighteen – which was smart thinking, because the following year she had the nervous breakdown.'

'Whoa, the impact on Aiden must have been enormous. His family caught up in the Irish troubles, his mother going over the edge and no father. No wonder he's fragile.'

'An aunt in Ealing became his legal guardian,' she went on. 'The nurse I spoke to at St Patrick's gave the impression that this aunt was only involved because a sum of money changed hands. I don't think she was interested in him. Anyway, he moved on when he was sixteen. He had plenty of money with so many family bereavements, so he wasn't on the streets. Rented a small flat in Pimlico. Enrolled to do A levels; art, English and history and got into Art college a year earlier than usual.' She'd reached the end of her fact-finding account. 'The rest, you know.'

'Thanks for filling me in, that's very helpful.' My mind went back to the sand tray exercise and I recalled the protective way Aiden had blown the sand off the Snow White figure he'd chose to represent his mother. The way he'd carefully put her in his pocket.

'There's one more thing,' Karen added. 'A few senior officers have been suggesting Aiden was discounted as a suspect too soon. He could be mentally unstable too, right?'

She'd hinted at this before. Hadn't Aiden been comprehensively cleared right at the start?

'Are you saying you've found something?'

She didn't answer.

'As far as I've been told, there's not one shred of evidence to pin the attack on him,' I said.

'Look after yourself,' she said stiffly. 'We'll keep you posted.'

I put the light out and laid on the bed, staring at the ceiling in the oppressive heat. I was wearing nothing but a silk camisole vest and couldn't bear even a sheet over me. Beads of sweat trickled behind my ears and I found my mind playing devil's advocate, trying to seek out ways in which Aiden could have been involved with Kora's death. I couldn't even get the idea off the ground. Kora had one of his scarves, but there was nothing to suggest he knew her. The police said some of the artists at CCAP had heard of him, but no one had actually met him. What was his motive? He was a gentle and sensitive man, blown apart by what he'd witnessed.

I changed tack and reflected on the text from Terry. In the last couple of days, my mind had brushed over thoughts of him more frequently than I'd expected and each time it sent a smile to my lips. He was undoubtedly a good-natured and brave man. I tried to imagine him at his first scuba-dive. I could picture him looking exhilarated and pleased with himself, not letting his injury get the better of him. That was Terry; cheery and upbeat, he wasn't the dark, brooding type. With him, what you saw was what you got. It made a refreshing change from the deep, introverted types I'd fallen for in the past.

I must have drifted off for a while when low moans coming from somewhere on the boat roused me. I sat up and listened. Nightmares, I guessed. I slipped on a long T-shirt and quietly slid the bolt back on my door, then crept toward Aiden's cabin. He sounded like a dog in pain. I slowly walked the length of the boat and came back again, hoping he would have stopped, but the muffled cries continued. I knew I shouldn't disturb him, but I couldn't bear to hear any more and gently tapped on his door.

When there was no response, I turned the handle. He hadn't locked it and I found myself standing over a bundle of dishevelled sheets on the floor. He must have fallen out of bed. The lamp was on, he never switched it off these days – there was always a slice of light showing under his door. He opened his eyes, but didn't seem surprised to see me. He breathed heavily, still caught up in the images inside his head.

'It's okay,' I said, crouching down. 'It's a bad dream.'

He reached out his hand and I held it briefly, then passed him a glass of water from his bedside table. He gulped it down in seconds.

'Are you okay?'

I waited while he grabbed the sheet around him and hoisted himself back into bed. I was about to leave when he stretched forward and pushed something into my hand. An open book. *The Hitchhiker's Guide to the Galaxy.* The deep wrinkles in the spine told me this wasn't the first time he'd read it.

'You want me to read to you?'

He nestled into his pillow, both hands under one cheek, his face primed with expectation. Given the story was familiar to him and therefore not about to deliver any nasty surprises, it was probably the ideal thing to do after his nightmare.

I sat on the edge of his bed and read to him for twenty minutes before I saw his eyelids flicker and heard the tell-tale click from the back of his throat. I left the book by his bed and crept back to my room.

Before I knew it, dawn was breaking.

Wednesday, July 11 - Day Six

Even though it wasn't the least bit chilly in the mornings, we still used the wood-burning stove for hot water. Sacks of logs were delivered regularly and I'd noticed there were only a few chunks of wood left in the basket. I decided to save Aiden the bother of getting a refill, so collecting the key from the galley on the way, I took the basket lined with old newspaper to the end of the boat.

With my mind only half on the job, I began grabbing bundles of logs, idly wondering how long the sheet of newspaper had been in the basket. I remembered finding an old suitcase belonging to my father under the bed once, lined with paper that went back to 1959. I'd smiled at the knitting patterns for men's cardigans, the adverts for a slide-projector and diet pills.

I uncurled the paper from the edge of the basket and realised this sheet wasn't old at all. In fact, it was dated less than a couple of months ago. Friday, May 25, to be precise. I was so busy looking at the print that I wasn't careful enough handling the rough logs and felt a sharp stab in my thumb. I'd pricked it on a large splinter. Before the blood ran everywhere, I snatched out the sheet of newspaper and squashed it around the wound. It was then I spotted Aiden's name buried in the print.

I straightened out the sheet and started reading an interview with him. It was a feature about how he had been asked to create an haute couture outfit in his trademark white for London Fashion Week. I was taken aback. What was something as prestigious as this doing lining his log bin? It should have been with his clippings.

I crept into the galley and found the tabloid PC Ndibi left behind a few days ago that we'd been using to start the stove. I replaced the one that had lined the basket, hoping that in his current state Aiden wouldn't notice it was fresh. I was brushing away the stray chips of wood from the page I'd removed when I heard a door creak. I quickly stuffed the sheet under a nearby cushion, just as Aiden emerged, yawning, from his cabin.

He squeezed my shoulder as he came past me and I watched his eyes, hoping he wouldn't look down. I stood the full basket beside the washing machine and hurriedly threw a few more logs into the fire, before he could do it himself. Then I found the first aid kit and hastily covered my thumb with a plaster.

After breakfast I brought out the sand tray again. Aiden had been doing lots of sketches on his own in the past few days, but I wanted us to have another therapeutic session together to see what came of it. After his torment during the night, he seemed subdued but in a calm, rather than forlorn kind of way. Perhaps today was the day we'd make headway. According to the big guns at Camden police, we only had one day left.

Aiden didn't even look at the sand box. He closed it and pushed it away. My shoulders fell. He wasn't in the mood.

I was about to abort the idea when I saw Aiden's eye trained on the tub marked 'miscellaneous'. He reached inside and began rummaging for something. It contained a collection of rubber bands, drawing pins, paper clips, nails and hooks. A moment later he pulled out a length of coiled wire and set it before him. It was my turn to look uncertain.

Wire.

A piece of wire, just like this, had led to Kora's death. I felt my nostrils flare as I sat back, trying to look only mildly interested. He didn't straighten it out, but began to shape the wire, twisting it here, bending it there, turning it over, tweaking it. Within a few moments he was finished. He stood the finished shape on the table. It looked like a bird. A seagull, perhaps, with its wings extended in flight.

'A bird?' I said quietly. 'It's beautiful.'

His head dropped. I'd obviously missed the point.

'Does it mean something, Aiden?'

He looked at it, ignoring me, changed the angle of the left wing so they were both symmetrical. He tipped his head from side to side judging whether he'd got it right.

'What's this in connection with, Aiden?'

He stood the intricate tangle of wire right in front of me.

'Is it an eagle, a blackbird? I don't know what it means.'

His hands became fists and he pressed them into his cheekbones, staring at the little creature he'd made.

'I'm sorry, Aiden.' I was lost for what else to say.

He tugged at a clump of his hair and got up. Dejected, he walked to the door at the stern and disappeared outside. I felt cross with myself. I'd alienated him, set us right back – but how was I supposed to know what he was getting at?

The door clicked shut and I heard his hollow footsteps on the roof of the boat. It rocked a little with the shift in weight then the footsteps stopped. I was on my own.

I returned to the cushion and pulled out the sheet of newspaper I'd hidden. I took it to my cabin and stuffed it under my pillow. I wanted to look at in more detail later.

Out of nowhere came a short electronic ping that made me jump. Aiden had left his mobile on the breadboard. The police had returned it yesterday when I was out for lunch, together with his laptop and tablet, having found nothing to connect him to Kora or CCAP. Instinctively I walked towards the sound, pretty sure Aiden wouldn't have heard it from the roof. It was an invasion of privacy to look at the text, but I couldn't help myself. Before I could change my mind, I was reading it:

Pippa still missing – police suddenly taking it more seriously now. Thought you'd like to know. Naomi – editorial assistant.

Chapter 26

I stood still, holding the edge of the sink with trembling fingers, listening for sounds on the roof of the boat. All I could hear was the gentle scrape of rope in a steady rhythm as we rocked against the pontoon. Aiden was directly above me, still engaged in his own private reverie.

I'd done a terrible thing. I'd invaded his privacy and read a personal message. And look where it had got me.

Naomi - editorial assistant.

I scuttled back into my cabin for the sheet of newspaper I'd dragged out of the log basket. I read the interview again and froze when I spotted something I hadn't noticed the first time; the byline at the top; Pippa French. Her interview with Aiden had appeared just three weeks before she went missing. Perhaps Naomi worked with her. She certainly knew there was a connection between Aiden and Pippa, why else would she leave a message for him about her?

Aiden's sketch had already indicated that he knew Pippa, but this was sending me towards a bigger question. How *well* did he know her? Aiden had drawn our attention to her, so why hide the interview in the log basket? I batted questions around inside my head. Why hadn't he thrown this article away, or kept it with his other press clippings in the shoe box? He'd treated this one differently. What did that mean? I had another read, it was an excellent review of his work; he certainly had nothing to be upset about.

I kick-started all the psychoanalytical cogs in my brain. Aiden was secretive – even his close friends knew little about who he really was. What if he'd taken a shine to Pippa but didn't want anyone else to know about it? What if he'd put the article where no one else would notice it? Where he'd see it every day, every time he lit the wood-burner? It was a possible explanation.

I gritted my teeth and returned to Aiden's phone, goading myself to take down the number the text was sent from. I didn't faff around for long. Before I knew it, I was back in the privacy of my cabin with a scrap of paper in my sweaty palm, my fingers tapping out the number.

'Hi, is that Naomi?' I said.

A cautious voice responded in the affirmative.

'I'm Sally Moore,' I said breezily, 'a friend of Aiden Blake, the young artist.'

'Oh, that's funny, I've just sent him a message. I sent one a couple of days ago, too. Is he okay?'

'That's why I'm phoning… he's not great, to be honest. He's not really in contact with anyone at the moment. I just wanted to let you know. He's been pretty down since it happened…'

'Since Pippa went missing, you mean?'

I decided in a split second to go along with her. 'Yeah… he's certainly been cut up about it.'

'Sure, I know. He rang a few times just after she first disappeared. Is he very upset? I hadn't realised it had… gone that far between them.'

'Well, Aiden plays his cards close to his chest,' I said.

I could hear voices in the background, the tinkle of a spoon against a mug, phones ringing, the chug of a printer.

I took a chance. 'You work with Pippa at *The Bulletin*, I take it?'

'That's right… who did you say you were again?' she asked.

I fudged a reply, telling her I was going into a tunnel, then in a panic, I cut the connection.

If I'd understood her correctly, she'd made it sound like Aiden and Pippa were actually *seeing* each other, in the early stages of a relationship.

I couldn't rest. I couldn't leave it like this. Nor could I face Aiden coming back inside and finding my guilt-ridden face.

Instead I did the *half*-decent thing and took the mobile out to him on the roof. I apologised and said I'd knocked his phone onto the floor and pressed a few buttons by accident. I handed it over and hated myself. Five minutes later, I left the boat, calling Natalie to tell her Aiden was on his own.

It was time to pay *The Bulletin* a visit.

I stood outside the glossy revamped offices at Charlington Street, near Blackfriars Tube and pushed the button on the silver intercom. After a click and echoing *Hello?* I asked for Naomi, saying it was a police matter about Pippa French.

A woman came clattering down the stairs to meet me at the reception, clutching a file to her chest. Everything about her looked inexperienced and flustered; the flyaway strands of blonde hair that were meant to fit snugly under the hair clips, the lipstick on her teeth, the stiletto heels that were too high and threatened to snap beneath her. I explained I was a psychologist working with the police and showed her my hospital ID. She seemed satisfied.

I followed her up the stairs to the first floor. Desks were uniformly laid out like a checkerboard; half-occupied, half-abandoned, but with items such as cardigans and packets of peanuts left behind to indicate ownership.

'We've got a lot of people out on stories,' she said, as if in answer to a question. She parked her backside against a desk without offering me a seat. 'The receptionist said this is about Pippa, right?'

'Most specifically about Pippa's interview with Aiden Blake.'

Her forehead puckered, clearly bemused at having his name crop up once again. 'What do you need to know?'

'The article that was published in *The Bulletin* on May twenty-fifth,' I said, 'do you know when she did the interview?'

She turned and led me over to a desk in the corner, reaching over to open a diary. 'Er... it was May twenty-first,' she said, running her finger down the page. 'They met at The Royal Court Hotel near his college.'

'Did they only meet once, for the interview?'

She shifted her weight to the other leg and seemed in two minds about answering.

'It's very important,' I insisted. 'She's still missing.'

'Pippa was clearly struck by him and she'd told a couple of us that she was meeting him again, you know, socially.' She snatched a stray biro from an in tray and began rolling it around in her fingers.

'Do you know how many times?'

'Once or twice, as far as I know. They had another date fixed up... only...'

'When was that?'

'Supposed to be on June sixteenth.'

'The sixteenth? The day *after* she went missing?'

'Yeah.' She was still holding the file against her chest like a shield. 'And there was a note from Aiden on Monday morning, the eighteenth.'

'A note?'

'Yeah – he'd rung the switchboard to leave a message for her asking if there'd been a mix-up, because she hadn't shown up. He couldn't reach her on her mobile, so he'd rung here.'

'And that was the first you knew she'd gone missing?'

'Guess so. She didn't turn up for work that Monday morning. It wasn't like Pippa; we all call her the hungry journalist. Someone called her flat and they hadn't seen her since she left for work on Friday morning. They'd already called the police about it that weekend.' She looked about her, ill at ease, sucking the end of the pen. 'The police think it's really serious now, don't they?'

'They don't know for sure,' I said, wanting to reassure her.

I noticed a series of photographs on a pinboard; pictures of *The Bulletin* team.

'Can I look?' I asked, already walking towards it. I recognised Pippa at once.

'Did Pippa ever go to his boat, do you know? In Camden... on the canal or at Limehouse?'

She shook her head. 'No, she mentioned she'd seen photos of it, but she hadn't been there herself.'

'Can I have a list of all the people Pippa interviewed in the last six months?'

Naomi stuck out her tongue as if to imply the task was gargantuan. I stood my ground, waiting. She thought for a moment, then turned to a computer terminal and typed in a password. Shortly after, she handed me a printed list and I made my farewells.

I had no idea in which direction I was heading once I stepped through the sliding doors out onto the street. I needed time to think. Once I'd got my bearings, I found my way to the Thames. It only took a few minutes to reach the glistening water, where I leant against the railing staring out blindly across the dancing ripples.

Aiden and Pippa were definitely dating. And he'd arranged to meet her on the evening after she went missing. But, why had Aiden drawn Pippa, not Kora, standing by the fence at the crime scene over three weeks later? The only explanation I could come up with was he was worried about Pippa and, knowing I'd pass the drawing on to the police, wanted to jolt them into cranking up the search for her. Perhaps that's all there was to it.

I stood for a while watching the boats pass on the water, then crossed Blackfriars Bridge and walked east to The Globe. I didn't have a destination in mind; I just needed to be outside and free, not cooped up on Aiden's boat. Time stood still as I watched the tide drag the water out to sea, mesmerised by the steady, relentless rhythm.

My phone buzzed.

'Hi, how's it going?' Terry's chirpy voice. I realised I hadn't replied to the text he'd sent last night.

'Oh, I don't know to be honest.'

'Anything more from Aiden?'

'No. I'm in a bit of a muddle.' I shouldn't have said that. He'd ask more and I didn't want anyone else knowing what I'd found until I knew exactly what it meant.

'Forget Claussen and Wilde with their ridiculous deadline,' he said. 'Just take your time and let Aiden open up when he's ready. Don't put yourself under pressure.' I was grateful he didn't press me. He must have realised there was only one day left before my ludicrous cut-off point.

'Thanks.'

I got lost for a moment in the turbulence of the river gathering speed, making its rapid escape east. His voice pulled me back. 'You okay?'

'I'm fine. I got your text and I'm afraid I'm letting the side down. I haven't given a holiday a moment's thought.'

He laughed. 'It would be nice to meet up again.'

'I'd like that,' I said. It was grounding to hear his firm but soothing presence.

'I'll call you soon. In the meantime, take good care of yourself.'

I held the warm phone against my ear after he'd gone, savouring the connection. I was starting to think there'd always been something between the two of us. I'd just never paid any attention to it.

That evening, after Aiden had turned in early for the night, I felt restless and left the boat to take a stroll around the marina. Aiden had re-moored, end on to the pontoon this time, as there'd been a sudden influx of residents claiming their berths. For a place cluttered with boats and hemmed in by apartments, it was remarkably quiet. I headed away from the water to the main street and into a pub across the road. There was a bracing view of the river from the sweeping terrace, so I took a seat, G&T in hand, and thought about Terry.

I wasn't sure I'd ever thanked him for all those times at university when I'd turned up in a state after an episode with Miranda. He'd been rock-solid. Kind. Always there when I needed him. I'd never fully appreciated his concern, nor taken the trouble to look below the surface. Meeting him again felt like a second chance to get to know him. Properly, this time. Ironically, I had Claussen to thank for that.

On my return, there was a heavy stillness in the air as if the world was holding its breath. As I got undressed, a strange roaring noise erupted outside my cabin and I realised a downpour had been brewing. I lifted the curtain and took a look outside, watching the rain scattering like marbles over the surface of the water. It pounded against the roof, battering the windows trying to get in.

It looked like we were in for a heavy storm. It was the perfect metaphor for what was about to happen.

Chapter 27

Friday, June 29 – Thirteen days earlier

Katarina Bartek got the call at the office. A policeman was in the foyer waiting to see her. As she hurried down the stairs her first thought was that it must be about the terracotta pots that had been smashed in the front garden at the weekend. As she reached the last step she realised that couldn't possibly be the reason. They wouldn't send a police officer all the way to her place of work about something so minor.

She knew it was serious when he asked her sit down. He held his cap under his arm. Hell. This was bad news. The officer was talking about her husband. He was trying to tell her that Lubor had died in an accident, but that couldn't be right. There must have been a mistake. He'd called her only an hour ago from his office to remind her to leave early that afternoon, so they could go for a drink.

The officer dropped his head and started again. 'Yes, he did make it into work, Mrs Bartek, but at about 11am, he left the office on foot and was involved in a road accident. I'm so sorry, but he'd already passed away by the time the ambulance arrived.'

Passed away? No, that couldn't be right. Lubor was always careful crossing the road.

'It can't be him. What makes you think it's him?'

'We checked his wallet and driving licence,' the officer explained. 'He was wearing a blue shirt and a red tie.'

No. The policeman still wasn't making sense. Red tie? Lubor would never wear a red tie with a blue shirt. Did he even have one?

He spoke again. 'There was an incident involving a bus. We're not exactly sure what happened, yet.'

She shook her head. They'd got it wrong. Her husband would never step out in front of a bus.

The only way she would believe it was if they showed her the body.

Katarina went to the hospital. At worst, she expected to see him with tubes coming out of his nose and a machine bleeping at his side. But she was shown into the basement towards a chilled room, instead. She hesitated as the cold blast of air hit her on the threshold, half-expecting silver hooks hanging from the ceiling and rows of swinging lumps of pink flesh.

There had to be a mix-up. Lubor couldn't possibly be in there.

They coaxed her inside to a body lying on a silver trolley covered with a white sheet. Someone steadied her as another folded back the cloth.

'We believe this is your husband...' The voice seemed to be coming from above her.

'It does look like him,' she whispered, 'but it can't be...'

Another voice said he was dead on arrival. 'There was nothing anyone could do,' they confirmed, guiding her away. 'It was very quick.'

After her initial shock, Katarina had to get a grip and face what came next. She had no idea how the system worked after a death in the UK; she hadn't been expecting to have to deal with anything like this.

A friend from work went with her to a Citizen's Advice Bureau and handfuls of leaflets were stuffed into her hand. She'd had to phone his family in Gdańsk. Tell her parents in Warsaw. She didn't get on with Lubor's family, so didn't want to have his body flown to Poland. The funeral would have to be here, so she'd have to organise it all on her own.

Outwardly, over the next week or so, she asked all the right questions and signed all the relevant forms. Internally, she was in a dreadful state. After the post-mortem, his body was moved to the funeral parlour she'd apparently chosen in Islington. Her friend said they would keep him there in a fridge until the date of the cremation.

The GP had given her sedatives and sleeping tablets to help calm her down, so the days slid past in a blur at first. She wanted a clear head for the day itself, so before long she stopped taking the medication. The day before the funeral she woke stricken with renewed panic. She still couldn't believe he was gone. It didn't make any sense to her. She hadn't been in her right mind when they'd shown Lubor to her in the hospital. What if they'd got it wrong and he was in a coma? She'd heard in the news about people who'd been accidentally pronounced dead. They were going to burn his body tomorrow and then it would be too late. She needed to see him again. Just one more time – to be certain.

Later that day, Katarina turned up at Dodd & Son Funeral Directors. She knew she was making a scene, demanding to see his body, but they weren't helping. They tried to fob her off, but she barged past the receptionist, looking for her husband. She tried every door, shaking off Henry Dodd, the man in charge. Someone called the police, but Dodd cancelled the call-out. He didn't want trouble.

By then, she'd stopped shrieking and was having a bit of a breakdown. They let her sit in the Chapel of Rest with a cup of sweet tea. They soothed her, told her how sorry they were. They said she could see him, but explained he wasn't ready yet. Said she should come back tomorrow and see her husband after he had been properly prepared.

Finally she left, but not for long. She didn't trust them. She was beside herself with distress and suspicion. Grief had done that to her, made her desperate. What if they didn't wait for her tomorrow? What if they shut him inside the coffin and screwed down the lid before she had the chance to see him? Anything could happen tomorrow – she needed to see him tonight.

Once it got dark, she went back. She prowled around the front entrance, but it was securely locked up. Of course it was – what was she thinking? She took a nearby side street that led round the back, coming up against tall wooden gates and a brick wall peppered with cut glass. A secure barrier under lock and key blocked her way. Loitering helplessly, she wondered how she could possibly get in. She jiggled the padlock in despair and that's when her prayers were answered. It slid open in her hands.

Chapter 28

My first thought when I woke the next morning was one of abject failure. The seven days were up and Aiden was as far from talking as I was from learning to fly. More to the point, he hadn't produced any drawings that could be taken seriously in terms of identifying the killer. Instead, we had drawings of a woman who was missing and a decorative bird made of wire that I couldn't decipher. Now, hanging over me, was the knowledge that he knew Pippa and was due to meet her the day after she disappeared. Furthermore, I was feeling guilty that I hadn't mentioned this to the police.

Before I took a shower I had a look at the list Naomi had given me of Pippa's interviews. She'd carried out over twenty for *The Bulletin* since January. Some were with names I recognised; actors, Simon Callow and Zoe Wanamaker, artist Tracey Emin. Others were new film directors, young playwrights and up-and-coming artists, like Aiden.

Kora Washington's name wasn't on the list, but I hadn't expected it to be; she wasn't in Aiden's league. I read through all the names, but nothing flashed at me with any relevance to the case. I folded it up again, not even sure why I'd asked Naomi for it in the first place.

I was about to go into the bathroom when I received a stilted call from DI Karen Foxton, informing me I was needed at the station. Her sombre tone gave me a bad feeling.

I got there just as officers were filing into the meeting room. I grabbed the chair beside Jeremy. He'd gone down in my estimation, not only for suggesting Aiden looked at the crime scene photos, but also for the manhandled lunch, yet he was still the closest person I had to calling 'a colleague' on this case. He passed me the plate of digestives, looking contrite, but I was too nervous to eat anything. Edwin Hall, Joanne Hoyland and DI Foxton pulled up their chairs around the central table. Neither Keith Wilde nor Elsa Claussen were there, a saving grace that allowed my blood pressure to drop a fraction.

'Just a general round-up,' said Jeremy, opening his file. Even more relief. Perhaps I'd been too paranoid, assuming the police knew I was withholding key information. 'As you all know, Kora Washington had traces of a strong laxative in her system when she was first admitted to ICU. By all accounts, it was definitely not the kind of substance she would have taken voluntarily. Sponge, her live-in partner, insisted that he'd never known her to need a laxative and would only ever have taken a herbal remedy if required.'

'So we're looking for someone who spiked her food that day?' I suggested.

'It's looking that way. If Kora was dashing backwards and forwards to the bathroom, it would have given the killer the chance to get hold of her phone to fob off Mr Kent when he turned up in the car park.'

'Anything else on *him*?' Edwin asked.

'There was no CCTV at the shop where Murray Kent said he bought groceries but, lo and behold, the sales assistant actually remembers him. A packet of crisps split open at the checkout, so Kent stuck in his mind. The time on the till slip was nine thirty, which is of course when Kora was on the towpath.'

'So, Murray Kent has an alibi,' I muttered, mainly to myself.

'And tyre tracks behind the fence don't match his van,' added Jeremy.

'Moving on... Simon Schiffer, the director of the Art Project, employs several cleaners on a duty rota,' said Karen. The name rang a bell; he was Miranda's personal tutor at CCAP and she often talked about him. 'I spoke to the cleaner on duty that night, Sue Reed. She said she thought Lou Tennison, the caretaker, and Kora were the only ones there when she left just after nine. Sue didn't see or hear anyone else.'

Jeremy raised his voice. '*Someone* must have seen Murray's van come into the CCAP car park and used Kora's phone to pretend to be the caretaker and send him packing.'

'Did Murray say it was a male or female voice on the phone?' I asked.

'Male,' said Karen.

'One more thing,' said Karen. 'Lou, the caretaker, doesn't drive. He always gets to and from CCAP on foot. We've checked and he's never owned a car and DVLA confirm he has no licence. There's no way he could have got to the boat to set up the wire in time, without transport.'

It was a complete conundrum. On the day Kora was targeted, everything seemed to have started with a strong laxative being given to her without her knowledge; although we couldn't know *for certain* that she didn't take it herself. Murray Kent said he had a call from 'the caretaker' telling him Kora had left in a taxi. Lou, the caretaker, said he hadn't used Kora's phone to call anyone. It was all he-said-she-said stuff, a jumbled series of statements that didn't fit together. A Rubik's cube.

I was glad I wasn't a detective. So much seemed to depend on personal accounts of who was seen, who said what, and what time it was. Trying to corroborate all the reports must be a logistical nightmare, especially when there was someone at the root of it who'd staged a macabre sleight of hand. It occurred to me that we were being presented with what the killer wanted us to see, not with what had actually happened. How the police were ever going to cut to the truth was beyond me.

I had no time to contemplate the matter further as the door swung open and Elsa Claussen stormed in.

'Listen up,' she said, clapping her hands together just like my mother used to do when I was little. 'We need to make some decisions.' She rounded on me. 'What progress have you made with Mr Blake? How close are you to getting a good sketch of the killer? Is he talking?'

'Not there yet, I'm afraid.'

'Right. Well, we haven't got time to wait weeks for him to recover. I'm taking you off the case. It's taking too long.'

I was stunned. 'What? You're giving up on him?'

'If you have nothing to show, it's over.'

Edwin Hall's chair squeaked as he leant forward, making a sound that could have been mistaken for an objection. She shot him a glare.

'We're going to focus all our efforts on other lines of enquiry,' she declared.

'*What* lines?' I hadn't meant to say it out loud. Especially not in such a snarky tone.

Claussen took two paces forward, then one back. She didn't have an answer.

'Thank you for your help and all that,' she said, 'but, it was a mistake to expect anything from this… artist guy. Mr Blake is obviously mentally unstable.' She gave me a plastic smile. 'If someone could show Dr Willerby out, then–'

'He's good,' I bleated. 'If anyone can put together an accurate likeness of the killer, Aiden can.'

'It's a big *if* though, isn't it?' Her hands were on her hips, reminding me of my mother, again. 'It's over. The police will handle him from now on.'

Great. As a reward for stepping in and giving up my holiday, the Ice Queen was ejecting me with the flick of her wrist. Aside from reeling from the affront, I was in turmoil. I couldn't abandon Aiden now. Not when he was in such a vulnerable state and had started to trust me. This wasn't some hit-and-miss experiment. You can't start intensive treatment then disappear halfway through.

Karen was on her feet, her arm out, indicating the door. 'It would be medically detrimental to the patient,' I said, taking tiny steps towards her, 'to just leave him in the lurch, like this.' I swung round and settled my gaze on Jeremy, waiting for him to speak up on my behalf. He returned my stare for a fraction of a second, then dropped his eyes.

'Well – get him to a psychiatric ward, then – let them sort him out,' snapped Claussen.

Just when I thought matters could get no worse, Spenser Ndibi charged inside the door almost knocking me over. He looked grave and headed straight for Jeremy. He stooped down to whisper in his ear and an icy anticipation gripped the entire room.

'Very bad news, everyone,' announced Jeremy, looking shaken. He sighed heavily. 'We have another body.' He turned to Ndibi. 'It could be linked. Give them the details, constable.'

Spenser Ndibi shifted his weight from one foot to the other. 'A body of an, as yet, unidentified woman has been found in undergrowth about three hundred yards from the spot Kora Washington was killed, by the steps at Medford Bridge. The body was found this morning and had been there all night.'

Everyone seemed to have forgotten I was supposed to have left. Karen hurried back to her seat, so I surreptitiously slunk back to mine. More details were exchanged, notes taken and fresh decisions were made, but I lost track. I was still struggling to believe everything I'd heard in the past ten minutes.

Another woman dead.

I didn't remember the meeting breaking up. I was outside in the car park, wandering towards the main road moments later, my head spinning.

There was a more immediate concern, however. The DCS had made the decision that I should abandon Aiden, but I'd still been fighting his corner when PC Ndibi walked in. Aiden's situation had now been swamped under the dreadful news of another body on the same stretch of towpath, but it still had to be addressed.

I walked to the Tube, then changed my mind about heading underground and rang Miranda.

I held my breath until she answered, then let it go with relief. At least she was safe.

'I don't want to row,' I said plaintively. 'I need a shoulder. Any chance it could be yours?'

'What time is it?' she whispered, without hostility.

'Nearly eleven. Coffee time.'

'Where are you?'

'Just outside Camden Tube.'

'Limo's on the high street,' she muttered through a yawn. 'Half an hour.'

I knew Miranda's half an hour would be nearer twice that, but I didn't mind. I walked along the high street, overshooting the café, carrying on to the canal at Camden Lock. There was a police jeep parked on the grass. Apart from that, you wouldn't know anything untoward had happened only a short distance upstream.

I walked down the ramp, through the market area to where it was quieter and leant on the railings watching the water. I mulled over the discovery of a second body; found so close to where Kora had been attacked. A week after the first he'd struck again. It was as though the killer knew I had a time limit and was making some kind of point. Was it another tripwire? Was the victim on her bike?

A pigeon hobbled up to a pile of discarded crumbs by my feet. A length of cord had been caught around its legs and it was taking wobbly steps, one foot a pink disfigured ball.

I wanted to cry.

I should never have accepted this impossible assignment. I'd waded knee-deep into a quagmire, unprepared, unfamiliar with the world of crime and police investigations. Furthermore, I'd given the situation my all and failed to come up with the goods in time. If only I'd got Aiden to draw the right picture. Found a way to get him talking. Another woman had been killed. And it was all my fault.

Chapter 29

Miranda swanned into the café wearing a short suede miniskirt and tank top, a long scarf floating from her neck. Her hippy appearance always made her look ten years younger than me. I felt a sting of jealousy. This was nothing new. She didn't carry any burden of responsibility on her face like most adults do. In fact, in most ways she still acted like a teenager; self-centred, impulsive, full of passion and rebellion. At times like this, I wished I possessed more of her wild, fighting spirit.

Her scarf made me think again about the white one made by Aiden that had been wrapped around Kora's neck when she was knocked off her bike. The police must have come to a complete dead end on that lead.

I bought Miranda a hot chocolate and we headed outside, taking a seat in the smallest courtyard you could ever imagine. There was one rickety table and three folding chairs around it. Piles of gnomes sat alongside a miniature golden Buddha on a tray-sized patch of grass and tinkling bells on ribbons hung from nails in the wall. I expected someone dressed as a wizard to squeeze through the back fence any second.

'It's called a dreamcatcher,' said Miranda, referring to the small hoop covered in netting and feathers that hung from the back door, batting around in the breeze.

I nodded, not really interested. 'We were *so* close,' I said, showing her the small gap between my thumb and index finger. 'Aiden was communicating… and he was drawing, using the sand tray and making little recognisable shapes.'

'Had he started talking?'

I scrunched up my nose. 'No, not yet.'

'Yeah, well, he never asked for therapy. Let the police deal with him.'

The air was rich with a pungent smell of Indian incense. So much so that even my coffee began to taste of it.

'I can't leave him in the lurch,' I told her. 'He's scared; he wanted me on the boat with him. He's vulnerable. Besides, I have a professional duty to follow this through.'

'I thought it was only supposed to be for a week.' She licked the chocolate froth from her lips, slowly and sensually. 'Are you hooked on this guy?'

'Don't be silly. He's nineteen, for goodness sake. He could be my son.'

She shrugged as if my argument held no weight whatsoever.

'In any case, what about me? I can't go back to my *normal* life at the hospital. Not with this going on.'

I slammed my cup into the saucer with a clatter. I wasn't ready to come back down to earth. Not yet.

'Have some time off, instead,' Miranda insisted. 'Get on a plane. Maybe you could salvage some of the holiday.'

Miranda's answers to problems were always 180 degrees away from mine. Largely driven by hedonism.

'I wouldn't be able to relax,' I said. I didn't tell her that being with Aiden filled a vacuum, that his canal boat had become the remote getaway I was supposed to have escaped to. I couldn't leave yet. 'Besides, they've discovered another body, just near where Kora was found.'

'Oh, God,' she brought her hands to her mouth. 'Who is it?'

'They don't know yet. Another woman. They only discovered her this morning. You mustn't say anything.'

'Why haven't they nailed the bastard? Surely by now they've got something to go on?'

I shouldn't have said a word. The entire case was confidential, but in the last few hours my allegiance to the police had been crushed to dust. I told Miranda about Kora leaving CCAP on her bike, about Murray Kent and the late arrangement to meet, and the caretaker who said he didn't make the call.

'So, it was him? This Murray guy?'

'No, apparently not. He has an alibi and other evidence doesn't match up.'

Before I knew it, I was telling her about Pippa and how Aiden was due to meet her the night after she went missing.

'Are you sure you're safe with this guy?'

'Absolutely. He can't have had anything to do with Kora's attack.'

'Why not?'

'I just know it. He's too sensitive. Logistically, he couldn't have killed Kora.'

I hesitated, suddenly not convinced by that last bit. I couldn't remember the exact reasons the police had given to exonerate Aiden. In fact, had they fully discounted him as a suspect? 'In any case, he was miles away with me at Limehouse last night when the second woman was killed.'

Miranda pulled a face that showed she wasn't convinced.

'Isn't it hard, staying with someone who doesn't say a word?' asked Miranda. 'Don't you end up talking to yourself?'

The question seemed ironic given Miranda's history of hearing random voices inside her own head. Memories flooded into my mind of times when they'd instructed her, cajoled her, into destroying things and putting herself in danger.

'You get used to it,' I said.

'And what about having to eat vegetarian all the time? Don't rubbery halloumi sandwiches make you retch after a while?' She pulled a face. 'I assume you're sneaking bacon sarnies into your cabin.'

I shook my head. 'Of course not – that's the least of my worries. I'm getting a taste for veggie, actually, apart from the halloumi, that is – I've never liked it.'

'Yuck, nor me.'

'Cooking without meat means you have to be more creative with flavours. It's refreshing actually.'

She tutted. 'Well, then. Keep on with his therapy and don't tell the cops.'

I gave the idea some thought.

Maybe this time she wasn't so wide of the mark. I couldn't abandon Aiden; that was becoming clearer the more I considered it. Perhaps I could take more time off work and continue with him until he was more stable. I could carry on at the boat, surrounded by still waters, floating inside my own bubble.

I reached over and planted a loud kiss on her cheek. 'Thanks. You've been a big help.'

'Bloody hell,' she retorted, 'I think that's the first time you've ever said that without being sarcastic!'

I laughed. Poor Miranda, I'm sure I hadn't been the most patient of sisters when we were growing up. I wish things had been different. There was so much about her I didn't know, didn't understand, but she was secretive and independent and getting past her garrisoned portcullis was a tall order.

I went back to the boat in two minds about telling Aiden there'd been another death. I rounded the first bend of the marina, then realised someone had got there before me. The blue lights from two police cars flashed at the far side of Aiden's pontoon. I ran along to *Louisa II*. Two officers I didn't recognise were climbing on-board and PC Ndibi, who looked embarrassed and wouldn't meet my eye, stood outside talking to another man.

'What's going on?' I snapped.

The man, dressed in a brown suit, stepped between Ndibi and me. 'I'm Detective Inspector Denton,' he said, without shaking my hand. 'You're Dr Willerby, I understand.'

'That's correct. Is Aiden alright? I need to see him.' I tried to peer past his shoulder into the boat.

'We'd like to ask you some questions, Dr Willerby. If you could step inside.'

He led the way. Half the boat had been partitioned off using the sliding doors and I couldn't see Aiden. DI Denton sat opposite me.

'Does Aiden own a vehicle? A car, a van?'

'No, not that I know of.'

I tried to think. Aiden certainly had a driving licence. I'd seen it one time when he'd opened a drawer in the Welsh dresser. The police could easily check government records, anyway.

'You slept on the boat, last night, is that right?'

'Yes.'

'When did you last see Mr Blake?'

I tried to remember. I'd been at the local pub. 'Must have been around eight o'clock.' I gave him the details.

'When did you return?'

'I'm not sure… around ten… ten-thirty?'

'Did you see Mr Blake when you came back?'

'Er… no. Aiden had already called it a day.'

'You have your own key?'

'Yes. I let myself in.'

'How did you know Mr Blake was on the boat when you came back?'

I felt my jaw retreat sharply. 'Well, he's *always* here.' I glanced up at Spenser Ndibi who'd followed us inside. He should know that. Hadn't he told them? 'Aiden's agoraphobic at the moment and can't go anywhere beyond the boundary of his own boat.'

'So he leads us to believe…'

'No, it's true.' I remembered something. 'His cabin light was on when I came back – I could see it under his door.'

I caught the hint of a sigh. 'Can you be certain he was on the boat all night?'

I didn't hesitate. 'Yes.'

'But, you said yourself, you didn't see Mr Blake at all… until when? This morning?'

'Er, no…' I faltered. 'He wasn't up when I left this morning.'

'You *assume* he was on the boat all night. Did you hear him?'

There'd been the raging storm and then I'd slept like a log. If Aiden had cried out during the night he hadn't woken me, for once. 'I don't know,' I said slowly. 'His cabin door was closed. I saw his mug on the draining board last night before I went to bed. He always leaves it like that before he turns in.'

'But you didn't hear or see him during the night?' he persisted.

'I don't think so, but I slept really deeply. I was tired.'

'Is it possible that Mr Blake wasn't on the boat? That he left sometime yesterday evening after you went out?'

I twisted round to try to find Ndibi again, but he had slunk back outside. 'I really don't think–'

'Is it *possible*?' He jerked forward so his face was inches from mine, his pale, windowless eyes unnerving me.

'Yes… I suppose, it's possible,' I conceded.

'There's been a witness who says they saw a man matching Mr Blake's description near the spot the latest victim was killed.'

'A witness? Who?'

'We can't tell you that, I'm afraid. We also know Mr Blake was dating another woman who's missing.'

A clatter could be heard and then Aiden appeared ashen faced from behind the partition, accompanied by a police officer. DI Denton stepped forward.

'Aiden Blake – I am arresting you in connection with the murder last night on the Camden Towpath and the disappearance of Pippa French.' I launched to my feet. *No!*

'This is ridiculous,' I yelled at them, trying to get in their way. 'He can't speak! He's suffering from clinical trauma, for God's sake…'

I knew what was coming next and how ridiculous it was going to sound.

'You do not have to say anything, but it may harm your defence if–'

'You're not listening,' I pleaded. 'He *can't say a word.*'

'…you do not mention when questioned something which you later rely on in court. Anything you do say may be given in evidence.'

'I must go with him,' I demanded. 'You can't question him like this. He must have an interpreter or a responsible adult with him in the condition he's in. It's his *right*.'

'We have a psychiatrist ready for him once he gets to the station,' said Denton, brushing me aside.

The ever-so-sympathetic Dr Melvin Herts, no doubt, if he deigned to give Aiden a few minutes of his precious time.

When the group got to the door there was a scuffle. Two officers pinned back Aiden's arms as he flailed around at the thought of having to leave the boat.

'He's *not* resisting arrest,' I shrieked. 'He's agoraphobic! This is outrageous! You're re-traumatising him.' I tried to reach out, to grab Aiden's arm, but he was hauled away. 'He's my patient. This is *completely* out of order. Where's DI Fenway? Who agreed the warrant for this?'

They all ignored me, even Spenser Ndibi, who had strategically positioned himself so there was always an officer between the two of us.

Aiden was utterly distraught at being dragged from the boat. His shirt split with a loud rip as he writhed and kicked. At one point I thought he might be having a fit. The officers practically had to carry him, one limb each, and the fracas brought other boat owners out onto the pontoon. I stood helpless as they bundled him into a patrol car.

I was on the phone to Jeremy straight away.

'What the *hell's* going on? Where are you!?'

'I'm sorry, Sam, there are more officers than just me on this operation.' He sounded cold and detached. 'And he's not your patient any more. We're just doing our job, whereas yours, I believe, has ended.'

The nerve of the man!

I was furious. I could scarcely speak without swearing at him. 'You... idiot... I can't believe you let this happen. You clearly don't understand what this could do to him.'

No objection or justification followed – it was clear my opinion counted for nothing.

'I spoke to Naomi Norton at *The Bulletin*,' he said matter-of-factly. 'Seems she's been talking to a Dr Willerby… working with the police. You had *no business* interfering with a police operation.'

'If you'd been doing your job, maybe I wouldn't have had to,' I spat out.

'I saw you as someone who cooperated, Sam,' he said in a patronising tone. 'I'm disappointed.'

Bloody hell, now *he* was sounding like my mother. To think, at first, I *liked* the guy.

'I can't just drop my professional responsibility towards Aiden. You have not only betrayed him,' I hissed into the phone, 'you have ridden roughshod over both of us.'

'Mr Blake will be in good hands.'

I wanted to scream that there was no way that was going to happen, but knew it was futile.

'I'm sorry, Sam,' he said, his tone softer. 'We have to play this by the book.'

I didn't reply. Instead, I took a breath. 'Who was the woman you found?' I asked tersely, as though I had a right to know.

I was surprised when he answered. 'She's just been identified in the last half an hour – Katarina Bartek, Polish woman, lived in Islington.'

Perhaps it was an olive branch, a small gesture to make amends.

'Is she an artist? A journalist?'

'Neither. She worked as a PA in a bank, south of the river, in Vauxhall. She'd just lost her husband. Lubor Bartek recently died in a road accident. She was waiting for his funeral.'

'Was it a tripwire?'

'No. She was strangled.'

'Your DI said there was a witness.'

'Listen, I've got to go.' That was all he was prepared to let me have. 'We'll look after Mr Blake,' he said, but I didn't believe one word of it.

Chapter 30

I stayed on the boat. It didn't seem right to abandon it.

Aiden's absence left a strange hollow emptiness. The space felt not only reduced in size, but flat and cold without him. I was used to hearing his padding footsteps, doors opening and closing, his latent struggle as he tried to come to terms with what had happened and put down on paper the tortuous scenes in his mind. Even in his silence, the boat had been bursting with his presence and saturated with his emotions. As I moved aimlessly from room to room, the memory of his tortured essence continued to mark the air.

I felt like an intruder and was reluctant to move things, take anything from the fridge or use any electricity. I had to remind myself that I *hadn't* barged my way in; Aiden was the one who had invited me here. At least I could make sure everything was in order for when he got back.

How long would the police hold him? How would he cope being away from the boat, unable to speak for himself? Who claimed to have seen him on the towpath in Camden last night?

Aiden was innocent. There's no way he could have left the boat and meandered over to Camden, when I'd gone out for a drink. The police had made a big mistake. If only I'd stayed put, last night – all for the sake of a lungful of air and a couple of G&Ts.

I should have been with him at the station. I was the only one who had any inkling as to what he was trying to convey. No one else would be able to understand him, they'd put his silence down to being stubborn and uncooperative. No one else would think of offering him a sand tray or a notepad. Dr Herts would defend him, wouldn't he? That's if he bothered to show up.

Then the solution hit me. I had to find something to clear Aiden's name. And I had to find it now.

From my brief conversation with Jeremy, it would appear that Katarina Bartek hadn't been connected to the art world; she was a PA in a bank in Vauxhall. Could Aiden have known her? I turned to my primary source of information; Aiden's shoebox. It was on the Welsh dresser, so I scoured everything again, looking for her name or any other clue to a link between them.

Nothing.

I returned to the list of names on Pippa's interview list and one caught my eye. Simon Schiffer. The director and Miranda's tutor at CCAP whose name had come up during my last meeting with the police. It turned out he'd been interviewed in March by Pippa French. I hadn't made the connection before, as Miranda hadn't used his surname. That meant Simon knew both Kora and Pippa, at least.

I made a call. Simon was working at the kiln, but a project user had persuaded him to come to the phone.

'I'm Samantha Willerby, Miranda's sister,' I said earnestly.

'Oh, yes?'

'I wondered if I could pop in and see you. I'm... a bit concerned about Miranda and hoped I might be able to have just a few moments of your time.'

I hoped my plea was hard to refuse, even if it wasn't strictly true. Miranda had taken Kora's death badly, but she hadn't done anything to worry me unduly.

'I'm busy just now, but you could come over later... say seven?'

The last time I'd been at CCAP was for their legendary annual dinner, the social high point of the year, held in April. Over a hundred people had been invited for a sit-down meal, champagne, music and dancing, culminating in speeches from high-ranking artists. I remember thinking at the time that Simon must have been maintaining a mighty-fine fundraising strategy to be able to put on that level of showcasing.

I stopped outside the front entrance. There was a new bronze sculpture that hadn't been there last time I was here. Positioned as a centrepiece in the walkway, it was a fountain with the Greek god, Poseidon, holding a conch to his mouth. The water corralled into a large scalloped shell, then gushed onto the rocks below. The plaque read: *Transformations*. Where had the money for that come from?

I eventually found Simon in the kitchen drying his hands.

'You've got a new addition at the entrance,' I said, after our initial introductions. 'Looks beautiful.'

'It was made by one of our very own tutors,' he said with pride. 'It's bringing a lot of people in, to be honest. It's the traditional, timeless look of it, I think. Helps visitors see that we're not so off the wall as they might think. "Transformations" – that's what CCAP is all about.'

I nodded. His voice was soft and welcoming. 'Thank you for seeing me,' I said. 'I'm a bit worried about Miranda, she doesn't know I'm here, by the way.'

'Let's go through to my office,' he suggested. He was tall and had a commanding stance, not falling into the trap that many tall people do, of hunching his shoulders in order to lose a few inches.

When we arrived, a woman was inside using the telephone. Simon made a sign to indicate she should carry on and he pointed me towards the art studio instead. A couple of project users in white overalls looked up and nodded as we came in. One was painting with oils at an easel, the other was moulding red clay. There was a radio on in the background playing reggae music, slightly off-station.

A man with a badly shaved head and a scar running down his cheek called out. He was holding a delicate unglazed vase which looked decidedly at odds next to his thuggish appearance. 'When's the next bisque firing boss?' he asked.

'Won't be today, Gazza,' said Simon. 'The kiln won't be back on until Monday.'

The man shrugged and sloped back to his potter's wheel.

Simon led me to a table at the far side. On each bench sat a series of unfinished items; unglazed vases, tangles of wire covered in wax, clay pots, beaded necklaces, the bust of a dog's head. Simon was wearing a blue suit without a tie, the top button undone. I held out a tissue when I noticed a splash of red paint near his jacket pocket.

'I hope it's not your best,' I said, pointing it out to him.

'No worries, white spirit will do the trick. It's not the first time.' He had a beaming smile. I could see why Miranda liked him. 'Don't touch anything,' he said jovially. 'More for your sake than anyone else's.'

The strong oily odour of the place made me feel light-headed. I blinked a few times before finding a stool to perch on. Although the streaks of orange on it looked old, I slapped a loose sheet of newspaper from the bench over it, just to be sure.

'It's been distressing for everyone,' he said, scratching the back of his head. 'I thought Miranda seemed to be coping pretty well.'

'She is. Well, she makes out she is. I was just checking to see if you were concerned about her at all. Whether you've seen a change in her, whether she's been turning up for therapy group and work shifts?' Miranda, like all the users, was expected to put in several hours each week at the café and gift shop in return for use of the extensive art facilities.

He rested his finger across his mouth. 'She seems fine,' he assured me. 'Upset, obviously, and a bit subdued, but she's coping, I'd say. She's been coming to the extra group sessions we've fitted in since it happened.' He undid another button on his shirt. 'That's helped everyone, I think. We'll have a special ceremony here in due course, and create some long-term tribute to our dear Kora. It's an absolute tragedy.'

'Miranda has certainly been very happy here.' I took in the whole studio space. 'You seem to be running a very successful project,' I added, aware that I needed to swing the conversation round to my real reason for coming. 'You had a piece in *The Bulletin* not that long ago, I understand.'

'That's right. Glowing review, for CCAP, not me. Not only about the therapeutic work we do, but the high standard of art we're producing.'

'An interview like that must have stuck in your mind,' I said.

'I do quite a lot with the press,' he said, without sounding pompous. 'Publicity for events, launching our artists into the real world, announcing shows, awards, that sort of thing.'

'I've heard of Pippa French,' I said, cringing inside at my inept attempt to direct the line of discussion. I was tired and anxious about Aiden, and wanted this over with. 'She does a lot of art interviews.'

'You an artist yourself?'

'No, no, far from it. Wish I was.' I picked at a blob of crusty red paint with my nail on the bench. It reminded me of dried blood.

'Everyone has some ability, you know. It just takes practice and dedication. You have to see where you might go with it. Take a risk.' His smile reached his eyes.

Damn. He was gracious, but he'd neatly avoided talking about Pippa. I had to try something else.

'Did you know that another woman has been found on the towpath?'

'I heard it earlier, on the news. Not one of ours, thank God,' he said, with only mild relief in his voice.

I stalled for a moment, completely stuck. I felt like a heavy-duty tractor blundering my way through a field of daisies, but I couldn't give up now. 'Can I see the interview you had in *The Bulletin*? Have you got a copy?'

'Oh, really?' He slid off his stool.

I couldn't believe he hadn't seen through my ludicrous questions by now. 'Marlene might have finished her call,' he said, leading the way back to his office. The room was empty.

'March, I think it was,' I said, trying to save time.

He went to shelves in the corner and lifted down a box file. 'Yes, here we are.' He pulled out a laminated sheet, carefully preserved for posterity, and handed it to me.

I skimmed it quickly. 'That's really positive. Miranda is certainly in safe hands.' Then as an apparent afterthought I said, 'Oh, yes, it *was* Pippa French, I thought she was the journalist.' I turned to watch his face. 'Do you remember her?'

A direct question he couldn't sidestep.

'Vaguely.' He shrugged and looked down. 'March was a busy month, what with the new entrance hall being finished. And as I say, I do a lot of interviews; students, press, parents.' He ushered me towards the door, looking like someone with better things to do. 'They all blur into one after a while.' He glanced at his watch and waited for me to take the hint.

I came away kicking myself. Just what exactly had I hoped to achieve by this charade? I walked to the corner of the grass and turned to look back, noticing the kiln flue smoking in a long white snake against the cloudless blue sky. That struck me as odd, given that Simon had told the man with the vase that it wouldn't be running again until Monday. Perhaps I'd misunderstood.

Reluctantly, I returned to the boat. My footsteps petered out as I stepped onto the carpet in the saloon, giving me a stark reminder of how empty it felt. I'd never been alone all night on a boat before. Aiden had reasonable security, but it would only take a few whacks with a sharp axe and an intruder could be inside in less than thirty seconds.

That was how paranoid I'd become after Aiden's arrest and the second murder. The idea of going back to my flat was sorely tempting, but I didn't know when Aiden would be sent home. I didn't want him thinking I'd deserted him.

I slid the bolt to my cabin closed, but as soon as I got into bed and put out the light, my brain began fizzing away. I sat against my pillows listening, but trying not to. I put my reading light on, then the radio, but decided it was a false comfort; if any sounds were going to alert me to danger, I needed to hear them. I waited, holding my breath. There was a distant police siren, a train rumbling over the arches and then nothing.

I started playing a game I often suggest to patients with insomnia. I call it a 'game' to make it sound fun, but it has short-lived amusement value. It involves running through the alphabet naming plants, countries, cities, actors – anything, to focus the mind on a simple, unemotional task. Working my way through vegetables I got as far as J and ground to a halt. My ears twitched. Then I heard a clatter. It was outside the boat, but close by. Someone was on the private pontoon.

I switched off the reading light and slid the curtain aside a fraction. Nothing but black-on-black. I craned my neck to try to see the front of the boat, but it was impossible at this angle. I waited to see if any of the shadows changed shape, but there was no movement, no sound.

I knew what I had to do. Check the boat. I pressed my hand over my chest in an attempt to make my heart slow down. It didn't do the trick, but I braved the gloom outside my cabin, anyway. Darting from room to room in my bare feet, I pulled all the curtains closed, including Aiden's cabin.

I shoved a chest of drawers in front of the external door at the bow end and barricaded the stern with a bookcase. I could hear every tiny sound; the creak of the woodwork as the boat rocked slightly, the rubbery thud as it grazed the pontoon, the patter of my feet. Perhaps the noise I'd heard had been a box flapping around in the wind or a rope coming loose. I couldn't be certain, so I switched on most of the lights and carried the full drawer of cooking knives with me back to my room, together with a hefty rolling pin. As a final precaution, I rammed a chair under the door handle before crawling back into bed.

Chapter 31

I was breaking out of a turbulent dream about Aiden when morning came. It left me wrung out and on edge.

I poured myself a mug of Earl Grey tea, put a crumpet under the grill and managed to get through to Karen Foxton.

'How is he?' I snapped. I wished I'd made more fuss when he was carted away. I should have made them see that, in the state he was in, he was a potential suicide risk.

'Er… distressed and emotional.'

My rage bubbled over. 'I *can't believe* you all let this happen! It's utterly appalling. Totally out of order.' Nothing came back. 'I don't suppose he's said a word?' I added.

There was a shred of hesitation; a reluctance to admit the shambles they were responsible for. 'No.'

The brief told-you-so silence felt justified. 'This could set him back months.'

'With due respect, Dr Willerby, we have to go through all the correct procedures.'

'So, what happens now?'

'Dr Herts is going to speak to him again today.'

'I'm sure that will be very useful,' I said dryly. 'You'll have to let him go after twenty-four hours.' I was about to end the call when Jeremy came on the line. I didn't particularly want to talk to him. I knew I'd get angry and say something I'd regret.

'Thought you might like to know about the second victim,' he said.

'I thought I was off the case?'

'I've been talking to the borough commander about that. It's turned into a slightly awkward political issue, in that the powers that be weren't properly consulted about removing you.'

'Elsa Claussen made the decision on her own?'

'This is all confidential, you understand, but it could work in your favour.'

'How?'

'We're not exactly sure yet, but it would be helpful if... you didn't disappear too soon. Where are you now?'

'On the boat.'

'Right...' There was a thread of humour in his voice.

'When is Aiden being released?'

'I can't say. He's going to be questioned, today. I thought DI Foxton just told you that.'

'You do know it's pointless keeping him, don't you? I hope you've got him a good lawyer.'

He ignored me. I heard him exhale heavily. 'DCI Wilde thought it could be useful if we shared certain bits of information with you... to see if anything Aiden has produced in your therapy could have a bearing.'

'Go ahead.'

'One of the last people to see Katarina Bartek was Henry Dodd, owner of Dodd & Son Funeral Directors in Islington. Do either of those names mean anything to you?'

'Not a thing.'

'The body of Katarina's husband was held there and she went over to try to see him the day she was killed. Henry says he has no links to any artists or CCAP and Aiden didn't react when he was shown his photograph. Katarina has no obvious links with art, hasn't been to the Camden project as far as we know, so far. No regulars there recognised her photo and her name isn't in the visitors' book.'

'Where was Murray Kent the night Katarina was killed?'

'We're checking his alibi now.'

'We don't know for certain, but it looks like Katarina was driven to the towpath and dumped. The post-mortem is this afternoon, so we'll know more then.'

'Why so close to the spot Kora was killed, do you think?'

'I don't know. Killer knows the area? He got away with it the first time?' he said wearily.

The conversation dried up after that.

I squeezed my eyes shut with a jolt of uneasiness. The deaths *had* to be connected.

I found myself mindlessly pacing up and down after that. I kept checking my phone, every hour, thinking the police should be contacting me. Keeping Aiden this long was diabolical. My phone rang at lunchtime, but it wasn't the call I'd been hoping for. Instead, it was Miranda inviting me over for a 'gathering' that evening. An offer like that didn't come too often from my sister; usually it was just the two of us, she rarely included me in her circle of friends. It crossed my mind that there was likely to be a catch. Nevertheless, my mind was made up when she said she was also expecting several members of CCAP to attend.

I arrived early to give her a hand, but Miranda looked irritated, rather than grateful.

'I said seven o'clock,' she muttered, throwing a duster over her shoulder.

The place was transformed; from warehouse to cosy dining room. Miranda had put strings of sparkly lights up everywhere and was in the process of stacking away all her painting gear under sheets.

I hung my jacket in the hall and helped her drag framed pictures behind the spiral staircase.

'Don't touch those ones,' she snapped, as I reached for more canvases.

'I'll be careful,' I said.

'Some of them are wet, that's all,' she added, softening her tone.

There were six places set around the circular table; she must have borrowed dining chairs from somewhere, because I'd never seen more than two in the entire flat. The napkins had been expertly folded to look like lilies and there was a red rose laid across each plate. Silver hearts had been sprinkled over the tablecloth. Miranda had always been one to put on a show when she felt like it. She'd certainly pulled out all the stops this time.

She tossed a silk throw over the ripped arm of the sofa and I turned to clear away newspapers from a side table. On the top was an old family photograph I hadn't seen in ages. Miranda must have been around twenty and I was eighteen. We'd spent Christmas in the New Forest and had been tramping through the woodland after lunch. Miranda was looking cold and grumpy and I was laughing at a stranger's dog at the edge of the shot who'd been rolling in the fresh snow. My hair was the longest I ever remember having it and I looked carefree with rosy cheeks – innocent and unflappable. A family blithely unaware that we were about to be given a diagnosis that would change all of our lives. In fact, this might have been the last picture we'd had taken as a family before Miranda was taken into care.

I was relishing the poignant moment, when the photo was whisked out of my hands. 'Leave that alone,' she scolded, hiding it from me. 'Why are you always snooping at my things?'

The doorbell rang before I could defend myself and a woman who introduced herself as Monica Tyler burst in giving both of us an overblown hug. She'd turned up in dusty dungarees and heavy Doc Marten boots, looking like she'd come straight from a building site. Designed to keep her bundle of jet-black ringlets at bay, a bright green scarf was wrapped precariously around her head. It merely created an unnecessary layer that threatened to topple down, so that she was constantly having to fiddle with it.

'Kurtis said we were having five courses, is that right?' she said, staring at the table.

'With strawberry pavlova for dessert, your favourite,' chuckled Miranda, her mood instantly brightened.

'Miranda doesn't do things by halves, does she?' she said to me in a stage whisper as my sister handed her a bottle of lager from an ice bucket on the floor. I smiled faintly, handing her an empty glass and picking up a full glass of red wine for myself from a cluster on a small table.

Others arrived. I dropped back to let Miranda greet everyone.

Goldfrapp was playing in the background and bowls of olives and peanuts had already got fingers active. Given how recently their friend, Kora, had died I couldn't decide whether this degree of excess was insensitive or could be excused on the basis of some kind of tribute. No one else, however, seemed to be bothered by any perceived tactlessness.

We all stood around waiting to be shown where to sit and Monica, hovering to my left, lifted her glass.

'To Kora,' she said, and the room echoed her words with gusto.

'Have an olive, darling,' said Monica, shoving a dish at me. 'This is Rachel…'

Standing to my right was the CCAP administrator, Rachel Peel. She looked almost the opposite of Monica; tall, prim and reserved, checking furtively over the rim of her glass as if she'd never met anyone here before.

'And this is Mark Ellerton,' Monica added, reaching out for his arm as he was about to walk past. 'He's a good-for-nothing in most areas, but he's a bloody good portrait painter.'

Mark gave a mock bow and threw his eyes to the ceiling when he straightened up.

'Hi, I'm Kurtis Mills,' said another man emerging from the hall, holding out his hand. Miranda had mentioned his name. 'I'm a tutor at the project.'

Frothy ginger curls you'd associate with a clown sprouted from beneath a flamboyant tam-o'-shanter tartan cap, warming me to him in an instant. As he wrapped his fingers around my palm, I glanced down and instantly yanked my hand away. Crawling towards his knuckles was a massive spider. I let out a sharp squeal, then did a double take, my brain needing a second to register that it wasn't real. An ingenious tattoo – as realistic as I'd ever seen.

'Most women have that reaction when they meet me,' he said playfully. 'I still can't work out why!'

I chuckled, my heart slowing down.

'Don't mind him,' Monica called over. 'He can't resist pulling one over on unsuspecting strangers.' She put her arms flamboyantly around his neck and gave him a loud *mwah* air-kiss beside each cheek.

As he flicked back his hair, I spotted another tattoo behind his ear; a cartoon caterpillar emerging from a 'hole' and another, a loop shape on the inside of his right wrist, although his sleeve obscured the rest of the motif. Unusual, clever trompe l'oeil skin art.

As he clinked his glass against mine, Kurtis saw my fascination. 'These are real works of art,' I said, lifting his hand to inspect it again. Even though I knew the spider was only a drawing, the way the shadows had been added under the bent legs still made me sense it was on the move.

'Have you seen the new bronze fountain outside CCAP?' Monica asked me. 'The statue of Poseidon?'

'I saw yesterday, as it happens... very impressive.'

She jabbed a thumb in his direction. 'It's a Kurtis Mills creation,' she said, looking pleased with herself.

'Really?' I wasn't sure if she was teasing me.

Miranda came through with the first starters; goats cheese tart with red pepper marmalade. 'Yeah, it's true,' Miranda chimed in. 'He's amazing.'

Kurtis smiled, appearing genuinely touched. He looked like he was in his thirties, his mellifluous Scottish accent light and cheery as he chipped in with witty, slightly barbed comments.

Miranda brought the final plates through and in the absence of any instruction otherwise, we each took the nearest seat. She'd taken off her apron and looked glowing in an off-the-shoulder chiffon dress; more glamorous than I'd ever seen her. It made me wonder if either of the men here tonight, Kurtis or Mark, were in her sights.

'Bloody hell, Miranda,' squealed Monica, her eyes stretched wide. 'If you weren't riding on the other bus, darling, I'd snap you up.'

Miranda laughed and gave us all a flamboyant twirl revealing enough cleavage to squeeze a lemon. The burns she'd suffered on her arms and shoulders from the fire, over a year ago, were barely visible.

She tapped a spoon against the side of her glass, drawing us to a hush. 'Now, you all know that we're here tonight to pay tribute to our good and loyal friend, Kora.' She put up her hand to show she wasn't finished. 'But we're also here for another reason.'

Chapter 32

Everyone was holding up their glasses in anticipation. I seemed to be the only one at the dinner party who didn't know what this was about.

'We're at this little gathering because we're a bit special,' announced Miranda. She giggled as the room erupted into a cheer. 'Simon says we're going to have proper ceremony at CCAP, but...'

I shuffled in my seat, not knowing what was coming next.

'...you all know that the prizes have just been announced for this year and I wanted to name names, so we can all celebrate our successes.'

Another cheer.

She slipped a sheet of paper out from under her plate and held it up.

'Mark Ellerton was runner-up in the Presner Award for best portrait.' A whoop and ripple of applause followed. 'Monica got highly commended for her installation, "Mortality".' Monica stood up and launched into a drunken happy dance, but almost fell over and had to be caught by Kurtis. She gave me a high five as she slumped back into her seat.

'Simon... he couldn't be here tonight, got the Warner Prize for his sculptures,' she snatched a breath. 'Kurtis was highly commended in the same category... yay... and that leaves... me – I got the Scott Award for abstract oils and a cheque for 500 quid – hence all the bubbly tonight!'

A roar broke out around me as they all jumped up and down, hugging each other. I joined in with loud cheering, forcing the biggest smile I could muster onto my lips.

Miranda hadn't told me. When did she know about it?

'Wow – that's fabulous!' I called out.

A round of individual hugs and kisses followed and when I was faced with Miranda, I did my utmost to clear the hurt from my voice.

'That's awesome. I'm really proud of you.' I hugged her close, wondering why we hadn't been able to share this special moment, just the two of us, first.

As the merriment died down and we tucked into our food, Monica reeled off several lewd stories about staff at CCAP. Mark took over, launching into a barrage of not very funny anecdotes about the art world.

Monica turned to me. 'Do you know much about the awards?' she asked, each word sliding into the next.

'No, not really,' I said.

'Well, Simon snagged the best prize – the Warner – there's a lot of prestige in that. Winners often get shortlisted for the bigger prizes.' She rolled her eyes. 'He *is* very good.' She stabbed at a gherkin three times with a cocktail stick before she managed to spear it, then gave me a nudge, dragging me close to whisper in my ear. 'Mark nearly didn't come tonight.' I glanced over at him without making it obvious. 'He was hoping to land *first* prize in the Presner Award. We all thought it was in the bag, but he only got second. Got some crap publicity just before the shortlisting and we reckon that's what did the damage.'

'What about you? Were you pleased to get highly commended?'

She wrinkled her nose. 'Sore point, actually. My installation was tampered with just before the judges came in. Someone had shifted a chair and moved the stretcher. I don't know who did it, but they ruined the whole bloody thing. *Bastards.*' After a tense pause, she laughed. 'I bet you thought all us artists were a sensitive touchy-feely bunch.' She leered close to my face so that I got a full blast of garlic breath. 'The truth is, when push comes to shove everyone's in it for themselves – we're all two-faced and bitchy.' She scrunched up her napkin on her plate. 'I need a pee.' She got up and tottered towards the spiral stairs.

I looked up at the others around the table. Rachel hadn't said much at all. Kurtis, on the other hand, had barely stopped for breath.

'Do you tutor many artists at the project?' I asked him as he finished a mouthful of spicy chicken.

'I've got lots of my own work on the go, so I only have three or four students, right now.' Monica returned to her seat and he waved a stick of celery at her. 'This madam, for one,' he said. 'She's a bloody handful, but very gifted.'

Monica put two fingers up at him and they both laughed.

'He's brrrilliant,' she said, chewing a jalapeno pepper, decidedly worse for wear in terms of alcohol. 'The best tutor we've got.'

He shook his head. 'No, that's got to be Simon the Great. Seriously, Simon Schiffer is excellent. A credit to the place.'

I wanted to cut through the banter with a specific question, but I didn't know how, without it sounding contrived. I decided to come right out with it and having given Miranda a warning stare I addressed the whole table and asked if anyone had heard of the artist, Aiden Blake.

Monica shook her head, Rachel shrugged, Miranda stayed silent.

'Seen his name somewhere,' said Kurtis, chewing a sprig of rocket. 'Up-and-coming chap, by the sounds of it. Textiles, isn't he?'

'I'm not sure,' I said. 'Someone mentioned him... as a local student... I just wondered if–'

'Yeah. At Chelsea, isn't he?' said Mark. 'Works in shades of white, I think. He won the Topping Prize hands down last year. That would have made him a good few grand better off.' He lowered his voice. 'Our prizes are small fry compared to his. Good luck to him. It'll still be a tough world once he gets out of college.'

I threw Miranda a grateful glance for not blowing my cover and the conversation drifted in another direction.

Kurtis handed me the jug of cream. 'Is "Transformations" representative of your work?' I ventured, as I tucked into the strawberry pavlova. It was surprisingly light and fluffy. As someone who had unfortunately been on the receiving end of Miranda's cooking in years gone by, I questioned whether she'd done all this on her own.

'It's the only fountain I've tackled, so far,' he said. 'I'm working on a piece with alien-looking seedpods for Kew right now and I also make commemorative monuments. I've just done a bust of Abraham Lincoln for a museum in Bath and got a miniature version of Stonehenge for a park in Milton Keynes lined up for next year.'

'And he's got a commission from Canary Wharf,' burst in Monica.

Kurtis sniffed, rolling over the edge of his napkin. 'Not quite. It was on the cards – they paid five percent – then changed their minds.'

'Oh, what a blow,' I said. 'Still, it all sounds remarkable to me.'

'Not really. Not when you consider what Monica's working on, eh?' He winked at her. 'Go on, tell her,' he coaxed.

'No, it's a secret. You *know* it is,' reprimanded Monica.

'In case you didn't realise,' he said in a low voice, 'Monica is something of an extrovert. She's the queen of performance art.'

Monica stuck out her tongue at him.

'See?' he said, reaching for the bottle to top up our glasses. Monica seemed to have several glasses beside her at once, with wine, champagne as well as lager on the go. She refused to say more about her project so that was the last I heard of it.

The music gradually mellowed into sombre ballads and inevitably, after more drinks, the topic of conversation turned to Kora.

'Kurtis might make a memorial statue for her if we can get together enough money,' said Miranda from across the table.

Kurtis held up his hands. 'Early days yet.'

Monica pulled my elbow towards her, eager to whisper once more.

'Kurtis has been hit pretty badly by Kora's death,' she said, her lips brushing my ear so only I could hear. 'His sister died only a few months ago and I think it's knocked him for six. She was an artist at CCAP, as well. Very gifted.' She hesitated. 'Drug addict… recovering, you know, like we all are. That's how Kurtis got involved in the place.' She straightened up with a sad nod.

'I didn't know Kora had a boyfriend,' said Rachel, tactlessly. 'The police said she was supposed to meet someone that night, a florist or something, but it all went badly wrong.' She sniffed into a handkerchief.

'She *wasn't* seeing anyone,' insisted Miranda. 'Kora would never do that.'

Mark chipped in. 'Maybe she turned the guy down and he lost his rag.'

'No, this was planned,' said Miranda, pursing her lips. 'Not an impulse reaction in the moment.'

'Yeah, well. I think he must have done it,' said Rachel.

'I spoke to Lou this morning and something doesn't add up,' said Mark. He'd had a lot to drink and had nearly fallen down the spiral staircase on his return from the bathroom. 'Apparently, Kora was supposed to be meeting this flower guy that night, only Lou phoned him and told him Kora had already gone home… except he didn't make the call.' He swung his glass in the air, then took a long swig.

Miranda got up to light an array of candles. I caught her eye, silently urging her to keep my involvement in the case under wraps.

'There must have been someone else in the building,' said Monica. 'Someone who *said* he was Lou, who knew Kora was meeting this flower guy, who got hold of Kora's phone and made the call to get rid of him. Then this same person must have told Kora she was supposed to go somewhere else… along the towpath. Miranda's right, it was all carefully set up.'

'Maybe they said her kid was ill…' muttered Mark.

'No,' said Kurtis. 'Lou said she wasn't going home. She headed in the opposite direction.'

'It certainly looks like whoever planned the whole thing *knew* Kora,' said Miranda. 'And knew her pretty well.'

She stared at me, as if to press home the point that the police should be pursuing that line of enquiry.

'Do you reckon it's a serial killer?' asked Mark. 'Another woman was found yesterday, wasn't she, near the same spot?'

'Different M.O.,' said Monica pretentiously. 'I caught the news before I came out. Police said it was a Polish woman, lived in Islington. Strangled. She wasn't on a bike.'

'Well, we must all be very careful,' said Kurtis gravely. 'If there is a lunatic in the area, we need to make sure any women we know aren't wandering about alone and certainly aren't anywhere near the towpath.'

'And who's to say he's just after women?' said Monica. '*Everyone* needs to be on the lookout.'

Rachel and Monica left together before midnight and Kurtis called a taxi for Mark, who was about to curl up for the night uninvited on the sofa. I picked up a tea towel and started drying dishes in the kitchen.

'No, you mustn't,' Miranda said. 'I can manage.'

'I know you can. I just want to make it easier for you.'

It occurred to me then that there had indeed been a hidden pretext behind my invitation that evening. Miranda had wanted to prove a point. She had wanted to show me how capable she was, how good a hostess she could be, how normal and efficient she was, even after the huge upset.

'You did a brilliant job,' I said.

'Thank you,' she said with vibrant triumph in her voice. She lowered her voice. 'I saw you chatting to Kurtis.'

I was aware he was still in the adjacent room, finishing his coffee.

'His fountain at CCAP is gorgeous,' I whispered.

'He tutors at CCAP for free, you know. Bet he didn't tell you that. He's one of the true professionals there and he does it for nothing.'

Kurtis brought his empty mug into the kitchen and I left to find my jacket. Now that the main light had been switched on, I saw a scrapbook, just like Aiden's, open on a coffee table in a corner. One of the others must have been flicking through it. Hearing the two of them chatting in the kitchen, I took a quick peek to see how it compared with Aiden's. This one was less artistic and more like Aiden's shoebox; full of press releases, newspaper clippings and photos. There was a printout of recent shots taken of the CCAP annual dinner and one of the new fountain.

I recognised Simon Schiffer standing beside a woman who was cutting a ribbon. There were pictures of Miranda's recent private exhibition and a copy of a flyer. Then another press photograph of Simon at a British Academy Award's ceremony. I carefully peeled away the clipping and held it nearer the light. The woman to one side of him. I recognised her. There was no question – it was Honoré Craig-Doyle, one of the missing women, who owned a gallery in Chelsea. I remembered her distinctive Latin appearance from the missing person's shot Jeremy had given me.

I stood reeling on the spot, affected by the alcohol, but more so by what this might mean.

Simon Schiffer knew Kora, Pippa – and now Honoré.

I dithered, not sure whether to take the clipping or not. The music had stopped by now and as I sidled back towards the kitchen to say goodbye, I overheard Miranda say my name.

'No, Sam hasn't got a clue,' she said, keeping her voice low. 'I think it'll be a real shock, actually…'

What would be 'a real shock'?

They spotted me before I could pick up any more. The urge to ask what they were referring to was almost irresistible, but I knew Miranda too well. She'd only accuse me of eavesdropping, be defensive and bluff her way through it, leaving the evening in tatters.

'I'm off now,' I said cheerily. 'Thanks for a wonderful time.' Miranda reached out and gave me a wrap-around embrace, splashing soap suds from her rubber gloves onto my jacket. I held her tight, relishing that rare moment. I was glad I hadn't said anything.

'Going to the Tube?' asked Kurtis.

I nodded and he joined me.

We didn't chat about anything significant on the way, but there were no embarrassing silences. He seemed self-effacing; slightly world-weary, with a wise core.

'Miranda's great, isn't she?' he said, just before we parted at the ticket machines.

I smiled. 'She's brilliant – but she's hard work too.' I lifted my shoulders. 'Complicated.'

'Look after each other,' he said, his eyes earnest on mine. 'Sisters are precious.' He kicked at a cigarette butt on the tiled floor. 'I lost mine.'

I pretended not to know. 'Oh, how awful – I'm sorry.'

'I'll tell you about it another time perhaps,' he said, patting my arm with a sad smile and turned in the direction of the signs pointing north.

It was only when I was on the train that I realised I had the press cutting from Miranda's scrapbook in my pocket.

Chapter 33

I was keen to get going the following morning. Rachel, the administrator, told me Simon Schiffer wouldn't be at the art project until after lunch. As my plan depended on his absence, that suited me fine. On the way over, I received a call from Jeremy.

'Where's Aiden?' I growled.

'St Anne's Hospital. Since he was released yesterday afternoon.'

'Yesterday afternoon? No one told me!'

I felt clammy and cold, all in one.

'He wasn't taking visitors,' he said smugly. 'In any case, we agreed we'd inform you when he was being returned to the boat.'

This man's attitude was increasingly getting up my nose.

'Is he okay?'

'He should be out after lunch. The detective chief superintendent wanted him sectioned, but Dr Herts said he couldn't sanction it. Apparently, he thinks Mr Blake is not a danger to himself or the world at large; he's suffering exhaustion and severe anxiety.'

'I'm not surprised,' I said, clutching my forehead. 'What have you done to him?'

Silence.

'I don't suppose he's spoken to anyone?' I asked dryly.

'No, as it happens.'

'I *told* you he wouldn't be able to help you.'

'He's not off the hook yet. He could have left the boat to kill Katarina. There is still the witness who said they saw someone matching his description on the towpath just before her body was found.'

'It can't have been him… it just can't.' I decided to spill the beans. 'I found a press clipping from earlier this year that shows

Simon Schiffer knew Honoré Craig-Doyle. Did you know about that?'

'We've got all bases covered, Dr Willerby. Leave it to us.'

I couldn't tell whether his tone was reassuring or patronising.

'Am I allowed to know anything more about this second murder?'

'I can't tell you much. The post-mortem indicates that Mrs Bartek was strangled elsewhere and dumped after the towpath gates were locked, sometime between around 11pm and 2am on the eleventh. She was dragged through a neatly clipped gap in the wire fence.'

'And Murray Kent?'

'He has an alibi. We've checked out Sponge, Kora's partner, and he looks clean, too.'

'Any *good* news?'

'I'm not sure whether you'll be glad about this or not… you're fully reinstated as consultant psychologist regarding Mr Blake, if you want the job back.'

'With Aiden as a witness *and* a potential suspect?'

'I know, it's complicated,' he conceded. 'We have to keep all avenues open. Are you up for it?'

'I'll need to check with work, first, they'll be expecting me back.'

'All done,' he said. 'Your locum is booked.'

I was aghast. My life didn't seem to belong to me any more. 'Until when?'

'Until we make some genuine headway, or you call it a day. Whichever comes first.'

'That's settled then. I'm not going anywhere,' I said. 'I'll be back on the boat at lunch time, waiting for Aiden.'

'There is one thing,' he said. He left an overlong silence. 'We don't think it's wise for you to stay with him. Our advice would be to leave the boat and go back to your flat. Visit him, for arranged appointments only and make sure someone knows where you are.'

'You're kidding me.'

'He's unstable.'

'So, he's well enough to be discharged, but not allowed to be around people?'

'Go back home. Dr Herts thinks he'll be no harm to anyone if he's left alone on his boat. We'll check up on him. Just drop in on him once a day to do your... therapy thing.'

'I can't do that. I don't want him left on his own. He's obviously in a very bad way.'

'We can't vouch for your safety round the clock.'

'I have to be with him.'

'I strongly advise you to reconsider, but I can't force you to leave the boat.'

'Okay then, I'm staying.' And with that the call was over.

I quickened my step. I wanted my mission at CCAP over with, so I could make sure everything was ready for Aiden back at the boat.

My pretext for returning to CCAP was to 'find' a pair of reading glasses I'd supposedly left behind when I'd been there to see Simon. I didn't use reading glasses, but no one needed to know that. The real reason for my visit was to dig around to see what I might be able to find out about his relationships with Kora, Pippa and Honoré.

When I arrived, Rachel led me into the large airy studio where I'd spoken to Simon. She stood out from everyone else around the place, dressed over-formally in a navy-blue skirt and jacket and a high-necked white frilly blouse. More suitable for a job interview than toing and froing within a hair's breadth of wet cavasses, spattering potters' wheels and dusty grey sculptures.

Inside, eight people in overalls had their heads down, immersed in their own intricate projects. Returning to the spot where Simon and I had chatted, I made a pretence of searching the bench and floor area.

'My specs aren't here,' I said. 'I must have left them somewhere else. No one's handed them in?'

'Not to me. I'll ask round. At least stay for a coffee while you're here,' she said. She led me along to the kitchen. On the way, we passed a door marked *Kiln* and an odd acrid aroma followed us along the corridor.

'What's that funny smell?' I asked innocently.

'Just the kiln. It's used for firing all the pottery the users produce. It's switched off now, but it stinks a bit all the time. Like burnt leather boots, I reckon. Simon will get it going this afternoon, I think.'

I'd remembered the kiln had been roaring away when I'd left late last time. 'Is it left on overnight?'

'Sometimes. It depends if there are items waiting to be fired. It's on complicated timers; it has to heat up to the right temperature and then cool down again or you can ruin all the pots. Each firing can take around twelve hours in all. Simon's in charge, he's the only one allowed to use it.'

'So, no one can fire their work unless he's around?'

'That's right. It's a health and safety thing. The users leave their work for him and collect it afterwards, but he's the only one who's allowed to open the door.'

She seemed more assertive today. It occurred to me that perhaps she wasn't a 'party person' and had been coerced into turning up last night to make up numbers. 'Miranda put on a great spread yesterday, didn't she?' she said, as she poured from the coffee pot. 'You two are totally different, aren't you?'

I gave a chuckle. 'Like chalk and cheese.' It was only then that I remembered Miranda had been confiding something to Kurtis last night when I'd walked into the kitchen. I knew it was about me.

'Sugar?'

'No, thanks.'

We walked round to her office. 'This place has transformed so many people's lives, as I'm sure Miranda will have told you,' she said. 'People come here lost and hopeless and they gain direction, motivation, a real sense of purpose and identity.'

She offered me a seat. Her office was neat and orderly, like herself. I imagined that everything was filed correctly and would be easy to locate.

'Simon seems to do a good job,' I said.

'Oh, yes, he's brilliant. I'm his PA as well as the general administrator here.' She swung her executive chair from side to side. 'Our funding has shot up since he joined us two years ago. I've been here forever; there's something about the atmosphere that's warm and calming. Everyone has a history – there's a sense we're all in it together.'

'You too?' I said softly. There was an air of isolation about her; as though she'd spent her life going it alone.

'I used to be anorexic. I won't go into details, but this place more or less saved my life. There isn't just art going on here, there are support groups, meditation, group therapy, one-to-one sessions – everything.'

I nodded. 'Simon must get to know a lot of local art people, local sponsors.'

'Definitely. I'm always arranging appointments for him to meet important people.'

'Must have run-ins with them now and again, though. I'll bet not everyone approves of this kind of project, or is prepared to support it, financially.'

'Are you interested in him?' she said suddenly. It caught me off guard.

I snapped my brain into gear. 'I'm always interested to know about people who have a hand in Miranda's well-being,' I said, shifting in my seat.

'I used to have a bit of a thing for him, too,' she said, misunderstanding me.

I decided to go along with it.

'I have to say, he's very attractive,' I said, meeting her eye with a coy look. 'Is he married?'

'Okay,' she said, clapping her hands together in excitement. She lifted her shoulders and squeezed her hands between her knees, reminding me of a teenager about to divulge a big secret. 'Let me give you the lowdown. He's single. Thirty-five. Keeps his private life to himself, but... I'm not sure if he might be taken, if you know what I mean.' I let her explain. 'I happen to know he's been seeing someone recently. Some art critic, I think. Pretty, dark hair.'

'Art critic?' I felt my stomach fold in on itself.

'From one of the arty magazines.' She tapped her lip. 'I can't remember which one.'

'They're definitely dating?'

'Yeah…' She dropped her gaze, looking apologetic. 'Sorry to disappoint you. I don't know how serious it is. I saw them in a restaurant on the South Bank at the beginning of June. I remember, because it was my birthday. It might have been a business meal, of course.' She inspected her nails. 'And, thinking about it, I haven't seen her for a while.' She was still for a moment, then suddenly got up, her cheeks flushing pink. 'Look at the time. I've got to finish this report. You're too easy to talk to!'

'Thanks for the coffee,' I said. I made a mental note that she could be well worth speaking to again.

I had to pass the kiln room on my way out. The door was ajar, so I slid my head around. There was no one inside, I stepped over the threshold. The kiln resembled a huge fridge with white bricks making a kind of fireplace inside; empty apart from two shelves and a scattering of ashes at the bottom. This was definitely the source of the smell; it reminded me of burnt hair on straightening irons.

I reached my hand inside to feel how warm it was and saw something small near the back catching the light. I thought at first it was a chip of marble or a stone from a piece of jewellery. I picked it up and played with it between my fingertips.

A tooth.

Animal or human, it was still incongruous.

Instinctively I took a step back, my other hand over my mouth. What was it doing here? Whatever the explanation, it didn't seem right. As I stood examining it, the sound of footsteps came from out of the blue. With nowhere to hide, I darted towards the space behind the open door, the tooth tight in my hand. The steps receded. Before I crept out, I took a scrap of paper from my bag and wrote down the make of the kiln, shown in raised lettering on the front. There was a label on the side that stated the capacity and model type, so I took that down too, before taking broad innocent strides towards the exit. The tooth bit into my palm all the way to the police station.

Chapter 34

Unfortunately none of the key officers I'd already met were available, so I stood in reception trying to work out what to do. I didn't want to hang around. I needed to get back to the boat to welcome Aiden. I had the choice of taking the tooth with me, or leaving it with the desk sergeant.

I wasn't sure how serious my find was. There could be a simple explanation, but it struck me as odd to say the least. Under what circumstances did a tooth belong in a kiln designed for firing ceramics? I opened my palm and stared at it again. It was human, I was sure of it; a human molar. I wanted rid of it, so I asked the desk sergeant for a small envelope and left it with a note in capital letters begging either DI Foxton or Jeremy to call me as soon as they could.

All manner of wild speculations swam around my head. Was someone using teeth as part of their ceramic designs? In a tooth-fairy necklace for a child perhaps or some kind of novelty fancy-dress costume for Halloween? Or had this tooth been part of some obscure sacrifice? Rachel had told me herself that Simon was the only one allowed to operate it. What was he up to?

A horrifying thought occurred to me. Was it actually *feasible* to burn a body to cinders inside a ceramic kiln? I shook my head. No way – surely I was leaping to a preposterous conclusion.

An idea came to me which could clear this up, one way or the other. If I was quick, I could get there and back before Aiden returned at lunchtime.

Dodd & Son Funeral Directors were easy to find, just off Islington High Street sandwiched between a letting agency and a Spanish tapas bar. There were sample headstones in the window, candles and flowers. They made death appear almost tasteful. Jeremy said this was the place Katarina Bartek's husband had been laid to rest before his funeral. It was where Katarina had been hours before she'd died. I wanted to get a look at the place, but it wasn't my main reason for going there.

The door gave an unexpectedly shrill ting as I walked in and a woman came through from the back, poised to offer her condolences.

'I'm sorry to trouble you,' I said. I lowered my voice to sound suitably mournful. 'My uncle has just died and I'm looking at a few places to see where…' I was surprised at how easily little white lies were slithering out of my mouth these days.

'You've come to the right place,' she said, adopting a stooping position in the manner of people trained to offer endless sympathy.

Probably in her fifties, she had a Princess Diana haircut that was fading to grey at the sides and held her hands clasped in front of her pleated skirt. She showed me to a seat at the desk. There were leaflets advertising different styles of coffins, tombstones and memorials, and others explaining services and cremations. The lit candle, surrounded by a wreath of white roses was a nice touch. As soon as I sat down, however, I realised the roses were plastic. The candle, too, was phony, its flickering flame powered by battery.

The woman pulled up her seat, pen at the ready.

'I wanted to ask a few questions, first, if that's okay?' I said.

She nodded sagely, as if she'd expected this.

'My uncle wanted to be cremated,' I said. 'This is going to sound really weird, but how hot does the temperature… get to, when the… you know…?'

She sat back. 'Goodness, that is an unusual question. Most people want to know what happens to the ashes or whether they are allowed to watch the coffin go into the cremator.'

'Grief does funny things,' I surmised, tapping a finger on her desk.

She got up and said she'd be back in a moment.

'Between 1,400 and 1,800 degrees Fahrenheit,' she recited, on her return.

'Does everything… go… even his teeth. Do they get destroyed too?'

She tried to hide a fleeting frown, but wasn't quick enough.

A man in a black suit came through from the back. He'd heard my questions. 'Interestingly enough,' he said, 'one part of the body that is often intact following cremation is the teeth. False teeth, too.' He held out his hand by way of a welcome. It felt dusty and too warm. 'Henry Dodd,' he said.

'Er… Pauline Watson,' I said, snatching at the first name I could think of. 'How long does it take?'

'It depends on the size of the person, but usually between forty-five and ninety minutes. Have we got you registered?' he said, turning to the receptionist.

'Can I see where he will be?' I said, ignoring them both. 'If the mortuary isn't in use, that is.'

'It's not normal practice to—'

'Oh, well…' I reached for my bag, ready to leave.

He rubbed his hands together. 'But I think we've got time this morning, Sally, don't you?'

Dodd led me through a corridor along to the mortuary. He opened the door and put on a bright strip light. The room was chilled and everything inside seemed to be made of brushed aluminium. The smell reminded me of a particular day at senior school when I'd walked into the biology lab to be confronted by rows of cloudy brown jars, each with a dead frog inside.

'The deceased are kept here,' he said, pointing to the long fridges. 'We offer embalming, if the family wish to view the body.' He pointed to various machines on wheels sprouting plastic tubes and a vessel resembling a bidet.

I noticed there was a back door leading into a rear car park, with tall wooden gates open onto the street. Two shiny black hearses sat in waiting. Presumably business wasn't brisk.

'You'd set off from here to the crematorium?' I said, peering out of the window.

'That's right. A standard hearse, or we can arrange a horse-drawn carriage, or whatever you like.' I felt sorry for him. He was trying his best to secure my custom.

We went back along the corridor and he showed me the chapel of rest. 'This is where you would view your uncle, if that's what you wanted. And that's it, really.'

'Thank you, that's really helpful.'

He was suitably over-effusive and left me in the capable hands of Sally at reception. She pulled out a set of forms and I began to wonder what sort of hole I'd dug for myself. I wrote *Pauline Watson* where it asked for my name and then stopped.

'I knew Katarina Bartek,' I said, without emotion.

'Really? Terrible business,' she said tutting.

'Her husband was here, wasn't he?'

'It was all very unfortunate. Poor grief-stricken woman insisted on saying one final farewell to him, but we hadn't got him into the chapel of rest at that stage, he was still in the mortuary – he wasn't ready.'

'Ah…'

'I didn't know her well, but she could be a pretty forceful woman, I understand,' I said, the pen still poised in the air.

'Too right. She barged in, I'm afraid. Very upset. Not sure she really knew what she was doing. We told her she'd have to come back and see him when he was ready.'

'You saw her leave?'

'Yes, it was just before we were closing.' She stopped and put her hand over her mouth. 'Then we heard the terrible news. Both of them dead now. Mr and Mrs. So extraordinary.'

I put down the pen.

'Listen, I'm very sorry, but I'm not feeling too well. Can I come back and finish this later?' I staggered to my feet and half doubled-over, made a dash for the door and ran out into the street. The bell reverberated after me as if to denounce my wrongdoing to the world.

Chapter 35

I flung my arms around Aiden's neck the moment he was helped on to the boat. He let me hold him; his body limp and bony. I was practically keeping him upright.

Two officers were with him, the more senior one indicating we should move inside. I dropped my arms, feeling unprofessional after my heartfelt welcome, then swiftly convinced myself it was the only decent, human thing to do after the ordeal he'd been through.

'I'm so sorry,' I said to Aiden. 'I couldn't stop them taking you away. Are you okay?'

He didn't need words to tell me that the answer was a resounding *no*. He looked shaken and terrified, just like the day I'd first met him. His body constantly trembling, his limbs jerking in spasms as he tried to stay on his feet. His pupils were too big and roved everywhere, but focused on nothing.

I poured him a glass of water and ushered him to a seat in the saloon, as if I was the one who owned the boat and he'd never been here before.

'I'm staying with you, okay?' I told him. 'I'm not going anywhere.'

The officers followed.

The younger one stood only a foot away from Aiden with his back to him, as though he wasn't even in the room. 'He's lost the plot, this one. Sure you can handle him?'

I raised my hand to swat away the ignorant comment.

In contrast, the older officer walked over to Aiden and raised his voice. He used simple words and broke each one down into punchy syllables as if Aiden was not only deaf, but also intellectually disabled.

'You're not to leave the boat, un-der-stand?' he said. My cheeks were on fire.

I rounded on them both. '*That* was all Aiden wanted, all along!' I exploded. 'And for your information, Aiden is not deaf, nor does he have any disabilities. He and I both find it insulting and patronising that you're treating him in this way. I will be speaking to senior officers about this.' I took their names, feeling a glimmer of superiority beneath my outrage.

'He's still a suspect,' said the senior one, straightening up, backing off a step. 'We'll need to check on his movements on a regular basis.'

'That won't be a problem,' I said. 'Call before you turn up. Now, I'd like you to leave.'

I caught the young officer giving the other one a look. They clambered out without another word and left us alone.

Aiden sat immobile in front of the television watching nothing but reflections in the blank screen. I made a mint tea and left it beside him. He didn't even blink, so I gave him some space and went into my cabin, leaving the door open so he could come to me if he needed anything.

The stray tooth had been on my mind ever since I'd discovered it. It *had* to be sinister. What acceptable reason could there be for a tooth in a kiln? I'd got half the information I needed from the funeral parlour, but I now needed to use the internet to get the other half.

I pored over my laptop, running key words through the search engine and clicking on various sites. Then I found the answer I was chasing. I was about to call Jeremy, when his number flashed up on my phone.

I burst in first. 'Have you checked the tooth I handed in?' I didn't wait for a response. 'The kiln at CCAP is more than capable of reducing a human body to cinders.'

'What exactly are you talking about?' There was a snide edge to his voice.

'Bisque firing requires 1,600°F, glazing usually around 2,372°F, but a human body needs only 1,000 degrees to burn to–'

'And because you found *one* tooth you think–'

'The missing women, Honoré and Pippa, you need to check.' It was my turn to cut him short. 'The tooth could belong to one of them.'

'No way,' he said. 'That's absolutely impossible.'

'What? How can you be so sure?'

'Because a constable has already taken your tooth along to a local dentist and found out it didn't belong to a human at all, that's why.'

All the air rushed out of my lungs at once. 'Oh. What is it, then?'

'It's part of a manufactured set of dentures. And a simple phone call to the dentists of both Honoré Craig-Doyle and Pippa French confirmed that neither of them had false teeth.' He waited for this sliver of information, flung at me like a lethal spear, to hit the target.

'But, maybe there are more women who've disappeared,' I stuttered. 'Maybe, the tooth is from a woman who hasn't been reported missing yet.'

'We can't carry out investigations on the basis of events that haven't yet taken place,' he said curtly. I could sense him resisting the urge to scoff at me. 'Besides, we've already carried out extensive searches at CCAP.'

I was taken aback. 'You've searched the place?'

Silence.

'*What's* going on?' I exclaimed.

'*Keep away* from that place,' he said, raising his voice.

'My sister works there,' I said smugly.

'You know what I mean. You had no business snooping around the kiln. That's not why you're involved. Your job is to get something out of Aiden, nothing else, understand?'

'Of course,' I said, my jaw rigid.

'*We'll* keep an eye on CCAP,' he said. 'There are all kinds of police operations going on you know nothing about, so *don't interfere*. In the meantime, let us know if Mr Blake comes up with anything.'

'On that subject,' I snapped at him. 'I want to put in a formal complaint about the way Aiden's arrest was handled. I don't know what they did to him after he was carted off, but he's come back looking like he's spent time at Guantanamo Bay.'

'Fine. I'll email you the forms.'

I was waiting for him to put up a fight. 'You're not surprised?'

'I agree, actually. It was handled very badly. I'm sorry.'

I opened my mouth, but nothing came out.

'Let's keep each other posted,' he said before hanging up.

When I crept back into the saloon Aiden was gone. A flutter of panic gripped my chest until a movement caught my eye from the rear of the boat. He was carrying the sand tray towards me. I went over to the sink and filled a kettle as he set the tray down on the table in the galley. I turned and watched as he took the wire bird he'd made a few days ago from one of the tubs and put it in the sand. He drew an oval shape around it and stared at the completed design.

The bird again. Was Aiden trying to communicate an aspect of Kora's killing? Or was he trying to express how he was feeling? That, was, after all, what the sand tray was originally designed for – to help patients express feelings they found too hard to put into words.

'Is this how you're feeling, Aiden?' I said gently. 'Like a caged bird?'

What happened next took me by surprise. Aiden grabbed the tray and with one violent action catapulted it into the air. The sand went all over the table and poured onto the carpet.

I got Aiden's message loud and clear; I'd got it badly wrong.

'I'm sorry,' I said.

I turned to the cupboards to look for a dustpan and brush. He rushed out of the stern door, but within seconds he returned holding a long-armed brush. He huffed and puffed, gathering the grains into one big pile, throwing his hair around, his limbs jerking this way and that, refusing to let me help.

Although breathing heavily and distraught, he didn't retreat to his cabin once he'd finished. Instead, he flung off his trainers and began doing stretching exercises. Fuelled by pent-up rage, he launched into a routine of athletic kicks, springing from one foot to the other, his extended leg reaching high as he kept his balance.

I'd seen a karate DVD in Aiden's rack by the TV, as well as various books around the boat about taekwondo, but didn't know how far his interest lay. Not a beginner, for sure.

After he'd finished, he sat in a yoga lotus position, his spine tall.

I'd been sitting with a book, barely reading a word, keeping out of his way. As he got to his feet, an idea occurred to me; something positive we could share.

'This might be unnecessary, Aiden, but if you ever needed to communicate with me, privately, there's something we could try.'

He drew his chin back gingerly.

'Nothing complicated. Let's say if you needed to get my attention or you had something to communicate, then you could put your hands together in a prayer position, just like you did in the yoga pose.'

He shrugged and gave me a slight nod. Shortly afterwards he padded towards his cabin and quietly shut the door. I went to mine and laid flat out on the bunk.

It was starting to look like four women were in the picture now; two dead and two missing. Kora, Honoré and Pippa appeared to have links to the art world, but Katarina was the odd one out. She worked in a bank. Then again, she *was* linked, because she'd been found at almost the exact same spot as Kora.

Pippa had been dating Aiden and Kora had been wearing one of his scarves. Furthermore, someone matching Aiden's description had been identified at Katarina's murder scene. How could that be? With his long blond hair and balletic frame, Aiden was distinctive – there was no mistaking him. Still – it *can't* have been him. I hadn't been on the boat that entire evening, that's true, but there was no way Aiden could have taken off and made his own way back to Camden. He was – still is – too traumatised to leave the boat.

I was in no doubt, however, that when you added it all up, it didn't look good for him. In one way or another, Aiden had links to three out of the four women. Jeremy had told me Honoré owned an art gallery in Chelsea. The police had been there and shown staff Aiden's picture, but no one had recognised him. Nor was he on Honoré's list of artists or clients. I rolled over onto my stomach. Aiden hadn't reacted when I showed him her photograph, but it didn't mean he didn't know her. I didn't like where my mind was taking me with this. Aiden was entirely innocent. I *knew* that.

I sat up. Did Aiden know Honoré, after all? If that was the case, it really would mean one coincidence too far.

Chapter 36

My phone saved me from further speculation.

'Terry, lovely to hear from you.' I wasn't lying.

'Thought I might risk asking if you might be free to meet up again?'

'That would be great. Not tonight, though. Aiden has just been released from police custody and he's in a bit of a state. I don't want to leave him.' A thought occurred to me. 'As I've got you on the line, I couldn't pick your brains about something, could I?'

'I haven't got long, I'm afraid,' he cautioned.

'Are you up to date with the two recent deaths in Camden; the women on the towpath?'

'Only in general terms,' he said.

'Neither Kora nor Katarina were sexually assaulted, which is uncommon in traditional serial killings, isn't it?'

'Mmm...'

'Both were well-to-do and would be immediately missed and Kora, certainly, wasn't a random choice – she was targeted.'

'That's true. Serial murders usually involve strangers with no relationship between the offender and the victim, but remember, that's a generalisation.'

'These two murders seem totally different, aside from the location.'

'Go on...'

'From a psychological point of view, I get the feeling that Kora's attack was carried out by someone who wanted to put on a show. It was audacious and almost theatrical, like a visual display.'

'I'd agree,' he affirmed.

'Katarina is different. It looks like she was killed out of necessity. No weapon, no set up, just the killer's own hands used to stop her from breathing – perhaps to shut her up.'

'Because the killer was caught off guard and had to act quickly?'

'Exactly – and perhaps he chose the same spot simply because it worked before. He knew the lighting wasn't great, the gates would be locked, there wouldn't be many people about and he knew how to get there.'

'Well,' he pondered, 'you could be right.'

'Everything comes down to motive,' I concluded.

'I can assure you,' he said with conviction, 'the Camden crew are nose to the grindstone on this. They're all racking up overtime.'

I heard a loud rapping on the door of the boat and told him I had to go.

We were being invaded once again. Couldn't Jeremy have warned me? DI Denton invited himself on-board, with Ndibi following on behind. He wore a permanently apologetic expression on his face. It would have been mildly endearing, if I hadn't known it was only skin deep.

'He's asleep,' I protested. 'You're not taking him anywhere.'

'We just want him to look at some pictures,' said Denton, sounding sincere. 'That's all.'

I heard a click and Aiden appeared barefoot and yawning in the saloon. As soon as he saw the officers, he tensed up and backed off.

'We want to show you some photographs, Aiden,' called out Denton. 'We're not taking you anywhere.'

Aiden stared at me as if to get my assurance that they were telling the truth. I couldn't blame him for being jumpy. I didn't trust the officers either.

'No photos of any crime scenes,' I hissed.

'Nothing gruesome, I promise,' said Denton.

'You'll need to show them to me, first,' I insisted, raising my voice so Aiden could hear.

'Absolutely.' Denton's tone was strangely acquiescent.

Aiden disappeared for a while, then joined us in the galley, wearing a long baggy cardigan even though the thermometer by the window read twenty-eight degrees.

DI Denton invited him to sit in front of the series of photographs laid out on the table. They were headshots of tutors at CCAP; Kurtis Mills, Rachel Peel, Monica Tyler, Mark Ellerton and several others I hadn't yet met.

I spoke first. 'Aiden, if the pictures disturb you or these officers touch you, I'll be straight on the phone to senior officers.'

Denton and Ndibi exchanged a glance. I had a feeling that since their last visit, there had been a long-overdue dressing down about Aiden's ham-fisted arrest.

'We just want to know if you recognise anyone,' explained the DI. 'Just point to any you recognise.'

Aiden didn't move.

'How about this man?' It was Simon Schiffer. Aiden didn't react.

'How about these?' It was Sue Reed, the cleaner, and Lou Tennison, the caretaker on duty the night Kora was killed. I'd seen all these pictures before from previous visits to the police station. A picture of Sponge, Kora's partner followed, then Murray Kent.

'Didn't you show him these photos when you took him away, before?' I asked.

'Yes, but we're hoping he might be in a more receptive mood this time.'

'What about this one?' It was an image of Henry Dodd from the funeral home.

Aiden lowered his head and turned away.

'Does that mean something?' Denton said, addressing me.

'I've no idea. It might mean Aiden has closed down and is unable to help you.' Aiden curled into a ball and hid his head under his arms. 'Because of what you've put him through, you won't know whether he's reacting because he recognises someone or because he's upset about this whole procedure.'

Denton had walked into his very own catch-22. 'Perhaps you can get some sense out of him,' he said. He got to his feet, leaving the pictures behind to see if I could do any better.

'Aiden is making perfect sense,' I insisted, herding them towards the door. 'He's telling you he can't cope with this, not after his recent ordeal in your cell. I thought that would have been obvious to anyone.'

Aiden and I shared a silent supper together. We'd had a delivery of fresh rocket, tomatoes and hummus earlier in the day, so salad was the obvious choice. The boat was so quiet that when I crunched a crispbread it seemed to fill the entire space around me with a sound resembling a threshing machine.

Beside our plates, several pages were scattered on the table. Drawings. It was the same design on each page. Variations on a theme of a bird inside an oval frame. I knew, therapeutically, that repetition was important. Aiden was trying to get something right, he was bugged by this image and was trying to get it clear in his memory. I took a quick glance at them without showing an obvious interest. I didn't want to push him, he'd had quite enough of questioning and probing for the time being.

At bedtime, I poured us each a glass of water and checked the doors were locked. When I turned round I found him standing right behind me. He placed his hand on my shoulder, offered a little squeeze. It was a simple and heart-breaking gesture. I mouthed a silent *thank you* and he padded away.

I went to my cabin to read more of the book on modern art I'd started. I left my phone on the bedside cabinet, then realised there was a text waiting for me. It was from Terry, inviting me for lunch the next day. I texted back to say I could make it.

I began a chapter on how surrealism shifted towards abstract expressionism, but I couldn't concentrate. I closed the book and sighed. Too many uncertainties were cluttering up my head. I had a niggling feeling that I was missing something. It wasn't only Aiden's bird image I couldn't grasp; there was something else hovering around the fringes of my comprehension. I just couldn't make out what it was.

Chapter 37

Aiden was looking calmer the next morning; his face softer with warmer tones than the day before. He gave a slight nod and poured me an orange juice. It was stuffy on the boat, early sun had already strewn shards of sunlight over the rugs and chair arms. I thought he was going to head for the roof, but he went straight to the sand tray.

He worked quickly, scooping the sand aside to create a bare strip and standing a model of a boat in the middle to indicate it was a stretch of water. He drew a line alongside the length of the river and stood sections of a fence parallel to it, from a model horse paddock. He added a little toy bicycle on its side. I didn't dare move, swallowing hard. It was a replica of the crime scene.

He took one of his model birds, wrapped around with wire to create the oval shape and stood it the other side of the fence. At that point, he appeared to get stuck. He couldn't bring himself to put in a figure to depict Kora, nor the tripwire, nor himself. More to the point, neither could he portray the attacker.

He stood up and looked at it from different positions. He hovered over the plastic tubs, but didn't pluck out any more items. He kept smashing one fist into the other hand, frustrated, at an impasse.

I decided to get involved. To take a risk.

'Your boat?' I said, pointing. 'And Kora's bike?'

He bit his lip.

'The bird is… behind the fence… in the car park.' My eyes were glued to his face, looking for any twitch, flinch, any sign at all.

He kept staring at the scene, his expression unchanged. I should carry on.

215

'The bird is… made of wire – and wire was the… the way Kora was hurt… is that significant?' I hoped desperately that I wasn't getting it all wrong.

He shut his eyes, flexed both hands, looking like he was about to step off a building.

'The bird is… connected to the assailant, is that it?'

Air rushed in and out through his flared nostrils. He banged his palms against his thighs and a tear bubbled at the corner of his eye. I reached over and squeezed his shoulder.

'You're doing really well, Aiden.' He opened his eyes and dropped his head, sinking into the seat as if he'd let me down. 'Is that it for now?'

To the untrained eye what he'd done might not have seemed of any value, but to me it felt like we'd reached a major milestone. Aiden was able to tolerate a direct reference to the killer. He had been able to replicate the crime scene. He was trying to tell me about something significant, something the other side of the fence, in the car park. But I wasn't getting it.

I forced myself to keep quiet. To stay calm and not pressurise him. It was *my* fault. I just wasn't grasping it. A bird in an oval, connected to the killer. It wasn't lighting up any circuits inside my brain.

I tapped on Natalie and Didier's boat a couple of hours later. It was one of those dry, dusty days when heat barges through every nook and cranny on your body. It sent droplets down my back, oozed between my bare toes, and kept forcing my sunglasses down the bridge of my nose.

There was a clunk and click, then Natalie opened up, wearing only a bikini top and denim shorts frayed at the edges. Her legs were tanned and shapely, revealing the curves of different muscle groups with every tiny movement she made. Dancer's legs.

'Sorry to bother you,' I said. A radio was blaring and Didier was singing along in a gravelly voice. 'I need to go out over lunch – any chance you could keep an eye on Aiden?'

'No problem,' she said with a sympathetic smile.

Lunch with Terry came as a welcome break. More than that – it felt like a lifeline. We'd arranged to meet outside the police station in Camden and as soon as I saw his smooth, boyish face I felt uplifted and liberated. I felt like I'd made an escape; like a third-former who'd managed to bunk off school for an hour.

'What do you fancy eating?' he asked, after an awkward hug that was too prolonged for friends, too clumsy for lovers.

In line with the spirit of truancy I suggested burger and chips, but in a smart pub, not a high street café. We found a place on a corner, five minutes away, but it was packed with family bookings. A note on the bar stated there was a forty minute wait for food. He pulled me out of the queue.

'I haven't got time,' he said. 'Sorry.' Terry was working even though it was Sunday.

'There's The George,' he pointed down the next side road, then came to a halt, 'but that's always busy.'

'How about the café at CCAP?' I suggested.

'I'd forgotten that place had a café.'

'Let's hope everyone else has too. We might get a seat.'

As soon as I mentioned CCAP, I realised our get-together wasn't going to be about a cosy relaxing lunch any more. It was going to be about getting more information. After all, why take time off, when I could be working? Story of my life.

Just like the art studio, the cafe was bright and airy and bubbling with chatter when we arrived. We clambered over two kids' buggies and a suitcase before gathering speed to skirt the children's play area in order to grab the only free table. Terry sat down, then stood up again, removing the bundle of keys from his pocket and dropping them on the table.

'Kora waited on tables here,' I said, keeping my voice down.

He gave me a strained look that said we shouldn't be discussing it. My line of thought carried on regardless, speculating on whether that's how Kora met Murray Kent, although according to the police none of the regulars had recognised him.

Our order for burger and chips came surprisingly quickly – bun a little soggy, chips spongy rather than crisp – but it filled a gap.

'I need to get back into exercise,' I told him as I held up a fat chip. 'I used to do a spinning class, but I missed a few sessions and got out of the habit.'

'Didn't you used to cycle everywhere?'

I nodded. 'I like cycling, but it's so crazy in London; it's more like an assault course than simply getting from A to B and certainly not relaxing.' I sat back. As I spoke I watched his eyes. They were always on mine, not drifting or distracted, but alert and intense, like he was listening with them, as well as his ears.

'What's your favourite way to switch off?'

'Riding through Richmond Park is good,' I replied. 'Walking along the Thames, films, theatre. Lunch with good friends...'

He gave me a bashful smile, scratching his nose in a little nervous tic.

Our conversation rolled along with ease. Light filled up spaces inside me that had been dark for a long time and for a short while I forgot the unsolved mass of tangles waiting for me.

'I'm trying mindfulness,' he said, 'but I'm not very good at it.'

'It can make you realise just how cluttered your brain is,' I said. 'I used to meditate, but I've stopped doing that, as well.'

'You're not scoring very well on self-care, Dr Willerby,' he said, with mock reprimand in his voice.

I smiled. 'I'm not scoring terribly well in many areas in my life at the moment,' I said, with a sigh.

'When was the last time you spent time away from London?' he asked.

'Oh, heck, it must be ages.' I gave it some thought. 'Probably my auntie's funeral in January.'

'That's not very impressive, either,' he said. He'd barely touched his burger, had fallen into a habit of picking it up and then putting it back down on the plate. I could sense he had something to say to me, something he was finding hard to broach.

'How about we go to Windsor one day for a picnic,' he said eventually. 'Or St Albans – that's not far on the train.'

Oh... a proper date!

'I'd really like that,' I said, flashing a big smile.

His face lit up before he glanced at his watch and moaned. 'Ugh – sorry, got to get back.' He reached out for my hand and raised it to his lips, then let it go when he saw the bemused look on my face.

'I hadn't realised we'd just had lunch in the court of Louis the fourteenth!' I said, laughing. 'Well, *I* had lunch, you barely touched yours.'

'Sorry,' he said again. 'I seem to be all fingers and thumbs, when I'm with—' He stopped and scratched his nose.

I caught hold of his hand again and squeezed it. 'Don't apologise. I'm only teasing you. This has been lovely.'

His lips quivered into a triumphant grin and he bent down for his briefcase. I noticed his keys had got tucked under his napkin.

'Don't forget these,' I said. He pulled a face at his absent-mindedness and scooped them up.

As I watched his hand close around them, I sucked in a breath that stuck in my throat.

A piece in this insane puzzle had just clicked into place.

Chapter 38

As soon as Terry left the café I typed two words into the search bar of my phone, then selected the *image* option and waited.

When Terry had picked up his keys from the table, it was the logo on his fob that sent bells ringing in my head. I could now see a full range of designs for vehicle logos in the UK; the familiar four rings of Audi, the chevrons of Citroen, the Vauxhall griffin. I scrolled down until I came to the one I was looking for. The shape Aiden had been showing me, time after time; a silver V shape, like a bird inside an oval. The Mazda logo. Is this what Aiden meant?

I needed to use the bathroom, so followed the signs, my sandals slapping my heels as I walked, sending the sound out along the empty corridor like the loud clicking of a clock. On the way back, a door to one of the studios was open and I could make out Miranda's voice. If she knew I'd been here without saying hello she was bound to read something into it, so I took a couple of steps inside.

She had her back to the door and was holding a sketch pad up to the light at the window. I heard another voice and thought there must be someone else out of sight, until I spotted Miranda's mobile on the table beside her and realised she was on speakerphone.

'I know. You must miss her terribly,' she said, not having heard me come in. 'I think the first birthday and first Christmas after someone dies are the worst.'

She hoisted herself up onto the edge of the table and rested her feet on a wooden chair, adding touches to her drawing with a pastel crayon. It was a private conversation. I should have walked away.

'…scatter the ashes,' the disembodied voice said, 'we still haven't done it.'

'Did she have a special place? You could always bury them in a box if–'

It was Kurtis Mills, presumably talking about his sister. His reply was so heavily dowsed in his lilting Scottish accent that I couldn't make out what he said.

'It's not up to them, though, is it? *You* were the closest one to her, so you should make the decision.'

Miranda dropped her crayon on the floor at that point and as I strained to catch what followed, all I could hear was the scrape of the chair as she bent down to retrieve it.

'…so upsetting… even now… find myself crying…' His words tailed off.

'Yeah, you must feel like you'll never get over it.'

He muttered something.

'Sure, listen, I should go,' she said, abruptly putting down the pad. 'I've got a class in a minute…'

I felt like a rabbit caught in headlights. She was going to turn round any second to catch me standing there, eavesdropping on her conversation. I took the longest stride backwards that I dared, placing my foot down carefully so as not to make a sound. Then another. Somehow, I got to the corridor and out of sight before she turned. I bolted for the exit.

Aiden was sitting cross-legged beside Natalie in the saloon when I came on-board. She had been knitting, but the needles lay abandoned by her side and she was passing a looped configuration of wool over to Aiden's outstretched hands. They were playing cat's cradle. I watched them twist the shapes back and forth. Then Natalie groaned as she wound the pattern the wrong way and the shape unravelled.

'I loved that at school,' I said.

She stood up on hearing me approach.

'Could I have just a moment with Aiden?' I said to her. 'Then I'm probably going to have to go out again. Sorry.'

'It's fine,' she said. 'I'm not rehearsing today. I might see if Aiden wants to sunbathe on the roof, later.' She disappeared and I took a seat beside him. His face seemed more alive than before, his eyes held more light in them.

I showed Aiden a blow-up photograph of the silver logo on my phone.

'Is this what you meant by the shape you made in wire, Aiden?' He nodded.

'It belongs to a car, is that right? The logo on the front?' Again, a nod.

'So, this was the car you saw in the car park when Kora was… hurt – a Mazda.'

He stood up and deliberately put his hands together – into the prayer position we'd agreed on if he needed to tell me something – and gave one final nod.

As soon as I was on the train back to Camden I put a call through to Jeremy.

'A breakthrough?' he queried.

'Definitely. Aiden has revealed something – I'm on my way.'

By the time I'd hurried around to the police station on Stanhope Street, an ad hoc meeting had been set up. Once they were all seated – Jeremy, Karen and Joanne – I broke the news. A ripple of approval filled the room.

'So we're looking for a Mazda,' said the DI. 'We'll need to check our witness statements from CCAP – see if we get a match with any regular cars there.' He scribbled in his notebook. 'Let's find out if this rings any bells for the cleaner or caretaker…'

'Mr Blake didn't give you the registration number by any chance, did he?' asked Karen dryly.

I smiled, refusing to let her spoil my moment of glory. Jeremy began tapping away on his tablet.

'Is this the logo?' he spun the screen round to show me.

'Yeah, that's it.'

'Means we're looking for a Mazda after 1997; that's when this logo first came into use.'

'He didn't hint at the colour of the car at all?' said Joanne hesitantly. 'Why didn't he draw the car?'

I tried to explain. 'Patients in his state can often only tolerate small segments of memory. They choose the parts they can cope with. I imagine Aiden can't bring himself to draw the car yet. That's why he's focused on one tiny remembered detail. It feels safer that way.'

'Perhaps you can get him to draw the logo using coloured crayons…' It was Karen being facetious again, but in fact, she wasn't so wide of the mark.

'Yes, I could try something with colours,' I said. I pressed my hands together into a steeple. 'It does lead me to an issue that isn't quite so helpful.'

Jeremy stretched himself out, ankles crossed under the table, arms behind his head. I noticed Karen watching him.

'I hate to say this,' I said, 'but what if Aiden didn't see the attacker's face. Maybe he was wearing a stocking, a mask, a hood… I don't know.'

Jeremy filled in the blanks. 'You mean we might wait and wait and then in the end, all Mr Blake draws is a run-of-the-mill and entirely unremarkable *dark coat*, because that's all he saw?'

The energy in the room dissipated in an instant.

'It's possible,' I told them, with gritted teeth.

Jeremy shrugged and got up listlessly. 'Thanks, anyway, Dr Willerby.'

'Yeah, thanks,' mumbled the others, as they disbanded.

Joanne was the only one left in the room with me. She was rocking the table and tutting.

'The piece of cardboard has come adrift,' she said, squatting down in an attempt to refit the wedge that was keeping the table steady. She straightened up with a groan. 'Take no notice of Karen, by the way.' She let the enigmatic statement hang for a second, then her voice dropped to a whisper. 'She had a one-night stand with DI Fenway a few months ago… off the record and all that. He says it was a big mistake, but she's still keen, apparently.' Her eyes fixed on mine. 'She might be a tad concerned that you are straying into her territory.'

'Ah,' I said. That would certainly explain why she'd been sniffy with me.

'Are you interested?' she added, pushing her chair back into place.

'Fenway? Me? Absolutely not,' I said, laughing loudly at the suggestion. 'Who or what has made any of you think I might be?'

'Me thinks she protesteth too much…' she muttered, collecting her papers.

'No, seriously,' I said. 'I'm not the least bit interested. Anyway, I'm seeing someone.' The assured statement came from nowhere, taking even me by surprise. My mind flashed to a picture of Terry in my mind's eye and I realised that my words didn't feel out of place.

'Oh. Good on you.' She tested the table again. Solid as a rock. 'Well, I think we're done here.'

I turned in early that evening. Soon after, I heard Aiden take a late shower. I was too tired to read; my limbs felt like they were filled with concrete, so I settled down, hoping to slip away into sleep without any fuss. After a few minutes, however, plans for tomorrow started niggling away inside my head. I had to find a way to help Aiden fit together the logo on the Mazda with the car itself. What was the colour? Was it four doors? Five doors? Could he recall any part of the number plate? I needed more details.

I threw myself over on to the other shoulder and my brain began leaping first this way, then that. I remembered I'd kissed Terry once at a party at university. I was trying to recall what it was like, but my memory-bank wouldn't reach that far back. I tried to imagine it now; how he'd tilt his head slightly, soften his silver-blue eyes, his lips meeting mine, his tongue… I drew my knees up to my chest and broke the spell. What was I doing indulging in daydreams? I had far more important matters to be working on.

My thoughts went AWOL for a while, then latched onto Miranda and the snippets of conversation I'd overheard recently after her dinner party and at CCAP. She seemed to be close to Kurtis, comfortable sharing emotional issues with him. I tried to fathom what it was I 'didn't know about' – a revelation which would come as a 'shock'. Had she done something rash that she couldn't bring herself to tell me about? Should I be worried? Was it connected to Aiden or the murders? Surely, if she knew something important she would have told me.

I stretched out and realised I was too hot, so much so that my sheets were getting damp. Not a normal summer night's response to the humidity, but a savage sweat. Before long, I was overwhelmed with shivering, a burning tongue, sandpaper throat. It slowly dawned on me that I had a fever. I reached out for my glass of water and knocked it off the bedside cabinet. My hands were shaking, my skin freezing on the outside, on fire inside. I stared into the flickering shadows around me and felt giddy; my eyelids drooping one moment, fluttering the next. Then I saw it. A shadow outside my window.

I stumbled out of bed and holding on to the sideboard, leant over and slowly lifted the edge of the curtain.

There it was again, sharply outlined against the moonlit sky. Someone in black. Poking around. Examining the boat.

Hang on a minute… is it Aiden? Why is he outside, I thought he'd gone to bed? Why is he wearing a long cape? Is he trying to frighten me? A face came right up to my window and peered inside, strands of blonde hair sticking out of the hood. I was crouching in the corner, my head down, my eyes shut, praying I was out of sight. *What's he doing? Am I going mad?*

I dared to look up and saw the figure retreat. Layers of black took his place. I threw myself across the mattress for my phone.

I couldn't find it. My shudder turned into a sob and I made myself sit up.

My phone buzzed amidst the confusion. I forced myself to stay still and listen to the source of the sound, then tumbled to the floor and groped under the bed, following the vibrations. It was Karen Foxton.

'Just thought you should know, we've come across a—'

'Help…' I whimpered, only the sound didn't come out.

'…property in Chelsea – a flat – owned by Aiden Blake. The boat isn't his only home. The flat is registered under O'Leary, his mother's name.'

I made a wordless sound that she must have taken to be a sign that I'd understood.

'We're applying for a search warrant. We strongly advise you to leave the boat, Dr Willerby, for your own safety…'

I tried to call out, but nothing happened. Karen said something I didn't quite grasp, then she'd gone.

The next thing I knew, Aiden was standing over me. I bristled with an unexpected quiver of panic. I thought he was going to say something, then he turned on his heels.

My mind raced. He was going to hurt me and there was nothing I could do about it. I was going to have to let him claim me – like Kora, like Katarina…

Chapter 39

When I awoke, I had a headache commensurate with going three rounds in the ring with an unforgiving prize fighter. To add to that, my body felt like it had been used as a doormat by a rhinoceros.

The first thing I recalled was Aiden pacing back into my cabin late last night with a cold wet flannel and two headache tablets. He'd straightened my damp sheets and fluffed up my pillows, before softly pulling the door behind him to let me sleep. In short, he'd been my guardian angel. As hours passed he brought me hot drinks, cold drinks, hot soup. He brought in a radio, his DVD player and later set up a small television which must have come from his own cabin.

My awareness came and went, with patches of fractured sleep interspersed between fragments of consciousness. I remember Aiden sitting beside me, keeping watch over me. At one point I thought I felt his lips brush my forehead, but I couldn't be sure I wasn't dreaming.

I didn't know how long he stayed each time. It occurred to me that I'd rarely, if ever, felt so utterly cared for. Growing up, Miranda used up all the attention in the family. Besides, my mother hated any form of illness; it was deeply inconvenient and she did her utmost to pretend it wasn't happening. In contrast, my father used to get himself into a frantic faff; disturbing me in my sick bed to take my temperature just when I'd managed to drop off to sleep, insisting I ate eggs – it was always eggs for some reason.

As an adult, I'd learnt to ride through minor ailments and cope on my own. It was pure fortune that I'd never been taken ill with anything serious. It crossed my mind that Aiden might have learnt his bedside manner from looking after his mother; he seemed to have an intuitive feel for it.

Rachel had sent over a handful of photos from the supper we'd had at Miranda's, but I was too dizzy to look at them. By 6pm I felt as if I was breaking through a crust of thick concrete and climbing out onto the surface. My head was throbbing, but clear – my thoughts seemed able to go in a straight line. Then I remembered the call from DI Foxton – it was real; Aiden owned a flat. Big deal. He hadn't ever denied it. Aiden joined me, noticing I was a little better. He lay beside me on the bunk and rested his head against mine. We stayed like that for some time, our breathing synchronised, neither of us in any rush to pull away. A moment that was too sweet to break.

It was my phone – my bloody phone – that ruined the tender aura of human comfort surrounding us. I could have let it ring, but by then the vibrating buzz had already broken the spell.

'It's DI Fenway,' came the clipped voice.

I sniffed and sat up straight. Aiden slipped away.

'It's about Mr Blake's flat in Chelsea. We haven't got sufficient evidence for a search warrant, but we want his permission to take a look. We'll need him to sign something. Can you ask him?'

I called Aiden back and explained. Aiden shrugged as if it was the least of his worries.

'Okay,' I said, 'but only on one condition.'

The DI drew a long patient breath.

'That I'm there too, from the point of entry to the point of exit, to check that nothing gets damaged and his home is treated with respect.'

'Fine. If that's how he wants to play it.'

I smiled up at Aiden. 'It's how *I* want to play it.'

'Karen said she phoned you earlier and you sounded… a bit out of it.' I could hear muffled footsteps in the background.

'You could say that. I've had some kind of twenty-four-hour flu thing.'

I hesitated, uncertain about whether to tell him I'd seen an intruder outside the boat last night. What exactly *had* I seen? I was still confused by it. Why was it *Aiden's* face I recalled every time I thought about the hooded figure?

'I'll be there tomorrow,' I said, aware I was keeping him waiting, 'no matter what.'

He gave me the details.

As soon as I turned the corner into Radcliffe Square, I could tell which house it was. The press were hovering around the front steps like kids outside an ice-cream van. They must have had a tip-off that the police would be here.

I strode onwards, feeling a million times better than yesterday morning, but still not a hundred percent. I'd barely slept a wink, not due to the fever this time, but because I couldn't switch off all the fretful questions that were burning holes inside my brain. Nevertheless, if anyone stepped over the line inside Aiden's home I'd be onto them in a flash. I was in no state to take any nonsense.

Jeremy climbed out of a patrol car and came to greet me.

'Teeming with vultures,' he said apologetically. 'Let's get this over and done with. Just say *no comment* if anyone asks you anything, okay?'

'I know.' I dangled the keys Aiden had given me in front of him and he took them before we ploughed into the mob. Jeremy got ahead of me straight away and I felt the crowd close around me like the jaws of a clam. There were too many legs in the way – tripods and elbows compounding the problem. It was like the first day of a Harrods' sale, only without the handbags.

'Is Mr Blake your serial killer, sir?' barked a voice, behind a microphone thrust into Jeremy's face. He pressed on and I ducked, narrowly missing losing a tooth.

'Is Blake the towpath murderer?' came another. He was an overweight guy, trying to manage a television camera on his shoulder as well as a furry microphone. His zoom lens nearly took my ear off.

The DI reached the top step and turned round. He straightened his tie and in a crisp, even voice called out, 'Nothing now, ladies and gentlemen, we're pursuing lines of enquiry and will keep you posted about any forthcoming press conferences.'

I found myself shoving with my fists, arms and knees, keeping my head down as Jeremy slid the key into the lock.

'Are you expecting to find more bodies at this address?' another voice persisted. 'Sources have indicated there are two missing women who are connected – are you expecting to find them here, sir?'

'Sir, why haven't–?'

'How long–?'

'Are the missing–?'

I slammed the door. Finally we were inside, squashed into the tiny entrance where there was space for only a mat and an umbrella stand.

'Did you bring the paperwork?' Jeremy asked, as he turned to face me. There was a line of sweat coating his upper lip. I pulled the emailed papers Aiden had signed out of my bag.

'Good,' he said. 'We need to stay here, until we can get kitted out.'

I nodded and made a move to go into the hall, but he grabbed my arm. 'No, I meant *here*, inside this tiny porch.'

We stayed where we were until the inner door opened and someone handed us the SOCO accoutrements we had to wear to prevent contamination; a white suit, rubber gloves, overshoes, face mask, the shower cap affair. As the other officers waited inside, we shuffled into our outfits in the confined space. I turned at an angle so we weren't blowing air into each other's faces and Jeremy sighed and looked up and down in the way people do when they're too close in a lift.

'I thought we'd be able to change in the front garden,' he said. 'Impossible with that mob outside.'

Finally, we shuffled into the lounge area. It was stifling in our suits and I almost keeled over. I narrowly avoided grasping

Jeremy's arm, making a grab for the edge of the sofa, in the nick of time.

That innocent act earned me a glowering stare from one of the forensic team. 'Don't *touch* anything,' she hissed.

'Sorry…'

There was no doubt about who owned the flat. Aiden's stamp was all over it. In fact, it was a more spacious version of his boat; luxurious, clean-cut and stylish at every turn. His distinctive pictures hung on the walls, photographs mostly, of snow, ivory piano keys, Greek columns, rice, radiators – all in shades of his trademark white.

Along the wall in the lounge was a long cabinet displaying a selection of textiles under glass, again mostly in white with touches of silver. Scarves, hats, gloves, ties, purses; each with a twist in the design to make them unique and striking in some way, but always elegant. Each accessory was designed to be worn to enhance; there was nothing garish or outlandish for the sake of it. I was itching to open the lid to touch the cool soft silks and run my fingers over the delicate silver adornments, but knew I had to keep my hands to myself.

I spent the first few minutes looking around in awe before I remembered what the police were there for. Then I clicked into psychologist mode. What could this space tell me about Aiden? He was proud of his achievements, that was obvious, and he had a deep attachment to white; the colour of beginnings, of beauty, purity, good taste and simplicity.

Skin deep, Aiden, himself, was certainly beautiful with humility and integrity, but what had I not yet seen about him? Carl Jung talked about us all having a shadow side; an aspect of ourselves that we keep hidden, traits we deny or are ashamed of. What was lurking in Aiden's shadow side? Was his moral compass as pure as his art work? Was he tainted with unstable and aggressive streaks like his mother?

The forms Aiden had signed stated that he agreed to fingerprints being taken from any surface in the property and for a thorough search to be made of all the rooms, including a cellar or loft if these existed, and any outhouses. Aiden's flat looked like it used to be part of a large Victorian townhouse. It was on the ground floor, with only a small concrete backyard. No attic, but chances were there'd be a cellar.

The scene of crime officers spread out, so it was impossible to keep an eye on all of them at once. The fingerprint guys worked meticulously, brushing powder over spots on chair arms and cupboard doors, lifting the prints with special tape, using ultraviolet torches on light switches and in places where prints would be less visible.

I followed the two officers heading towards a door under the stairs, instead. The skin on the back of my neck prickled as an officer sank a key into the lock. All of a sudden, I wasn't so confident about what they might find down there.

The first officer flicked on the light switch and we clomped in a line down the wooden steps. In the centre of the cellar, a table tennis game was set up, complete with net and bats, and behind it, a wine rack ran along the whole of one wall. Neat piles of household junk; the sort you'd expect to find in any cellar, filled the floor space; crates containing tins of paint, rusty tools, an old kitchen cabinet in the corner, empty glass bottles ready for recycling. There were no manacles and chains hanging from the walls, no chairs with restraints or bodies wrapped in black plastic. No chest freezer. No smell of rotting meat.

One of the officers was picking with a sharp tool at the mortar between the bricks.

'What are you doing?' I asked.

'Checking if any of the brickwork is new. People build hidden rooms or false walls inside their cellars.' He looked up scanning the ceiling, then took out a small item like a torch that threw a thin red beam across the space, checking measurements from one wall to the other. 'I want to see whether the space down here matches the floor design above.' He said something into his radio, then turned back to me. 'We'll get fingerprints taken down here, too. Then we'll move everything, open everything, make sure everything is what it says it is.'

'Looks too tidy down here, to me,' said the other officer.

I shuddered, aware of the damp chill. After my recent bout of flu, I retreated back up to where it was warmer.

In the master bedroom, a female officer was looking under the vast four-poster bed, while another was tapping the walls. Waiting for that telltale hollow sound that signalled a secret hidey-hole, no doubt. She moved on to the wardrobe, to the cases above it. I started to feel stupid standing about; totally redundant. Everything was being examined with precision and care.

By the time we left, it was impossible to tell that anyone had been snooping around.

'Satisfied?' said Jeremy, as we changed out of our white suits and wandered outside. The paparazzi had gone. It was an ordinary summer morning for the Chelsea hoi polloi, on their way to their coffee mornings and business lunches.

'Find anything?' I said, ignoring the arch question.

'Our labs will tell us what we need to know.'

'But nothing obvious?'

'Our killer isn't an "obvious" kind of person,' he said, giving me a direct stare. A patrol car drew up at the front steps for him. Before he got in, I had to hand over a signed form to confirm that the police hadn't wrecked the place. Barely had the sheet of paper left my hand before the door of the car slammed shut and he disappeared.

I headed back to the underground, feeling alone and strangely unnerved.

Chapter 40

Instead of going back to the boat I caught the Tube to Waterloo and from there, the overland train to Clapham Junction. I hadn't been back to my own flat in more than ten days. So long, in fact, that the door jammed as I tried to push it open; a pile of mail wedged underneath. I wrestled with the envelopes and took an armful to the kitchen table. The place felt sterile and unfamiliar, as if it now belonged to someone else.

I separated the bills from the junk mail and put them in my bag, before pulling some fresh clothes out of my wardrobe, although it wasn't my main reason for coming back.

I dragged myself to the bathroom and ran a bath. I'd missed soaking in a tub. More than that, I was constantly on my guard at Limehouse, watching Aiden in case he was able to bring a crucial memory out into the open, checking he was okay. I needed a few moments to myself.

I was starting to miss the hospital, too. My line manager had sent an email letting me know that they'd consulted with the police and I shouldn't worry about how long I was away. But how many more days was this going to go on for?

It was tempting to consider not going back to the marina. I could stay where I was for the next day or so, follow the advice from the senior officers. Steer clear of the boat, the police – everyone – and have some much-needed downtime. Let Natalie and Didier watch over Aiden.

I sank down into the water and let my body flop. Only then did I realise how utterly exhausted I was. Even before recent events, I was long-overdue a proper break and in the end I'd never had one.

Then I thought again of Aiden and my defiance melted. I was the only person he had a connection with, right now. He trusted me and we were making progress. I couldn't leave him. It was as simple as that.

As I rubbed myself down with a towel, a conversation I'd had several days ago with Miranda flashed through my mind. She'd asked me how it felt being around someone who didn't utter a word. But she'd said something else. A twinge of disquiet caught me by surprise – it was the tiniest of pinpricks. It was some other statement Miranda had made about being on the boat with Aiden.

But it wouldn't come to me.

I pulled on fresh jeans and a clean silk top, grabbed my belongings and set off.

I sat down with Aiden to explain where I'd been.

'The police were very careful at your flat,' I assured him. 'It's beautiful, by the way. They didn't mess anything up.' I searched his eyes. 'They didn't find anything, but they took samples away.'

I watched his face carefully as I spoke. The only emotion I could find there was relief.

When I'd come back on the boat he was finishing off a series of yoga exercises. There was a plate drying on the draining board. He must have made himself lunch. A good sign. He seemed refreshed and emotionally stable.

That's when it hit me.

A few days ago, Miranda had asked me about being vegetarian on the boat, about what it was like having to eat halloumi cheese all the time. It was very specific. Halloumi cheese. How did she know that about that? I'd certainly never mentioned it.

I took out my phone and scrolled through my photo gallery until I found a photo of Miranda and I. Like other users at CCAP, Miranda said she'd heard of Aiden, but had claimed she'd never met him. But what if that wasn't the case?

I showed him the screen. 'This is Miranda Willerby, my sister. Do you know her at all?' He considered the picture for several seconds. 'She works at CCAP. Paints oils.'

He shook his head, but a trace of concern shaped his features. 'It's not a problem. She's fine. It doesn't matter.'

Perhaps Miranda had read about Aiden's eating habits from a magazine article, or something.

Aiden yawned and stretched his arms above his head, probably the most relaxed I'd seen him. It certainly seemed worth having another go at identifying the Mazda. I brought Aiden's sketch pad and pastels to the table and made a passable sketch of the car logo. Using a stub from his wooden box, I shaded in the background in a pale grey colour, then showed it to him.

'Is that the colour of the car?'

He shook his head, so I held out the box of colours for him to choose. He ignored the pastels and picked up a stick of charcoal instead. To my astonishment he began sketching the shape of the whole car itself, then filled it in with colour. I sat back, holding my breath until he'd finished.

I was straight on the phone to Jeremy.

'It's pale blue,' I said as soon as he picked up.

'I take it this is Dr Willerby,' he mused.

'Yeah. Sorry.'

'I was about to contact you, as it happens – you first…'

I got up and wandered out of Aiden's earshot. 'The Mazda car in the car park when Kora was attacked was pale blue.'

'Good work. We'll get on to it.'

'I can send over a photo of what Aiden has drawn. It might help you work out the model, it's pretty detailed.'

'Even better, although we're chasing our tails on that front, to be honest.'

'How do you mean?'

'We've re-questioned everyone working at CCAP at the time of Kora's death. No one seems to drive a Mazda or knows anyone who does. Murray Kent drives a Ford van for his flower deliveries, Sponge doesn't have a car, or a licence. Neither does Sue Reed, the cleaner.'

'And you already know Lou doesn't have a licence.'

'Yup. Kurtis Mills goes everywhere on public transport, too. Simon Schiffer drives an Audi.' I pictured the Audi logo. You couldn't mistake four rings for the Mazda insignia. 'No regulars, users or staff at CCAP drive a Mazda,' he continued. 'We've had a watch on CCAP's car park, just in case, but drawn a blank.'

'What about local car hire firms?'

'We've already got a list of locals who hired a Mazda over the period in question. At least now we can narrow it down to pale blue and cut down the leg-work.'

'You said, when I rang, that you were about to contact me,' I prompted.

'Yeah. I'm sending you a photo. During our recent search of Henry Dodd's funeral parlour, we found an earring.' He cleared his throat, pointedly. 'Given you were there yourself not long ago we need to check it isn't yours. Otherwise we'll need to identify it.'

'Okay, email it over and let me look at it.'

I got straight back to him once it pinged into my inbox.

'It's not mine,' I said. I looked at it again. 'It definitely doesn't belong to me, but–'

'But, what?'

'I'm not sure. There's something slightly familiar about it.'

'Okay, so it could be a lead. Let me know straight away if it rings a more definite bell.'

'Is there anything else? Any other leads?' I was hankering after any results from the samples they'd taken from Aiden's flat, but it was probably too soon.

'We've got Henry Dodd in for questioning again. Forensics discovered traces of a substance containing formaldehyde on Katarina's clothes.'

'Formaldehyde?'

'It's used in funeral parlours to make the bodies presentable. We know Katarina was there the afternoon she died. She managed to barge past the reception and ended up in the chapel.' He sniffed. 'I'm sure you'll remember the layout of the building from your little escapade.'

'Mmm…' I wasn't going to apologise for it. 'Surely, if corpses are regularly going in and out, wouldn't that explain the formaldehyde on her clothes?'

'Two things,' he said. 'No one can account for the *large amount* of the substance on her clothing, especially around the collar.'

'And she was strangled…'

'Exactly. A trace of it here and there from touching a door handle would be understandable, but not around her neck – and she didn't even get as far as seeing her husband's body.'

'And the second thing?'

'It isn't formaldehyde, itself. It's a substance *containing* it. Not pure embalming liquid. Something else.'

'Do you know what car Dodd drives?'

'A red Volkswagen.'

'The killer could have borrowed a friend's car,' I added unhelpfully. We left our conversation there.

Buoyed that Aiden had provided the police with at least one small piece of valuable information I decided to call Miranda.

'Are you still on that bloody boat?' she chided.

'I'm fine,' I said. 'There's nothing to worry about.' Despite the admonishment, I was touched she bothered to have me in her thoughts.

I'd meant to see how she was doing, but found myself asking a different question instead. 'Do you remember seeing a pale-blue Mazda, five-door, at the Art project any time?'

'The police have already asked me about a Mazda.' She stopped to think. 'Pale blue? It doesn't ring a bell, but I don't tend to notice cars.'

'Ask around and have a think,' I said. 'It could be helpful.'

'Is that the car the killer used?'

It would have been churlish not to answer. After all, the police had already questioned her about it. 'Looks like it was at the scene, in the car park behind the spot on the towpath where Kora was injured. It would explain how the wire was set up – someone could have parked the car and got over the fence in a matter of seconds.

Then after Kora came off her bike, he could have rushed back for the wire and been back over the fence again before driving off.'

'He must have been pretty fit,' she mused. 'The fences around there are high and made of criss-cross wire with no footholds.' She was right. 'And the second woman?'

'Same stretch of towpath, but further along. The fence was cut that time.'

'Do the police think it was the same guy?'

'It's looking that way, although the second victim doesn't seem to have any connection to the art world, whereas the others all had a link in some way.'

There was a chill in her voice. 'Others?'

'Ah…' I made a sucking sound. Damn! I shouldn't have been telling her anything. It slipped out. 'I'm not meant to tell you this, but there are two women missing who could be connected. You *must* keep it to yourself. One is a journalist who did an interview at CCAP recently and the other is the owner of a gallery in Chelsea.'

'Shit…' I could hear her breathing, hoarse and ragged. 'So, has this bloke on the boat come up with anything useful?'

'Yes, as it happens. That's why I'm asking about the car.'

'Is he going to remember more?'

'Hope so. Things are starting to come out into the open. Fingers crossed.'

'Anything that will help catch the bastard who did that to Kora,' she hissed. 'You're doing great, Sammie.' My nerve ends tingled at the thought that in that brief moment, my sister and I were actually on the same side. 'Keep me posted, okay?'

I said I would, but I was already feeling guilty about flouting professional procedures. I shouldn't have been informing my sister of any inside information, but I couldn't help it. Finding out who'd killed her best friend was paramount.

I ordered a takeaway curry from the local Indian restaurant for supper. Aiden had marked out his favourites on a leaflet and left it on the draining board, so I knew what to choose.

His eyes lit up when the containers arrived. The waft of cumin and garlic claimed the entire boat and I was aware of a gnawing hunger I'd not experienced in days. The aubergine dish was succulent. Aiden quickly fried a sliver of halloumi to go with it, while I stuck with the paneer. It was squeaky and chewy with a tandoori kick. The whole meal was sumptuous and even though I was full, I kept wanting just one more spoonful.

Two hours later, Aiden was doubled over in agony with stomach cramps. It happened so fast. Within minutes he could barely stand and I was forced to call an ambulance. He didn't resist being removed from the boat this time; he was so delirious he had no idea what was happening.

I was allowed to go with him. I think the paramedics assumed he was my son and I didn't bother to put them straight. The first thing they asked when the sirens began to wail and we raced through the London streets was whether Aiden had taken an overdose. Once that was concretely dismissed, they asked more questions.

'You say he paints – has he been working with any unusual substances today: paint, solvents, glue?'

'Not that I know of.'

'Is he epileptic?'

'No.' That certainly wasn't listed on the medical reports I'd seen.

'Has he reacted to nuts or bee stings in the past?'

'You mean anaphylactic shock?' I remembered Aiden happily eating pistachio nuts a while back. 'I don't think so.'

Once we arrived at A&E, Aiden was trundled at speed down the corridor, a red blanket over the trolley and a nurse alongside jogging to keep up, holding an intravenous drip bag above his head. It was looking serious.

I found an alcove with chairs nearby and waited while the evening limped along under the flickering strip lights. In spite of the lingering heat from the day, the radiators were on, creating a cloying heat; the perfect breeding ground for viruses. I couldn't sit still for long and trawled up and down the blue-veined lino squishing down the blisters with the toe of my sandal, watching them pop up again.

I stood around, I sat, I walked aimlessly about. I sat again. I leant my head back against the wall and closed my eyes. Then I sensed someone beside me.

'Mrs Blake?' I opened my eyes. 'I'm Dr Weir.' He sat down alongside me. 'Aiden has been in and out of consciousness, but he's stabilized. What exactly did he have to eat today?'

'We had an Indian takeaway and red wine, at about seven this evening,' I told him. 'Before that...' I tried to think back. It had been a long day and my brain was lagging a few minutes behind. I was in Chelsea that morning, Clapham in the afternoon. 'I've not been with him much,' I said. 'Aiden usually has grapefruit and toast... coffee... for breakfast... and I don't know what he had for lunch.'

Dr Weir was leaning forward, his hands around his knee caps, mulling over what I was saying. '*You* feeling okay?'

I rubbed my stomach as if to check. 'I think so.' My voice was tight and shaky. 'Can I see him?'

He got up wearily. 'Not yet.'

'Is he going to be alright?' My voice broke.

He didn't answer. 'You acted quickly. I think you should go home and we'll call you if there's any change.' He nipped his lips together into a forced smile. 'And don't throw away any of the packaging from the food you both ate – just in case.'

'Really?' I was too befuddled to work out what that might mean.

'By the way,' I said, making myself look up into his eyes. 'I'm not his mother... I'm his therapist.'

'Ah,' he said, patting my knee.

I got to my feet and staggered back to the entrance, feeling like I was ploughing through waist-high water. At the sliding doors I waved over a black cab and climbed inside. Go home, Dr Weir had said. I hesitated when the cab driver craned his neck to hear me state my destination. Home? Nowhere felt like home. The boat had become a dangerous place, my flat was sterile and empty and there was something prickly and weird going on with Miranda. I genuinely felt like an orphan.

'Where are we going, love?' asked the taxi driver again, tapping his fingers on the wheel.

'Limehouse Marina,' I said finally.

Chapter 41

I'd just snuggled under my duvet when there was a hammering at the front door. Two scene of crime officers I recognised from the search of Aiden's flat stood on the bow, Jeremy was behind them. I pulled the belt of my flimsy dressing gown tighter around my waist, stood back. Jeremy spoke first.

'Sorry it's late, but I'm afraid Mr Blake's incident is a police matter.'

'What's happened? Is he worse?'

'In a bad way, but stable,' he said. 'Your quick actions might have saved his life.' He brushed past me and headed for the galley. 'I hope you haven't thrown away any packaging from today's meals.' His tone was overly harsh in my mind. Not for the first time, I was having trouble working out how DI Fenway regarded me. As a necessary evil? A thorn in his side? He'd invited me to call him Jeremy when we first met, but I was more inclined to refer to him now by his official title. 'The doctor thinks he was poisoned,' he said, striding through to the galley. 'Signs of acute toxicity.'

I tried to keep my voice steady. 'I've left everything where it was. Like the hospital asked me to.'

The sink area looked as if it belonged in a squat. I hadn't even washed up our dishes, which sat under abandoned aluminium cartons, stray lids and a torn naan bread. He looked down at his shoe. He'd just crunched half a poppadum into a hundred pieces.

'Great…'

He instructed one officer to empty the bin, the other to start taking samples from the cartons and plates. 'We'll need to see everything Mr Blake ate and drank today.'

I ran through a list of all the likely items I could think of. At least we didn't need to consider anything he might have eaten outside the boat.

'Thank you, *Mrs Blake*.' He punched out the last two words, out of earshot of the others.

'I did tell Dr Weir… eventually.'

He gave me a glare as if to suggest he was within his rights to issue a verbal warning of some kind, but thought better of it.

'I'd get someone in to check the gas installations,' he advised. 'Get a new carbon monoxide monitor, make sure everything is how it should be.'

I felt a chill skim down my spine. He was concerned that something else on the boat had been tampered with.

The officers continued to poke about, then Jeremy came over to join me on the banquette. I pulled my knees into my chest, making sure the dressing gown didn't leave any gaping holes.

'No one has identified the earring, yet,' he said. 'It certainly doesn't belong to Sally, the receptionist at the funeral home. We're doing DNA tests to see if it's a match for Katarina. Also, Henry Dodd appears to have a solid alibi for the nights Kora and Katarina were killed.'

'What about the pale-blue Mazda in the car park?'

'We know that Aiden's sketch is of a five-door model, produced between 2005 and 2010.'

'And…?'

The DI leant forward and rested his elbows on the table. 'Nothing.' He banged his fist in time to his words. 'No one owns one. No one saw one. Zilch.'

'It's not looking good, is it?' I sighed.

'Not great, to be honest.' He sat back, patting his abdomen and yawned. 'The witness who said she saw Mr Blake near Katarina's body is having second thoughts. She thinks she might have got the gender wrong.'

'What?'

'She says it might have been a tall woman with blonde hair she saw in a black hood.'

'Golly. Does that fit? Could the killer have been a woman?'

'It's certainly possible. In both cases, actually. Kora's deathtrap with the tripwire required no specific strength and Katarina's body was pushed through a hole cut in the wire fence, rather than being tipped over the top. We know Katarina was strangled somewhere else and driven to the car park. A strong woman could strangle another of smaller build if she was taken by surprise. Katarina was small, around five feet two. Kora was five feet four, she weighed only 108 pounds.'

'Less than eight stone, that's tiny,' I mused. It was also the same weight as me.

'We're starting to think the witness just saw a late-night stroller with insomnia, not the killer at all.'

'But the figure ran away. Why bolt like that if they had nothing to hide?'

He shrugged and tucked his hands under his knees like a small boy. 'We found tyre prints, by the way, matching the type usually fitted as standard to a Mazda5. In the mud right by the fence. The car was parked so close that someone would only need to drag the dead weight a few feet.'

'What about Simon Schiffer and that tooth I found?'

'That's ongoing,' he said stiffly. 'Keep out of the way, with that.'

I heard a shuffle from the galley and one of the scene of crime officers called Fenway over. They conferred about something. The DI beckoned me over.

'When did you last have a grocery delivery?' he asked.

'This morning.'

'Did you bring it in?'

'Er, no. I was with you in Chelsea when it arrived. Aiden must have brought it in.' The two men exchanged glances.

'Did Blake have this halloumi cheese with the curry?' he said, pointing to the packet the officer was holding with protective gloves.

'Yes, a tiny bit for himself. He knows I don't like it.'

'It looks freshly opened,' he said. 'Was it in the latest delivery?'

'I can check.' I went back to the saloon and opened up the site on Aiden's laptop where we'd requested the last order. 'Here it is. Yes, three packs.'

'Looks like he only took a small amount.'

'There's definitely an overtone of something chemical,' said his colleague, holding up the pouch. 'We'll get it to the lab.'

A sharp pain gripped my throat. Someone had tampered with our food. They'd got in through the locked security gate and had rummaged through our delivery.

'I suggest you clear out all the cupboards, tomorrow, to be on the safe side,' Fenway said. 'Throw everything that's unopened away. We'll take the rest for more tests.'

I nodded.

He moved away to examine the locks on the doors at each end of the boat. 'I'd get these changed, as well,' he warned. 'I've seen too many burglaries where this brand of lock has been picked. Contact the station to get one of our specialists round or ask a locksmith for the best security available.' He sniffed. 'Mr Blake can afford it.'

He examined his cuffs, then glanced down at my dressing gown. 'I wouldn't stay here on your own.'

'I suppose police protection is out of the question?' Fear made my voice sound flimsy.

He let out a staccato laugh. I should have known the answer to that.

'We can take you back to Clapham, if you like.'

'It's okay. I need to sort a few things out and get changed. I'll get a taxi.'

'Suit yourself.'

Chapter 42

I woke at 3am with a cricked neck and pins and needles in my arm. After clearing up the mess once the police had gone, I must have fallen in a heap in the saloon and dropped off. By then I was too groggy to think about ordering a taxi, so I repeated my elaborate tactic of barricading heavy furniture across the main doors and leaving the lights on. Then I slunk to my cabin and bolted the door.

As soon as I heard the nearby fountain bubble into life signalling daybreak, I rang the hospital. Aiden was a lot stronger and the nurse suggested I could pick him up, but not before 4pm, as they needed to run final tests. In the meantime, I requested emergency call-outs from a local electrician and gas engineer, then made a fresh grocery order; basics like bread, cereals, milk, butter and cheese to be delivered the same day. I did as DI Fenway suggested and cleared out the fridge, freezer and all the food cupboards.

After that I sat and waited, turning every creak on the boat into the footstep of an intruder, every tiny shift in the light to the shadow of a prowler on the pontoon.

I stared out of the window at the idyllic scene; the gentle pebble-dash sheen on the water, the glossy white boats with their silver railings catching the sunlight, but I couldn't feel any of it. Our tranquil sanctuary had been violated.

The locksmith came at lunchtime to fit a better system with extra bolts at both ends of the boat, and the electrician and gas engineer turned up and checked everything over. There didn't appear to be any problems, but they replaced a few pieces of cable and threw in a few technical sounding terms to justify the extortionate fee they charged.

I set off to collect Aiden at mid-afternoon. He was able to stand, but couldn't straighten up, shuffling along the corridor like an old man, clutching his stomach. I looped my arm around him, half holding him up as far as the taxi. I handed over a new set of boat keys, told him about the visit from the police and how our cupboards were bare.

Aiden sat hunched over in the cab, his breathing laboured, his skin a dry greyish-yellow like a dead moth.

After we got back, the groceries arrived and I made Aiden some dry toast. He had two bites and had to leave the rest before dragging himself to bed.

There was something I'd been meaning to do ever since yesterday afternoon, but I hadn't had the chance until now. I tapped on Natalie and Didier's door. Didier was doing some research at home and said he'd stay with Aiden.

'I wouldn't leave him like this,' I said, 'but I just need to check on my sister.'

What I really meant was check *something* with my sister.

Miranda took a while to answer the door. I could tell by the way she opened it that she had company. I was angry. I thought I'd made it clear that I wanted to speak to her on her own.

'You're early,' she said accusingly.

Her visitor was out of sight, clinking dishes in the kitchen. Miranda asked if I wanted tea. I accepted and took a seat. I felt like I was in a waiting room anticipating some horrible medical procedure. I heard footsteps before a man came into view. It was Simon Schiffer. His sleeves were rolled up and he was drying his hands on a tea towel.

'Hi, again,' he said, offering me his hand. It wasn't quite dry. 'How are things? Miranda said you needed a chat.'

I was stumped for words. My life was consumed by one of the most complicated and unnerving situations I'd ever come across and he was implying I'd be sharing my inner turmoil while he was around. I was damned if I was going to discuss any of it in his presence.

'Yeah, I'd like to speak to her in private.' I couldn't be bothered to beat about the bush.

As Miranda walked past him, bringing my mug of tea, she gave his sleeve a subtle brush with her little finger. It was easy to miss, but I'm highly attuned to signals such as these. They were seeing each other – and not as tutor and student. I had been trying to figure out why Simon hadn't been at the meal the other day, but now it was obvious. Meetings between the two of them were undoubtedly of a secret one-on-one nature.

A knot tightened in my stomach. How much detail had I inadvertently blurted out to Miranda about the case? Had I mentioned the tooth? How much had Miranda passed on to him? Most of what I'd said wasn't common knowledge and should not have been divulged to anyone, least of all someone who already had a veil of suspicion cast over them. I knew for certain that I'd let it slip that Aiden was starting to piece Kora's murder together in his mind. Had Miranda told Simon? Was it Simon who had poisoned the cheese?

I wanted to ask about the kiln... about how a tooth could possibly have shown up where it did, but I managed to keep my mouth shut, supped my tea instead.

'I'll leave you to it, then,' said Simon. 'I just popped over to see how Miranda was coping... you know, with...' He tailed off. The implication that he had merely 'popped over' was somewhat belied by his retreat up the spiral staircase to fetch his rucksack. One of the drawbacks of having an open-plan living space.

Miranda went to the door to see him out and spent too long for it to be a straightforward goodbye. I wondered how long their relationship had been going on. Surely a fling between Simon and Pippa now seemed less likely.

Miranda came back, her hair ruffled.

'He's nice,' I said innocently. 'You been seeing him long?'

'Oh, no, I'm not... we're not, you know. He's just been very supportive.'

Miranda made a habit of never revealing anything about her love life to me and I imagined, given he was her tutor, that made her more reluctant than normal.

'It's a little bit obvious,' I said.

She scrunched up her nose. 'It's okay, he's not married.' She toyed with the skin on the edge of her thumbnail. 'You mustn't say anything, though.'

'Why would I?'

'It's against the CCAP rules.'

'You're both consenting adults,' I said, knowing full well why such a policy would exist. There were vulnerable individuals at CCAP.

'What did you want to see me about?' she said. 'Has that art student remembered something else about Kora's attack?'

'No, it's not about that.' I finished the tea and put the chipped mug on the floor beside my foot.

'Aiden Blake, the *art student*, how well do you know him?'

'I don't know him at all.'

'Have you met him at the project or at an exhibition, maybe?'

'No. I told you, I don't know him. Never met him.'

I took my phone out and showed her a photo of him from a recent feature on the Chelsea College of Art & Design blog. She shook her head and reached down for my empty mug.

I decided to cut to the chase. 'How did you know Aiden loves halloumi cheese, that he's vegetarian, for that matter?'

I tried to stay focused on her face, to be ready for any sign of discomfort, but she took the mug and turned away. 'I don't know. *You* must have told me.'

I knew I hadn't.

'Listen,' she said, changing the subject in a flash. 'I've made a decision.' She'd been heading for the kitchen, but she turned around, tossing the mug from one hand to the other. 'Now we're not going, I actually think the holiday in Greece was a bad idea.'

'Okay, well, we can think about going somewhere else. Where did–?'

'No. What I mean is, let's not... let's scrap the whole holiday idea, shall we? It might be better if I go away with someone else.'

'Oh, Simon, you mean?'

'Not necessarily.'

'Right. So when did you decide this?'

'Recently, but it was always a bad idea, don't you think?' She huffed with impatience as if we were going over old ground.

'No, not really. I thought it was a *good* idea.' My words were coming out clipped with hurt. 'We've never been away, just the two of us. I thought it would be... fun.'

She laughed.

'I was never allowed to be different growing up, was I?' she said. 'I was never allowed to do things my way or have my own ideas about things. I've always been *watched*.'

I was searching for an explanation in her face, but she was on the move again, heading towards the front door this time, keen to show me out.

'What? I don't understand,' I said. My words broke off, but I stayed where I was.

She put the mug on the ledge by the front door and stabbed her hands into her hips. 'That's the problem.'

'Did you think I suggested going on holiday with you, just so I could keep an eye on you?' Inwardly I cringed. It wasn't that far from the truth. I *had* intended the break as a way of finding out how well she'd been doing after the hit and run.

'I want to branch out on my own and not feel...' She cleared her throat and started again. 'I want to do my own thing a bit more and feel like you trust me.'

'I *do* trust you.'

She made a funny clucking sound with her tongue to indicate she didn't believe me.

'I don't know why you're pushing me away like this,' I said, as tiny shards splintered the back of my eyes. 'It's very... hurtful.'

'I'm sorry. I'm trying to be honest. You always say that's the best way to do things.'

She moved towards the front door, looking purposeful.

'I need to break free, that's all. Anyway, Simon's coming back any minute. I think it might be best if...'

The ensuing silence was hollow and unforgiving. *She doesn't want me in her life!* Our family was damaged enough without this. Now it felt ripped to shreds. I got my things and left without another word.

On the way back to the underground station, I called Terry. His was the only voice I could think of that could possibly make me feel better.

'Miranda hates me,' I said. 'She's basically told me to fuck off out of her life.'

'What? What's happened?'

'Nothing, really. That's why it's so awful. We didn't have a fight or anything. She's got a new boyfriend and she doesn't want to go on holiday with me and she wants me to back off and stop...' My voice cracked. Shapes of the shop fronts were swimming through my tears.

'Oh, Sam, it's not you. Miranda's always been a bit...'

'Messed up?'

'Well, yeah.' He was still at work; I could hear the thrum of activity around him.

I growled into the phone. 'I can't believe it – my own sister. She doesn't want me anywhere near her.'

I'd been holding it together pretty well until that point and then the waters broke. I stepped into an alleyway between shops and blubbed something about love, ending up wailing incoherently.

'Families are the worst, Sam. You're a psychotherapist – you should know that by now.'

I could hear him batting away demands at his end with quiet grunts, but he let me blather on, as I repeated over and over the whole *I can't believe it* thing that people do when they've had a nasty shock.

'You sound like you need a... full debriefing,' he said. 'How about dinner tonight?'

'I'd love to, but I can't leave Aiden. He's just come back from hospital. Someone tried to poison him.' My professional side kicked in at the mention of Aiden's name. I got a grip on the situation and swiftly dried my tears.

'I heard.' There was a lengthy pause. 'In fact, are you sure you should be there with him?'

'I can't leave him.'

'I'm worried about you,' he said. 'There's a maniac out there.'

'I know,' I conceded, 'but it's not Aiden.'

A threat hung over the boat now, like a dense fog. Whoever the killer was, he – or she – was still free, desperate for Aiden not to reveal their identity. Weren't they likely to try again?

'Can I suggest something?' He faltered. 'You can say no.'

'What?'

'I'll come and join you both, just for tonight. I'll sleep in the saloon of course, bring a sleeping bag. I know I've got a gammy leg, but it would make three of us, if anything happened.'

'Terry, I can't ask–'

'You didn't.'

'Are you sure?'

'Absolutely. I'll eat before I get to you so I won't be in the way and I'll need to get away early in the morning. It won't be a particularly sociable event – but it might mean you get some sleep.'

I was hit with a surge of sheer relief. For the last few nights, decent sleep had become a precious gift given only to other people. 'Thank you. That would be brilliant.'

'Anytime.'

Chapter 43

I could tell from the lack of dishes that Aiden hadn't eaten anything, but he looked marginally better. He was drinking a mug of plain hot water, leaning against the kitchen sink in his towelling bathrobe.

I thanked Didier for looking after him and he discreetly disappeared.

'You're still feeling rough, aren't you?' I said to Aiden.

He was struggling to hold his head up, his eyelids puffy, his silky hair hanging in rats' tails over his eyes. He managed a white-lipped smile.

'You must try and eat something,' I said. 'Something really light. A boiled egg? Marmite on toast?' I glanced at the fruit bowl. 'A kiwi?'

He nodded and reached out for it before I could. Seconds later, he'd managed to cut his finger while slicing it. I found the first aid kit again and brought him a plaster.

'No knives for the time being,' I suggested.

He put on his sunglasses, even though I'd drawn the curtains to keep out the late shafts of sunlight, and he sat to eat, labouring over the fruit as though it was a three-course meal. I told him that Terry, a friend who worked in the Met was going to stay the night with us for extra security. I didn't see any reaction, either way.

My phone rang, so I left him stretched out on the banquette.

'We've completely wiped out the forensic budget for this year in order to fast track that sample of halloumi through the labs,' Fenway said, as if I was to blame. I waited. 'It was poisoned with a substance containing formalin. That's a watered-down version of formaldehyde, capable of causing sudden death if consumed. One more slice and Aiden could be dead by now.'

'Bloody hell,' I whispered, walking further away from Aiden's earshot.

'We're treating it as attempted murder.'

'But, formaldehyde? Why couldn't he smell it?'

'It was in an odour-reduced solution – clever. We reckon it was used by someone who knows this substance inside out.'

'Formaldehyde again. That *has* to be significant, doesn't it? You said it was found on Katarina's clothes.'

'We've traced those samples to the same type used in Henry Dodd's mortuary, but it's a common brand. It's used in a number of funeral parlours in London. Also used in certain types of paint.' He cleared his throat. 'This is strictly confidential, by the way – the earring we found at Dodd's – guess who it belongs to?'

I was hardly in the mood for games.

'Kora? Katarina?' I said flatly.

'Pippa French.'

'Pippa?! Jeez, that's a huge breakthrough isn't it? What was *she* doing there?'

'Who knows? The woman you met at *The Bulletin* confirmed it, Naomi Norton. Pippa was wearing the same distinctive earrings in her staff photograph, pinned to their noticeboard.'

Ah – that's why it looked vaguely familiar. I recalled seeing the same headshot.

'Dodd still has two solid alibis for the times of the towpath deaths,' he continued talking. 'He was at his mother's eightieth birthday for the first, and for the second he was caught on CCTV at a late-night supermarket. The evening Pippa French went missing, he wasn't even in the country.'

'Damn…'

'He's been in and out of our interview rooms like a yo-yo – we've just got him back in again. We're waiting for his solicitor. He definitely knows *something*.' I heard a siren wail in the distance.

'I'm only telling you this in case any of Mr Blake's sketches shows a connection.'

'Of course. As far as I know Aiden hasn't touched a sketch pad since he was poisoned.'

Fenway ended the call.

I made a mug of calming chamomile tea for Aiden and as I placed it in front of him he stood up. I waited, expecting him to move past me or reach for something.

'Do you want to show me something? Do you want the sand tray? A sketch pad?' I craned my neck trying to locate them.

He stood there, unmoving, but not at ease. He took another step towards me until his toes touched my slippers. His eyebrows drew together slightly, his eyes questioning and searching. Then, before I knew what was happening, his face drifted towards mine and he was kissing me on the lips. A delicate, testing kiss. I drew back, but my reaction should have been quicker. He was my patient and he was vulnerable; he wasn't thinking straight… and for a snap second, neither was I. Fortunately, I came to my senses.

'Aiden,' I whispered, taking a step back from him. 'We can't… this is…'

He put his hand on his heart and gave me an imploring look.

I needed to be coherent and clear about this. 'Aiden, I'm so sorry, but this can't happen. I am a professional trying to treat you. That's the extent of our relationship. I'm in your personal space on the boat and that is very strange – no doubt for both of us.' I sighed. 'However, our boundaries must be very clear. *That* must never happen again.'

His eyes fell away and he backed down the corridor. The next sound I heard was the faint click of his cabin door.

I sank to the sofa. I should have seen it coming. Pulled away sooner. Even though we'd scarcely touched – it should never have got that far.

I was already in my dressing gown when Terry arrived. I'd removed my make-up and been confronted by plum-coloured shadows hanging under my eyes that took me by surprise. My hair had gone flat and I felt nowhere near my best. He came through with his rolled up sleeping bag and rucksack, looking like a tourist passing through. We were ill at ease with each other, at that awkward stage of a relationship nobody can really define. As a result, I was finding it hard to make eye contact. Finding it hard, in fact, to keep my eyes open. I was exhausted.

'Aiden's already gone to bed,' I whispered. 'Fancy a hot drink?'

He shook his head. 'No, I'm fine.' I was actually glad he refused. Whilst overjoyed that he was there on one level, I was running on empty. The situation was not one in which anything could develop between us, anyway. I was 'on duty', with a patient in the next cabin and Terry was our bodyguard. There was no room for any overtones of romance. Furthermore, I was still reeling from the kiss Aiden had given me. He'd caught me entirely off-guard.

I handed Terry pillows and he rolled out his sleeping bag over a spongy layer of padded seats in the centre of the saloon floor.

He approached me as I was about to say goodnight and brushed a strand of hair out of my eyes.

'You okay?'

'Just tired. Thank you so much for this.'

'Shush.' He put a finger over my lips and let it stay there. I gave his arm a friendly squeeze and he took his finger away. 'See you in the morning,' I said. 'I owe *you* a meal at The Dorchester now.'

He smiled and held the palm of his hand up for a high five.

I woke with a jolt during the night, not sure if the sound I heard was real or had seeped out of a dream. I grabbed my phone so I could call 999 in a hurry, then remembered Terry was in the saloon, keeping guard.

I zombie-walked towards him, yawning.

Terry was curled into a motionless bundle on the floor, his face hidden. A small table lamp had been left on giving the space a dim glow. I watched his shape rise and fall, hoping he wouldn't stir, then tiptoed along the corridor to Aiden's cabin door. It was closed, his light on as usual, given away by the thin slither of brightness underneath. I stood still and listened. Not a sound, other than the familiar gentle knocking of the boat against the pontoon.

When I returned to the galley I noticed that the sand tray on the table had been disturbed. It looked as though Aiden had tried to recreate the crime scene as he had before. Something must have come to him during the night and he'd left it here for me. There was a tiny model bike on its side again, the sand scooped away to show the canal with a boat in it, and one of his wire birds in an oval shape depicting the Mazda insignia stood behind the fence. I got that much. Then things started to get more obscure.

There was a tiny glove, from a set of fashion items for dolls, laid between the boat and the fence. Resting on the glove, almost obliterating it, was a collection of animal's teeth from one of the boxes. They had been carefully positioned, forming an interlocking pattern. I stared at it, had absolutely no idea what it meant. A glove and teeth.

Was this connected in some way with the dentures in the kiln? Was it a link to Simon? Something more symbolic?

Whatever the message, I wasn't getting it.

The towpath, the fence, the wheels of the bicycle began to flood into a blur in front of my eyes. How did the glove fit in? What did the pattern of teeth mean? Had the killer been bitten? What on earth was Aiden getting at?

I was getting nowhere, my eyes finding it hard to fully focus – hardly surprising as it was just gone 4am.

As I crept back to my cabin, I came to the sure-fire conclusion that the killer had to be an attention-seeker. Kora hadn't been attacked in some remote back alley, she'd almost been decapitated in a dramatic fashion right out in the open, as if her death was a performance.

Terry and I had both agreed that Katarina's death seemed different; she'd been strangled, a method without gore or theatrics.

The first was planned, the other was about expedience. While it was understated in comparison to Kora, nevertheless the body had been moved to almost the exact spot on the towpath, sending a message of sheer effrontery to the police. Put together, the deaths were the grotesque work of an exhibitionist – if not one killer, then two who were working closely together.

Beyond that, I had nothing. My brain had come to a standstill.

I awoke to find my phone vibrating under my fingers. I must have been clutching it all night.

It was DI Fenway. 'I thought I'd better check up on you both.' I might have been touched by his concern had I not heard the disdain in his voice. 'How is Aiden after yesterday? Do you have any delayed symptoms?'

'I'm fine,' I said breezily. I wandered towards Aiden's cabin and heard drawers closing, then his en suite shower running. 'Aiden seems to be up and about.'

I walked into the saloon. Terry had gone. He'd returned the cushions to the seat and left the pillows on top. I sat down beside the place where he'd slept.

'For your information, Simon Schiffer has been arrested and charged,' he said.

'Wow!' I was on my feet before I realised he wasn't sharing my euphoria. 'What's wrong?'

'We've had him under surveillance for a while and carried out a raid at CCAP last night. It looks like he's been using the kiln illegally to fire porcelain dentures on the cheap.' 'The tooth…'

'Not only that, in order to keep CCAP financially afloat, he's been involved in selling cheap dental supplies overseas.'

'Seriously?'

The tooth, the kiln – *that's* what it was about?

'He's on bail.'

'You've let him out?'

His response was flat-packed. 'We've got nothing connecting him to either of the murders. This looks completely separate.'

'He knew Kora. He knew Pippa – she interviewed him. He knew the other missing woman, too – Honoré, from the gallery.'

'His alibis stack up – he was in Chichester the night Katarina was killed. He'd just finished giving a lecture in Fulham when Kora was attacked.'

I couldn't believe what I was hearing. 'So, Simon's not even a suspect?'

'Not at the moment. It's a different charge altogether.'

'Making false teeth? Is that it?'

'It's a serious offence.' He muffled a yawn. 'Want some better news?' He sounded more upbeat. 'Looks like the net is closing in around Henry Dodd. After scrutiny, one of his alibis isn't quite so sound as it should be and, apparently, he's been leasing his mortuary out, overnight.'

His words turned my stomach. 'What? Letting other people use his mortuary? Why? Who?'

'That's what we need to know. He says it's a little earner on the side – he gets cash up front and doesn't know any names, but I don't believe a word of it.'

'What on earth is someone using his mortuary for after dark? Why would you regularly need a mortuary, other than to store dead bodies?'

'We don't know yet,' he said with exasperation. 'Apart from Pippa's earring, the place came up clean.' He seemed to have nothing more. 'Any progress your end? Aiden spilling the beans yet?'

'He did leave some kind of message for me during the night, but I don't understand it,' I admitted. 'He's set up a replica of Kora's crime scene with a glove and teeth in a pattern over the top.'

I squeezed my fists tight during the pause that followed, silently beseeching a light to flick on in at least one of our heads.

'Means nothing to me,' he said wearily. 'What do you make of it?'

'No idea.'

I heard him suck air through his teeth. 'Listen – glad you're okay. Got to go.'

I stood over the sand tray scrutinising it again. A glove… with small teeth running over it. Had the killer been wearing gloves with a distinctive design on them? I cursed myself for being so dim. I suddenly thought of Miranda – she and Simon were a secret item. How would she be coping after his impromptu arrest?

I called her mobile, but it was switched off. She might have decided she wanted nothing to do with me, but I still needed to know she was okay. I tried CCAP. Rachel answered, sounding upset.

'Something awful has happened,' she spluttered. 'The police have–'

'Is Miranda there?' I butted in.

'It's Simon… the police have–'

'Arrested him. I know. Is Miranda at CCAP?' I persisted. 'It's Dr Willerby, her sister.'

'No,' she said. 'Actually, I'm trying to reach her. She's not answering her phone. I texted everyone for an emergency meeting this morning and she hasn't shown up. It's not like her.'

'Can you ring me back if she arrives?' I urged.

I made myself sit down and closed my eyes. Everything was one big muddle. Simon Schiffer had been on the police radar for some time. No wonder Fenway didn't want me poking my nose in about the tooth I'd found. They *knew* about that. Simon had committed a crime by using the kiln to produce dentures on the cheap, but there was nothing to link him to either of the deaths. We were back to square one.

Or rather, the landscape had radically shifted. I had to get a grip on what this new information meant in terms of the whole picture, a picture in which my own sister may be playing some unexpected part.

I took slow deep breaths to calm myself down, but my head was buzzing. Bright lights flickered in the black space behind my eyelids.

I had the feeling the answer to everything was right under my nose.

Chapter 44

Aiden emerged from his cabin earlier than usual, looking refreshed with better colour in his cheeks. I pretended not to watch him. I still felt awkward after the kiss. He didn't appear perturbed in the least, but for once I was glad he wasn't speaking – I only wanted to forget it had ever happened.

I stood over the scene he'd made last night in the sand tray. I had so many questions.

'The glove… the teeth,' I said. 'I don't understand. Can you show me more?'

He frowned, pressing his knuckles against his mouth as he stared at the tableau. I had to be careful. I didn't want to push him. At times, he looked deceptively calm and assured, but I had to remember how broken he was inside.

I had an idea. I left him for a second and went to the back of the boat where I'd seen a number of jackets hanging up. I checked the pockets until I came across what I was looking for.

'Did you see someone by the boat wearing gloves that night?' I asked him, placing the pair of gloves next to the tray. 'The person who came to unclip the wire?'

Nothing.

'Did the gloves have a pattern on them? The teeth?' My words fizzled out. I didn't even know the right questions to ask him. I opened out my hands in a gesture of helplessness, inviting him to do something with the gloves to make me understand, but he stared at them as if they were dangerous and began to tremble.

'It's okay,' I said. I led him away from the table, left him sitting on a stool in the sun, outside the front door.

I sat by a window, feeling impotent, waiting for the police to make up their minds about Henry Dodd. Waiting for them to find that vital bit of evidence that would point the finger to whoever the towpath killer was.

As the gentle breeze wafted over my shoulders I went back to the beginning. Using my phone, I skimmed through all the art-related features I could find that were written by Pippa French. Could there be a clue within them we'd all missed? I reread the one with Simon Schiffer at CCAP; but there was nothing unusual about it. No one knew then where most of his funding was coming from.

I read another with the painter Shire McGann. He'd been taken on as a client at the Craig-Doyle Gallery in Chelsea and, as a result, his career had hit the big time. That created a link between Pippa and Honoré Craig-Doyle, so I looked him up, but he was living in Bonn. I glanced through several more features with writers and playwrights, but could find nothing that stood out.

I'd been concentrating on her interviews for *The Bulletin*, but after a few more searches, a new set of features came up written on a freelance basis, for magazines such as *Tatler* and *Vogue*. They were mainly about screen celebrities, but there was one that caught my eye. It referred to an artist whose stick-thin sculpted figures had been criticised by the journalist for being a 'pale shadow' of Giacometti's:

"We're not seeing anything new here," says art critic, Norman Brandt. "I'm not the only connoisseur to describe his work as unimaginative. Perhaps he should stick to his neo-classical garden pieces."

Ouch. The artist in question was Kurtis Mills. When compared with most of Pippa's other interviews, it was harsh. But surely, all artists got bad reviews from time to time. It didn't mean much in itself.

I skimmed through the rest of Pippa's interviews and noticed one name cropping up more than most; Honoré Craig-Doyle. She had taken on a number of up-and-coming artists in the past year and Pippa appeared to think highly of her gallery. They certainly knew each other.

It was time to pay her place a visit.

Before I left, I asked Aiden if I could take some samples of his work with me.

'I'll bring everything back in one piece, I promise,' I said. 'I need to jog a few people's memories.'

He made no signs of objection, so I went ahead and trawled the boat for portable examples of Aiden's best work and, together with a selection of his photographs, put them in the carry-case he left out for me. Before I left the boat I made a quick call to Didier. He confirmed he'd be around all day and would watch Aiden.

On my way to the station I tried Miranda's phone, but it was switched off again. I cut the connection. As I hopped on the Docklands' train, I called CCAP once more. No one had heard from Miranda and, quite out of character, she hadn't turned up for her therapy at 11am.

I felt a quiver of worry run through my body as I slipped the phone back in my bag.

The Craig-Doyle Gallery was a classy affair; immaculate high walls, with larger than life silver dome lampshades dangling from the ceiling. The parquet floor was polished to a shine that reflected the sunlight, but which also gave it the patina of black ice. After two steps I was forced to grab hold of a chair – a plastic one curved into an 'S' shape. All so very state-of-the-art, but desperately impractical. I managed to slip and slide to the reception desk and was greeted by a woman who looked like she'd walked straight off the set of a *James Bond* production. Sleek hair scooped up into a French twist, a plunging neckline and retro winged-spectacles propped on the end of her nose.

'I know I should have made an appointment,' I said, 'but I wondered if I could have a few moments of your time.'

'Mr Kilroy is busy at the moment. What's it about?' The response matched the look; pouty with a touch of frost.

'I have some work here you might be interested in. My client wants to remain anonymous for the time being, but he's won various national awards and shows tremendous potential.' I unzipped the case and placed a couple of Aiden's sketches in front of her.

'He's your client?' she queried.

'I'm his publicist. You're the first gallery I've approached because of your... reputation.'

'We normally expect an introduction in writing,' she said, snootily. 'We only offer an interview if we're interested.'

'I understand,' I said. 'Only, Honoré told me to come in, before she–'

'You know Honoré?'

'Personal friend,' I said. 'We met at Fitzwilliam College. Chess club.' I'd read enough of Pippa's features to know a few facts about Honoré by now. The Bond girl melted a fraction. I held out my hand. 'Emma Watson,' I said. I'd come prepared this time; providing a name I knew would bombard her with hits should she try to Google me.

'Mrs Perez might be able to see you,' she conceded. 'Just hold on.' She disappeared through a frosted glass door. Moments later another woman appeared.

'Come through, Mrs Watson,' she said. She shook my hand and led me to a spartan office. On the smoked glass door was a sticky rectangle of glue, as if a sign had been recently removed. There was a wooden filing cabinet in the corner and a laptop set up on the desk. That's all. Either she'd just moved in or business was slow.

I leant the case against the desk and began showing her Aiden's work. Mrs Perez hummed and hawed in a non-committal fashion, stroking her over-made-up cheek with glossy red talons. As she did, I allowed my eyes to wander, settling on a large cardboard box on the floor to my left. Inside were personal belongings; a mug, desk-diary, picture frames and a make-up bag. Sticking out at the top was a sign that matched the sticky shape on the door. I was able to make out the first few letters: *Hono…*

The agency had decided she wasn't coming back.

'The theme of "white"…' she said in a vague manner. 'Isn't there a new kid on the block already doing this somewhere?' Her up-to-the-minute knowledge took me by surprise. I'd need to tread carefully. 'Honoré's been to view his work,' she said. 'At one of the London colleges, I believe.'

A bubble of panic caught in my throat and I took the opportunity to turn it into a debilitating cough, the kind my pipe-smoking grandfather would have been proud of. I needed to play for time.

She waited in vain for me to compose myself.

'Glass of water…' I croaked, hacking uncontrollably.

She disappeared. Once her spine-like heels had clacked into the distance, I shot over to the filing cabinet half-expecting it to be locked. I had the list of names with me; artists Pippa had interviewed as well as the ones Miranda had announced at her special dinner party. If any of them had ever applied for representation here, there should be a record of it, somewhere. Had any of them felt badly treated by Honoré? Could that be a motive?

The top drawer, labelled simply 'A–H', glided towards me, half-empty with flaccid files. Most of the details were probably in an online database. I shut it carefully and turned to the computer.

Fortunately, Mrs Perez was already logged in. I made a few clicks to reach the full list of documents, then frantically scanned through them to find details of submissions. *Catalogues… Current clients…* I scrolled down to 'S'. *Submission Guidelines…* then *Submissions.* I opened the one for this year and scrolled down.

There was no file for Mark Ellerton, so I carried on. *Manson, Mendez… Mills, Kurtis.* I didn't have time to read it, so I grabbed the memory stick I always carried with me from my bag, slotted it into the USB port and copied the files over. I heard the clack of heels and was about to snatch it out again, when they stopped. Mrs Perez began speaking to someone in the corridor. I still had

Simon Schiffer and Monica Tyler left to check, further down the alphabet. I ran through the files at break-neck speed. Simon – no. Monica – *yes*. I copied that one, too. By now, the heels were almost at the door.

Willerby. What about Miranda? She would be right at the end.

There wasn't time. I ejected the stick and held it in my sweaty palm, hurriedly restoring the screen to the last document she'd been working on.

Mrs Perez found me leaning on her desk, past the worst of my manufactured coughing fit and into the throat-clearing and laboured breathing phase. I drank greedily from the glass she handed to me and thanked her. For the next ten minutes I played out the charade of submitting my client's work for representation.

After a short period, during which time Mrs Perez pretended to think about it, she turned me down.

'This is just too similar to the work of this student we've already got our eye on… Aaron or Eamonn something.' I didn't correct her.

I pulled together all the sketches and photos, and got out of there as quickly as I could.

I walked for a while so that I was no longer in the neighbourhood and found a quiet café. At the back, over a coffee, I took out my tablet to look at the two files I'd copied.

Monica's file held all the submission data you would expect; scanned copies of letters, a CV, images of her installations, links to websites. A PDF file contained a scanned contract signed two years ago with the address of their sister gallery in New York at the top, but it was the document dated three months ago that jumped out at me. To my untrained eye it seemed to outline a breach of contract. Beneath it, was a letter to Monica stating that following legal advice, unfortunately the gallery in New York was terminating her contract. It had Honoré's signature along the bottom.

Kurtis Mill's file was more straightforward. The same submission details, together with the address of his workshop in Kentish Town, a small map, then the name of the foundry he used in Surrey. He was interviewed in April and offered representation, only there was a big black line drawn through the scanned copy of that letter. Another page followed in the same PDF file, dated May, explaining to Kurtis that in light of the Canary Wharf commission having been retracted, the gallery wanted to reconsider their position. A handwritten note across the top stated 'offer withdrawn'. Kurtis must have had his hopes raised, then horribly dashed.

I rang Fenway straight away.

'Yeah – we've covered this ground, Dr Willerby,' he said, sounding weary. 'We've examined the client files from the gallery. We've already considered that the two missing women might be the product of a bruised narcissist taking revenge, like you suggest, but Kurtis Mills has solid alibis for the deaths of Kora and Katarina.' I remembered Fenway at some point saying Miranda was one of them.

'What about Monica Tyler? We concluded that both attacks could have been carried out by a woman, right? The witness who described Aiden near Katarina's body later changed her mind and said it could have been a female figure, didn't she?'

As soon as I said it, I knew there was a problem. If the mysterious figure on the towpath matched Aiden's description – with fair hair and a tall, slight frame – there was no way it could have been Monica.

'In theory. As it happens, Ms Tyler hasn't been able to produce an alibi for the two nights in question. Said she was on her own at home sketching and watching television.'

'Any link between Kurtis or Tyler and Henry Dodd?'

'No – not a sausage. Kurtis had certainly met Pippa for a magazine interview, Kora at CCAP and Honoré, through the gallery – but there's still the question of Katarina.'

'And Monica?'

'She knew Kora, of course; really good mates, according to statements we got from other users and no history of any public clashes between them. She *hasn't* done an interview with Pippa, but some photos on Pippa's Facebook page show Monica with her arm around her, although Monica claims it was at a party and she doesn't remember her. Again, no apparent link to Katarina at all.'

The Polish PA. She kept being the odd one out.

I took a sip of coffee, but it was cold. We kept taking two steps forward and one step back. I pulled a notebook from my bag and drew what I could remember of the scene Aiden had left in the sand; the glove with the pattern in teeth over the top. As I sketched, I realised that the glove he'd left was palm up. Was that important? A pattern of teeth…

Where do you find teeth? Interlocking teeth?

In a flash it struck me. *A zip*. Was this what Aiden had been trying to tell me? Was there a zip on the inside cuff of the killer's glove?

I sat back, unconvinced. Surely Aiden wasn't trying to say the killer wore gloves with a zip – it was hardly a vital piece of evidence. There must be lots of styles of gloves made with a zip and besides, the killer would probably have destroyed the gloves he or she had used days ago. I was missing something.

I ordered another coffee, looking around at the people in the café, preoccupied all the while with zips. They were everywhere; on the woman's purse at the till, on the jacket of the man by the window, on my handbag. I thought about the people who frequented CCAP – almost everyone had a zip somewhere; Monica had a big zip printed on one of her T-shirts, Kurtis had been wearing a zip-up top, the other day, Simon had zips on his trainers. What, exactly, was Aiden getting at?

I was heading towards the Tube when my phone buzzed. I answered thinking it might be Miranda, but there was only silence.

'Hello?' I said. Nothing. I ended the call, not recognising the number. It rang again. 'Who is this?' I snarled.

This time I heard sounds coming from the other end. The tinkling melody from a musical box.

Chapter 45

The strains of 'Love Me Tender' jangled in my ear.

'Aiden? Aiden?' I bellowed.

Oh, God. *Something had happened.* Either he'd found something or he was in danger. Where was Didier – wasn't he supposed to be looking after him?

I called his number straight away. Didier sounded so flummoxed when he answered, he was having trouble sticking to one language.

'Aiden? Oui,' he said. 'It's true – il est parti. Just now.'

'Didier in English, please.'

'Ah. Pardonnez-moi. Aiden – he left just one minute ago.'

'He left the boat?'

'I know he's been – how you say… *agoraphobe* lately, but suddenly he looked purposeful, like he had somewhere he wanted to go.'

'Was he upset?' I demanded, 'distressed?'

'Mon Dieu. He was in a rush, certainly,' he said. 'It was hard to tell – he took his jacket and ran. Did not speak, of course.'

I was jogging now. 'What had he been doing just before he left?'

'Er… he was looking at printed sheets from the computer, I think.'

'Okay, if you think of anything else or he comes back, please ring me straight away.'

I didn't like this one bit. Aiden had *never* left the boat of his own free will since the incident. My mind flooded with dread.

I tried DI Fenway once more to tell him Aiden had gone, but the call was diverted to the desk sergeant who told me there was nothing they could do.

'But, he's agoraphobic, he can't speak and he's not well,' I protested.

He asked me to hold the line and I heard the mutterings of voices in the background. 'I've spoken to one of the officers on the case,' he wouldn't tell me who, 'we know the situation, but the thing is Mr Blake left of his own free will, you said it yourself. Sit tight. He'll be back before you know it.'

He promised to pass the message on to DI Fenway in person, but I didn't like the lack of conviction in his voice.

Aiden had certainly left the boat in a hurry. A bundle of A4 sheets were scattered on the table with a pair of scissors left to one side. He'd found something. He'd tried to alert me, but must have decided it was too urgent to wait. Then I spotted the knife drawer was open.

The sand tray looked the same as when I'd left, he'd not altered or added to it from what I could make out. The sheets beside it looked like they'd come fresh from his printer. He must have made some new connection.

I skimmed through the first sheet, from an arts page of *The Independent*, dated February of that year, but there didn't seem to be anything that hit a nerve. Picking up the sheet next to it from another website, I read about a new artist from Norfolk and there was a short piece about Aiden's latest prize. The next minor heading read: *Promising Artist Dies*, but it stopped there. An L-shape was missing from that page. Aiden had cut something out.

I went back to the glove in the sand with what I now thought to be a zip at the cuff. I closed my eyes. *Think!* I visualised everyone I'd met from CCAP, then remembered Rachel had emailed me a batch of photos on Monday, from our gathering at Miranda's. I flicked from one to the next; Monica retying her headscarf then throwing her arms around Kurtis, Miranda making Mark dance, Kurtis topping up our drinks, Mark and Miranda turning to laugh at something I must have said.

Then it hit me. *How stupid...* how could it have taken me this long?

I sprang to my feet so quickly the chair toppled backwards. I left it where it was and made a dash for the door. As soon as I got outside I called DI Fenway's number again. It went to voicemail. I tried DI Foxton. Same thing. Then I tried Camden police station, explaining who I was and insisting I speak to someone – anyone – involved in Kora Washington's murder case. After a series of clicks that threatened to cut me off, I was put through to the crime scene manager, DS Edwin Hall. The new guy with rosy cheeks who'd looked out of his depth in the case meetings.

'Ah, Dr Willerby.'

'Where is everybody? Where's DI Fenway?'

'You'll be pleased to know that the team are out searching Dodd's mortuary again – looks like that undertaker is in a lot of trouble,' he said, sounding animated.

'No, no!' I shouted. 'They need to be looking for someone else. You must let me get through to them,' I pleaded.

'I can't do that, I'm afraid,' he said politely, 'but you can leave a message.'

'No. Forget it.' I cut the connection. I didn't trust Edwin with what I had to say.

There was only one way forward. I had a journey to make.

Chapter 46

Wednesday, July 11 – Eight days earlier

Katarina pressed open the tall gate and slipped inside. No security light came on, but there was a faint glow inside the funeral parlour. It was hours after the place had closed, nevertheless someone was in there.

A van was parked by the open back door and a lone figure was going back and forth into the building, carrying cloths and blankets. She braced herself and made a rush for the entrance, catching the person who was at work completely off guard.

'My name is Katarina Bartek,' she said, out of breath, 'and my husband is here. I need to see him.' She was already inside the door, rapping her fingers on the edge of an aluminium sink.

She was calm at first, giving her name, insisting on telling the whole story; about how the police had come to her office with news that Lubor was dead, how she'd been to the hospital and then had to wait for the post-mortem.

'You've no right to be in here.'

No one would have been best pleased at such an untimely interruption.

'I was here this afternoon, but they wouldn't let me see him. I need to find him… don't you see? Check one last time. I don't believe this has happened. I won't rest until I know he's really–' She dropped her head.

'Get out of there, you hear me? I'm busy and I can't help you. You'll need to come back tomorrow morning when the place is open for business. I've got work to do.'

But she wasn't listening and paced further inside. She stared down at the gurgling machine, staggered past the trailing tubes, holding on to the empty casket beside it. She started whimpering, poking about, randomly lifting plastic sheets on a mission to find her husband.

How was it possible to maintain a sterile environment with this stupid creature flailing around? She was ruining everything. The only way to handle it was to play along and look for her husband. Maybe direct her over to the stacked fridges where they could check them together. Once she'd got a good look at his corpse, she'd see sense and be on her way.

But Katarina didn't move when invited to keep walking towards the back of the room.

'What the hell are you doing here?' she gasped. 'This isn't right…'

She'd been warned. She'd been told not to look at what was on the trolley. There hadn't been enough time to grab a sheet.

Bereavement should have blinded her to what was going on, but Katarina took a long hard look at the sight before her on the stainless steel trolley and screamed. It was a piercing and extended shriek from deep within her. She howled something in a foreign language, then spun round and jabbed her finger in the air.

'Where's my husband? What have you done with him?' Her legs gave way and she grabbed the rim of a nearby sluice.

She was verging on hysterical now, making far too much noise. To be fair, from an outsider's point of view, the whole set up probably didn't look too good. It's not every day you see the body of a naked woman with her arms stretched out above her head. Stiff as a board and not such a good colour. It wasn't a scene for the faint-hearted, but the job wasn't finished, that's why.

She kept on wailing, partly from her own personal grief, partly because of what she'd seen on the trolley. Katarina was in the company of death and she didn't know how to cope with it. She wouldn't shut up. What else was there to do? The alternative was to risk this crazy woman alerting a bunch of local busybodies, having them burst in to see what all the fuss was about.

The surgical gloves were already in place.

It wouldn't take much.

It was the only way to keep her quiet and it didn't last long. She flopped in a heap in under twenty seconds.

The surfaces she'd touched were wiped, everything tidied up, before she was bundled into the van. All back to normal, but she'd taken up valuable time. It would mean having to come back later to finish what had been started.

Just one final touch, in case someone got a good look or there were CCTV cameras on the way – so easy to alter one's appearance these days and vital when people were already jumpy around here.

Now behind the wheel, the driver took the van to the canal. It was the obvious place. Best to go past the first car park; the police might have sealed off sections of the fence after what happened. Try the second parking area. Different vehicle this time, the Mazda was too risky; the transit van came courtesy of an old chum and was plain white with muddy number plates. Like thousands of others. Inconspicuous.

With a fresh pair of gloves on, the killer dragged Katarina's body from the van and, using the wire cutters from the toolbox, clipped upwards from the bottom of the chain-link fence. She was too heavy to hoist over the top, but she could be pushed through at ground level. The aim was to get the body into the water, it would play havoc with forensics. It was a good spot; better than the last one. Darker with no boats moored nearby. No need for a boat. No need to tie up a tripwire, not this time. Just bend back the small section of ragged wire and squash Katarina's limp body through. Easy.

About to squeeze through after her, the killer spotted a shape moving in the distance. Time to go. Better to back away – leave her where she was, on the path. To risk coming face to face with a passer-by was too dangerous, even though the disguise was pretty good.

Chapter 47

Present Day – Thursday, July 19

'Nineteen' was written in large white numbers in paint which had dripped down the brickwork. Next to it hung roll-down security shutters, the ones you find on shop fronts in the high street, only this was no row of enticing boutiques. This ugly cul-de-sac in Kentish Town was home to a row of storage spaces and garages. It was the sort of dubious area you'd stumble upon if you'd taken several wrong turns. There was a soggy sleeping bag discarded in a doorway and a wheelie bin on its side disgorging litter at the kerb. Beside it was a sideboard, the top curling up after repeated soakings in the rain. It wasn't a place to loiter.

On the far side of the shutter a door stood slightly ajar. By now, I'd left a message on Fenway's voicemail to tell him where I was, but I couldn't afford to stand out here and wait. In any case, it didn't feel safe on the street and I wanted to make sure I'd got the right place.

I stepped inside where a narrow corridor led to a huge, concrete, echoey space lined with trestle tables. There were fresh art materials everywhere; tins of paint, brushes, rollers, ladders, boards and empty barrels. A bright overhead light at the back drew me towards many items I didn't recognise; machines with tubes and pumps next to vats containing caked on substances. The toxic odour – a dense mix of paint solvents and some sort of adhesive – was so strong I could taste it, each inhalation making me more light-headed.

At the far side, directly under the light, was a huge silver cauldron sending up rising steam. I stepped gingerly towards it, making sure my heels didn't make a noise, and stood in the cone of heat that surrounded it. The substance inside was a gloopy green liquid on the verge of bubbling; the smell reminding me of children's crayons. I backed away.

Behind it, several coats hung on hooks on the wall, there was an unplugged electric fire, and mugs and a kettle on a bench. I touched the side of the kettle. It was warm. Beside it stood a pair of sunglasses. My stomach lurched as I recognised the silver design on the side. Aiden was here.

There was a tall hardboard partition behind the bench, the sort that folds up in a zigzag. I crept to the edge, holding my breath and poked my head round.

She was lying flat out on a beaten up old sofa, covered in a sheet, her arms stretched out above her head. I recognised her spikey blonde hair and I nearly laughed out loud – Miranda taking an afternoon nap. What was she doing here? I was about to call out her name, but stopped myself. Something wasn't right. Her arms continued to reach up, locked in an odd, stiff posture. As I moved round into the light, reality hit me. She was too still.

I staggered back making a whimpering sound, trying not to scream. Every sinew in my body was yelling at me to get out of there as fast as possible, but I couldn't turn away. I couldn't leave her like this. With my hand over my mouth, I took a step closer to the body, then another. I eased back the sheet. That's when I realised her hair looked too dry, too yellow. This wasn't Miranda.

The figure was naked, with skin below the neck the colour of mahogany, the texture not like skin at all. It was taut and crisp with a glossy finish. The hair was a wig. The body had been elongated so that her arms stretched above her head, her feet pointed. It looked like an exquisitely detailed mannequin. I stared at the gruesome form and couldn't work it out. Her face looked like it was made of plastic. So human and yet not right at all.

The overpowering smell of formaldehyde forced me to back off, but I couldn't take my eyes away, I was both mystified and horrified. What was this? A very clever model – a perfect replica, like you'd find at Madame Tussauds? For some reason, I wasn't convinced. Perhaps it was the smell, perhaps it was the fact that it was too realistic, too good. And then, when I looked down, I saw her nails were black.

At that point, I forced myself to look properly at her face. The vision sent bile, burning into my throat. Her gunmetal grey eyes were staring back at me, but they were covered in a cloudy film and were flaccid as though punctured at the back. I knew then, without a doubt. This was no waxwork figure.

Strands of dark hair trailed down from under the blonde wig and by then, I knew the face. I threw a hand over my mouth as my stomach clenched, but there was no stopping myself from throwing up.

Chapter 48

I had to get out.

No sooner had I hurriedly begun to retrace my steps, when I heard movement behind me. I stepped behind a tall board propped up against the wall. Miranda appeared wearing her painting overalls. Someone was behind her holding his hands over her eyes. I froze to the spot hoping they couldn't see me.

'Keep them shut,' he said jovially to Miranda, letting go of her. 'But stay where you are.' He adjusted the partition a fraction so that she couldn't see the body of Pippa French on the sofa.

'This is so exciting,' she squealed. 'Urgh, it stinks, though. What is it?'

'You can open them, now.'

She looked around expectantly. 'What am I looking for?'

His hands were in the pockets of his overalls, flapping the sides around.

'Be patient,' he said chuckling. 'I'll show you in a minute.'

I was craning my neck out of the shadows desperate to see what was going on and Miranda, her eyes on the lookout for some promised surprise, looked straight at me. I shook my head in an urgent signal not to give me away, but she moved forward, squinting, trying to see beyond the bright light above her. There was nowhere for me to go.

'What are *you* doing here?' she called out.

'Hello, Sam,' came the melodious Scottish accent, as he stepped out into the light.

'Are you okay?' I burst out, striding towards her.

'Of course I'm okay,' she snorted.

'That's because Miranda understands,' said Kurtis, his hands covered in white latex gloves.

'Understands what?' said Miranda, fiddling with her earring. 'All this.'

'What is *all this*, exactly?' she asked, turning her nose up. 'It smells foul.'

'Welcome to my latest project,' he said congenially. 'A tribute to those who make the lives of artists like me a misery. You understand, I know you do.' He threw his arm out towards me. 'Tell Sam how they drove my sister to suicide…'

'Oh, yes,' said Miranda. 'His sister was a brilliant painter. She died earlier this year – heroin overdose – totally tragic.'

'It was the critics who made her life hell,' snarled Kurtis. 'They are the ones who killed her. Zena had everything going for her – she'd even got herself clean. That was until she got that crappy review in a national paper. She was about to be shown at a newcomers' exhibition at the Tate Modern, but they withdrew the offer.'

'That's terrible, isn't it, Sam?' said Miranda. She turned to Kurtis. 'I *do* understand. They drove her to it. Anyone can see that.' Miranda folded her arms. 'So, where's the surprise?'

He turned to me, ignoring her. 'Same thing happened to me. My commission for Canary Wharf was withdrawn after that cow Pippa French wrote an appalling item on me in that blasted magazine. My career went up in smoke. She called me a pale shadow of Giacometti. Then a gallery in Chelsea did a U-turn – that snotty bitch, Craig-Doyle, didn't give me a chance to explain. Since then, I've been reduced to the status of "craftsman".' He stamped his foot. '*I don't think so. I'm an artist.*' He bellowed the words, punching the air with his fist.

Miranda went to him and touched his cheek. 'I know – you've had a terribly rough ride. You've been treated like shit by people who hold all the power.' She turned to me. 'He's brilliant. He's working on a bronze statue of a diver for a couple in Dorset.'

'But that's just the point, isn't it?' hissed Kurtis. 'My work shouldn't be beside a rockery or hidden inside some pokey conservatory. My sculptures should have pride of place on plinths you can see from the motorway – on the top of high-rise buildings or on the beach – seen and admired by everyone.'

'I know,' said Miranda soothingly. 'And maybe, one day, that's exactly what's going to happen.'

He shook his head. 'It's too late. The damage is done. Don't you see?'

She looked like she was trying to, but hadn't yet worked out the gruesome truth like I had.

'I had to do something to fight back,' he said.

Kurtis strode purposefully towards me and ushered me out of Miranda's line of sight. I tensed my body ready to run.

'May I borrow your phone?' he said, snatching my bag from my shoulder. 'Don't even *think* about screaming,' he hissed in my ear. 'There's no one else around to hear you.'

'The police are on their way,' I said, trying to tug the phone away from him. He got the better of me. He gave me a disparaging look and tapped several words into a text on my phone, pressed send, then pocketed it.

'By the way, the police are looking for Honoré Craig-Doyle, but you know exactly where she is,' he said tauntingly, out of my sister's earshot. 'She was all set to take me on, then had the nerve to send me packing. You've been walking past her for the last few weeks.' He waited for my reaction. I blinked hard. 'Not worked it out yet? Here's a clue. Let's say it was quite a transformation.' He laughed and walked back to Miranda.

Transformation… oh my God, the new fountain outside CCAP. The figure of Poseidon. It couldn't be, could it?

Kurtis took Miranda's hand and led her round to the sofa. As soon as she saw the outstretched figure, she screamed and pulled away. Then, just as I'd done, she took a step closer, convinced the figure must have been cleverly constructed.

She laughed. 'Kurtis – it's amazing!' She stared in awe. 'I thought it was *real*.'

They both looked down at the preserved corpse of Pippa French, who, with her arms stuck straight up above her head, was destined to be encased in metal and forever dive into a rock pool in a couple's garden in Dorset.

'Miranda, come away,' I said.

I glanced over at the door. The police should have been here by now. 'Kurtis has *killed* people. That's not a sculpture, it's a *real* body. It's one of the women who went missing.'

She scoffed at me. 'Don't be silly. Kurtis is an artist. He's done all this by himself.'

I thrust my hand towards the huge vat in the centre, which gurgled and popped as bubbles broke the surface with a splat. 'Look at what's in here, Miranda… it's wax…' I edged closer to her, hoping that as soon as she twigged the truth, I'd be able to drag her free from Kurtis. 'He's been using a funeral parlour to–'

She laughed again. 'He needs the wax to make the figures, don't you?' she said, rolling her eyes at him.

I wanted nothing more than to run for it, but not while Miranda was still being so clueless about what was going on. I couldn't leave her with this maniac.

'Sit down, Miranda,' said Kurtis, pulling up a wooden chair for her, 'and let me tell you the whole thing. I think you'll be rather proud of me.' She took a seat and wrapped her arms loosely around her knees, totally at ease.

He cleared his throat. 'A guy called Henry Dodd and I used to be in the navy together, many years ago. He skipped duties once and was having a sneaky ciggy in a strictly no-smoking area of the ship – and by the time he got back to our cabin, the whole place was on fire. I didn't give him away and ever since Henry's owed me one. When I was organising Zena's funeral I found out he was based in London, running a funeral home. So I dropped in on him. Henry agreed a deal so I could use his premises overnight. I had this place, but it was the embalming equipment and freezers I needed.'

Miranda was chewing her nail, looking bewildered. 'Embalming equipment? Why would you need that?'

I wandered over to her chair and stood behind it protectively, waiting for the moment she finally understood. I kept glancing towards the door, expecting a storm of blue uniforms to come charging in.

I was trying to think back to the message I'd left on DI Fenway's voicemail. I'd given him the number of the workshop and said it was behind the Kentish Town baths. I'd told Kurtis I'd called the police, so why hadn't he fled by now?

'What better place to hide a body than inside a statue,' he continued. 'The main concern is the smell and the possibility of – not to put a finer point on it – leaks. Wouldn't want Pippa seeping out all over the conservatory carpet now, would we? Or Honoré attracting the Camden rats?'

My toes curled taut inside my sandals, my fists throbbing; every muscle in my body coiled into a spring. We had to go – *now*.

Only, Miranda had her mouth wide open, but she still hadn't grasped the truth.

Chapter 49

I watched helplessly as everything began to unfold in slow motion. Kurtis went over to the wall and unhooked a heavy chain that was attached to a pulley above the steaming cauldron. 'I know you'll understand about Kora,' he said, returning to my sister.

'Kora?' said Miranda.

'It was very unfortunate. She started asking questions about how I made my statues. She was a sculptor herself, of course, and I think she was scouting for tips. I was working late at CCAP and she found me trying out fixative on the leg of a horse. I was trying to get the right strength of embalming fluid. She laughed and accused me of being a second-rate Gunther von Hagens – you know, the guy who sets up preserved bodies to play chess and throw the javelin?'

Miranda looked puzzled. 'The artist who preserves *real* bodies…?'

He went on. 'She started asking too many questions and threatened to talk to Simon.' He clapped his hands together. 'She had to go, I'm afraid.'

The disbelief took the colour from her face. 'You… killed Kora?' she whispered, slowly rising from her seat.

'She *laughed* at me,' he said. 'She was going to tell Simon, then my whole scheme would have collapsed. So I set up the wire and sent her off down the towpath. It was all very quick and tidy. Or it should have been. She wasn't meant to survive.'

'*You* killed my best friend!' Miranda was glaring at him, her eyes bulging, her hands shaking.

'Hey, hey,' he protested, reaching towards her. 'You're supposed to understand, remember?' She recoiled. 'You know how I've suffered at the hands of people who didn't value my work.'

He took hold of her arm, but Miranda snatched it away from him, sobbing in convulsions. 'I can't believe you did this… I can't…'

Kurtis carried on. 'That Polish woman was a fly in the ointment, too. She found me at Dodd's mortuary preparing Pippa and started screaming the place down. I had to stop her.'

Miranda's legs gave way under her and she sank back into the chair. She'd been reduced to a crumpled wreck, incapable of speaking. I put my hand on her shoulder.

'Don't touch her,' said Kurtis, his words stabbing the air. I kept my hand where it was. 'Don't you want to know all about it? The surprise?' He looked over appraisingly at Pippa's body on the sofa. 'For long-term preservation, not just for a twenty-minute viewing at a chapel of rest, you have to use an embalming fluid containing concentrated formalin with glutaraldehyde and phenol. It's a brand-new formula and I'm the first to use it. I'm a pioneer!' He thumped his chest with his fist. 'The fluid is injected into an artery under high pressure to swell and saturate the tissues. I don't like the "embalmer's grey" discolouration, so I added a stain to give Pippa a healthy tan.'

Miranda glanced over at the sofa with revulsion. 'It's disgusting,' she wailed. 'What you're doing isn't art – it's monstrous!'

'I've got a bronze cast all ready for Pippa, at the foundry. She'll be put inside, just like Honoré in Poseidon at the fountain. The statue is in two parts, the joins will be welded together afterwards.' He allowed himself a chuckle. 'Pippa French said my work was derivative and passé – but now she'll become part of one of my pieces. Some sort of poetic justice, don't you think?' His mouth curled into a smug grin. 'Like Honoré, her flesh will rot, but she'll forever have perfect bones.'

Miranda had stopped crying and was staring at him. I could feel her entire body shivering through the back of the chair.

'You disgust me,' she spat.

He leant towards her and before I could stop him, he gave her a sharp slap, so hard that she toppled off the chair. I dropped down to her, checking she hadn't been injured by the fall.

'I'm okay... I'm fine,' she mumbled, looking startled.

As I straightened up, I scoured the trestle tables behind her, searching for something I could use as a weapon. Before I could grab anything, Kurtis came up behind me and kicked the back of my knees. As I went down, my head struck the chair Miranda had been sitting on and the world turned into the inside of a coal bunker.

Chapter 50

Iheard my ring tone and, still dazed, patted my pockets for the phone. But, of course, it wasn't there. I sat up and watched Kurtis take my mobile out of his overalls. He let my voicemail take the call, then listened to the message.

'It's Fenway,' Kurtis said cheerily. 'They've found a light-blue Mazda in my ex-wife's garage, the car I borrowed for Kora, and Dodd has finally told them I'm the one leasing his mortuary.'

They were onto him – thank God. I tried to get up off the floor, but he was over me before I could move. 'You stay where you are,' he snapped.

I looked over at Miranda curled in a foetal position on the floor, her cheek turning a deep shade of purple. While I'd been out cold, her hands and feet had been bound with cable ties, her mouth covered with brown tape. I certainly couldn't leave her now.

'I knew it would only be a matter of time,' he admitted. 'Looks like poor old Henry is going to be charged with obstructing the police. They've also sussed that my alibis were porkies as well.'

'They'll be here any second,' I told him defiantly.

'Er, not exactly,' he said, with a smile. 'Fenway also said they'd turned up near the swimming pool, like your message instructed, but there are *two* swimming pools in Kentish Town and it looks like they went to the wrong one. They couldn't find the workshop. Shame.'

'But, they'll realise, soon enough, that there's another pool.' I wanted to push him aside and get to my feet, but my head was spinning.

'It will be too late by then,' he clucked.

Kurtis gave me a shove that sent me back down to the floor again. He pulled my hands together behind my back and tied them with another self-locking cable tie. It cut into my wrists. The duct tape smelled of vomit as he wrenched it from the roll and slapped it across my mouth. I couldn't work out why he was so unconcerned. The police were closing in on him, they *knew* he was the killer – he knew they knew – and yet he was acting like he had all the time in the world.

Kurtis disappeared behind a long velvet curtain and came back dragging a typist's chair behind him. I gasped when I saw there was another figure sitting on it, bound and gagged.

'Mr Blake hasn't been feeling too well – we can't trust him to stay conscious. Never mind, saves me a job.' Aiden's eyes were red and puffed up, his head lolling against his chest, blood dribbling from his nose.

'You've hit him!' I tried to shout, but it came out like three feeble moans through the duct tape.

Kurtis dragged Miranda and I towards the bubbling vat and pushed us into two wooden chairs before clipping my ankles together with more black ties. He went back for Aiden and wheeled him beside us.

'As soon as this liquid wax is at the right temperature, all three of you are going in it,' he declared. 'That's the surprise! You will all be saved for posterity inside my work. What an honour.' He ran his hand through his clown-red hair, the latex gloves covering the tattoos I'd so admired on his hands the first time we'd met. He looked down at Aiden. 'The talented artist-of-the-moment can become a piece of art in his own right. Let's see how things are cooking.'

Taking a small wire basket, Kurtis tested the temperature of the wax by dropping my phone inside.

While he was preoccupied watching the bubbling liquid I took a look at Aiden. One eyelid slid open and he lifted his head slightly so he could see me. He'd only been pretending to be out cold; he must have heard Kurtis's footsteps. His ankles were bound like mine, but his hands were tied in front of him and his fingers could move a little. He extended his hands into a prayer position. I stared at him. Was this a signal? Did he have something he wanted to say? He nodded as if answering my questions. I waited.

He made both hands into fists, then extended a finger – the one he'd cut recently. Then he looked deliberately down at his left foot, hitching up the leg of his chinos, then rubbed the finger against his other hand. It was certainly some kind of message. *A knife... in his sock?*

'Not quite ready,' said Kurtis, examining the gooey mess that was my phone. 'A few more minutes.'

Using his index finger, Aiden jabbed four or five times in the air in a little square and stared down at his pocket. Kurtis glanced over and straight away Aiden's head went down.

What was Aiden trying to tell me? That he had a knife in his sock and a phone in his pocket?

Kurtis dragged the three of us together in a line with Aiden in the centre, his head flopping against his chest.

'Who's going to be first?' he said, slapping his hands together as if we were all playing a party game. 'Of course, I'm going to have to ask you all to be naked.'

He was utterly deranged. When I'd first met him, I thought his mild-mannered approach and lightness of touch was natural charm. Now, I could see it was a well-practised act, a superficial crust covering a sadistic paranoia. In his mind, art critics and connoisseurs had killed his sister. They were out to bring *him* down, too. He, in turn, had to punish them. For him, it all boiled down to a petty game of tit for tat.

And us three? We had just got in the way and needed to be disposed of.

Kurtis turned to me with a smile. Normally I'm pretty good at anticipating what people are about to do, but I was totally out of my depth. 'By the way, I forgot to say,' he said conversationally, 'when I used your phone earlier, I sent a text to Fenway to say that you'd found nothing at the workshop, but you'd moved on to the foundry in Surrey and had found me there – up to no good. I left him the exact address.'

The police weren't coming. They were miles away.

I had to act now before things got any worse. Aiden had given me a lifeline; I had to use it.

Slipping off the chair, I flopped forward as if I was fainting, landing just in front of Aiden.

'Whoops-a-daisy,' said Kurtis, glancing over. He was using a large spatula to stir the boiling liquid, wafting the rising steam towards him with his other hand as if it was a delicious soup. 'Feeling a bit faint, are we?' I was horrified by his mounting psychotic flippancy.

In the split second his back was turned, I reached towards Aiden's trouser leg.

Kurtis bundled me back onto the chair and I worked quickly. Squeezing the knife I'd managed to grab from Aiden's sock, I tried to rub the blade against the plastic cable tie behind my back. My fingers were slippery with sweat so I wiped my palms against my backside, desperate not to drop the blade. As Kurtis stirred and sniffed the mixture, I rubbed to and fro, to and fro, trying not to make it obvious. The knife was sharp and I kept catching my skin with painful slashes. There was a little jolt as I finally broke free, but I kept my arms rigidly behind me to hide my achievement.

I waited for Kurtis to check the thermometer on the side of the vat, then bent down and slashed the ties around my ankle. Still seated, I reached over to slice Aiden's hands free.

Aiden delved into his pocket and handed me his phone, just as Kurtis was turning round. I hurriedly pushed it up my sleeve out of sight, the knife now tucked between my knees. I hadn't had time to cut the tie around Aiden's ankles.

'Right,' said Kurtis giggling. 'I think we're ready.'

Squatting before Miranda, he snapped the tie around her ankles with a pair of clippers and started hacking at her overalls. 'These will have to come off,' he said.

'No, take me,' I moaned, through the duct tape. I toppled deliberately across Aiden, pushing his chair backwards. Then I threw myself at Kurtis, lashing out at him with the knife. Caught off balance, he took two steps backwards and fell into a table. As Aiden and Miranda broke each other free, I ripped the tape from my mouth and managed to punch two digits – 9… 9 – into the phone.

That was as far as I got.

Kurtis reacted faster than I'd expected. He regained his balance and with only a minor stab wound on his arm, knocked the phone out of my hands. As Aiden aimed a punch at him, Kurtis seized his arm and sent an emphatic kick into his shin. Aiden went down. Kurtis grabbed me roughly and threw me against a set of shelves to one side, before punching Miranda hard in the stomach. She fell back with a grunt.

As I tried to get to my feet, Kurtis reached over me, claiming the knife I'd managed to grab from the floor, and in a single movement yanked me upright pressing the blade against my neck. In seconds, beads of warm blood began trickling down inside my collar. I stared in horror as drips made their way to the floor, forming pools the size of five pence pieces. With them came a sharp pain and wave of nausea.

'Anyone moves and Dr Willerby is going into the wax in tiny pieces,' he declared.

Aiden was clutching his leg, looking weak and disoriented. Miranda sat on the floor, her legs splayed out, sobbing at the state I was in and staring longingly at the phone several feet away. She hadn't had time to make the call, either.

Pain tore into my flesh and blood continued to leave my body. I was on the verge of blacking out.

With the knife still at my neck, Kurtis instructed Aiden to tie Miranda up again.

'And do it properly, or I'll cut off your fingers,' he snapped.

Kurtis then told him to retie my arms and ankles. Aiden did so, as gently as he could, before Kurtis let me topple sideways and

I sank to the floor. From that position I watched Aiden hold out his wrists ready to be tied up again.

In a split second everything changed.

As Kurtis approached him, Aiden braced himself and sprung unexpectedly, his left foot sending a high kick into Kurtis's chin. Kurtis, taken unawares by this sudden display of martial arts, was sent arching backwards, hitting the floor with a thud. It took him a few seconds to get to all fours to catch his breath. It was long enough for Aiden to rush to a pile of cans on the shelves behind us. He was looking for something. I tried to sit up, I wanted to help, but the room was pulsating. I couldn't move unaided, in too much pain from the cut in my neck to do anything.

As Kurtis began to rally and stagger to his feet, Aiden found what he was looking for. He unscrewed the lid and threw the contents into Kurtis's face. He let out a blood-curdling scream and doubled over, clutching his cheeks. Behind his fingers I could see the damage the paint stripper was already doing, chewing up his skin on contact. I looked away.

Miranda was still tied up, so Aiden grabbed the phone from the floor. I tried to shout to him, to tell him to pass the phone to me, but a strange gurgling sound came from inside my throat. Kurtis was thrashing out towards Aiden like a blind zombie, brandishing the knife, screaming murderous rage. I knew the phone was worthless in Aiden's hands. He looked at it as if he'd never used one before.

I closed my eyes.

Then it happened. A miracle.

'This is Aiden Blake with Dr Sam Willerby — police and ambulance needed immediately at...'

I gasped.

Kurtis finally came to a stop, his hands over his streaming eyes, howling in pain. Aiden pushed him into a corner.

'They're on their way,' said Aiden, in a soft Irish accent.

At the sound of his voice, tears flooded my vision joining the blood splatter on the floor.

Chapter 51

Four days later

I didn't remember much after that. I was peppered with bruises and needed four stitches in my neck, but I was incredibly lucky. The surgeon told me there's a lot of structure around the throat that isn't vital; muscles, connective tissue. Had the incision been a centimetre to the right, I wouldn't have made it to the hospital at all.

Visitors came and went, but they all blended into a sea of worried faces. I was finally sitting up in my bed, able to differentiate individuals from the blur of general ward activity, when DI Fenway and DI Foxton came in to see me.

'Kurtis gave us a complete confession,' Fenway said. 'In fact, he was rather smug about his plans. He'd given Kora a strong laxative the day he set up the wire, so he could get his hands on her mobile when she rushed back and forth to the toilet. He'd been helping out in the CCAP kitchen that day and merely stirred the powder into the soup she ordered at lunchtime. She'd told him she was meeting someone about a new project later on and was expecting Kent to pick her up. Kurtis threw the phone in the canal, after telling Kent she'd already gone home.'

'What made her cycle so fast in the wrong direction?' I croaked, my throat burning.

'Kurtis found her after her last dash to the loo and spun a story that the police had rung the CCAP office with news of a dreadful accident. Some rubbish about Raven, her son, having fallen in the canal. Of course, she didn't have her phone to check by then, so she took off to try to help. Kurtis had hidden her helmet, so she'd be unprotected.'

Karen stepped in. 'That's when Kurtis jumped straight in a car, the Mazda he kept at his ex-wife's place, and got there ahead of her.' She was looking particularly refined in an off-duty summer dress. 'Kurtis wore a ski mask and a black hood. He knew he'd been seen at the boat, but was convinced he couldn't be identified.'

My mouth fell open. 'So, Aiden would never have been able to draw Kurtis's face, after all,' I said, 'because he'd never seen it.'

They both shook their heads, mirrors of each other in their grim solemnity.

In short bursts, I told them how I'd finally worked out the killer's identity.

'I'd seen Kurtis's clever tattoos,' I whispered, 'but not the full "zip" design on his right wrist. When Rachel sent me photos from Miranda's supper, it clicked. That's what Aiden had seen under Kurtis's glove when he unhooked the wire from the boat.'

Fenway chipped in, 'If Aiden had been able to tell us that, it would have been an instant giveaway. Kurtis had more sense than to leave the spider on his hand visible, but he'd made one big mistake. He hadn't realised the "zip" tattoo on his wrist could be seen when he reached forward.'

'Although, I still can't work out why he went back for the wire…' interjected Karen, 'he could have easily slipped away unseen.'

It was my turn to offer an answer. 'I think it was because Kora was specifically targeted – Kurtis wasn't killing randomly. Perhaps too, he went back for it because he thought he was invincible.' I snatched a ragged breath. 'I saw such an audacious arrogant side to him when we were trapped inside his workshop.'

Fenway sat down on the edge of my bed, pulling the bedclothes too tight over my ribs. I let out a yelp. 'Sorry,' he said, standing up again.

'What I don't understand is why Aiden didn't just point to a zip on his own clothes or show you what the *teeth* actually meant,' he said, rubbing his chin. 'You might have made the connection sooner.'

'Or why didn't he just draw *exactly* what he'd seen?' added Karen.

'That's why my job is so interesting,' I said, straining to be heard. 'People don't always do the obvious or logical thing… especially when they're psychologically distressed. To put it bluntly, Aiden wasn't able to think in straight lines at that point. In fact, a lot of what he was trying to show me was off the wall. It took me ages to work out the *bird* was a logo for a make of car.'

Fenway blew air out of his cheeks. There was more. 'Once Kurtis realised Aiden was getting too close to revealing what he'd witnessed that night, he tried to scare you off the boat by creeping around outside your cabin. He described you as Aiden's "bodyguard" and wanted you out of the way, so he could target him. Then when you didn't leave, he contaminated the cheese in an attempt to kill him. Miranda had told Kurtis you didn't eat it.'

'So, Kurtis was the intruder by the boat?'

'He'd spent time hanging around the security gate and managed to get a good look as various residents punched in the code to unlock it.'

'But his hair…' I said, my voice reduced to a rasp, 'I thought it was Aiden.'

'Apparently, he's always been a bit of a showman.' I took my mind back to Miranda's party again – the floppy tam-o'-shanter I'd smiled at when I met Kurtis. 'He wore a blond wig to disguise his distinctive hair. He hoped you'd doubt Aiden's story about not being able to leave the boat. Hoped you'd leave, so he could get to Aiden and make sure he'd never be able to reveal any more information as a witness.'

Soon after, DI Fenway bade his farewell. Karen gave me a weak smile and withdrew after him. In the wake of her dreamy perfume, I silently wished her well in her conquest of him. She certainly didn't have to worry about any competition from me; the DI and I had ended up rubbing together like two pieces of sandpaper.

Aiden arrived shortly afterwards holding a tiny package.

'What is it?' I asked, peeling open the wrapping paper.

He didn't say a word; watched me find out for myself.

'Oh, Aiden – it's lovely.'

It was the musical box, just like the one I'd had as a child.

It had turned into a lifeline between the two us. A lifeline we didn't need any more.

'It's yours,' he said, sitting carefully on the bed. 'I don't know how I can possibly thank you. For everything.'

I was still getting used to the sound of his voice. Each word he uttered continued to feel precious to me. Those mellow tones I'd longed to hear break the silence for what felt like an eternity.

'What happened to make you leave the boat that day?' I asked him, 'what exactly did you find?'

'Everything came together in my head,' he said. 'At first I thought I'd mixed things up in my memory and the zip was on a glove, then I realised what I'd seen was actually drawn on the killer's *skin*. I knew I'd heard about someone with that tattoo somewhere. I checked my press cuttings as well as online and found what I was looking for – there was a picture of him with his sister, a short news item after her death. I had his name. I looked him up and found out about his workshop. That's about it, really. I was worried about you. I thought you might have made the crucial connection around the same time and got there first.'

I took his hand. 'It was your actions – at the workshop – that saved us all.'

He looked just the way I'd seen him on film; bashful and unassuming – and breathtakingly attractive.

'Do you happen to know about that police witness – the one who claimed they'd seen you on the towpath when Katarina was left by the canal?'

'A passer-by gave a description that could have been me, but it was actually a tall woman with blonde hair.' He lifted a clump of his own hair and shrugged.

'Why didn't she come forward? It would have saved so much trouble. You wouldn't have been arrested.'

'She didn't want to get involved. Simple as that. Someone persuaded her to come clean in the end.'

A nurse came to the bedside and suggested it was time I had some rest. Aiden squeezed my hand. I closed my eyes for a moment and when I opened them, he'd gone.

Chapter 52

Terry arrived not long after the nurse had woken me to change my dressing. As soon as I saw his troubled face, I knew the view I'd had of him for all these years had been entirely lopsided. Terry was far more than a good mate. There was a depth to his character I'd never taken the trouble to see; a warmth, kindness, trustworthiness, selflessness. The list could go on, now I'd had time in my sick bed to reflect properly.

He hovered over me awkwardly, not knowing how to greet me, then reached into his pocket and handed me an iPod.

'To help you while away the hours during your recovery,' he said. 'I'm sure your taste has changed a lot since university days, but there are some old favourites to take you down memory lane.'

'I can't believe you remembered what I used to listen to...' I said, my voice breaking.

'I paid attention,' he said simply.

His eyelids flickered when he looked at me, as if I was too bright for him. He hesitated, then reached out his hand and tenderly stroked my cheek. A sprinkle of stars tingled up my spine. All too soon, he drew away. 'I won't stay long,' he said, 'you must be tired.'

I was about to insist that I should be the judge of that when I spotted Miranda peering over his shoulder. Terry sensed he should leave us alone. I wasn't sure if he heard my husky voice calling after him, urging him to come back in a while.

Miranda leant forward as if to kiss me, then took a good look at my face instead, mustering a fleeting smile. She straightened up, her shoulders hunched. I wasn't sure which way things were going to go between us. I couldn't bear more hostility. I wanted everything to be back to normal, but I didn't know what normal was any more.

'I suppose you'll be champing at the bit to get back to that mental health unit of yours,' she said with forced brightness.

'When I'm ready,' I replied. 'Thanks for coming. It's good to scc you.'

She squeezed my hand, but didn't look me in the eye. I noticed hers were bloodshot. 'You okay?'

'Just a bad night,' she said, rubbing them with her knuckles like a child. 'I've seen Simon.'

'What's the latest?'

She ran her finger along the shelf above my bed checking it for dust. 'So-so. Simon's solicitor thinks he could get six to nine months, if he's lucky. The lawyer called it *counterfeit false teeth*.' She sniggered. 'Sounds so hilarious. He did it to keep CCAP afloat; did it for us. He's a good man.'

I didn't want to argue with her.

'Did you know?'

'Of course not! Simon never told me anything about it, but CCAP wouldn't have survived if he hadn't managed to find extra money from somewhere. What he did wasn't harming anyone; he was doing the local dentists a favour. It was a health and safety breach, that's all.'

'And Kurtis?' I nudged.

She looked miserable as she sank down on the chair beside the bed. 'He did it out of grief for his sister, didn't he?'

'I think it started out like that, but he was also angry at the way his art had been overlooked. He was obsessed with his own crazy mission of revenge, killing individuals he thought were responsible for degrading him, as well as the ones who got in his way.'

'I'm afraid I did give him a false alibi. After Katarina's death. He said it was to protect someone from getting hurt and I believed him. It's incredible how you think you know someone.'

I heard her exhale and she grimaced, looking around for something to help her change the subject.

'He saved our lives, didn't he?' she said. 'That boy you were treating.'

'Yes, he did.'

'That was one hell of a karate kick,' she added. We shared a smile, but she was the first to look away. Her harsh words from last week still rang loudly inside my head. She didn't want to go to on holiday with me – ever – and had thought the whole thing, on reflection, had been a stupid idea. Was that the 'shock' she had in store for me? Making it clear I was cramping her style so I'd back off and leave her alone? Or was there another shock still to come?

She pulled a bag of salted cashews from her pocket and casually offered me one, as though this was a day like any other.

I shook my head. 'There's one thing I haven't been able to work out,' I said. 'I know I never told you myself, so how did you know Aiden had a thing for halloumi cheese?'

'Ah…' She wagged her finger at me. 'I saw your supervision notes when I went into your bag.'

I blinked fast. 'You looked in my bag?'

'Yeah, to borrow some money.' She sniffed. 'I was going to give it back.'

'Wait – you rifled through my bag, read my confidential notes about Aiden *and* pinched some cash.'

'Yeah, it was just once and only twenty pounds,' she huffed. Indignant as ever.

I shook my head in despair. I wanted to find something amusing to say to lighten the mood, but before I could get my brain into gear, she patted the bed, stood up and made a vague suggestion that we might meet up 'sometime'.

'You're going?' I reached out my hand, but she'd already turned away.

'Got an appointment,' she said, like a slap in the face.

I closed my eyes until I could no longer hear her clipped footsteps. We were never going to be the same again – I could tell.

A nurse called my name and I opened my eyes. She was pointing to the foot of my bed. 'Someone left their shopping,' she said, lifting up a carrier bag. She brought it alongside me. 'What do we have here?'

She reached inside and slid out a thin canvas. 'Ooh... I say!' She held it up so I could see. 'It's you, isn't it?' she said, taken aback.

It was a portrait, the oil paint barely dry. Broad, bold strokes had been lashed across the image, but on the face itself were fine intricate details; in the eyelashes, the irises, the creases in the lips. It had a vivid sense of intimacy that took my breath away. Startling in its accuracy, it also captured something wistful and bleak.

'It's stunning,' she said, 'such an amazing likeness.'

A lump lodged in my throat. I couldn't take my eyes off it. There was a strange smoky hue painted in wispy brushstrokes around my hair. It made me look like an angel.

'Who left this for you?'

I fought back tears, struggling to speak, but they got the better of me. Finally, I gave in to them and let them fall.

THE END

About the Author

AJ Waines is a number one bestselling author, topping the entire UK and Australian Kindle Charts in two consecutive years, with **Girl on a Train.** Following fifteen years as a psychotherapist, the author has sold nearly half a million copies of her books, with publishing deals in UK, France, Germany, Norway, Hungary and Canada (audio books).

Her fourth psychological thriller, **No Longer Safe,** sold over 30,000 copies in the first month, in thirteen countries. AJ Waines has been featured in The Wall Street Journal and The Times and has been ranked a Top 10 UK author on Amazon KDP (Kindle Direct Publishing).

She lives in Hampshire, UK, with her husband. Visit her website at **www.ajwaines.co.uk** or join her on **Twitter (@AJWaines), Facebook** or on her **Newsletter** at http://eepurl.com/bamGuL